Tomorrow
MAY NEVER COME

Tomorrow
MAY NEVER COME

LINDA HUDSON-SMITH

BET Publications, LLC
http://www.bet.com

NEW SPIRIT BOOKS are published by

BET Publications, LLC
c/o BET BOOKS
One BET Plaza
1900 W Place NE
Washington, DC 20018-1211

ISBN: 1-58314-296-7

First Printing: September 2003
10 9 8 7 6 5 4 3 2 1

Printed in the United States of America

This book is dedicated to the loving memory of my wonderful father,

Jack Hudson

Thank you for your unconditional love.
Anyone can be a father, but not everyone can be a daddy.
Daddy, you earned in spades this honorary title.

This book is also dedicated to all the wonderful dads around the world!

This novel is a loving memorial to my dear cousin,

Clifton Norris

We will always miss your smile and the sound of your laughter.

Sunrise: July 7, 1950

Sunset: May 25, 2002

ACKNOWLEDGMENTS

Black Images Book Bazaar, Mrs. Emma Rodgers—Thanks for such a warm welcome into your prestigious store. It was a pleasure and an honor to sign there. Your graciousness precedes you.

Romance Noir Book Club, Dallas, TX—A super-special thank-you for hosting my signing at Black Images in Dallas. You ladies outdid yourselves. It was a wonderful event. Thanks for all the love and support I received from each of you.

Shrine of the Black Madonna, Houston, TX—Aneika: Thanks so much for having me as a guest author in your beautiful store. It was a pleasure to sign there. I want to thank all of the wonderful Houstonians who came out to the Shrine to support me.

The Sister Circle Book Club, Houston, TX—A heartfelt thanks goes out to each of you. Thanks for driving all the way to Dallas to join up with Romance Noir to make my signing event such a memorable one. Thanks for all the love and support I received from each of you.

Friday's Pages Book Club—Houston, TX—It was an honor to be a guest at your very first official book club meeting. Thanks so much for such a heartwarming welcome. I also thank you for choosing *Ladies in Waiting* as your first novel. A special thanks to Sylethia Jones for pulling everything together to make our meeting happen and for handling the travel arrangements.

Single Sistah's Book Club—Memphis, TN—Thank you for allowing me to invite myself in to participate in your book club meeting via the airwaves. It was truly a delightful experience to chat with everyone via speakerphone. I thank you for selecting *Ladies in Waiting* as the club's novel of the month. A special thanks to Paris Ducker for making this wonderful event happen.

WINE Book Club (Women of Intelligence Now Empowered) Smyrna, GA—Thanks so much for allowing me to be a part of your book club meeting, my very first one via the telephone. It was an honor to be among you in voice and in spirit. A special thanks to Judith Griffith for organizing the momentous event.

I STILL HAVE JOY

In my lifetime I've stumbled and tripped over many a jagged stone,
Bitter tears have flowed when I felt lost and alone;
Been racked with pain so deep, I've felt it down to the bone.

Though I've been tossed around on the sea of life like a rubber toy,
Because Christ resides deep in my soul, I still have joy.

Many of trials and tribulations have caused me to despair;
So often I've had to pray to Jesus for my very life to spare;
Can't even count the times when I thought no one cared.

Though I've been tossed around on the sea of life like a rubber toy,
Because Christ resides deep in my heart, I still have joy.

No way, no how did I have the strength to keep my demons at bay,
There have been instances when I didn't known the time or even
the day;
Not to mention the countless hours that I'd totally lost my way.

Though I've been tossed around on the sea of life like a rubber toy,
Because Christ resides in my life, I still have joy.

His teachings have taught me to call on His precious name;
I can even recite the multitude of reasons as to why He came.
Through His preaching, I've learned He loves me too.
I now know there's nothing too hard for Him to do.

I'm no longer bouncing around on the sea of life like a rubber toy;
Because Christ now has complete control, I still have joy.

©Linda Hudson-Smith

CHAPTER ONE

"**I** need to see Nicholas Reynolds."

"May I tell him who's here to see him?" asked Lynda Frasier, the office manager.

"Isaiah Morrell, his son." Young Isaiah looked like he could kill a brick.

Lynda appeared shocked. "There must be some mistake. Mr. Reynolds doesn't have any children." In taking a clearer look at the young man standing in front of her, Lynda saw that he was the spitting image of her boss, just a taller, younger version of one of the best-looking black men in southern California. With silky hair that curled at the ends, jet-black bedroom eyes, a warm autumn-brown complexion as smooth as a newborn's, the gorgeous young man's bio could easily be filed under "heartbreaker."

Isaiah, fondly known around the NBA as Ike the Psyche, smiled wryly. "You're right. There was a mistake. And I'm it. The mistake he made with my mother twenty-two years ago—when he got her pregnant. Now that I've satisfied your curiosity can you go and get the sorry-butt man in question?" Isaiah sat down on a chair and propped his size-thirteen Nikes up on the antique magazine table.

Lynda shot into an inner office like a bullet fired into the night, careful to close the door behind her. "Oh, my God," Lynda gasped, "Nick, there's a young man out there claiming to be your son. He's asking to see you." Lynda was Nicholas's right arm and his dearest friend.

Tall, handsome, and stately, with slight graying at the temples of his silken curly hair, Nicholas looked perplexed. "What are you going on about, woman? No such animal exists."

Disliking the tone he'd use with her, Lynda snorted. "Oh, he exists all right—and he's out there in your waiting room looking like a fire-breathing dragon. If I were you, I'd get out there before he burns the door down."

"Lynda Frasier, if you don't calm down, you're going to suffer a cardiac arrest."

"I think you're the one who's gonna suffer a heart attack. Especially when you try to explain a twenty-one-year-old son to the estranged Mrs. Reynolds. Don't be surprised if she doesn't change her mind about suing you for alimony after she learns that you may have a son."

Nicholas frowned. "You're serious, aren't you?"

"As serious as any war that was ever fought."

The door burst open just as Nicholas reached for the knob. Looking into the face of the young man who looked just like he did at that same age, Nicholas blinked hard and swallowed even harder. Perspiration began to soak through Nicholas's silk shirt. It felt so weird being face-to-face with himself, without a mirror.

"So you're the piece of crap that broke my mother's heart twenty-two years ago, the same son of a gun that ran out on her when you learned she was pregnant. I thought you'd be all that, but my mother must've been wearing blinders back then. You don't look like nothing, brother. You don't have one darn thing going for yourself."

Nicholas snatched the young man by the collar of his sports team jacket. "You *will not* disrespect me in my own space, young man. If you want to talk to me, you'd better change your attitude. Otherwise I'm going to throw you out of my office on your ear."

"Then why don't you step out of your space so I can give you a good old-fashioned butt kicking, 'cause that's exactly what you need. Your space don't mean nothing to me, old man."

"That's it," Nicholas thundered. "You step off, or I'm going to call the police. You're trespassing on private property, not to mention extremely dangerous ground."

"Call them, you no-good coward. You were a coward back then, and you're still one."

Lynda quickly stepped between the two men. "Both of you need to calm down. This is no way to act with each other. You all need to go into the private office, sit down, and talk this over. I don't think either one of you knows what's going on here. For sure, I can tell that you two don't know anything about each other. Perhaps it's time to at least get acquainted."

"I don't have nothing to say to that no-good lying jerk."

"Yes, you do," Lynda interjected, "or you wouldn't have come here. You came here because you needed answers. So stop the name-calling. Go on and get your needs met by asking the hard questions you've been thinking up all these years. You just might accomplish something. Your anger didn't build up overnight and it's not going to subside in a couple of minutes. Now are you ready to sit down and talk about this like the man I think you are? Or are you going to keep standing here being disrespectful? Whoever your mother is, I don't think she raised you to act like this. What's it going to be?"

Without waiting for an answer, Lynda opened the door to Nicholas's private inner office. "I'll get some coffee. I got a feeling you two might need it."

Nicholas looked extremely nervous. The more he looked at the angry young man, the more he saw himself. He'd been angry at that age, too, angry that his daddy had died on him. Shot in the line of duty, Detective Nicholas Reynolds, Sr. had been murdered by a cold-blooded killer during a failed bank robbery attempt. Nicholas still ached for both his father and mother.

Lynda popped back into the room, set down the coffee tray, and made a hasty retreat.

Looking pensive, Nicholas sat down behind his desk. He then thought better of it. The desk would only further distance them from each other. As Nicholas sat down on the sofa, his expression grew soft. He actually saw strong characteristics of the kid's mother in him. Beautiful, defiant, feisty as hell, yet so shy, Asia Morrell had been the one woman that he hadn't been able to tame. From all indications, it appeared that he was definitely the kid's father. He'd never seen a child who looked more like the alleged father than this one did. This young man was a carbon copy of himself.

"Now that we've calmed down a bit, do you want to tell me the reasons you came here today? I'd like to hear what you have to say." Nicholas filled a cup with coffee and sat back.

Refusing the offer of coffee, Isaiah looked at the chair but didn't sit. "I came here to ask why you haven't contacted me in all these years. Why didn't you at least pay child support if you didn't want anything to do with me? Why did you make my mother struggle all these years when it's obvious that you have so much?" Isaiah's hands swept the room, encompassing all the fine furnishings and beautiful accents making up the lavish decor of the large office.

Nicholas stroked his chin. "Would you believe me if I told you I never knew you existed before this very moment?"

Isaiah's eyes grew bright with surprise. "Hell, no!"

Nicholas smiled. "Didn't think so. Nonetheless, it's the truth. You're telling me something I never knew before today. Whether you believe me or not, I believe that you are my son. You look just like I did at your age. But since I look like nothing, I guess that's not much of a compliment to you. Sorry. Wish I could've passed on something better to you than unattractive looks."

Isaiah stared hard at the man that wasn't the least bit resisting the paternity charges made against him. He hadn't expected that. Since he hadn't seen any pictures of his alleged father, he hadn't expected to look so much like him, either. The looks Nicholas had passed on were far from unattractive, but Isaiah saw his own good looks as a curse. Women, old and young, wanted to spoil him because of his looks, wanted to give him anything and everything he wanted, wanted him at all costs; all he ever wanted was a good man in his life, his real daddy. Without that, he'd never really thought himself worthy of being loved by anyone, with the exception of his mother.

Asia Morrell loved him more than she loved anything else in the world. She'd done her level best to be both mother and father to him. She taught him everything he knew. Though she'd constantly talked to him about the things boys had to learn in order to become good men, she couldn't show him how to be a real man simply because she wasn't one herself. It certainly hadn't been from lack of trying, Isaiah knew. Her uncle had also been a great influence on him.

"How is your mother?"

"You don't even know who my mother is, do you?"

"I believe I do."

"Then why didn't you use her name?"

"How is Asia? Is that better?"

That was something else Isaiah hadn't expected. He'd convinced himself that his father had slept with so many women and had gotten many of them pregnant, so many that he wouldn't possibly know which one of them had given birth to him.

Isaiah got a proud gleam in his eyes. "My mother is a successful lawyer now. After years of toughing it out on her own, she finally went back to law school. She could kick your sorry behind in a court of law any day. I think it's kind of funny that you're a defense attorney and she's a prosecutor. I don't know why she hasn't sued you all these years for child support. My mother is one hell of a woman. And don't you ever forget it."

"So, we're back to being disrespectful. I won't sit here and tolerate that from you. Do you want to continue with this discussion? Or would you rather come back when you're feeling a little less angry?"

"If I waited until I felt a little less angry, I might never come back. According to my therapist, the anger inside me is the result of years of suppressing my anger. I don't understand any of it. If you didn't know you had a son, you're saying my mother is a liar. A liar she's not."

"I never said your mother was a liar. I said I didn't know you existed. Did your mother ever tell you that I knew about you?"

"My mother never told me much of anything about you until a couple of years ago. I just recently decided to start looking for you. In fact, I hired someone to find you."

Nicholas raised an eyebrow. "How could you afford to hire someone to look for me?"

Isaiah glared openly at his dad. "I'm Ike the Psyche of the California Wildcats. The best point guard in the business of professional basketball. My pockets are as deep as my skills."

Nicholas did a double take. While he'd heard a lot of talk about Ike the Psyche, he'd never found time to watch any of the games. Besides owning and running his own private practice, he took on a fair amount of pro bono cases, which he worked on after his regular office hours. After a nightly workout at the private health club, he went straight home, showered, and jumped right into bed. Each day's schedule was rigorously demanding.

"A professional basketball player, huh? Are you any good?"

Isaiah's spitting-nails glare made Nicholas flinch. "I'm the man! Don't you watch television? I guess not. If you did, you'd know me by sight. I can't believe you've never seen so much as a picture of me. Do you think you would've wondered about me had you seen one?"

"Possibly. It is uncanny how much you look like me, especially when I was your age. I was cocky as hell, too, just like you. I was also one hell of a basketball player."

"Why didn't you go pro?"

"Because I was more interested in becoming a lawyer than a jock. I wanted to make money so I could do great things with it. I had dreams of becoming a philanthropist. I wanted to be in a position to offer educational scholarships to underprivileged minorities. No one other than God would beat me at giving."

"That's an interesting statement coming from you since you haven't given any monetary support so that your own child wouldn't have to suffer."

"You suffered? Somehow I doubt that. If I know your mother like I think I do, she'd never let you want for a thing. Asia would've sold her soul to the devil to meet your needs."

"She did sell her soul to the devil! She worked two jobs and continued with her education. She used to take me to her school and to her night job 'cause she couldn't afford a baby-sitter. My mom struggled back then. That's why I decided I was going to make something of myself. I was going to make enough money so that my mom would never have to work again unless she wanted to. I did what I set out to do. Mom couldn't be prouder. I could've gotten caught up in gangs and drugs, but that would've broken her heart. I couldn't do that to her. You'd already broken it and left her life in shambles."

Nicholas ignored Isaiah's accusation. It wouldn't do any good to challenge him. Isaiah had his mind made up about him, but Nicholas was going to move heaven and earth to try and change it. "I don't know if it means anything to you, but I'm also proud of you."

"It doesn't . . . it doesn't mean a damn thing." Isaiah started for the door. "Now that I've seen you, I hope I can put everything from the past to rest. But seeing you hasn't changed a thing for me. You'll never be anything more to me than a stranger, nothing more than a sperm donor."

Bleeding from the wounds sliced into his heart, Nicholas leaped to his feet. "Son, don't walk away like this. We need to talk. I promise to answer any questions you might ask of me. I'll be as honest as I can with you. Won't you please give us a chance to get to know one another?"

Unable to believe his ears, Isaiah looked stunned. "Why should I do that?"

"Because we're blood relatives. I'm your father and you're my son."

"Are you saying you don't want to have a paternity test to see if you can discredit my mother? Are you trying to tell me that you actually believe I'm your son?"

Nicholas jumped up and marched Isaiah into the private bathroom where he stood him in front of the mirror. "A judge would jail me if I tried to deny you. Look at yourself, son. Then look at me. No, I don't need a paternity test. I just need some time with my boy. I can't make up for the lost years, but I don't want to miss out on another second. Let me buy you dinner, son."

Isaiah checked his emotions. This was just something else he hadn't expected, at all, not in a million years. "I'll have dinner with you as long as you don't ask me to call you dad. That's something I'll never be able to do."

"Never say never, son. We have to live in the moment. Let's get out of here. I know a quiet Italian place that serves great meals. Do you like Italian food?"

"It's okay." Isaiah loved Italian food with a passion, but he didn't want Nicholas to know that. It seemed too personal. "What about you?"

"I love it! My favorite is Italian sausage smothered with onions, bell peppers, lots of mozzarella cheese and thick, spicy tomato sauce. Spaghetti is next, followed by lasagna. One trip to Tony's Place, and you'll love Italian food, too."

Isaiah was amazed to learn that he and his father loved the same foods in the same exact order. Asia had learned to cook all of Isaiah's favorite Italian food. Though he loved his mother's cooking, he liked it best when Asia allowed him to take her out to his own favorite Italian restaurant. He loved to pamper her, loved for them to spend quality time together, more than loved it when they had each other's undivided attention.

Excited because he was possibly going to learn more about his son, Nicholas grabbed his suit jacket on the way to the door. He didn't try to touch Isaiah but he was curious as to whether he'd ever feel his arms around his son, feel his heartbeat thumping against his own. He wanted desperately to feel that sort of soulful connection with his only child.

Isaiah refused to leave his shiny black sports car in the parking structure, opting to follow Nicholas to the nearby restaurant. When their dinner was over, he didn't want to come back to this place. His mission would be complete. He had a hard time believing he'd even accepted the invite. Oddly enough, Isaiah somehow felt glad that he did.

On the other hand, Nicholas couldn't believe the blessing. Being a very spiritual man, he knew that none other than God had ordained this meeting. *Father, help me,* he prayed in silence. *Help me to be open and honest with this young man, who, no doubt, came here to condemn me to hell. Instead, by the miracle of your love, we're going to break bread together.* "Father, I thank you for this divine opportunity," Nicholas whispered.

Soft lighting brightened the near-empty restaurant where candles burned at each table. Red-and-white checkered tablecloths added warmth and a brighter touch to the atmosphere. A well-stocked bar, with assorted glasses hanging from overhead racks, took up one entire wall. With all of the bar stools vacant, only one tall figure stood at the bar, the burly-looking bartender.

Ernie nodded in the direction of the two patrons entering the restaurant. "What's up, Nicholas? Who's that you got with you?"

Nicholas looked at Isaiah's scowling face. How in the world was he supposed to answer that? But it went deeper than what was actually asked of him. How Isaiah would want him to answer it was his real dilemma. "Are you telling me you don't recognize this fine young man?" Nicholas took in a deep breath at the look of relief on Isaiah's face. His expression appeared to say, *I'm glad you didn't have the gall to tell someone I'm your son.*

Ernie came from behind the bar to peer into Isaiah's face. "Well, I'll be darned if it ain't Ike the Psyche." Ernie thumped hard on Isaiah's back with an open palm. "I'm honored to meet you, young man. You sure know how to handle that darn B-ball. Keep setting the NBA on fire. The best of luck to you!" Ernie pumped Isaiah's hand and then Nicholas's. Without further ado, Ernie turned back toward his workstation.

The restaurant wasn't as crowded as normal, Nicholas noted. He was glad for that. This way, they wouldn't have to try and talk over loud conversation and laughter. After seating themselves at a table near the rear emergency exit doors, Nicholas studied his son's handsome features. The large dark eyes shone brightly with a heart-melting sadness. The full mouth, firm but pouting, was turned down in a slight frown. The ends of the long lashes, dark with fringe, curled upward.

Nicholas laughed inwardly. The unruly curl hanging in the middle of Isaiah's forehead reminded him of how he'd chemically relaxed his own unruly curl—the one that had once annoyed him to no end; Asia had loved it. He grew full at the crazy memories of yesteryear.

"Want to let me in on it?" The sound of Isaiah's voice brought Nicholas back around, but the arrival of the waitress kept him from responding to the question. Menus were handed to each of them, but Nicholas already knew what he wanted to order.

"Number-five sampler," he told the waitress. "Extra mozzarella on the sausage. You can hold my salad and serve it with the entrée."

The number-five sampler dish consisted of all the things Nicholas mentioned loving, Isaiah saw, as he read the menu: Italian sausage, lasagna, and spaghetti. He ordered the same, only asking that the salad be served as soon as possible.

Isaiah watched after the waitress until she disappeared, more out of feeling awkward than from any personal interest in her. After all, he'd never before sat across the table from his father. Oh, but how he'd wished for that very thing, time after time, especially during his adolescence.

"So," Nicholas said, breaking the awkward silence, "how'd you get the nickname Ike the Psyche?"

Isaiah's gentle smile softened his brooding expression. Nicholas saw that the credit for his beautiful smile went to his mother. Asia had a way of lighting up any spot she occupied. One smile from her could render him senseless. Her brilliant mind was what had attracted him to her in the first place. But it was Asia's quiet spirit that had made him highly curious about her.

"The sports commentators dubbed me with it. I've been known to completely psyche out my opponents. Pretty much like Rodman used to do. I'm exceptionally good at it. What can I say?" Isaiah wished he could psyche himself up right about now just to get through this dinner.

"Are you always this cocky?"

"Always. I just happen to believe in myself. If that's cocky, I'm guilty of it."

Since he was a chip off the old block, Nicholas was somewhat amused by his son's arrogance. "What do you average per game?"

"I'm only in my second year, but my point average is about twenty-six per. I'm consistent and my teammates can count on me in clutch situations. My point average was even higher in college, twenty-eight per. But I'm romping with the big boys now. The NBA's no joke. Still, I'm tossing big numbers into the hoop each game."

"What about your grade point average?"

"Four point oh. Graduated from the University of North Carolina with honors. I took my studies seriously to prepare for life after hoops. Besides, Mom would've thrown a major fit if I hadn't. She didn't play when it came down to my education." The liquid softness in Isaiah's eyes was a strong testimony to the love and admiration that he felt for Asia. "As kindhearted as she is, she was pretty hard-core about the importance of a good education. She's a great mom."

Damming up his emotions came hard for Nicholas. It was doubly hard for him to hear about all the things he'd missed out on. "Damn you, Asia," he cursed under his breath. He couldn't help thinking of how things could've been different for all of them. His boy had grown up without the benefits that come with having a father around the house, a good father. There was no doubt in Nicholas's mind that he would've been a great dad to his son.

A mother could teach her son all the things he needed to learn about nurturing, even about respecting women, but it took a strong, positive male to teach a boy how to become a responsible man. But he had to admit that Asia had done a magnificent job in raising their son alone. In fact, a lot of single moms had done great jobs with their young men. Was Asia married now? He wanted to know, but thought asking might cause Isaiah's anger to rise all over again.

They ate in silence, each wondering what the other was thinking, but too afraid to ask. Isaiah was still overwhelmed by the fact that his father was seated right across from him. What would it feel like to touch him, to hug him, to hear him say that he loved him? *That can't ever happen,* he told himself. He hated the man with a passion. At least, that's what he'd been telling himself for years now. The hate inside him had blossomed like nature in spring during his teen years. That he didn't feel as bitter and angry as he normally did surprised Isaiah.

"Would you like a beer, or something else cold?" Nicholas asked Isaiah.

Isaiah raised his hand in a declining gesture. "I never put anything in my body that could prove hazardous to my health. My anger is the only thing I've ever allowed in that could threaten my life. I'm now much better at managing it since I began therapy." He thought about the near uncontrollable anger he'd displayed at Nicholas's office. "That is, most of the time."

Nicholas acknowledged his son's message, saw the regret over his earlier behavior awash in his dark eyes. He was glad that Isaiah had the type of eyes that he could envision his soul through, eyes very much like his own. Angry, yes, but nonetheless a good kid, Nicholas assessed. He was proud of his son's glowing accomplishments. Nicholas hoped Isaiah could look into his eyes and read what he'd read in his.

"I drink, but not much, a glass of wine now and then. I don't like to have my mind blurred since I use it to make a living. A drunken lawyer is usually an incompetent one. He may do well for a short spell, but the effects of drinking will eventually show up in one way or another."

Isaiah wanted to ask Nicholas if he'd been drinking when he'd gotten his mother pregnant, but that was too crude a question, not to mention too personal. He didn't want to know, anyway. It would hurt to know that he'd been conceived under the influence of alcohol or drugs. He knew college kids back then did a lot of puffing on the all-time party favorite, the old MJ, as well as other psychedelic drugs. Unfortunately, his generation of college kids was into hard-core drugs.

"Say, Da . . ." Isaiah nearly choked on his tongue, hating himself for almost using the name he'd promised to never use. Terribly uncomfortable with his blunder, he got to his feet. "I think I'd better go now." He hated admitting that he was enjoying spending time with this stranger who just happened to have fathered him.

Looking panic-stricken, Nicholas got to his feet, too. "I thought we'd shoot a game or two of pool, as well as a little more of the breeze, before you moved on."

The idea was tempting to Isaiah. It showed in his eyes. He gave the idea a few seconds' more thought before he agreed to stay a bit longer. When both men sat back down, Nicholas looked relieved. He actually felt giddy with delight. He was going to shoot a game of pool with his very own son. *His very own son*, his brain reverberated, his heart loving the sound of it.

The check was paid, Isaiah's treat. He didn't want anything from Nicholas, who'd let him pay the bill because he sensed that Isaiah wouldn't allow him to do it. Letting the young man keep his dignity was a must for Nicholas.

Nearly identical in height and build, Isaiah being an inch or two taller than Nicholas, the two men moved into the billiards room.

"Want to rack 'em?" Nicholas asked Isaiah.

"Sure," Isaiah responded in a casual tone.

Nicholas won the first game and Isaiah won the next two. Father and son talked trash the entire time. They'd even laughed at each other's missed shots. Nicholas's reactions to Isaiah weren't even close to what Isaiah had imagined. He had set himself up for the worst-case scenario. Though Nicholas had threatened to kick him out of his office earlier, Isaiah was aware that it was only because of the disrespect that he'd shown toward the older man.

Had Asia known that Isaiah had found his father she would've warned him to mind his manners. *Don't make him think that I didn't raise you right*, she would've demanded of her son. *I don't want him to think that we did anything but fine without him*, Isaiah imagined Asia saying.

Since Nicholas hadn't rejected him, Isaiah wondered why Asia had kept him such a secret. Every time he'd ask about his father, she'd say, "Let's not visit that issue. Some things are better left unsaid." While she'd never said anything bad about him, Isaiah had assumed that the man was so horrible that she couldn't even stomach talking about him. But he was puzzled since Asia had actually given her son Nicholas's last name as his middle one: Isaiah Reynolds Morrell.

Isaiah hadn't pushed his mother on the subject of his father because he'd feared the things that she might reveal to him. Such as, your father didn't want you, he wanted an abortion, or even if he said the baby couldn't possibly be his. If any of those things had been said, Isaiah didn't want Asia to relive the pain. Besides, they'd done just fine without the great legal eagle Nicholas Reynolds.

"Do you have any other kids?" Isaiah asked Nicholas.

"Just you." Nicholas said that as though he'd always known he had a child.

"Why'd you never have any?"

"Oh, but I did. You."

Nicholas truly wanted to relay to Isaiah that he accepted him as his own flesh and blood, without any reservations whatsoever. Nicholas always knew that he'd been Asia's first and only lover. Just the fact that Asia was Isaiah's mother was enough for Nicholas to go on. Isaiah's age was just another convincing factor. Undeniably, Isaiah's looks mostly came from him.

Isaiah lowered his head. Anger had eaten him up so badly that he'd never felt some of these new emotions that kept coming at him. He actually felt like crying, something he hadn't done out of pain since he was a teenager. He'd cried like crazy when he'd learned that he'd received both academic and athletic scholarships to the University of North Carolina, Chapel Hill. And he'd also cried buckets when his name was announced as the first draft pick in the NBA. Crying didn't come easy for him, and it had nothing to do with being a man.

For the next hour or so conversation between father and son flowed freely, although awkward moments came upon them from time to time. They had taken up the corner table in the billiard room to polish off a medium vegetable pizza between them.

Isaiah drained the last of his Coke and got to his feet. "I need to stop by my friend's place in Ladera before I call it a night. Troy Dyson and I have been best friends since childhood."

Nicholas stood. "Okay. I'd better move in the direction of home, too." Nicholas took a business card out of his wallet. "Every number where I can be reached is on that card, with the exception of my home number." Nicholas then wrote down his private home number on the back of the card and handed it to Isaiah. "I hope you'll decide to use those numbers one day. We shouldn't let it end now that we've gotten through the beginning."

Isaiah stuck his hand out for Nicholas to shake. Instead, Nicholas pulled his son into his arms. Isaiah's anger at Nicholas forcing physical contact on him arose like a firestorm. The rage in his eyes cast Nicholas into hell's lake of fire. Cursing under his breath, Isaiah broke the embrace and walked away. Stopping at the exit, he turned and looked back.

As though he had no control over his long, sturdy legs, they carried him toward his father. So happy to see his son coming back to him, Nicholas didn't see the punch coming. Landing in his chest, the powerful blow knocked Nicholas backward, yet he somehow managed to stay on his feet. Nicholas didn't move a muscle as Isaiah came at him again and again. Bracing himself anew after each blow, Nicholas flexed his muscles in order to prepare himself for Isaiah's next powerful jab, even though most of the wild punches were barely connecting.

Yelling something totally incoherent, Isaiah flung himself into Nicholas's arms. Sobbing like a little boy with a broken heart, Isaiah clutched hard at his dad's back and shoulders. Holding this boy-man of his tightly in his arms, Nicholas dropped down to his knees bringing Isaiah with him. Two loudly sobbing men brought the owner rushing into the billiard room. When Nicholas put up his hand in a halting gesture, Tony walked away, closing the door behind him. He had simply read in his old friend's eyes the pleading request for privacy.

Not daring to pull apart, father and son kissed, cried some more, hugged, and sobbed harder, blubbering unintelligible things all the while. Crying harder than they'd ever cried before, the two men promised each other to work on building some sort of a relationship. Laughter came briefly—and then came more tears, hugs, and kisses. Promises of more tomorrows were made.

Isaiah and Nicholas ended up nearly closing the Italian place down. Having crammed several years into a few hours, they promised to keep on talking until all the gaps and holes of yesteryears had been filled in. So much more needed to be said, but so much had already been felt between this father and his only son. But Nicholas now felt sure that there was so much more in store for them. The time had been granted for them to spend more time together. Silently, Nicholas thanked God for yet another miraculous blessing.

Nicholas loved Isaiah simply because he was his flesh and blood, because fathers were supposed to love their children. Just as naturally as parents loved their children, children also naturally loved their parents. Nicholas believed that the Creator loved all of which He'd created. The Creator had ordained him as Isaiah's father. Although Satan had somehow thrown a monkey wrench into the Creator's plan,

Nicholas knew that the devil couldn't do any more than he was permitted to do by God. Nicholas also knew that God would reveal to him in His own time why there had been such a delay in him meeting his son; for unto everything there is a purpose.

Isaiah was so emotionally full by the time he got in his car he had to sit quietly for a few moments just in order to pull it all together. As the tears rolled down his cheeks, he thought of all the things that had transpired over the past few hours. How could a meeting that had started out so badly end up turning out to be one of the most wonderful experiences he'd ever had in his life? Spending time with his dad had been awesome.

As much as he hated to admit it, he realized he had spent years hating a man who didn't seem to have deserved his hatred at all. Isaiah had the hardest time trying to figure out why his mother would deny him the opportunity to know such a seemingly wonderful human being. Something in Nicholas's spirit had reached out to Isaiah in a way that he'd never be able to explain. Isaiah had been around enough evil to know that Nicholas wasn't in any way an advocate for the devil. Still, he didn't know why a loving God had allowed this to happen.

Perhaps over the years Nicholas had gone from being an irresponsible boy to a very responsible man. Maybe Asia hadn't told him about their child because she hadn't trusted him to do the right thing back then. She could've believed that he was incapable of taking on the responsibility of a child while still in college. Something serious had happened to make his mother decide to keep father and son apart. Asia wouldn't have done something like that without just cause. She wasn't that type of woman. He didn't know what had occurred between Asia and his father, and he couldn't go back and change it if he did, so he decided to just count this phenomenon as another blessing.

From the way it looked, he was going to have both his mother and father in his life. How could he ask for more than that? While unsure of God's intent, Isaiah had turned to prayer off and on for many, many years. Isaiah now felt that his prayers had finally been answered.

Wearing a bright smile, he finally pulled out of the parking lot.

Feeling as though he would burst inside if he waited until he saw Asia to tell her about his encounter with his father, he reached for the cell phone. He hoped that his mother wouldn't be hurt by his news or feel betrayed by him. Deep down inside, he knew that she would be happy for him. On the other hand, she might not be too elated with him after he told her how he felt about her deceit.

CHAPTER TWO

U nable to sleep, Nicholas sat up in the king-size four-poster bed and felt around for the remote control. After finding it between the top and bottom sheets, he pushed the red power button to turn the television on. A flash of blinding white briefly lit the darkened room. Then the screen came into view in full color.

Nicholas wiped the corners of his eyes where the salt from his tears had dried and caked. He'd washed his face before going to bed, but he had begun to cry again the moment his thoughts had wrapped around a young man named Isaiah Morrell, better known to the entire sports world as Ike the Psyche, his one and only child, a son.

A breaking news story flashing across the wide screen gripped Nicholas's immediate attention. After plumping the pillows, he laid his head back against them and made himself comfortable. Seconds later he sat straight up when he saw the badly twisted metal of what appeared to have once been a car. It seemed that the driver of the black BMW convertible never had a chance to steer the car out of the path of destruction. According to the news reporter, a commuter train had smashed right into the car, knocking it several yards away from the tracks.

"While we haven't come up with any confirmed information on the driver's identity, the license plates are still in good condition. There are reliable reports that this car belongs to NBA superstar Isaiah

Morrell, fondly known as Ike the Psyche of the California Wildcats. The plates on the car read IRM-CW. We understand that the first three initials stand for his first, middle, and last names, and that possibly the CW stands for the name of his team."

Horrified at what he'd just heard, Nicholas could barely breathe. He'd actually felt the blood draining from his face when Isaiah's name was mentioned. A moan from somewhere deep within him escaped his lips. Doubling up on the bed, he held his stomach, hoping to quash the nauseous feelings violently rising up inside him. Fearing for his son's safety, he felt sweat pouring profusely from him.

The phone rang but Nicholas was in too much pain to even attempt to reach for it. As the answering machine came on, he prayed that Isaiah was the caller, that the previous scenario was nothing more than a horrible nightmare. Rocking back and forth in agony, he moaned loudly.

"Nicholas," Lynda Frasier called out, anxiety lacing her voice, "good God, Nicholas, please pick up the phone." She paused for a few seconds to see if his voice would come over the line. "Please call me as soon as you get this message. Please, Nicholas, it's urgent!"

Writhing around in total agony, Nicholas let loose with a haunting, bloodcurdling howl. Like a pack of crying wolves, his mournful howls crashed into the silence of the early morning hours as he fought hard to try to gain control of himself and his emotions. *Perhaps the media report was dead wrong,* he tried to convince himself. *Maybe the car had stalled on the tracks and Isaiah had gotten out before the train had actually hit.* His eyes suddenly grew blurry.

The very moment Asia came to mind, the howling started up again. Though he detested what she'd done in terms of keeping his son away from him, he could never hate her. She was the only woman he had ever truly loved. If he felt this horrible after a few hours of knowing that Isaiah even existed, how was the woman who'd actually raised this kid going to feel? If it was Isaiah in that car, Asia was going to want to die herself. He knew that much about her. Asia wouldn't want to survive this, but she'd have to. And he'd have to be the one to see to it.

The beautiful, tall, slender Asia was dressed in a simple cream-colored silk blouse and black denim jeans, as she stood motionless looking down at the near lifeless body of her beloved son, who lay so still in the narrow hospital bed. Bloody, battered, and bruised, Isaiah's body looked like it had been put through the wringer of an old washing machine. Bending over the railing of the bed, she gently kissed her son on the lips, praying that they both might awaken to find that this was only a bad dream. That Isaiah wasn't lying in bed fighting for his life had been her constant prayer all the way to the hospital. Reality had come all too soon.

Through the blur of her tears, she looked around the private room, hating the etherlike smell of it. The thought of colorful fresh flowers brightening this room and possibly chasing away the sterile odor occurred to her. Having his own comforter set brought from his bed at home would also lift the spirit of this space. A cheerful atmosphere would help matters.

Still matted with blood from the deep gashes in his head and forehead, Isaiah's silky black hair curled around his head like a thick, protective covering. A coma, she'd heard the doctors say, as Isaiah was moved from the emergency room to the intensive care unit. It's a touch-and-go situation, very small chance for survival, she'd been informed.

Impossible, she screamed inwardly. Her tears bubbled and broke on her lashes. Feeling like she wanted to curl up in a ball and die, she sat down and pulled her knees up to her chest, resting her feet on the very edge of the chair. Asia thought of how she would gladly take Isaiah's place there in that too-small bed. She'd be willing to give him every vital organ that her body possessed if that was required to save his precious life. She would die for her only child.

She didn't care if he never dunked another basketball, though she somehow knew that her son would do exactly that. She just needed Isaiah to live, to laugh again, and to continue to give her his undying love. No mother could ask for a finer son than what she had in Isaiah.

Regrets, she mused. She had so many. That she hadn't told Isaiah everything there was to know about his father was her biggest regret. She was sure that telling Nicholas about Isaiah would've kept him in her life by force. Nicholas would've readily taken responsibility for his son. But she also knew that Nicholas would've felt obligated to her, even to the point of marriage. A marriage in name only wasn't something she'd wanted back then, or ever. That wouldn't have worked for her. She truly loved Nicholas. Not to have his love in return would've been her undoing. It was better this way, she'd told herself. The one time she'd convinced herself to find him and tell him, she'd heard he was engaged.

In many ways she still had Nicholas in Isaiah, the spitting image of his father. He even walked and talked like Nicholas. Curious as he'd been about his father, Isaiah had never really pressured her into talking about him. If he had, she wasn't sure that she would've been able to bear the pain of telling him all the wonderful things that she knew about Nicholas Reynolds.

It was rare for her to deny her son anything he desired, but she allowed only that which was good for him. She had never indulged Isaiah in mere whims. But she had foolishly denied him one of those good things, had denied him what he had truly needed most in his life: his father.

The gentle hand on her shoulder instantly liquefied her insides, the same way its owner had melted her heart years ago. Without looking up, she knew that Nicholas stood behind her. Her thoughts took her back to the phone call she had received earlier from her son. The joy in Isaiah's voice had brought tears to her eyes. Isaiah had tracked his father down and he couldn't have been happier about it. He had cried during the entire conversation, which made it impossible for him to tell his mother everything. He had decided to come to her house first, before stopping by his friend's place. What had eventually occurred between them had turned out to be anything but pleasant. She never got to fully explain her reasons for keeping his father at bay. Terribly upset over her not telling him the truth about his father, Isaiah had stormed out on her. Asia felt totally responsible for his accident.

Without hesitation, her small hand reached back and covered his. "I know that Isaiah found you, but I don't know all the details." *His out-of-control anger caused him to shut me out.*

"I laid my eyes on him for the first time this evening, quite a few hours before this tragedy occurred. Angry as hell, he came to my office to confront me over my absence in his life for the past twenty-one years."

"I'm sorry, Nicholas."

"I'm sure you are, Asia. But now that I'm here, please don't ask me to leave."

"I wouldn't think of it, Nicholas."

"Are you here alone?"

"It has always been just Isaiah and me. Now that you're here, I don't feel alone anymore. I'm not used to being in a room with Isaiah without conversation. We love talking with each other about everything you can imagine." *Except the subject of you being kept away from him.*

"I can only imagine. I've only just met my son. Now tomorrow may never come."

The hurt in his voice stung her hard. "I know that I owe you an apology, which would never, ever be enough. I'm so sorry, Nicholas, so sorry that I didn't tell you about our son."

"Not now, Asia. There will be plenty of time for us to discuss this. Just know that I'm here for our son, here for you, as long as you need me to be."

His words were very comforting to her but they hurt. As long as you *need* me to be, resonated through her brain. As long as you *want* me here would've kept Nicholas there with her forever. That's how she'd always desired it to be, but circumstances hadn't allowed her desires to be fulfilled. Asia Morrell had never stopped loving Nicholas Reynolds.

"What are the doctors saying, Asia?"

Asia closed her heart to the words that had cut her so deep. That she'd have to repeat them again and again was burdensome. There were many people that cared about her precious Isaiah, a well-liked, highly respected young man. Upon her arrival, the media throng that she'd had to endure had been a challenge. Microphones had been shoved in her face from the moment she arrived at Cedars Sinai Hospital. Many other people were going to want to know, too. No doubt the media would also bombard Isaiah's girlfriend when she returned to Los Angeles from visiting her family in Chicago. Supermodel Torri Jefferson's screams haunted Asia still, as she thought of Torri's reaction when she'd earlier phoned to give her the bad news.

Although Asia hadn't turned around to look at him, Nicholas could imagine the pain filling her beautiful pecan-brown eyes. Her rich chestnut-brown hair was much longer than the pixie-cut style that she'd worn in college. The heavy silky curtain of shiny hair hid her elegant neck. Even though he couldn't see her figure, since she was seated, he doubted that she weighed any more than the one hundred twenty-five pounds that she had carried around in college. Her slender, five-foot-seven frame couldn't handle much more weight than that, anyway.

"Come and sit down, Nicholas."

Once he pulled up a chair and situated himself comfortably, her delicate hands took hold of his in a warm caress. The memory of his tender touch on her flesh was instantaneous.

"It's not good, Nicholas. He's in critical condition. Touch-and-go for now is what I've been told. The prognosis is not what you and I would hope for. The healthy vibrant Isaiah that once was may be lost to me, to us. Still, I want him alive, no matter what. I simply can't stand the thought of losing him. To never hear his voice or to feel his touch would be unbearable."

"God is in control of this situation, as He is in control of everything in this world, Asia. He will have the final say. Man cannot give life, therefore he can't take it away."

Asia had to look closer at him now. A man of conviction, a man of God had spoken those very words. That surprised her in some way, even though Nicholas had always been somewhat of a spiritual being. Not religious per se yet filled with the purest of spirit.

His breath caught as her bright eyes connected with his. She didn't look a day older or any less stunning. Though maturity had claimed her in many other ways, the features on her tawny-brown face were still as delicate as they'd ever been. Her eyes still had an angelic glow.

Her heart wept. Nicholas was every bit as good-looking as he had been over twenty-two years ago. The graying at the temples made him a distinguished-looking gent. Tall and stately, Nicholas still had the physique of an athlete, the same body she used to love finding herself lying beneath in the bed in his dormitory room. At forty-three years of age, a year older than she, he was still able to hold his own in the department of outward appearances. Though only dressed in casual gray slacks and a black cashmere polo sweater, Nicholas looked elegant and debonair.

In slow motion their fingers came together and entwined. After she stood up, slowly, he brought her slender frame toward his slightly trembling body. There, in his arms, he held her tightly.

The warm caresses, only comforting in nature, were over much too soon for both of them. When Asia returned to her chair and pulled it

alongside Isaiah's bed, Nicholas pulled a seat up on the other side of
where their son lay motionless. Before seating himself, Nicholas stood
over Isaiah and passed a few words of humble and meaningful prayer.

Nicholas and Asia had sat in stony silence for the rest of the night
and for the better part of the next day, though they had nodded off
for short periods of time. Each had stayed lost in musings of past
times together and in the prayerful thoughts of their son. Nurses had
come into the room quietly and had gone out the same way, but not a
word had been spoken.

Nicholas looked at his watch, surprised at how the time had flown.
It was already after one o'clock in the afternoon. He then glanced
over at Asia. "What about us getting something to eat? We do have to
keep up our strength."

"Thank you, Nicholas, but I can't leave Isaiah's side. He needs me
here."

"Yes, he does, but he also needs you to remain healthy. I'll be right
back." Without further comment, he kissed the top of her head and
left the room.

Tears fell from Asia's eyes before Nicholas could even clear the
doorway. This was a strange happening. The very man she'd kept out
of her life, her son's life, was now here offering her every comfort.
His kind ways hadn't changed a bit. God, what had she done to him?

He should hate her. Instead, he had embraced her and had also
voiced sincere concern for her health. But weren't those the very
same qualities in Nicholas that she'd fallen in love with so many years
ago? At the tender age of eighteen, a quiet, soft-spoken Asia Morrell
had fallen head over heels in love with one Nicholas Reynolds, the
black athletic wonder for Howard University. Nicholas could've had
his choice of any female on the university campus, but he had chosen
her.

Although their coming together had occurred through an unusual
set of circumstances, nonetheless she had become his choice. Yet,
after nearly four years of exclusive dating, she still hadn't grown as
confident in his love as he had been in the love she'd obviously felt
for him.

Learning that she was pregnant with Nicholas's child in the latter part of her junior year of college had caused her to run far away. Asia had sacrificed her own goals in life so he could fulfill all of his dreams and aspirations. Isaiah had been born in Ohio, Asia's home state, soon after her twenty-first birthday. Asia had only moved to California after Isaiah was signed to the Wildcats. While settling down in her new home, she also began fulfilling her requirements for taking the California bar.

Thirty minutes later Nicholas came back into the room carrying a plain brown shopping bag. Placing the bag on the small round table, he reached into it and came up with two sectioned Styrofoam containers that held Italian spaghetti and meatballs, a garden salad, and two slices of buttered garlic bread. Nicholas and Isaiah weren't the only persons who loved Italian food. Asia loved all sorts of pasta, especially spaghetti drenched in fresh marinara sauce.

She smelled the spaghetti sauce the moment he opened the lid. The aroma was divine.

After taking the plastic utensils out of the clear wrapper, he walked over to Asia and handed her the Styrofoam container. "This will help you keep up your energy. I hope you enjoy it. It came from an authentic Italian place right down the street from here."

She smiled. "Thank you. I saw that you had two containers when you emptied the bag. Are you going to join me?"

"If you recall, I have a tendency to get a little messy when eating. Therefore, I'm going to sit at the table over there. I'd love to have you join me."

She did recall, with crystal clarity.

"That's fine with me, Nicholas." As Asia got to her feet, Nicholas took the food from her hand and carried it over to the table. Once she was seated, he sat down and passed the blessing.

Asia said, "I see that Italian food is still high on your list of favorites. Isaiah loves it, too. There's a lovely little Italian place that he loves to take me to. It's really close to where I live out in the San Fernando Valley."

Nicholas appeared surprised. "Funny you should mention that. I took Isaiah to my favorite Italian place last evening. When I asked Isaiah if he liked Italian food, he didn't seem overly thrilled by it. I later thought about his response after I saw how much he was enjoying his choices. I find it very interesting that Italian is a favorite of his, too."

"Isaiah loves Italian food almost as much as he loves basketball. There are many things about Isaiah that remind me of you, Nicholas, numerous things."

"I just hope I get a chance to see those things. He certainly looks like his old man."

"Do you want to talk about it, Nicholas?"

"Talk about what?"

"Why I didn't tell you about Isaiah."

"At some point in time, Asia, but not right now. My emotions aren't stable enough to deal rationally with anything more than Isaiah's health." He closed his eyes. "I'm scared, Asia. So scared for all of us."

As he opened his eyes, she saw how deep his fear ran. Asia reached over and massaged the back of Nicholas's hand. His skin felt soft to the touch, but his hands held untold strength. Nicholas loved to work with his hands in a creative way. He was always building something, she recalled. She smiled at the memory of the wooden birdcage he'd made for her. The funny part was that she hadn't even owned a bird. She ended up filling the intricate cage with silk flowers and all sorts of lush artificial greenery. The birdcage now hung from the ceiling in her bedroom.

"As for the time you spent with Isaiah at the restaurant, how'd you get him to go?"

Nicholas frowned. "It wasn't easy. I think he agreed to go more out of his curiosity about me than anything else. He came into my office full of hate, filled with anger. But I thank God that we parted with hopes of building some sort of relationship. Father-and-son relationship or just a casual friendship?" Nicholas shrugged his shoulders. "I don't know. We didn't really say." He looked thoughtful. "I'd like to know what you told him about me that made him dislike me so much. I never knew that I'd done something to hurt you. Did I unwittingly make you hate me?"

She blinked hard. "It's not what I've told him that has him so angry. It's what I didn't tell him about you, which wasn't much of anything. As for hate, I could never hate you. If it's any comfort to you, it wasn't anything you did that caused this outcome. However, Isaiah seems to have made a lot of negative assumptions about our relationship. That's my fault."

Nicholas sighed with relief. Asia's statements about him not hurting her had brought him a touch of comfort. "That may be it. He certainly had some pessimistic views about me. It has just occurred to me that possibly you ran off because you were pregnant. But what I don't understand is why. But I'm not sure I'm ready for the answers just yet. You and I have a lot to discuss, but Isaiah's health is all that I can concern myself with right now. Are you thirsty? In my confused state of mind, I didn't think to get us anything to drink."

Asia reached for her purse as she got to her feet. "There are several vending machines down the hall. Orange, right?"

He smiled gently. "Orange was definitely the drink back then. My taste buds have matured a bit. Ginger ale has been my only soft drink flavor of choice for more than a decade."

"Ginger ale it is." Asia excused herself and then left the room.

Totally overwhelmed at seeing Asia again, in complete awe of his actually having created a son with her, Nicholas began to sob. Pulling himself up from the chair, he crossed the room to where Isaiah lay so still. With tears falling from his eyes, he buried his face against Isaiah's chest, mindful of his son's fragile state. "Come back to your daddy, boy. Fight with everything that's left in you. We've got so much to look forward to. Reynolds men don't give up. Don't you dare to be the exception to that rule. Please don't leave me, son," he sobbed brokenly.

"I desperately need someone to share all of this pent-up love that's buried so deep inside me. In loving your mother so long, I was never able to feel anything for anyone that even came close to what I felt for Asia." With tears still streaming down his face, he looked upward. "Now that I have a chance to love that way again, even though it's in a much different way, Father God, please don't take that away from me," he prayed. "Please don't deny me the much-needed fulfillment that loving my son will bring to my soul."

Wiping his eyes with the heels of his hands, Nicholas had to work hard at pulling himself back together before Asia returned. He had to rein in his emotions before his badly broken heart gave way to anger. The spiritual side of him was telling him that he had to treat Asia with a gentle hand because of the tragic situation. But the human side of him, with all of its extreme flaws, was telling him to vent his anger and make her hurt the way she'd made him hurt all these years. Asia would hear from him. When she did, there would be no one that could shut him up, not a one to stop him from demanding the answers that he needed. But right now Isaiah needed positive energies around him, not negative currents. Nicholas couldn't even afford to think negatively for fear of passing bad energy on to his child.

Being a spiritual man, Nicholas didn't like having these unsettling feelings. It went against everything he stood for. *Love your neighbor as you love yourself* kept popping into his head. But he did love Asia, much more than any neighbor. While she'd hurt him deeply by not telling him about his son, she was the very woman who'd given birth to Isaiah. Through Isaiah she had also given birth to a second chance at happiness for Nicholas.

Asia had come back into the room so quietly that he hadn't heard her, but he now felt her presence. He turned around as she set down three cans of soda. Walking back to the table, he took his seat. Knowing he couldn't hide the fact that he'd been crying, he didn't try to, but he found it hard to look her in the eye. She had always been able to read his heart through his eyes. But if that had been the case, why hadn't she seen the depths of his feelings for her? If she read what he was feeling right now, anger and contempt, he was afraid it might hurt her.

"I know what you must be feeling, Nicholas. You shouldn't try to hide it," she said, as if she'd read his heart, the very thing he knew she was capable of. "I know how I'd feel if you'd done to me what I've perpetrated against you. Again, I'm sorry. And I still know that sorry will never be enough to ever take all the pain away." *I never got to tell Isaiah how sorry I am.* Asia's biggest fear was that her son might die without them making amends. That frightened her silly.

"You can't possibly know what I'm feeling, Asia, but that's not something I want to discuss right now. We will, though, in due time. Nicholas tells me that you're a savvy prosecutor as a deputy D.A. I'm surprised that I never ran across your name somewhere in the halls of justice. How do you like your job?"

She shrugged. "It's okay, but I do give it all that I have. I've been thinking of switching sides. I want to go into private practice. It's not so odd that you wouldn't hear my name around since we work in different counties. Besides that, I've only been in California for a short time. Isaiah insisted on buying me a home out here. He could no longer stand us living on separate coasts. The four years at college was enough of absence making the heart grow fonder for him. I used to repeat that expression to him when he called home crying that he was homesick. I know that you're a defense attorney. From very credible sources, I've heard that you're the very best attorney that money, or no money at all, can retain. Actually, I know for a fact that you're a very famous attorney."

Absence definitely made the heart grow fonder, but it also knew how to kill the spirit, Nicholas thought. "I've heard a few people refer to me as such. Since I own the firm, I can make the decision to take on a lot of pro bono cases. Despite all the other brilliant legal minds in my office, I practically work twenty-four-seven. I simply love what I do."

"That's half of the battle. I've become restless with being a prosecutor. But I'm torn. It's tough either way. Hard to prosecute the innocent, doubly tough in defending the guilty. It's not something we have a choice in when we become lawyers and take an oath. We have to give nothing less than our brilliant best." She looked closely at him. "How do you manage to maintain a marriage working twenty-four-seven?"

"How'd you even know I was married? Isaiah and I didn't discuss it."

"I heard about it many, many years ago."

He raised an eyebrow. "That can't be. I've only been married less than two years."

She looked surprised. "Your first one?"

"First and only."

"Were you ever engaged?"

"Briefly. Things went awry within a month of the official announcement."

"I see." His engagement must've been during the same time frame when she'd decided to look for him and tell him about Isaiah, she mused. A mutual friend of theirs from college had told her about Nicholas's engagement. She'd been told that Nicholas and his fiancée were head-over-heels in love. Not wanting to interfere in his happiness, she'd aborted her disclosure plans.

As more and more time had lapsed, Asia finally made the decision to never tell Nicholas. Fear of his wife rejecting Isaiah was at the forefront of her decision. Though it was something that she herself could handle, now that she was a mature adult, she couldn't imagine the pain that could be caused if a young new bride were to learn that her husband had already fathered a child by another woman. It was one thing to know about if before the engagement, but it was an altogether different matter to learn it after the wedding.

With the question he was dying to ask stuck in his craw, he swallowed hard. The absence of a wedding ring didn't necessarily mean that she wasn't married. "Are you married, Asia?"

"I've never even been engaged. I always backed off when it looked like things might get serious. I'm better as a friend than I am as a lover. I have way too many issues for one man to deal with. I won't lie and say that there weren't times that I didn't have my physical needs met, but I never felt good about it afterward." *Never anything akin to what I felt like with you.*

"Besides that, I didn't want to expose Isaiah to a string of men that would only be in his life for a minute. I didn't want him to get that attached to anyone. He would've only gotten hurt when the relationship ended. I kept my social life completely away from Isaiah. He had enough to deal with without having to deal with men who might not guard his precious heart."

"I commend you for that. You had a very mature attitude for someone so young. Who were the male role models in his life?"

"The first of the two men who had the most influence in his life early on was his childhood basketball coach, Raymond Wilkes. Then there was my Uncle Thomas. He loved Isaiah as if he were his own. Unfortunately he died before Isaiah was drafted into the NBA."

"I'm sorry to hear that. I recall how fond you were of him. Your mother's brother, right?"

"Right. Thomas Carlton was the main influence in Isaiah's life. My baby was pretty broken up over his death."

"I can only imagine." All he could do was imagine anything and everything that had to do with his son's life. Knowing that he would've been everything in Isaiah's life, if only he'd been given the opportunity, was making him start to feel bitter. "What about your father? Didn't he have an important role in Isaiah's life?"

"My father and I were estranged for many years, but I don't care to get into all the reasons why it was that way. That made my father unavailable to Isaiah for a very long time, but by his own choice, not mine. However, Isaiah and my father grew very close before his death.

My mother is also gone." She smiled to acknowledge the sympathy that Nicholas's eyes held for her. "You mentioned that Isaiah didn't know you were married. Did he ask?"

"He only asked if I had other children. I think there was already enough tension for us to get through without me discussing my marriage with him. Besides, I'm getting a divorce. I had planned to see Miranda, my wife, to tell her about Isaiah. That was before I heard the news on the television about his accident. I do want to tell her before she hears it on the news. It's just a matter of time before it gets out. The media in this metropolis are savages, at best. I will not hide from anyone the fact that I'm Ike the Psyche's father—and it has nothing to do with him being famous and possibly rich. It has everything to do with who I am as a man. I'm Isaiah's father in every sense of the word. But more than anything in this world, I desire to become Daddy to him. Folks are just going to have to get used to me being around, including you, Asia."

"I'm happy about that. Even if you did deny it anyone that sees you here is going to immediately know. Your son happens to look just like you. You are a famous lawyer with a famous son. I can already see how that's going to play out in the media. It's unfortunate, but it's going to happen. We won't be able to stop it." Asia itched to know more about his pending divorce, but she wouldn't think of questioning him on it. It really wasn't any of her business. But she couldn't imagine any woman agreeing to divorce Nicholas. He was the total package.

"The accident is very unfortunate, but I couldn't be more ecstatic about the whole world learning that I'm the proud father of NBA superstar Isaiah Morrell. Thank God my divorce isn't going to be one of those messy proceedings that the media love to have a field day with."

"Isaiah Reynolds Morrell."

Immediate tears came to his eyes as he wondered if he'd heard her correctly. Was she saying that she'd given Isaiah his last name as his middle one? Then he remembered the reported initials on the license plates: IRM. Maybe she'd been telling the truth when she said the decisions she'd made weren't a result of anything he'd done wrong. Then what had it been?

Perhaps she hadn't loved him enough, hadn't loved him the way he'd loved her? That would hurt, but he could live with it now that he knew he had a son, a son that she was the mother of. The irony of it all was that he couldn't think of a single soul outside of Asia that he'd rather have as the mother of his children. Maybe that was the reason he'd never had any.

His soft gaze caressed her face like a warm afternoon breeze. "If you're saying you gave Isaiah my surname as his middle name, I'm honored. Thank you, Asia. There are so many things I have to thank you for where Isaiah is concerned. You've done a wonderful job in raising him. My only regret is that I wasn't there to share in the parental duties along with you. But I'm here now. By the grace of God, Isaiah and I will soon have our day in the sun."

"You're welcome, Nicholas. I can tell how proud you are of him. The whole world will know of your relationship to Isaiah very soon. I'm surprised that someone hasn't already leaked it to the press. He had plans of calling on one of his very good friends after he saw me. Juicy news travels very quickly when tongues start to wag. I know there will be plenty of calls coming into my office once the news hits the AP wires. Can you believe the nerve of these guys?"

"What I don't believe is that you can't believe the nerve of them. If the story were to get out this soon, I'm sure it would be a generously paid for leak. It would be such a shame for someone close to Isaiah to give up his personal business for the almighty dollar. I can't imagine him telling his news to anyone that he wasn't somewhat close to." Nicholas nearly drained the can of ginger ale in one long gulp. "If that happens, they better hope that I don't find out who they are. It'll be the last story they'll ever sell to the tabloids."

"Well, it hasn't happened yet, so maybe we shouldn't speculate. We have to think of Isaiah, Nicholas. We can't do anything that will bring any negative press his way. I know how you feel, but violence is never the answer." In watching his reaction to her remarks, she saw that her chastising tone had lit a spark of anger in him. Who in the hell was she to chastise him? That was the question she'd read in his expression.

"You can't possibly know how I feel, Asia. So do us both a favor by stop saying that you know my feelings when you don't." Wishing he had bitten his tongue, Nicholas got up from his seat and crossed the room. It wasn't like him to lash out at others, but Asia's tone had irked him.

Asia looked after him as he went over to Isaiah's bedside and pulled up a chair. The open line of communication with him had been lost. Nicholas simply had to regroup. He'd rather bite off his tongue than get into a bitter argument with someone. That was only one of many admirable things that she recalled about Nicholas Reynolds. He had always been a staunch advocate for peace.

As he sat quietly at Isaiah's bedside, he asked to be forgiven for snapping at Asia. It wasn't that she hadn't earned his wrath, because she had, but now was not the time for such a display of anger. Was there ever really a right time for it? It suddenly came to his mind that he hadn't seen a hospital staff member in quite a while. Unsure of how he should play out his role with Asia or the staff as Isaiah's deeply concerned father, he looked over at her. "Don't you think someone should be in here checking on him? It's been several hours since the nurse was in here last. Do you mind if I go out to the nurses' station and voice my concerns?"

"Why would I mind?"

"I don't know, Asia. I'm not sure how you want me to play out my role in this situation. This is all so new for me. I've never been a father before. Maybe you should tell me what the boundaries are. I don't want to do anything to upset you."

"There are no boundaries, Nicholas. Isaiah is as much your son as he is mine. Do whatever comes naturally for you. You've been deprived of your rights long enough. In fact, I'm glad to have you here to take control of this tragic situation. It feels good to have someone around that I know I can count on. I'm afraid that I don't have the strength to go through this nightmare alone. I just hope that I don't lean on you too hard. Thanks for being here."

"Thanks for allowing it. When you feel depleted of your strength, lean on me as hard as you need to. I promise that I won't let you hit the ground."

"Hearing you say that makes me feel a hundred times better. With that settled, I'll sit here with Isaiah while you go talk to his nurse."

"I'll be right back."

Asia was so sorry that Nicholas was being hurt yet again. It seemed to her that he hadn't had any luck with any of the women after her. A broken engagement and now a divorce after less than two years of marriage was quite surprising since every girl in college would've given up a limb just to have him look in her direction. He'd only been the most popular guy on campus.

Asia and Nicholas had passed each other in the hallway every single day for several months during her first year at Howard, but he rarely even looked at her. She'd be with her friends and he'd be with his. The small group of girls she hung out with would whistle and make flirtatious remarks at Nicholas when he passed by. That was something she couldn't do despite how handsome she thought he was. The evening that he actually came to her room to see her was quite a shock for her. His reason for being there shocked her even more. That evening was the start of something she never would've believed possible.

If she could only take all of his hurt away, especially the pain that she had inflicted upon him by her reckless decisions. But it was too late for all of that. They were now two totally different people. Getting their son through this crisis was the only thing that they had in common. Years and years had come between them and no one could give them back any of the time they'd missed out on. But there was only one thing that could keep him and his son apart, the one thing that she couldn't bear to think about: death. The death of Isaiah would also separate her from her son permanently, without the hope of him ever forgiving her. If he lived, she knew he'd eventually come to absolve her. They loved each other too much for them not to reconcile.

Nicholas sat at Isaiah's bedside, right where he'd stayed the whole night through. In looking at his son, he was still amazed at seeing the mirror image of himself. For the past several hours all he could think of were the things he and Isaiah could've done together. Nicholas hadn't taken very much time off from work over the years, especially for anything that had to do with fun or social activities. But with having a son, he would've taken all the time that was needed to love and nurture Isaiah. As sporting events came to mind, Nicholas nearly broke down and cried. Someone other than himself had encouraged Isaiah in playing basketball. For him to be in the NBA, his coach and Asia's uncle had to have been the dominating force and a major influence in his son's life. That hurt so badly. He should've been Isaiah's mentor in everything he took on.

Since Nicholas had once loved and lived for every kind of sport there was, he could only dream of what it might've been like to assist Isaiah in developing his numerous skills. It disturbed him that he hadn't taken the time to watch one of the sports he loved so much. Perhaps had he seen Isaiah on television he might've questioned the fact that he looked so much like himself. But watching television was a rarity for Nicholas. The last name of Morrell could've also possibly sparked an interest but only when combined with Isaiah's looks. From the first moment he laid eyes on Isaiah, he had not one second of doubt as to the issue of paternity.

Isaiah was his son, all six feet, five inches and one hundred eighty pounds of him.

Nicholas began to pray over Isaiah, his eyes filling with tears. "Father God, I thank you for allowing me to know my son for however brief it has been. It is my prayer, Father God, that you may have so much more in store for Isaiah and me. Please spare him, Lord. Let me have more time with him. I need to know this child; I need him to know me. I can accept your will, whatever that might be, but all I ask is that you consider my heart in this, Father God. If these things I ask are thy most holy will, I ask them in the name of Jesus. Amen."

Nicholas opened his Bible to the Book of Job. As if Isaiah would hear him, and he believed that he could, he began to read aloud the story of Job, one of Nicholas's favorite books of the Bible.

Surprised to see him so early this morning Asia quietly observed Nicholas's interaction with their son as she stood in the doorway of Isaiah's room. While she listened to Nicholas read from the Bible, Asia's mind drifted backward in time to where the hallways at Howard University were a flurry of activity.

Asia had nearly been knocked down twice already by students rushing by trying to make it to class. She was pretty much a loner, and still was. She'd had one girlfriend at school, and she only had one now, but she hadn't been quite sure of Lynette's loyalty to her. Lynette had the tendency to be wishy-washy with Asia when they were in the company of other females. When they were alone, she had been very attentive to Asia and had shown genuine concern for her.

Asia remembered how stunned she'd been when Nicholas Reynolds, a star athlete, had bumped into her, knocking her off balance. Before she could regain her footing, Nicholas was steadying her with firm but tender hands. He had apologized immediately. For the first time ever, he'd actually looked at her, a very up-close and personal look. Then he'd asked her name. She had responded in a timid voice. All of a sudden, it had looked as if he was impressed by her.

It was later in the evening on that same day that Nicholas had come to Asia's room, asking her if she'd tutor him in one of the classes he was doing poorly in. He was in dire need of someone to study with, someone who could help him out. After she'd given him her name during the earlier incident, he'd recalled seeing Asia's name on the Dean's list numerous times. So his initial interest in her had merely been in her brilliant mind. Although he was always the gentleman, she was disappointed to find that his only interest in her had to do with his studies. She'd later found out from him that it was her smile that had taken his breath away.

The sound of the chair scraping against the floor captured Asia's attention. As she looked up, she saw Nicholas bending over the bed. The sight of him kissing his son gently on the cheek brought a gasp to her lips and tears to her eyes. The sound of her gasp caused Nicholas to turn.

He looked surprised to see her. "How long have you been here?"

"Not long." She didn't want him to know that she'd heard and seen everything he'd done over the past several minutes. She had no desire to embarrass him. Asia stepped into the room. "Have any of the doctors been in yet this morning? I'm afraid I slept a little longer than I'd planned. Cramped up on that couch in the waiting room right down the hall, I didn't think I was going to get any sleep. But it looks as if I overslept."

"Only the nurses have come in to check his vitals. His signs are good but there's been no change in his condition. Are you going to be here awhile?"

"All day. And I plan to stay overnight again. Why do you ask?"

"I'd like to run home, take a shower, and hopefully grab a few hours of hard sleep."

"Are you saying you've been here all night?"

"Every second of it. I couldn't sleep last night so I came back. It was a little after ten o'clock. I was told you were already gone. I had no idea you were asleep in the waiting room. It won't take me long to run home and do what I have to do. I'm glad to know that you were with him before I got back. Like you, I don't like him being alone."

"What about your job, Nicholas?"

"I'm my own boss, Asia. Until Isaiah comes around this is going to be my second home. I'll be back later on." He hugged Asia and left the room.

Glad for Nicholas's presence in both her and Isaiah's life, Asia sent upward a quiet supplication of thanksgiving to the Lord. If she'd ever needed a man in her life, this was definitely the time for it. The miracle for her was the man that the Lord had chosen to send.

CHAPTER THREE

Inside his posh Pacific Palisades home, upstairs in his magnificently appointed family room, Nicholas was seated on the teal-green leather sofa next to his estranged wife, Miranda. In waiting for her reaction to the news he'd just shared with her about Isaiah, he saw that her toffee-brown complexion had gone pale. But it was the look in her warm brown eyes that puzzled him most: anger mixed with the green of envy. He couldn't figure out why she'd feel either emotion.

He touched her hand. "What's the matter, Miranda? Aren't you going to say anything?"

Tears forming in her eyes, she shook her head from side to side. "I don't know what to say. But I'm having a hard time believing that you didn't know you had a son."

Her statement really stunned him. He couldn't believe that that was all she had to say to him, especially after learning that his son was lying in a hospital fighting for his life. Granted the news of him having a son had great shock value, but what was more shocking was Miranda not voicing or even showing any concern for him or Isaiah. "What? Do you think I'm lying?"

She studied his handsome, scowling face. "I never said you were lying. I said I found it hard to believe. Who is the mother?"

"Asia. Asia Morrell, my girlfriend in college. But you already know who she is."

Her mouth dropped. "The only woman you've ever confessed to loving."

The sarcasm in Miranda's tone had Nicholas completely stumped. She knew exactly who Asia was because she was the only person he'd ever poured his heart out to about his broken heart. Miranda was only a friend to him at the time he'd shared the details of his heart-surrendering romance with Asia. Miranda had also shared with him many a woeful tale regarding her numerous unsuccessful relationships with the opposite sex, one thing they had in common.

"How long have you known about Isaiah?"

"Only hours before the accident."

"How long have you been back in contact with his mother?"

"A few hours after the accident."

"Really. I find that odd."

"What's so odd about it?"

"Everything. You have a twenty-one-year-old son, yet you haven't talked to his mother in all that time. That's what I find so odd."

"I didn't know about him. That's how it happened. Weren't you listening to what I told you? I don't know what you're getting at." The look he gave her was fraught with impatience.

She snorted. "It's nothing more than curiosity on my part. How is your son doing?"

"I thought you'd never ask. He's in a coma. The most recent information we got on his condition is that he may have a spinal cord injury. Since he hasn't moved any of the muscles on the lower portion of his body, there's a good possibility that he may be paralyzed. But no matter what the doctors say, God is in control of Isaiah's health and his future."

"Always the optimist, aren't you?"

"Complete trust in God is the answer to that."

"I hope to have that type of trust one day. If you'll excuse me, I'm going to use the bathroom. Then I have to be on my way."

"And if I don't?"

"Don't what?"

"Excuse you. Are you just going to wet yourself?" He thought a bit of humor might lighten up the tension that had suddenly loomed between them, but the look in Miranda's eyes told him he'd figured wrong. Without comment, she got up from the sofa and left the room.

While waiting for Miranda to return, Nicholas went over their conversation in his mind. Something was bothering her, but he wasn't sure what it was. Miranda was a wonderful woman but her negative thinking had puzzled him on numerous occasions.

When he first met Dr. Miranda George, a psychologist, they were both looking to make changes in their lives. Both were hard workers and neither of them had much in the way of an active social life. Moderately attractive rather than pretty, Miranda was an overachiever, a brilliant doctor with a brilliant mind. Her mind was what had first attracted Nicholas. He liked intelligent women, especially the ones that could communicate on his level. He'd met her during a legal conference she'd attended with a girlfriend. They'd been assigned seating at the same banquet table. Engaging conversation had revealed that she also lived in southern California.

That knowledge had led up to the discussion of a first date; their relationship progressed from there. Nicholas later thought that his lack of interest in sleeping with her should've told him something, but he really hadn't paid much attention to that.

In short, they had been in dire need of steady companionship. No great love affair had developed between them over the next several months, yet they'd made the decision to marry. Time was running out on them and neither had wanted to grow old alone.

Miranda's biological clock had run out of time several years prior to their meeting, so having children hadn't been a motivating factor for marriage. Plain and simple, loneliness had brought together two very different people. The inability of each to relieve the aching loneliness for the other had caused them to decide on divorce. Each had confessed to being just as lonely as they'd been before the marriage.

Miranda's stimulating intellect and sharp wit had easily gotten them through many evenings. However, after less than two years of having nothing in common but intelligence and sharp wit, Nicholas began to see their marriage as a big mistake. Apparently Miranda had also come to the same conclusion since she was the one who'd approached him about considering a legal separation. Filing for the divorce had come a few months later. Nicholas had initiated that phase.

Miranda came back into the room and immediately reached for her purse. "I've got to run, Nick. I'll keep you and Isaiah in my prayers."

Since Miranda was a Christian woman, he found it strange that she hadn't included Asia in her prayer list. Perhaps it was an unintentional oversight. "Thanks. Please pray for his mom, too. She's hurting something terrible. Isaiah is her whole life."

Her spine stiffened. "She's not married?"

"Never has been. Like I said, Isaiah is her life. If he doesn't make it, she's going to fall completely to pieces. Her state of mind is very fragile."

"Sorry to hear that. I'll talk with you soon, Nick."

"One more thing before you go. Don't forget to have your attorney contact mine to schedule an appointment to sign the divorce settlement. Now that we've gotten everything in order and down in writing, we can move forward."

"I don't know why you're in such a hurry all of a sudden to finalize things, but I guess it wouldn't take a genius to figure it out. I'll do as you wish."

Knowing exactly where she'd gone with that remark, he decided that it was best not to comment on it. No good would come of it.

He got up and followed her downstairs so he could lock up. Miranda no longer had keys to the home he'd purchased long before they'd ever met. She had moved back into her own home right after her tenant's lease was up. It wasn't that he didn't trust her when he'd had all the locks changed. He'd had it done for his own peace of mind.

At the front door, he pecked her cheek. "Have a good day, Miranda. Drive carefully."

"Good-bye, Nick."

Nicholas closed the door and walked into the newly decorated gourmet kitchen where he brewed just enough coffee for two cups. While waiting for his coffee, he read over a legal brief that he'd brought home from the office. He smiled when he thought of Lynda. She had shown him her strength on numerous occasions. He was pleased with the fact that he could count on her in his absence from the office. She ran his firm quite effectively, with every confidence in her ability to do so. With her always on top of everything, he had nothing to worry about in that area.

The moment Asia's lovely image popped into his mind, Nicholas looked at the wall phone. He was worried about her. She wasn't holding up very well. He was glad she didn't know that he wasn't handling things so well, either. Both were worried sick about Isaiah's serious injuries. Even though Nicholas trusted in God, he knew that God would not hesitate to take Isaiah home if He thought it was the best course of action. If that were to happen, Nicholas would know in his heart that God had done what He saw best. But that was not the outcome he desired. As it was with matters concerning life and death, Nicholas was well aware that he had no say in the matter. But prayer brought about miracles. Therefore he would stay on his knees on Isaiah's behalf. He'd stay on his knees until they were swollen and bruised, twenty-four-seven, if that's what it would take to bring Isaiah back from the brink of death.

The phone rang just before Nicholas picked it up. Upon closing his eyes, he prayed that it wasn't bad news about his son. While the time wouldn't ever be right for such a call, this was definitely not the moment for it. His strength was all but depleted even though revitalization was a mere prayer away. For him to lose Isaiah after just finding him would mean losing his sanity.

"Nicholas, can you talk a moment?"

Even though she sounded worn down, the softness of Asia's voice was so sweet to his ears. "Has something happened over there? You don't sound too hot." Praying with his mind, he held his breath in nervous anticipation of her response.

"Nothing has changed, Nicholas. Isaiah still hasn't come around, but I know that he's fighting like crazy to do so. Our son is very much a fighter, just like his dad. Just need to know how long it's going to be before you come back to the hospital."

"As soon as I drink my coffee. Do you need me to do something for you?"

"Actually, I do need a favor. I have to go into the office for a couple of hours this afternoon. Since they think I'm superwoman, and that I can catch up without any difficulty, the crew has a tendency to allow my cases to fall by the wayside if I'm gone more than a day or so. Can you come sit with Isaiah?"

"I'll be on my way. In fact, I'll stay the night so you can go on home and get a good night's sleep in your own bed."

"That's such a generous offer, but I'll be fine. This cot they just brought in is terribly uncomfortable, but I'll manage to get in a few good winks. They won't let us both stay."

"I'll have my say on that matter. There are a few strings that I can tug hard on. But I'll take the cot tonight. No argument is taking place either. We rotate from here on in. See you in a little while. Asia, stay strong."

"Thanks, Nicholas. You do the same. Oh, one other thing. The media attention hasn't begun to peak, yet it's already out of control. They're everywhere in and around this place just waiting to get a glimpse of anyone from the basketball team, or me, so they can pounce. A few of his teammates and their coach failed at trying to slip in here unnoticed, right after you left. It quickly became a media circus. Afterward, when things calmed down, the doctors asked my permission to do a press conference to try and appease their curious appetite for Isaiah's condition. I told him I had to confer with his father. What do you think?"

That she had even considered him in making this important decision overwhelmed him. He hadn't been sure of how she was going to take it when she first learned that Isaiah had made contact with him, but it seemed that she was more than willing to share their son with him. It was a huge relief. "Thank you for your consideration of me. I think it's something we have to do. Isaiah is a world-renowned sports figure. We can't let his fans down. Those that genuinely care about him are going to want to know what's happening with their hero. I promise to be right there by your side during the conference. Is that okay?"

"I guess you didn't hear that huge sigh of relief. Now that you're here, I don't know how I've managed things without your help. It's greatly comforting to know that you're going to be here for both Isaiah and me."

Her voice had cracked. That instantly alerted Nicholas to how much emotional distress she was in. Like him, she was trying her best to hide the fragility of her state of mind. It nearly killed him in thinking that their time for any sort of personal relationship had come and gone. That he still cared deeply about her came as no surprise to him. He'd never stopped caring. But how did someone bridge twenty-two years of separation? It simply couldn't be done.

"It's time for me to let you go. See you later, Nicholas."

Discreetly, Asia's hand went up to her eyes. She didn't want Nicholas to see her crying all the time. She had to be stronger than that. Nicholas needed her to be strong whether he knew it or not. Isaiah needed to draw from their combined strengths.

Nicholas saw that Asia had been crying as soon as he'd stepped into the room. Fearfully, he looked over at Isaiah. It looked as if nothing had changed since their conversation. Then he looked at the little cot that Asia would be forced to sleep on. He made a mental note to talk to someone about making the room semiprivate by adding another hospital bed. The room was certainly large enough to accommodate the change. Asia should have somewhere comfortable to lay her head. He could afford to pay the cost for an additional bed. He didn't know why he hadn't thought of it before now. All the hospital administration could tell him was yes or no.

Asia got to her feet and went over to Nicholas. He looked surprised when she reached out to him, but he didn't hesitate a moment in taking her into his arms. He had clearly seen her need for solace. For several minutes they stood in total silence, embracing each other with tenderness and warmth. Nicholas and Asia only pulled apart when they heard a sound. Nicholas looked over at the door and saw a scowling Miranda standing there. He and Asia exchanged puzzled glances.

Asia had no idea who Miranda was, but she had a pretty good idea when Miranda's arms went around Nicholas's neck in a loving embrace. How she'd been able to gain access to Isaiah's room without her consent caused Asia concern since she'd initiated certain rules for visitations. Perhaps Nicholas had given his consent for her to be there. She had allowed him that freedom. Asia tried to deny her burning feelings of jealousy, but she couldn't turn away from the truth.

Miranda's embrace felt weird to Nicholas since she wasn't an openly affectionate person. Then, when she planted a lingering kiss on his mouth, he understood. She was staking a claim to her right to be affectionate with her husband, estranged or not. It was now that he realized Miranda felt threatened by Asia being back in his life. The things that she'd said and done during her last visit with him all made sense now. He and Miranda hadn't shared anything more than friendly kisses on the cheek and light hugs for several months. They'd stopped making love long before she'd moved into one of his three guest bedrooms until her place became available. Their intimate moments had been few and far between during the entire marriage.

Without further speculation, Nicholas introduced the two women. Asia extended her hand to Miranda, but Miranda seemed reluctant to take it. The hesitation was brief but it didn't go unnoticed by Nicholas and Asia. As far as Nicholas was concerned, this would be Miranda's last visit to the hospital. Her motives for being there were very questionable and he was almost certain that they weren't pure. It didn't take him long to consider leaving when he saw and felt the tension. It wasn't a good idea.

He quickly decided on another approach. He retrieved the chessboard from the suitcase he'd packed it in. After pulling the round table and a chair up as close as he could get it to Isaiah's bedside, he set up the chess game. As if he and Isaiah were the only two people in the room, he started to play the game.

The two women looked at one another and shrugged. Both couldn't help smiling even though they thought Nicholas had lost his mind.

Several minutes into the game Nicholas began taunting and baiting Isaiah as if he could actually hear him. "Scared to make the next move, aren't you? You know I got something for your bad butt, don't you, boy?"

Nicholas was making the moves for both himself and his son. It was really something beautiful to see. A man playing chess with a son who was in a coma was a rare sight to behold. Not only did Nicholas move Isaiah's game pieces, he also answered the taunting questions he'd asked Isaiah.

"Okay, old man, I know you think you're the best chess player in the world, but I'm here to show you that you're no Bobby Fisher. This young blood is about to dethrone you."

"If that's what you really think, son, you've set yourself up for bitter disappointment. Not only am I going to whip the pants off you, I'm going to put a few holes in your underwear too." As his back was to them, the women couldn't see Nicholas's tears falling as he continued on as if what he was doing weren't anything other than natural. He had tuned everything out but the game of chess that he and his son were playing. This was the reality he'd chosen to indulge himself in.

"So, how long have you and Nicholas been back together?" Miranda asked Asia.

"Back together? I don't know what you mean by that, but he and I only recently saw each other for the first time in twenty-two years. There are times when it seems longer than that."

"That's what he told me."

"Then I'm surprised you had to ask me the same thing. It also sounded as if you don't believe either of us. Nicholas and I have no reason to lie about anything."

"You must admit that it's a hard one to believe, especially regarding two people who once loved each other so much."

"Where did you hear that?"

"From Nicholas. He told me a lot about you. Maybe he meant it when he said that he'd come to hate you. I didn't believe him. Kept secrets can bring deep hatred to the secret keeper."

As hard as it was for her not to, Asia didn't bite into the poisoned apple that Miranda had just shoved up to her mouth. Still, she could taste the acidic bitterness of it. Asia was in no doubt that Nicholas was disappointed in her, but he'd made it clear to her that he didn't hate her even though she thought he should. Miranda had intentionally set out to hurt her with that remark; the reason for her desire to cause pain was obvious. She wasn't over Nicholas. Asia was getting the impression that Nicholas's divorce wasn't going to be as cut-and-dried as he originally thought.

Asia looked over at Nicholas, who was still having a hearty conversation with Isaiah. As sick as he was right now, Isaiah was a beautiful black man. His good looks had been solely inherited from his gorgeous father. Asia checked her watch. Torri should've been here by now, she thought. Her brow creased with worry as she looked toward the doorway. She hoped nothing had happened to Isaiah's girlfriend during her travels from Chicago. It was probably just the numerous delays that had come as a result of the events of September eleventh.

Asia felt Miranda's eyes on her. They made her feel uncomfortable. She hadn't intended to be rude to her, but Asia had to turn her attention on something else to keep her tongue in check. Miranda had insulted her terribly. Under different circumstances, Miranda's remarks wouldn't have gone unchecked. And Asia's response would've come swift and in no uncertain terms.

Asia was surprised that Nicholas had even chosen Miranda as his wife. She seemed a bit mean-spirited, the exact opposite of Nicholas. Men didn't come any kinder than Nicholas Reynolds. In being honest with herself, Asia failed to see what Nicholas saw in Miranda. Looks weren't as important to Nicholas as attitude was, and Asia sensed that Miranda had a negative mind-set. However, she still planned to give his wife the benefit of the doubt. This situation was hard on everyone concerned and Nicholas was still Miranda's husband since the divorce wasn't yet finalized. At any rate, Asia had boundaries that Miranda should be very cautious in crossing.

Looking like a breath of fresh air, the stunningly beautiful Torri Jefferson swept into the room, but not with as much grace as she always took to the runway. She was a tall wisp of a girl with moon-bright, almond-shaped hazel eyes and long sandy-brown hair. Her caramel complexion was flawless with a permanent blush of a desert-rose color in her cheeks. Asia could see that Torri had spent some time crying. Her slightly swollen eyes were a dead giveaway.

Torri went straight to Isaiah's bedside. Laying her head on his chest, she closed her eyes as her fingers reached up and nestled in his naturally curly hair. A few minutes later, when she opened her eyes, she gasped at seeing the man who looked just like her beloved Isaiah. Torri stared at Nicholas for several seconds. "The only person that you can possibly be is Isaiah's dad. He called me after he called his mom to tell her that you two had dinner together. I'm happy that he decided to find you." Her eyes filled with tears.

"And now this. How sad for all of us, especially my boo." Torri wiped her tears. "I'm sorry, but here I am crying all over the place and I haven't even introduced myself. I'm Torrianne Jefferson, Isaiah's girlfriend of four and a half years. Everyone simply calls me Torri. Isaiah and I met at college."

Torri had quickly earned a spot in Nicholas's heart. There was no doubt about her sincerity. He didn't sense one pretentious thing about her. Nicholas didn't know how he knew it, but this woman loved his son with a passion; the same way he and Asia had once loved. He couldn't imagine that Isaiah's feelings for this beautiful creature weren't mutual.

Nicholas embraced Torri the instant he got to his feet. "So nice to meet you, Torri. I'm sure Isaiah is glad that you're finally here."

Seeing Asia for the first time, Torri smiled as she went into Asia's arms. The two women comforted one another as Nicholas looked on. Miranda had been all but forgotten until Torri noticed her. Without expression, Torri looked at the female stranger. "Hello. I'm so sorry for not speaking to you. I didn't see you until now. Are you somehow related to Isaiah?"

"I'm his stepmother, his father's wife."

"Oh, I see. Nice to meet you." Torri failed at not looking disappointed at the revelation. "Thanks for caring." There was something about Nicholas's wife that Torri instantly didn't like.

Nicholas raised an eyebrow. That Miranda had dared to refer to herself as Isaiah's stepmother had stunned him. It hadn't even sounded right to him. Perhaps it was the passionless way in which she'd voiced it. Miranda was becoming a complication that he could very well do without at a time like this. He couldn't help wondering where she'd left her spirituality.

Miranda crossed the room and stood face-to-face with Nicholas. "I've got to leave now. I only wanted to stop by and see how things were going before I started with my busy evening. But I hate leaving you all alone. I'll come back here if it's not too late. Or I'll stop by the house later tonight. I want to be here for you."

"That's not necessary, Miranda. I won't be alone. God is always with me. I won't be at home this evening because I'm staying here at the hospital tonight. Please don't worry about me. I'll be just fine. Just keep Isaiah in constant prayer."

The kiss Miranda gave Nicholas was deep and passionate. All for show, he knew, since he'd never before experienced that kind of kiss with her. Miranda didn't so much as nod at the other two women as she left the room. He didn't know how she'd managed to get into Isaiah's room in the first place, but he knew she wouldn't be coming back. He was going to see to that. This was a side of Miranda that he'd never seen before. He didn't like it one bit. She hadn't given him a second thought until after she'd learned about his son and Asia. The only reason she was at the house earlier was that he'd invited her there to share the news about his son.

Nicholas stood outside the doorway and looked after Miranda until she'd disappeared around the corner. If she had found it necessary to turn around and come back, he would've gone out to meet her to keep her from returning to the room. Satisfied that she was gone, he walked back inside. The first thing he observed was Asia and Torri embracing each other with love and affection as they looked down on Isaiah. After a couple of minutes of whispering between them, a conversation that Nicholas couldn't hear, the two women crossed the room and sat down at the table. It was then that Nicholas joined them.

Asia smoothed Torri's hair back from her face in a loving gesture. "How was your flight, sweetheart? You look worn out."

"Horrendous. All I could think of was Isaiah. I've been a nervous wreck from the moment I learned of his accident. I am very tired from so little sleep. Have there been any changes in his condition since our last phone conversation?"

Asia took Torri's hand. "None, my dear. But we aren't giving up on him. Isaiah is strong, very strong."

"He has so much to live for," Nicholas said. "With the three of us pulling for him, he won't want to do anything but live."

"The four of us," Asia corrected Nicholas.

"Four?" Nicholas asked.

Asia's eyes went straight to Torri's stomach. "I know about your own health concerns, Torri. I know everything. I'm extremely glad you didn't go through with your plans."

Embarrassed to no end, Torri felt the tears spring to her eyes. "I see that Troy Dyson has been bending your ear but good." One hard sob shook Torri's body. "I'm still not convinced that I'm doing the right thing by sticking around. What if Isaiah doesn't want this baby? For me, an abortion is totally out of the question, even if it means raising my child alone."

Finally, Nicholas completely understood the exchange of words between the two women. Even as an outsider he didn't dare to keep quiet on the subject. It seemed that history was repeating itself and allowing him to witness it. Isaiah and Torri meeting at college was a single similarity of many. He just hoped his input wouldn't upset the lovely Torri. "Whatever you do, don't run off. He has the right to know that he's a father. Even if he decides that he doesn't want the child, which I doubt will happen, he should know. Don't try to second-guess him and don't shut him out. Let him in on this."

Torri looked from Asia to Nicholas. "Can you two accept this baby?"

Nicholas and Asia reached for Torri's hand at the same time. Neither of them pulled away as the three hands entwined in a tender embrace.

"I think that I can speak for both Asia and myself. You're carrying our first grandchild. Of course, we can accept the baby."

Asia cupped Torri's face in her two hands. "I'm only sorry that you had to ask the question. There's nothing in this world that could keep me from accepting this child."

Nicholas looked upward to heaven as he reunited his hands with theirs. When he closed his eyes, Asia and Torri did the same. "Thank you, Father, for another magnificent blessing, the gift of a new life that shall soon be added unto us. I hope this doesn't mean you're shutting the door on Isaiah, since you've obviously opened up another one for us through his precious baby. Please, Father God, let Isaiah live to see the birth of his child. Two additional miracles will be a breeze for you. Thank you, Father God, for hearing my selfish yet humble plea."

Nicholas carefully guided Torri over to the bed. Taking Isaiah's hand in his own, he held it in place against the flat of Torri's abdomen. "Go ahead and tell him the good news, Torri. He'll be excited over it."

As Torri moved Isaiah's hand over her stomach, she did very little to fight off her tears. "This baby was created from our love. I hope you're as happy as I am. The baby needs both of his parents, Isaiah. Please stay with us so that we can be a real family. You don't have to marry me, Isaiah, though I'd like that very much. I just want you to be in our child's life." After gently placing Isaiah's hand back on the bed, Torri leaned over and kissed him full on the lips, her tears splattering onto his cheeks.

While wiping her tears with a tissue, Asia's nails on her left hand dug into her thighs through the slacks she wore. This entire situation was pure hell for her. If only she had been as brave as Torri was being right now. According to Isaiah's best friend, Troy, Torri had planned to disappear from Isaiah's life because of her fears of interrupting just the beginning of his success; just as Asia had run from Nicholas so as not to interrupt the flow of his future. The similarities in her and Torri's stories were uncanny. It was as if a portrait of the past were being painted in brilliant colors for the world to see all of the unforgivable mistakes she'd made. *Your sins will surely find you out* rang with resounding truth in Asia's ears. Failing to enlighten Nicholas of her situation was the biggest mistake she'd ever made in her life, one that she could never undo.

Nicholas put his arm around Asia's shoulders. He'd read the expression of sorrowful regret on her face. "I'm here now, Grandma." The three of them laughed. "You have reinforcements at your disposal around the clock. You go ahead and take care of your business. If you're too tired to come back, you already know that I'll be here for the entire night."

Without any intent on her part, Asia's smile charmed him. "Thanks, Grandpa, but I can't imagine me not coming back here as soon as it's possible." Asia then shared with Torri all the things that she had to take care of.

"I'll be here, too. That is, if you don't mind Mr. . . . ." Torri suddenly looked embarrassed. "I'm afraid I don't know your last name. I don't know if Isaiah mentioned it or not."

"It's Reynolds, Torri. But it would do my heart good if you'd just called me Nicholas or Nick. Formalities aren't necessary with me."

Torri looked to Asia with a soft expression. "Hey, that's Isaiah's middle name. Does he know that he has part of his dad's name?"

"He does. Nicholas is the one that didn't know about his name, but he knows now, too."

"I'm thrilled about that. Thanks for your kind offer regarding your name, but I was raised to always put a handle on the names of adults. How does Mr. Nick sound to you?" Torri asked.

Nicholas grinned. "Charming."

"Okay, Mr. Nick," she enthused. She turned to Asia. "That's the reason I've always addressed you as Miss Asia, but Isaiah would have a fit if I addressed you in any other way. He hates it when he hears young kids call grown-ups by their first name. He always corrects the kids he works with when they call him by his first name. Mr. Ike the Psyche to you," Torri scolded in a gruff voice. Asia and Nicholas laughed at her very good imitation of Isaiah.

"I've got to get out of here, but this has been a wonderful atmosphere to surround Isaiah with. Thanks to both of you." Asia stepped forward and kissed Nicholas on the cheek and then she hugged Torri. "See you later this evening."

Asia's heart was near bursting as she headed for the elevator. It was now confirmed for her that she was going to be a grandmother. She couldn't have asked for a lovelier mother for her first grandchild. Torri had been so easy for Asia to love simply because she treated her son the right way and she had loads of respect for him as a man and as a professional athlete.

Asia could clearly see that Torri genuinely loved her son. Isaiah also loved Torri Jefferson, but it had taken him a while to figure out his true feelings for her. And it had hit him like a ton of bricks when he realized he was madly, crazily in love. Isaiah had been ready to run scared until he thought about what it would mean to never see her again. It was then that he decided he didn't want to lose her. Asia had lost count of the times that Isaiah had confessed to her his love for Torri. Perhaps his child was a key to his recovery. If for no other reason, she was sure that Isaiah would want to live for his unborn child.

Every day that she had to see Isaiah so still and lifeless made her past serious errors in judgment even more blatant. She had robbed the two people she loved most in the world, had virtually stolen their rights to be a family right out from under them. Her actions back then were abominable. But it was now a new day and it would do no one any good for her to continue dressing herself down as a she-monster. God had apparently forgiven her; Nicholas had also. Now it was time for her to forgive herself. Isaiah's forgiveness was what she needed most.

Her desire to talk more in depth with Torri about the baby was strong. Torri had to be reassured that she was doing the right thing. She still seemed somewhat unsure of what she should do and Asia wanted to be there for her since Isaiah couldn't be. The thought of her becoming a grandmother sent shivers up and down her spine. Another little Isaiah to love and spoil would make these hard times easier to bear. No one could ever replace her beloved son, but she definitely had lots and lots of unoccupied space in her heart for his child.

Although Isaiah talked about loving Torri, he'd never brought up the subject of marriage. While she would love to see them happily married, with his future so undecided, she thought it wasn't something she should entertain. For the moment it was time for her to turn her energies toward her job as deputy D.A. Holding her head up high, denying her tears a release, Asia walked out of the hospital and into the cool morning air.

Nicholas couldn't help noticing how lovely a woman Torri seemed to be. She actually reminded him of Asia. They were both quiet-spoken but each had self-assurance along with the ability to turn on a strong air of defiance. It appeared to him that Isaiah had searched for and had definitely found a woman with the same endearing qualities as his mother. While the nurses had come in to check Isaiah's vitals, she showed her concern for him in the many questions she'd asked them. She had even helped them wash him up and get him into a clean hospital gown. It looked as if she was more in the way than anything, but the nurses seemed to understand her need to help Isaiah in any way she could.

Nicholas smiled when Torri's hand gently pressed against her abdomen in a loving, motherly gesture toward the unborn child she carried. *Had Asia caressed her stomach in the same gentle way when she was filled with Isaiah?* His heart ached to have been a part of that whole process of creation. "How far along are you?"

She beamed at him. "Only six weeks. Having a horrible time with morning sickness, though. My doctor wrote me a prescription but it isn't helping to ease the nausea one bit." She suddenly looked pensive. "Since you've only met Isaiah, how are you so sure that he's going to want this baby?"

"He's my son. I would've wanted him back then. I want him now. He's also very much his mother's son; she wouldn't have considered any other option than the one she took. I'm just sorry that she chose to exclude me. I thought Asia knew me as well as I knew myself." He looked chagrined. "I'm sorry. This isn't something I should be discussing with you, especially when I haven't even gotten my issues out in the open with Asia."

"Perhaps she did know you, maybe even better than you think. What if she thought you'd give up everything for the baby and then later come to regret it? I know that in my consideration of bailing out on Isaiah I've been thinking of his future, giving no thought to my own. That's kind of crazy, huh, Mr. Nick?"

"Not so crazy. Women have a tendency to put others before themselves, especially those they love. What career field are you in?"

"I'm a high-fashion model, but I'm also a licensed registered nurse. I'm not employed as a nurse, but I do volunteer twenty hours a week to a local hospital."

In thinking back to the medical questions Torri had asked the nurses—and how she'd worked alongside them in a thorough manner, he now understood that she was only doing what she had been trained to do. So, she hadn't just been in their way. Still, he didn't think the nurses knew that she was one of them.

"When I start to show, I'm going to have to give up modeling."

"Why?"

"Who will want to employ a pregnant model? To be more specific, a black pregnant model."

"For one, a business that sells maternity clothes. You're a beautiful pregnant model."

Torri blushed. "Thank you." Her eyes suddenly filled with tears. "I just pray that Isaiah turns out to be just like you in terms of wanting this child. I think you're going to be a wonderful grandfather to our baby. I'm really sorry that you and Isaiah didn't have the chance that this baby may have at getting to know his father and his grandparents. But the fact that you're here now means there's still a good chance for you to become a father-and-son team and to become the best of friends. I believe that can happen, Mr. Nick."

Nicholas wiped Torri's water-filled eyes with a handkerchief and then he dabbed at his own. "Thank you, Torri. I also believe in that. Wholeheartedly."

CHAPTER FOUR

Nicholas was having a hard time believing his own ears as he listened to his personal attorney, John Wilder, speaking over the phone line. "Did she say why she's doing this?"

"According to her attorney, Miranda is accusing you of adultery. I'm glad you called and told me about your son before her attorney did. She says you're divorcing her to be with Asia Morrell, the mother of your son. She refuses to sign the settlement that's been agreed upon and already drawn up. She's also suing for alimony and half of your pension plan. She may get the alimony, but as far as state law mandates, she hasn't been married to you long enough to lay claim to any pension funds or any of the property you possessed before marrying her."

"This is too much, John. I never dreamed that Miranda would ever stoop to this level. She has to know that I'm not having an adulterous affair with Asia. Something else is making her do this, but I don't know what it could possibly be."

"Money is usually the only motivator in cases like this, Nicholas."

"But she had the opportunity to go after the money in the first place. We had amicably decided on a settlement that we could both live with. If this is settled in the courts, she's not going to fare as well as she did in our private settlement. We haven't acquired anything of any real value together. I already owned everything I have before she came along. Miranda and I have never had so much as a checking or savings account together. We wanted it that way."

"Perhaps she didn't think she had a good enough excuse to go after the money in the beginning. It seems she feels that Asia and your son came first and that you never gave her what she needed from you because you were involved with another family all the while. Are we going to fight her on this? Or do you want us to try and reach a new settlement?"

"The first thing I'm going to do is talk to Miranda and find out what's going on."

"May not be a good idea, at least, not without representation present. If she's making these allegations of adultery against you, the chance that she'd speak with you in the absence of her attorney is slim. I advise you to completely abandon the idea."

Nicholas sighed hard. "John, I need to think about what you're advising me to do. I've been married to Miranda a little over two years and we've barely spoken an angry word between us. Surely we can resolve this matter without the assistance of our attorneys. This is another sorrowful day for me. I don't understand Miranda doing this, especially knowing that my son is fighting for his life. If I don't confront this situation, I may very well go stark raving mad."

"As your attorney, I can only advise you. The ultimate decision is yours. Let me know what you decide."

"Sure thing, John. Thanks for the call."

"You bet. We'll talk soon."

This couldn't wait, Nicholas decided as he hung up the phone. He looked at his watch. Miranda would be in her office, but it was near the time she normally took for lunch. Hoping he could get to her office before she left; he grabbed his car keys and suit jacket.

Upon entering the popular restaurant, Nicholas saw that it was crowded. His visit to Miranda's office had been futile, but her secretary had been able to tell him where she was having lunch. Mack's Deli, one of her favorite eateries, was located right across the street from her office. It only took him a couple of seconds to spot her. He was glad that she was alone.

Miranda looked startled when Nicholas took the seat across the table from her. She looked around her, as if she was looking for an easy escape route. She hadn't thought that he would seek her out in a public place. There was little doubt in her mind that he'd already learned she'd backed out of the settlement. The sorrowful look on his face was indicative of that.

"What's this all about, Miranda? Why?"

"We shouldn't have this discussion without legal counsel. I'll have my attorney arrange a meeting time for us with your lawyer. This conversation will have to wait until then."

He shook his head. "That won't do. Something has happened to make you go back on your word. What is it?"

Miranda looked Nicholas right in the eyes. "Asia happened. If you're expecting me to believe that she just suddenly reappeared in your life, it's not going to happen. I honestly believe that you've been having an affair with her behind my back. I can't stomach that."

"You don't believe that, Miranda, not for a second. You know me better than that. I'm not the kind of man to run around on his wife even if we'd had a terribly unhappy marriage, which we didn't. We simply aren't compatible. Are you jealous of Asia, of our history?"

She gave Nicholas a hard look. "How dare you say something like that to me? You do wrong and then you attack me to justify the wrongdoing. I'm not going to allow that."

"There has been no wrongdoing on my part. The first time I saw Asia was at the hospital while I was there to see about Isaiah. The last time I saw her before that was over twenty-two years ago. Why is that so hard to believe?"

"By your own admission, she's the only woman you've ever loved."

"I'm sorry if the truth hurts. And you somehow feel threatened by that truth, don't you?"

"This is not about how I feel, Nick. It has to do with how you're trying to make a fool of me. You're the fool if you think you can get away with it."

"Okay. Let's say that you're absolutely right about me. What do you want?"

"Compensation for pain and suffering?"

"You want compensation for less than forty-eight hours of pain and suffering? You only learned about Asia a short time ago, so you haven't been in pain for very long. At any rate, is money really going to be enough?"

"It's a start."

"I see. Draw up your demands and send them over to my attorney through yours. I'll give you whatever it is that you want. Money is only paper. Paper burns easily."

She looked surprised at how easily he'd given in to her demands. She didn't like that. "It's really not about what I want, Nick. It's what I don't want that's driving me."

"What don't you want, Miranda?"

"The divorce. I think we should give our marriage another try. We've given up on us way too easily."

He closed his eyes briefly. "Miranda, you came to me about a legal separation. I filed the paperwork several months ago, but only after *we* decided that a divorce was the best course of action for us. I didn't decide that on my own. We came to the conclusion that this marriage wasn't right for either of us. I don't know what has happened to make you believe otherwise. And if you believe that I'm having an illicit affair, why would you want us to try and save the marriage? I wouldn't think that anyone would want to stay married to an adulterer."

Miranda pushed back her chair from the table, but she didn't attempt to get up. "The covenant of marriage is sacred. So these are things we should discuss with our pastor. Howard will be glad to counsel us. He's your friend and he'll tell us what we need to do to stay within the accordance of God's law. It can't hurt us to get some badly needed guidance. We probably should've gone to him before we separated. Will you agree to see him with me?"

Unable to endure her gall for another second, Nicholas stood up. "Set up the appointment if you think it might make a difference. Just know that I think it's hopeless."

"Why do you think that?"

"Because months ago we both decided that the marriage was doomed to failure, agreed upon the fact that we simply don't do it for each other. You're acting way out of character, not to mention that this is an incredibly selfish act on your part. You know the difficulties I'm going through right now. My son is fighting for his life and you're fighting for a marriage that we both agreed should end."

His laughter was derisive. "This is a no-win situation for me and we both know it. I'm damned if I do and damned if I don't. Please try to remember that you came to me wanting a legal separation; this entire situation was initiated by you. I just finished up with what we both decided should be the final outcome, a divorce."

Nodding his farewell, he walked away from the table and headed
for the exit. That he didn't verbally tell Miranda good-bye told him
just how upset he was with her. All of this unpredictable garbage of
Miranda's had come right out of the blue. Just thinking about it made
him hot under the collar. Miranda wasn't playing fair or with any
amount of integrity. Her accusing him of adultery burned him up in
more ways than one.

Finding Isaiah alone in the room came as a big shock to Nicholas.
That Asia wasn't there puzzled him. Something very important must've
interrupted her normal routine. Perhaps she'd gone down to the
cafeteria, he mused. That thought didn't completely satisfy his curiosity since Asia hated the idea of Isaiah being alone for a mere minute.
Maybe she'd come to the reality that no one person could be with
him twenty-four hours a day. While they both had staying power, they
had to be careful about depleting their strength at the gate when the
road ahead looked long.

After looking down on Isaiah for several seconds, he pulled up a
chair next to the bed. Before taking a seat, he leaned over and kissed
his son on the cheek. "You're looking a little better today. Your skin
actually has some color back in it. You have to hurry up and get out of
this bed. I have big plans for us. Check this out."

Nicholas took a deep breath to keep his emotions from spilling
out. "I have a great town house in Sedona, Arizona. There are a lot of
amenities on the property, such as a swimming pool, full basketball
court, tennis courts, lakes loaded with fish, and lots of other good stuff.
We'll go there for a long weekend, say from a Thursday to a Monday."

Nicholas took a handkerchief out of his pocket and blew his nose.
Just thinking of him and Isaiah spending quality time together had
him all choked up. There were many times in his life that he'd wished
for a son to do guy things with. Had he known that he had one, long
before Isaiah had become a superstar athlete, his life would've been
almost complete. Resentment of Asia welled up inside him, but he
tamped it down. Not only had she taken Isaiah away, she had taken
her love from him. Asia had probably done what she'd thought was
best. He had to stop blaming her. He again reminded himself that
there'd been no malicious intent on her part.

Nicholas got up and went into the bathroom, where he retrieved a plastic basin and a bottle of antibacterial soap. After filling the container with hot water, he carried it back into the room and set it down on the tray table. Once he lathered a white washcloth with the liquid, he washed Isaiah's face, and each of his hands, drying them afterward with a large white towel.

Washing Isaiah's neck was a delicate process, but he only dared to do the front part. He then cleansed Isaiah's feet and thoroughly dried them off. Removing a couple of Q-tips from the nightstand drawer, Nicholas cleaned behind and around the outer part of Isaiah's ears. He then applied a soothing lip balm to his son's dry, cracked lips. His son didn't so much as twitch.

Before removing the basin, he had bathed as much of Isaiah's body as was possible. He couldn't turn him over. That was too risky. He'd have to leave that job for the nurses. After emptying the water out, he went back to the bed. Squirting a generous amount of body lotion into his hands, he massaged it into Isaiah's face, hands, legs, and feet. Isaiah's body appeared lifeless.

Touching his son this way brought tears to his eyes. He had to wonder what it would've been like to care for baby Isaiah. He could only imagine bathing him with infinite tenderness and then rubbing down his little body with baby oil, following up with a dousing of sweetly scented baby powder. Nicholas inhaled, as if he could smell the mixed scents of baby oil and powder. It hurt to have had his rights so badly violated. Did Asia realize how much she'd hurt him? She may not have realized it at the time, but he was sure she was now deeply aware of his pain.

Nicholas had always believed in the power of prayer, but he'd been praying harder than ever over the past few days. Time couldn't run out on him and Isaiah now. It was the last thing he wanted to have happen. "Father God," he prayed, "please team up with Father Time on my son's behalf. I know that time waits for no man, but I just don't want it to completely run out for us. We have so much yet to discover. Father God, please hear my plea."

Tears fell from Nicholas's eyes as he covered up Isaiah's body with the extra blanket he'd retrieved from the bottom of the bed. Nicholas looked behind him when he heard a noise. The two black males entering the room carried medical charts under their arms. One man was relatively young. The other gentleman appeared middle-aged.

The older man extended his hand to Nicholas. "I'm Dr. Anderson

Woolridge. I've been consulted to do a neurological workup on Mr. Morrell. Are you family, sir?"

Nicholas looked puzzled, as if he didn't know how to respond.

"I ask because I see only one name written as next of kin, Asia Morrell, his mother."

Nicholas's heart ached with deep regret. He also thought Asia had given permission for him to be consulted. "I'm Isaiah's father, Nicholas Reynolds. Pleased to meet you."

"Same here. This young man is my colleague, Dr. Simon Whiteman. We'll both be looking after Mr. Morrell until our workup is complete. Is Mrs. Morrell around?"

"Miss Morrell," Nicholas corrected without thinking. "She hasn't come in yet, but I know she'll be here. Is there something important that we need to know about Isaiah's condition?"

Dr. Woolridge looked uncomfortable. "I'm sorry, sir, but we can only discuss Mr. Morrell's health issues with his mother, as she's the only person showing as next of kin. I wish—"

"It's okay," Asia said from the doorway. "He's Isaiah's father. Mr. Reynolds has every right to know what's going on with his son. He has the same rights as I do when it comes to making decisions about Isaiah's health care. It has been my intent to sign the necessary paperwork giving the staff permission to discuss with him their concerns and findings. I'll make sure to take care of that today. Isaiah would want that."

Dr. Woolridge nodded. "The charge nurse can help you out with obtaining the proper forms. Now that we have that settled, I'd like for us to sit down and begin discussing your son's case. Several of his test results are now in."

Asia smiled nervously as everyone took a seat around the table. "Thank you. Do you have any good news for us?" she asked.

Dr. Woolridge looked to his colleague, Dr. Whiteman, to answer the question.

Looking regretful, Dr. Whiteman wrung his hands together. "I wish we did. In viewing the X rays of Mr. Morrell's swollen spine, we fear that he may have suffered a spinal cord injury. He may be paralyzed, which would explain the absence of muscle movement."

When Asia gasped, Nicholas's arm stole around her shoulders before she could draw her next breath. Knowing she had to remain strong in the face of adversity, Asia silently prayed for grace sufficient enough to get her through this moment and beyond.

Dr. Whiteman went on to explain the latest medical findings.

"If he is paralyzed, is the paralysis permanent?" Nicholas questioned.

"We're not sure. We can only speculate at this point. If he comes out of the coma, we will then be able to gather more specific information regarding his injuries," Dr. Woolridge responded. "At this point in time, your son's case isn't an easy one to call."

"*When* he comes out of the coma," Nicholas said. "Asia and I have to believe that. We don't dare to believe anything else."

"I understand your feelings, sir, but you both should prepare yourself should the worst occur," the younger doctor advised.

"We'll deal with it should that time come." Asia had relayed her remarks with calm, but her inner workings were in a messy state.

"The amount of drugs found in your son's system makes this case even more confusing and complex—"

"Drugs!" Asia shouted at the older man, jumping up. "I beg your pardon? Where are you getting this information? Dr. Chance Lowery, Isaiah's regular sports physician, hasn't mentioned anything about drugs to me. Besides, Isaiah has never used illegal substances in his entire life. That's a fact." Asia looked dumbfounded as she dropped back down in the chair.

Dr. Woolridge appeared both perplexed and embarrassed. "I'm sorry that you hadn't yet been informed about the drugs. The toxicology reports only came back a few hours ago. I've obviously overstepped my boundaries as a consulting physician. I'll make immediate contact with Dr. Lowery and apprise him of this unfortunate set of circumstances. But let me say this, it could very well be the drugs that have rendered your son immobile. If that's the case, the paralysis could be temporary. To help cleanse the drugs from his system, additional IV therapy is indicated as part of his treatment. A nurse will be in shortly to get the treatment under way."

The doctors stood, shook hands with both Asia and Nicholas, and then left the room.

Nicholas took Asia into his embrace. "This nightmare is only getting worse by the second." He looked into her eyes. "Thanks for including me in the decision-making process where Isaiah's health is concerned. I really appreciate all the kind consideration you've given me." Nicholas was having a hard time accepting that Isaiah may have used illegal drugs, but he'd wait for Asia to bring up the subject. She looked very disturbed by the allegation.

She touched his face for a brief moment. "That's the way it should be. Since Isaiah found you, and then later accepted your invitation to dinner, his heart has the desire to know you." Her voice began to break under the emotional stress she felt. His hand to her back soothed her as the circular massage calmed the troubled waters threatening to engulf her.

"What if he doesn't come out of this, Nicholas?"

He gently cupped her face between his hands. "We won't use the word 'if.' I hope you don't mind. Using that word is leaving his health to chance. Saying 'when' he comes out of it keeps hope alive."

"Sounds like a positive approach. I'll remember what you said." She looked apprehensive as she stared down at the floor, wondering if Isaiah's anger at her had caused his accident. "He has never used drugs, Nicholas. I hope you don't believe what the doctors implied. It's not true."

A thoughtful expression settled in his eyes as he recalled Isaiah telling him that he never ingested anything harmful into his body. That particular response had come from Isaiah when Nicholas had offered him a beer at the restaurant.

"If it's any comfort to you, I don't believe one word of it. However, if the test results haven't somehow been contaminated, we're going to have to look into how the drugs got into his system. We first need to get confirmation from his regular doctor before we decide on the next course of action. Both you and I have plenty of professional resources at our disposal to launch a thorough investigation. We'll get to the bottom of the allegations. I can promise you that much."

"I've been wondering how this could've happened. With drugs coming into play, I'm thinking this may not have been an accident. But I just can't think of a single person that would want to hurt Isaiah." Asia couldn't bring herself to voice the possibility that Isaiah may've gotten himself into difficulty with the wrong crowd after he stormed out of her house. If that was the case, they hadn't just hurt him, they'd tried to kill him. But why? Her heart began to race.

"We'll have our plates full, but we'll come up with the answers, Asia. We have a lot of friends in high places. This case will be solved.

If there is foul play involved, the guilty party or parties will be brought to justice. That's a certainty."

"Thanks for the encouragement, Nicholas. I'm suddenly feeling very tired."

"Were you able to get all of your business handled?"

"Most of it. I have a really tough case that I'm prosecuting. I could use a couple of dozen more paralegals to help me out with this one. The county budget won't allow for that. Thank you for being here during the times when I couldn't."

"You're welcome. Is there something I can do to help you out with your caseload?"

She smiled softly. "That's a very generous offer from you. With you being a defense attorney, we think quite differently, so I don't know how you could help me. There's so much about this case that disturbs me."

"What's the charge?"

"Murder-one, three counts. Children allegedly murdered by their mother. Lethal doses of sleeping pills were found in the children's bodies. Being both a woman and a mother, I'm so torn. The mother swears she's innocent, but the evidence leads to her as the only suspect. The grand jury felt there was enough evidence to return an indictment. This case already has me on an emotional roller-coaster ride. Isaiah being hurt has turned this ride into one with cyclone force. I wish you could help me out, but I don't want to trouble you. I know you're very busy."

"You mentioned that we think differently as a prosecutor and defense attorney. I think our different perspective is a good thing in this instance. Give me copies of the discovery and I'll play the devil's advocate as the opposing counsel. What do you think?"

"Sounds intriguing. Brilliant as you are, I know you'll come at me with both barrels blazing. Sure you can find time for this?"

"To be here with Isaiah, I decided to take some time off. The other legal eagles in my firm can handle most anything that comes up. But I'll remain available to them. I can study your case while I'm sitting here with him. In fact, I've already arranged for them to move another bed in here. I don't like you sleeping on a cramped up cot. Since the request hasn't been filled yet, I think I should go and see what's the holdup."

Asia nearly jumped out of her seat before Nicholas could make it to the door. Her sudden rush toward Isaiah's bed had startled him. He watched as Asia leaned over their son, watching him closely. She thought she'd seen his eyelids fluttering. For several minutes, she stood stock-still, staring into the beautiful face that she loved so much. Nicholas didn't know what was going on, but he, too, remained deathly still, watching Asia as closely as she was eyeing Isaiah.

Her breath tumbled from her lips. "I thought his eyelids moved. It looks as if I was wrong. Oh, Isaiah, please give us a sign that you're in there just resting." She laid her hand in his. "Squeeze my hand if you can hear me, darling. Mommy's right here for you." She began to sing the words to "Mockingbird," one of the songs she'd sung to him as a child, the same song that had been sung to her when she was a little girl.

Nicholas listened to the voice of an angel as she sang so sweetly to her son, their son. Though he and Asia weren't bonded together in matrimony, this was as much his family as any married man with a child had a right to lay claim to. Suspension by distance and time hadn't broken the connection between him and Asia. The fact that they'd produced a son made the bond an even stronger one. Isaiah was his flesh and blood. No one would ever deny him his rights again. Closing his eyes, he thanked the Lord for allowing the physical connection to be made between him and his son and for help in understanding Asia's twenty-two-year-old bad decision.

Asia's disappointment was obvious by the look that Nicholas saw on her face. He could see that she was doing her level best to remain brave and optimistic, but the dark shadows of pain and fear were etched on her lovely face. He felt sorry for her, regretful that she had to go through these tough times, more saddened for what Isaiah had to endure now and in the past.

"Do you need to talk about what you're feeling, Asia?"

She shook her head. "It might help if I knew what I was feeling, if I knew what to say. I'm numb with trepidation. My brain is in a fog."

He walked over to her and took her in his arms. "That's understandable. I think we both should get out of here for a short time. We need to get some fresh air to clear our heads. If you'll agree, I'll call my office manager, Lynda Frasier, and have her come sit with Isaiah."

"That won't be necessary, Mr. Nick," Torri said as she popped into the room. "The little one and I are here now. We'd love to spend some time with Isaiah while you two get away to collect yourselves. You've been here around the clock." Torri embraced Asia and then Nicholas.

Asia gently rubbed Torri's belly. "How is the little one?"

Torri smiled with pride. "He or she is doing just fine. I saw my doctor this morning. Miss Asia, if you don't mind, do you think you could go to the doctor with me in two weeks? I feel a little intimidated by this pregnancy. Perhaps Mr. Nick will stay with Isaiah while we're gone."

Asia squeezed Torri's hand. "I'd be delighted, Torri. Let's hope that Isaiah won't need us around the clock when that time comes. If we are required to be here, could you help Torri and me out, Nicholas?"

"Without a doubt. Torri, we're glad that you're here. We're going to take off for about an hour or two unless you need us to come back sooner than that."

"I don't have anything else to do. I cleared my schedule of personal things to do and I'm also on a five-day work break. Go on and get out of here."

"Thanks. Asia, get your purse. We're going to find somewhere close by to wind down and chill out for a short spell."

"Nicholas, I don't want to interfere in your plans, but I'd like to go to Isaiah's place. I want to make sure everything is okay over there. My keys to his home are in my purse. I brought them with me in case I got the chance to check things out. It's something I need to do."

"Wherever *over there* is, I'll drive you. Is that okay?"

"That'll be fine. He resides in Toluca Lake. Are you familiar with the area?"

"Very much so. I have friends that live there." Nicholas wondered if he would've noticed the uncanny resemblance between himself and Isaiah had he seen his son somewhere in the vicinity of where a few of his close friends resided. It still amazed Nicholas that he had a famous son that had lived and worked for nearly two years in the same state as he did yet he'd never laid eyes on so much as a picture of him. Though he had heard plenty about Ike the Psyche.

Nicholas walked around Isaiah's home in utter amazement. Elegant but furnished with extremely comfortable-looking furnishings and masculine accents, the lovely house was located in an extremely pricey neighborhood. That their taste in decor was so similar astounded him. The colors in Isaiah's place were Nicholas's favorites, shades of gray and teal spirited with various shades of white. The entire house had a cool, breezy feel to it, and Nicholas felt Isaiah's spirit as he wandered around the place familiarizing himself with his son's environment. It felt as though he was walking on hallowed ground. From the look of things, Isaiah had been richly blessed.

With her heart breaking for the man she respected and loved dearly, Asia watched Nicholas touching his son's belongings as if they were precious gems. Fingering Isaiah's valuable treasures helped Nicholas stay connected to Isaiah's heartwarming spirit, which seemed to beckon to him from every nook and cranny in the place.

Concerned for him, Asia walked up to Nicholas and took his hand. "Are you okay?"

It took him a minute to find his voice. There were so many deep layers of pain for him to cut through. His heart was battered and badly bruised. The bitterness he felt was hard to swallow. He somehow managed to bite back the sarcastic retorts stinging his tongue, but he didn't know how much longer he could go on like this. His anger for the hand of injustice that had been dealt to him was dying to burst loose from within.

Unable to withstand the physical longings caused by the softness of her flesh, he withdrew his hand from hers. "I'm all right. Just astounded that our taste in furnishings and colors are so similar. I'm amazed by how two people can be so much alike without one ever knowing the other." He dropped down on the teal-green leather sectional sofa, almost an exact replica of the one in his home. "Go ahead and do what you came here to do, Asia. I'm going to sit here and get in touch with my feelings. I seem to get overwhelmed at each new item of discovery."

Hoping Nicholas would be fine, Asia stood quietly for a moment. He sounded so distraught, but she certainly understood why. Nicholas had suffered much trauma within such a short period of time. It seemed that his world had been turned upside down and inside out, and all of it in an instant. Before daring to move on through the house without offering him her support, she put her hand on his shoulder. "He's more like you than you could ever imagine. Isaiah is definitely his father's son, in every way possible."

When Nicholas didn't respond to her comments, she sensed his need to deal privately with the feelings overpowering him. She'd also perceived his anger. Gently, she squeezed his shoulder. Asia then moved down the long hallway leading to the master suite.

He hadn't responded because what he thought about her comments was indeed sinful. Struggling with the forces of evil was becoming a constant battle for him, especially when he was around Asia. He didn't understand how she could even tell him how much Isaiah was like him after denying them access to each other for so many years. He was beginning to think she had no idea of how much she'd hurt him despite her voicing deep regret. Since he'd have to be in her presence, at least until Isaiah pulled through this crisis, he was going to have to find a constructive way to deal with his deep-seated feelings of anger and frustration.

Seated on the king-size four-poster bed inside Isaiah's personal suite of rooms, Asia looked over at the nightstand to glance at the caller ID box. Isaiah had numerous messages. She couldn't help wondering if there might be a clue on one of them as to what had happened to her child. Intruding in Isaiah's private space wasn't something she'd even consider under normal circumstances. But there was nothing normal about this situation. The drugs found in Isaiah's body deeply concerned her. If the test results proved to be accurate, someone out there in the big, bad world had all the answers to her unending questions. She just had to find out who they were and why they might want her son dead. If her son hadn't taken the drugs willingly, an attempt to kill him was a certainty. Isaiah was not an illegal substance user or abuser.

She wouldn't hesitate to bet her life on that fact.

After reaching for one of a dozen pens and a message pad from the stack of yellow pads that Isaiah kept next to the phone, she began writing down the names and phone numbers that appeared on the caller ID box. As she went through the list of calls, she noticed that Isaiah hadn't checked his messages for at least twelve hours prior to the accident. Asia was a sharp prosecutor, highly revered. She had the ability to zero in on minute things in the cases she prosecuted, clues that seemed so insignificant to others and had gone totally unnoticed by seasoned investigators.

Isaiah's every step on the day of the tragedy would have to be retraced. Asia was most interested in the events that had occurred before and after the time Isaiah had spent in Nicholas's company. His hours with Nicholas were already accounted for. Nicholas had told her the exact time Isaiah had arrived at his office and the approximate time they'd parted company at the restaurant. She also knew the time that her son had called her and the hour he'd left her house.

A time line for his other movements needed to be established immediately. How to accomplish that without Isaiah being able to tell her where he'd gone that day made it a tough assignment. But knowing how to contact all of his close friends and teammates provided her a starting place. Troy Dyson would be the first person she'd call on. As Isaiah's best friend, he could probably fill in a portion of the gaps in time. Troy would surely know the hour that Isaiah had left his place since he still had planned on going there. *Had Troy's been his last stop?*

As Asia got up from the bed, she spotted the heirloom photo album she'd put together for Isaiah. She had presented her precious gift to him at the surprise twenty-first birthday party that she and Torri had thrown in his honor. The picture book chronicled his entire life. Thinking that the pictures would help Nicholas to draw closer to their son and possibly assist him in getting to know Isaiah better, she picked up the thick album and carried it back to the family room.

With his back to her, Nicholas stood in front of the marble fireplace looking at the numerous fancy framed pictures neatly arranged on the mantel. She smiled at the fact that looking at photos had occurred to both of them. Pleased with her decision to show the album to him, she sat down on the sofa. "Nicholas, I have something here I think you'd love to see."

As he turned around and looked at her, she stifled a gasp. His eyes were bloodred from crying and the dangerous glint in them frightened her. Taking on the expression of a scared rabbit, all she could do was sit there and stare back at him. This unsettling episode wasn't what either of them had in mind when they'd left the hospital to take an emotional break, Asia thought. It seemed that the attempt to clear their heads had backfired. Nicholas looked like he wanted to snatch her up and snap her in two with his bare hands.

Stuffing his hands deep into his pockets, as if he needed to control them before they wrapped around her graceful neck, he crossed the room and dropped down beside her on the sofa. "What is it you want me to see?"

Although she no longer thought the idea of showing him the album was a good one, she handed it to him anyway. "These are pictures of Isaiah from birth up to the present."

Knowing what magnificent beauty he'd find on the pages of the album, and how much it would hurt to see exactly what he'd missed out on, Nicholas closed his eyes to battle against shedding more tears.

This was just another cruel twist of fate. He couldn't help wondering if Asia was getting some sort of sick pleasure out of tormenting him this way. Even though it didn't fit the character of the woman he'd fallen in love with, he didn't know whom she'd become. Perhaps the difficulties she'd had in raising a child as a single parent had turned her bitter and vengeful. If her desire was to make him pay for his part in impregnating her, she was doing a good job of it. He hoped that he was dead wrong in his thinking. Tarnishing the angelic image of her that he'd carried around in his head and in his heart for so many years didn't at all appeal to him.

Opening his eyes, he looked directly at her. "Will you allow me to take this home and look at it when I'm in a better frame of mind? I promise to take good care of it and return it as soon as possible. Right now isn't a good time for me."

"As you wish, Nicholas." Though she was disappointed that they wouldn't share in looking at the photos together, a thoughtful expression crossed her face, instead of one that spoke to her disenchantment. "I think it's time we get back to the hospital. What about you?"

He got to his feet. "I agree with you."

Asia suddenly remembered that she hadn't looked into Isaiah's refrigerator to see if anything needed to be thrown away. He kept a lot of perishable items at home. Isaiah loved most fresh vegetables and fruits so his refrigerator was always loaded with his favorites. He also drank a lot of milk. It wasn't unusual for him to have at least two gallons on hand.

Asia sensed that Nicholas wanted to get away from her as soon as possible. With that in mind, she quickly decided to stay behind and drive one of Isaiah's other two cars, the black Lexus sport-utility vehicle or the metallic-silver Mercedes Benz convertible. She knew where he kept all of his spare keys. In fact, she knew where Isaiah kept everything, the important and the unimportant. Isaiah shared with his mother most of the things in his life. She'd earned the title of confidante early in his life. But if he'd known that someone wanted to hurt him, he certainly hadn't shared that important piece of information with her. Asia had to believe that Isaiah couldn't have been aware of the danger he'd come to face one day.

"Nicholas, I think I should clean out Isaiah's refrigerator before I leave. It's one of the things I came out here to do. You can just leave without me. I'll drive one of Isaiah's cars back to the hospital. I know you must be anxious to be on your way. I'm sure you've suffered long enough in my company."

"Asia, once again I'm going to warn you about assuming things. You don't know my feelings, anxious, suffering, or otherwise. Stop trying to second-guess me. You're not inside me; therefore, you can't possibly experience my emotions. The last thing we need to do is create more complications for ourselves. Life itself is problematic enough. I'll help you clean out the refrigerator. Then we'll go back to the hospital the same way we came here, together."

She didn't like the brusque, matter-of-fact tone he'd used with her, but she wasn't going to stand around and trade sarcastic remarks with him. In case he'd forgotten, she'd hate to have to remind him that she had hot buttons, too, several of them. And his clipped comments had already pressed hard into the one known as belligerence. "Follow me," she instructed, her intonation no less snappish than the one he'd used with her.

CHAPTER FIVE

Mentally denying everything being said regarding her son's medical condition, Asia rocked back and forth in her seat at the press table, continuing to listen to the negative information the doctors were feeding passionlessly to the throng of media personnel. It appeared that every television station in the nation was present. She had attended many press conferences with Isaiah, but none of them had been anything like this one. None had been for sad occasions.

Isaiah was completely relaxed and confident in the presence of the media. On the other side of the coin, Asia found very little comfort among these man-eaters. Several of them looked ready to devour Isaiah's stellar reputation just to satisfy their voracious appetites for reporting vicious lies, vulgar gossip, and unfounded innuendos. She'd never dreamed that her son's reputation would one day end up on the media's dinner plates. The mention of the drugs found in Isaiah's body was what had unleashed their insatiable thirst for his blood. She was grateful that Nicholas was seated next to her. Her body tingled all over every time he squeezed her hand to foster reassurance.

Nicholas wasn't buying into the report that Isaiah might never walk again. He wasn't accepting any unconfirmed diagnosis, couldn't accept it. He didn't care about the mentioned odds, which didn't favor his son. If it was in God's plan for Isaiah to do so, he would recover and walk. Only by the grace of God could Isaiah be made whole again.

Asia saw that Torri wasn't faring too well either. She looked pale, nervous, and emotionally upset, yet she was hardly a stranger to the media. Considering Torri's own delicate health condition, Asia wished she had encouraged Torri to skip the press conference. At any rate, she would've eventually seen it on every television channel in America and heard it on numerous radio broadcasts, repeatedly, Asia considered. It was impossible to protect Torri from any of it.

"As for the drugs found in Isaiah's system," one reporter shouted from the back of the room, "what types of drugs were found and have you yet been able to determine if he's a recreational user or an addict?"

Asia quickly pulled the movable microphone stand toward her. "I'll answer that question. Isaiah Morrell is not a drug user or a substance abuser. If drugs were found in his system, there will be a plausible explanation, and we will find the answers. Until we learn the truth, I urge you not to report that which is unfounded and unconfirmed. Isaiah deserves your respect."

"Ms. Morrell, many of us certainly recognize the great legal mind, Mr. Reynolds, who's seated next to you. But would you mind telling us if you've retained his services in the event that your son needs legal representation to defend against the drug charges?"

Nicholas stood straight up. "What drug charges?"

The reporter didn't so much as flinch at Nicholas's caustic tone. "Ones that will be filed if he's guilty of illegal drug use."

"I think you're getting way ahead of yourself with that line of questioning. Let's simply deal with the facts."

"According to a reliable source, we've received information that says you're actually Isaiah's father. Can you confirm or deny those allegations?" another reporter shouted.

Even though he'd known this day would eventually come, the question had caught him off guard. Trembling inwardly, Nicholas saw red, but he wasn't about to lose his composure. He was a professional with immeasurable experience in fielding unfair media inquiries. Defined as one of the most brilliant trial lawyers in the country, Nicholas had tried innumerable serious cases in the state of California. Many clients that kept Nicholas on retainer were of the high-profile variety.

To name a few, music moguls, movie stars, and professional athletes were on his list of wealthy clientele. The media often referred to Nicholas as the Celebrity Counselor.

"What source would that be?"

"I'm not at liberty to divulge that information."

Nicholas raised an eyebrow. "When a source has irrefutable evidence of the information he's sharing, he shouldn't mind being quoted. Any source that you aren't free to name, in my opinion, isn't a very reliable one." The other reporters laughed, which hadn't been Nicholas's intent. This was hardly a laughing matter and he wasn't about to let this conference turn into an unruly media circus. His son's hard-fought-for reputation was at stake here. Nicholas knew all too well how a black man had to fight harder than anyone else to earn genuine respect. Keeping that reverence alive was also a major uphill battle.

From the research he'd recently done on his son's college and pro careers, Nicholas had determined that Isaiah was held in high regard from those involved in all aspects of the media, men and women alike. As with several Internet sports profiles, every newspaper and magazine article that Nicholas had thus far read on Isaiah had nothing but great things to say about the superstar athlete. That alone was commendable when one considered all the high-profile athletes who seemed to seek out trouble and wear it as if it were some sort of honor badge.

There had been a number of times that Nicholas had taken the media to task for insensitivity, but he had to remain mindful of what was at stake right now. The walk through this press conference was layered with thin eggshells. If he wasn't careful with this wording, he was quite aware that the already fragile path could suddenly turn into a playing field littered with land mines.

"I am in fact Isaiah's father, a very proud one. The relationship between my son and me is private. When he's out of the woods, perhaps we'll both be willing to answer your more candid questions. As many of you know, Isaiah has always been media-friendly. However, this press conference was called for us to share information about Isaiah's health. Under such grave circumstances, I'm afraid we're not prepared to have personal questions fired our way. I only ask that you respect our position and to please write only those things that are based on fact. In view of what my family and I have had to and still have to endure, I feel compelled to bring this meeting to an end. Thanks to all of you who've shown and voiced heartfelt concern for Isaiah during this most difficult time. Good day, ladies and gentlemen."

Extremely confident in his position as the designated spokesperson for Isaiah's loved ones, Nicholas stepped back from the microphone. Smoothing his silk tie in place, he waited at the edge of the podium for Asia and Torri to join him. Hands entwined as they walked off the dais with their heads held high, totally ignoring the barrage of questions from the scrambling throng of reporters shouting desperate questions at their retreating forms.

Asia squeezed Nicholas's hand. "You handled that brilliantly, Nicholas. Isaiah would be so proud of you."

"He could end up being mad as hell at me for announcing to the world that I'm his father. I can live with that as long as he stays down here on earth where I can continue to reach out to him. If God was only willing to grant me one more blessing in this lifetime, I'd opt for more time to show my son how much love I'm capable of giving him."

Weary with emotion, Torri laid her head on Asia's shoulder. "I know what you're saying, Mr. Nick, but God never puts limits on His blessings. And I also have to agree with Miss Asia. Nicholas really would be proud of your performance today."

"I hope so," Nicholas responded. "I pray that he'll one day be as proud of me as I am of him." With his emotions nearly getting the best of him, he had to find a way to temper them. "How about us getting a bite to eat?"

Asia nodded her approval. "I'm all for that as long as we can get something from the hospital cafeteria. I'm anxious to get back to Isaiah. Your assistant must be tired of just sitting by now. I don't want to take advantage of her kindness." Asia was actually overanxious about returning to the hospital. Isaiah had been left in the hands of someone that was a virtual stranger to her. Isaiah had only met Lynda Frasier once. Asia knew that because Nicholas had told her about how Lynda had encouraged Isaiah to sit down and get some of his questions answered.

Nicholas grinned broadly, his fondness for his assistant apparent in his expression. "Don't worry about anything like that regarding Lynda. She's one of the kindest people I know. Lynda is the kind of woman that would help anyone who needed it."

Asia eyed Nicholas curiously, wondering if he was involved in more than a professional working relationship with Lynda. The look on his face was radiant when he talked about her.

"Lynda Frasier is like a sister to me. I'm extremely fond of her, as you can probably tell. We have gone through a lot together over the years. She's a very loyal friend and employee."

Asia breathed a sigh of relief at his explanation of his relationship with Lynda. His being involved with Lynda on a personal level wasn't at all pleasant for her. Her body shivered as she thought of what it would be like to kiss his sweet lips again. She was sure that it would prove to be nothing less than divine. Even though she knew there was no chance for her and Nicholas to take up where they'd left off, she couldn't help how deep her feelings still ran for him. Just as he'd been during their time together in college, and in all the years afterward, Nicholas Reynolds was still very much her hero.

Asia had very few male heroes in her life. Nicholas was one of the strongest black men she'd ever come to know. In her opinion, her father had also been very strong, but he'd shown his weakness when he'd learned that she was pregnant. His disappointment in her had weakened him considerably. And, for years, he'd dared to cut his daughter completely out of his life. What was most troubling for Asia was that her parents had been in the very same position as she was. Her mother hadn't been married to her father when she was conceived. But that was a family secret, one that Asia had accidentally overheard being discussed by family members. Asia had kept the secret locked away in her heart even after her parents had turned her out cold.

Out of all the people in the world, she had expected Wilkes Morrell, a Christian man, to be her tower of strength, her bridge over troubled water, the one person who'd understand and offer compassion. Instead, he'd turned his back on her for nearly fourteen years, only reconciling with her a couple of years before his death. For a man who'd believed in God, one who believed in and had preached the true meaning of forgiveness, he had come up very short in that area.

Her mother, Virginia, had gone along with Wilkes's wishes to completely cut Asia off, therefore abandoning her daughter in her most desperate time of need. Although Virginia had periodically kept in touch with Asia, she'd done it covertly. Virginia had failed to stand up for her only daughter. In doing that, Virginia had shown weakness, too. Virginia had passed away less than a year after her husband's death, leaving Asia and Isaiah alone in the world. Besides Isaiah and Nicholas, Asia's uncle Thomas was the only other hero in her life until his death.

Seeing Miranda seated in Isaiah's room with Lynda caused Nicholas to fume. Without uttering a word, he placed the Styrofoam boxes of food on the table. He then propelled Miranda from her seat, leading her out of the room, and down the hall to an empty waiting room.

Miranda pulled her arm away from Nicholas's tight grasp. "Why are you manhandling me like this?"

"Sit down, Miranda."

The contempt in his eyes caused Miranda to quell her desire to ignore his demand. But she was happy that she had at least managed to capture his undivided attention. She had gotten him alone and she planned to keep it that way for as long as she could. From the television set in her office, she had seen the live press conference. His referring to Asia and Isaiah as his family had provoked her impromptu visit to the hospital despite Nicholas's pleas for her to stay away.

"Why do you suddenly keep popping up in Isaiah's room, especially after I asked you not to do that? It's apparent to me that you couldn't care less about my son. If you did, you'd respect his right to privacy. He's a very ill young man, Miranda. This crisis with my son is separate from anything to do with you and me. What don't you understand about that?"

"I believe it's you that's lacking in understanding. You need to understand that I won't sit by and watch you publicly humiliate me."

"Publicly humiliate you? What are you talking about now?"

"In case you've forgotten, Nick, I'm still your wife, the only family that you have legally. You've never been married to Asia and your son doesn't even carry your surname. For you to get on national television and call these imposters your family is a vicious slap in my face, one that I don't take lightly."

Nicholas had to take a deep breath to keep from exploding all over Miranda. This was not the time for them to have this kind of discussion, but he saw that he had no other choice in the matter. Nicholas was so angry that he began to tremble. He wasn't a man who allowed his tongue to have control over his head and heart very often, but he wasn't above responding in an unkind manner to personal attacks on himself and those he loved. His internal rage made him see that he had to take a moment to calm down and try to pray his way through this ugly confrontation. Two wrongs never equaled a right. Besides, he rarely allowed others to have his power.

Miranda took his silence as an attempt to ignore her. Taking a pink message note from her purse, she slapped it on the table. "This is the appointment time for us to see the pastor for our first counseling session."

Her boisterous tone caused him to abandon his moment of reverent prayer. He looked up at her with a stunned expression on his face. This woman seated before him was one that he apparently didn't know at all. What the new Miranda seemed capable of was growing more and more unsettling. The woman all of a sudden seemed to be possessed by the redheaded devil.

"I expect to see you in Pastor Jones's office at seven-thirty this evening. Don't disappoint me, Nick. I don't take disappointment too well."

All he could do was watch her storm out of the room. In all his years of engaging in legal combat, he couldn't even figure out where to begin in mounting an effective defense against the woman he had deep respect for, professionally and personally. Using unattractive forms of ammunition against her went against his moral fiber. He couldn't stoop to that level, nor would he allow his lawyer to use unethical defense tactics. There had to be another way. He thought of not showing up at the counseling session, but he quickly changed his mind. He couldn't live with himself if he didn't do everything possible to turn Miranda back in the right direction.

Nicholas already knew that it wasn't going to work out between them, that the marriage was over, but he felt that he somehow had to convince Miranda of that. He had to find a way to respectfully appeal to who he thought was the real Miranda. It was clear for him to see that there was no way to appeal to the selfish she-devil who'd completely taken Miranda over.

As he got up to go back to be with Isaiah, Asia came into the waiting room. Seeing her beautiful face caused bitter feelings to rise. If she hadn't excluded him from Isaiah's life, his own life wouldn't be in so much turmoil. Asia was responsible for all of the unpleasantness that was now taking place in his life. He had lost count of the times he'd recently begun to wish that he were capable of hating her, an impossible feat for him since he still loved her so much.

Asia took the seat directly across from him. "I came to check on you. I saw Miranda storming past the door as if she was enraged. I was concerned for you."

"Don't you think it's a bit too late for your concern? About twenty-two years too late?"

For the first time in his life, he was scared of himself. His anger was nearly out of control. It wouldn't take much more to push him over the edge. He had a hard time seeing Asia looking so cool and calm knowing she was the producer of all his insanity.

Asia got to her feet. "Maybe I should leave you alone with your thoughts. I'm sorry. I didn't mean to intrude in your private affairs."

Before she reached the doorway, Nicholas jumped up from the chair and blocked her exit. "I can't believe you're just going to run out on this conversation. When are you going to face up to what you've done, Asia?"

Deep regret showed in her eyes as she sat back down. "Repeatedly, I've told you how sorry I am about everything. If you can't accept that, I'm sorry for you. I don't know what else I can do to convince you of how much I regret my past decisions, Nicholas."

"There's nothing you can ever do to undo all the hurt you've caused. But you can tell me why." He dropped back down in the seat. "I've waited and waited for you to explain things to me, but you haven't even tried to speak on it."

"That's not true. I did. In the beginning, but you stopped me, said you weren't ready to hear it . . ."

"That was when I first saw Isaiah lying there broken, battered, and bleeding," he interjected. "We didn't know if he was going to live or die. The timing was wrong. You were already in enough pain. I didn't want to add more discomfort by bombarding you with hard questions about your reasons for keeping our son a secret."

"Nothing has changed for any of us since that night, Nicholas. The conditions are all the same. So why have this confrontation now?"

"I beg to differ. Everything in my life has changed. And I suddenly have a burning need to know why you kept my son away from me. If Isaiah hadn't taken the initiative to find me, regardless of his motivation, I still wouldn't know that he existed. What did I do to deserve such disrespect from you? If I did something that hurt you, I've never been able to figure out what it could be. I was extremely careful with your heart. I guess it was stupid of me to think that you and I had a future. Did you even love me, Asia? I'm not so sure you ever did. Am I right?"

Asia's heart couldn't break into any more fragments and it couldn't ever be put back together again. To see Nicholas hurting so badly was killing her inside. He looked so vulnerable. She wanted to bring his head to her breasts and hold his body against hers. His violent trembling scared her. *Please, Lord, don't let him have a heart attack. I couldn't bear it,* she prayed silently.

"Of course I loved you, Nicholas." *I've never stopped.* Anguished, she wrung her hands together. "I was scared. I knew what you'd do if I told you I was pregnant."

"And what would that be? Don't tell me you thought I'd run out on you. If that's what you thought, you didn't know me, Asia. Not at all."

"I did know you, Nicholas, very well. I knew you'd drop out of school in order to take care of your responsibilities. But I was more afraid that you'd later come to hate me after you realized how I'd ruined your life, that you'd eventually blame me for everything going wrong. I ran away to ensure your future, not to take it all away from you."

A perplexed mask of pain and anger distorted his features. "Who the hell did you think you were to try and decide my future? Who gave you permission to take away my right in deciding what I might want for myself? You made decisions for me that have challenged my manhood. But you're right about one thing. I would've done whatever it took to take care of my responsibilities. That's how it should've been."

"Nicholas, you have to understand. All I could see is you dropping out of school and later blaming me for it."

"I don't think I would've had to drop out of school. But if it had come to that, I would've taken it all in stride. That's what a real man does. The first time I ever made love to you, I'd already made up my mind about what I'd do if something like that happened. Asia, I would've done the right thing by you, but not because it was the right thing to do. I was in love with you, woman. I would've given up my life for you, Asia. But all I got in return was you taking mine from me. You stole my boy away from me. You denied me the most important responsibility a man can have, which is taking care of his own. You can never justify your actions, not in a million and one years."

Seeing how angry that he was, that he couldn't be reasoned with, Asia got to her feet. Perhaps they could resume this conversation when he didn't look ready to kill her. In her attempt to leave the room again, she got no farther than a couple of steps away from the table.

He grabbed her arm, digging his fingers into her tender flesh. "You've run out on me for the last time. You need to sit your beautiful behind back down so we can talk this through. This conversation is long overdue." Seeing the painful expression on her face let him know that he'd brought both emotional and physical harm to her. He immediately loosened his grip on her arm. An apology was on the tip of his tongue, but he couldn't seem to get the words out.

Instantly, Asia returned to her seat. It was obvious to her that he wasn't in the mood to have his demands denied. His eyes were dark with the rage he'd kept pent up inside for too long. This clearly wasn't the time to challenge him. His voice had already assaulted her ears like an unexpected thunderstorm. It sounded strange to her since she'd never heard him raise his voice before.

"I hope you've been listening to me," he finally managed to say, rather loudly.

"I'm listening to you, Nicholas, but I'll only continue to do so if you stop yelling. I'm not deaf and it's disrespectful of you to talk to me that way. I won't sit still for that kind of abuse."

He shoved a trembling hand through his hair. "I'm sorry I've let my emotions run wild. But, Asia, I need to understand what made you do such a terrible thing as this. Whether you knew or didn't know I'd do the right thing by you, why couldn't you let it be my decision? Why'd you feel you had to make up my mind for me? Help me before I go insane over this."

The sorrowful look Asia gave Nicholas made it impossible for him to continue feeling angry with her. It was his guess that she was already paying a high price for her past mistakes. Asia was the kind of person that took everything to heart, but he'd never known her to wear it on her sleeve. The Asia he once knew had always taken responsibility for her decisions, good or bad.

"I don't think there are adequate words to explain my negligence. I now know that what I thought to be right was dead wrong. What saddens me the most is I can't go back and change it. I finally did make the decision to look you up when Isaiah was around two. Like I've already told you, I thought you were married. I didn't think it was right for me to disturb your life. Even though you weren't married at the time, I thought you were; you are now. And I must admit that I was very surprised when you told me about the divorce."

"I'm sorry you never learned the truth about my broken engagement. I didn't get involved with anyone for a couple of years. I didn't know it for a long time, but I was still on the rebound, still unable to get over your walking out on me. I had a hard time dealing with your sudden disappearance. No one at school knew where you'd gone. It was like you'd vanished without a trace. Since I hadn't met your family, I really didn't know how to contact them. I even tried to get the information from the administration, but that proved impossible due to the privacy act. I tried to move on when it seemed I'd never find you. It was a year or so later that I met Trina. Our relationship was great up until we got engaged. Shortly after that I began to question my feelings for her. That's when I realized that I still loved you. I couldn't commit to Trina knowing that. Though she believed I'd come to love her one day, I knew better. You were the only woman for me, the only woman I couldn't have, the only woman I'd ever love. Knowing that I have a son by you still overwhelms me at times."

"No one knew where I went because I never told anyone I was leaving school. I didn't utter a single word to anyone about being pregnant. As for my family, I know you often asked me about meeting them, but I grew up in a very religiously strict household. I was too embarrassed to tell you that my parents would never allow me to bring anyone home for a visit, let alone a young man. I rarely spoke about my parents or my difficult upbringing to anyone. I was ashamed to admit how unreasonably sheltered I was. I was only at Howard University because I rebelled against their dictatorial style of parenting once I turned eighteen. While I know it will never be enough, my deepest regrets are all that I can offer you. I'm glad that you finally found love, but I'm sorry for you that it's ending. Why *is* your marriage over, Nicholas?"

"For the same reason no other relationship has worked for me. There's really nothing wrong with Miranda, though she's acting pretty strange as of late, but we married for all the wrong reasons. Love never was a part of our relationship. We were lonely and neither of us wanted to grow old alone. We married for companionship, only to discover that we were lonelier together than we'd ever been when we were single. We never became a comfort to each other. Being set in our ways was another issue: too old to change and too tired to try any harder."

"I'm sorry that you're going through all of this compounded misery, sorry that your marriage isn't working out. I just hope you can forgive me for all the hurt I've caused."

"Forgiveness will come. It just may take a little more time for me to work through everything that's happened. As for my marriage, Miranda has suddenly decided that she doesn't want the divorce. She wants us to try harder, or so she says. But I don't think her change of heart has anything to do with trying." He laughed cynically. "She thinks I've been having an affair with you the entire time we've been married. She's accusing me of adultery, yet she wants us to stay together. Doesn't make sense, does it?"

"What do you want, Nicholas?"

Asia was ashamed of the fact that she didn't care a hill of beans about what Miranda wanted. The one confrontation she'd had with Nicholas's estranged wife was enough to let her know that Miranda didn't deserve a wonderful man like him. The woman seemed so self-absorbed. Mrs. Reynolds had shown total disregard for Isaiah's serious health issues and the obvious emotional pain that Nicholas was in because of them.

"It doesn't matter what I want, but I agreed to work on our marriage. It wouldn't do any good to argue about it. She'll come to realize there's nothing for us to hang on to. In the meantime, I won't try to take away her dignity. The truth is that you threaten her. If you hadn't come into the picture, she would've signed the divorce papers and we probably would've remained good friends. Always the optimist, I'm sure Miranda and I will get through these bad times. I believe she'll agree to the divorce once she realizes why she's really doing this."

Looking thoughtful, Asia formed a steeple with her hands. "Seems like I'm responsible for a lot of the heartbreak going on around here. I don't know what to say. That's a lot for me to take responsibility for. I'd change all of our circumstances if I could. We both know that I can't." Asia couldn't contain her tears no matter how hard she tried. Tears rolled from the corners of her eyes and splashed onto her cheek before she could wipe them away. How anyone could envy the position she was in now went way beyond her understanding.

Nicholas never could stand to see her cry. Unable to deny her need for compassion, he stood up and drew Asia into his arms, kissing her tears away. A sudden flashback of them making love instantly awakened his latent desire for her. His lips, salty with her tears, crashed down over hers in a kiss that nearly shocked both of them senseless. Embarrassed by his stupid, juvenile display of uncontrollable desire, he pulled himself away and rushed out of the room.

Still reeling from the sensuous feel of his lips on hers, Asia touched her fingertips to her mouth, as if to savor the passionate kiss. Feeling the fiery heat of the deep passion they once shared, Asia dropped down in the chair. Nicholas's kiss had taken her breath away.

As she thought about the probing kiss, she came to realize that she couldn't read too much into his show of affection. This was an extremely emotional time for them. She was sure the kiss had come as a result of his emotions running so high. They were no longer carefree college students with the world at their fingertips. As they'd done on so many occasions, she and Nicholas couldn't escape the bustling activity of campus life to go off and find a secret place to make love. They were now a grown man and woman with numerous adult complications and a mountain of problems to solve. Nicholas was married to an attractive woman who wanted to hold on to him forever and Asia was committed to her son as well as married to her job.

Nicholas and Lynda weren't in Isaiah's room when Asia returned, but Torri was still there. Torri reading something to Isaiah from *Sports Illustrated* made Asia smile as she pulled up a chair and sat down. "How's it going in here?"

Torri looked at Asia with concern. "Fine in here, but whatever happened out there is what has me worried. Mr. Nick seemed so upset when he left with his assistant. Are you two going to be okay?"

Asia gently patted Torri's knee. "We'll be just fine. Nicholas and I had to get through some unfinished business. Nothing for you to worry about. What are you reading?"

"Mr. Nick told me to try reading some of these sports articles to Isaiah. He seems so sure that Isaiah can hear us. What do you think?"

"I've heard that comatose patients can hear what's happening around them, but I don't know that it's a proven fact. I'd like to think it's true and that he can hear us. Nicholas won't allow himself to interact with

Isaiah in any other manner. He truly believes that Isaiah is tuned into us. It's probably part of what keeps Nicholas going."

"He seems like a very positive man, a spiritual one. I hope Isaiah gets the chance to really know him. Do you mind if I ask you a personal question or two, Miss Asia?"

Asia nodded her approval, hoping the questions being considered weren't too personal.

"I'm curious as to why you never told Mr. Nick about Isaiah, especially since you've encouraged me to stay and share the news of my pregnancy with Isaiah."

"It's a simple answer, Torri. I loved him that much."

"I kind of figured that. But I guess I'm asking about what factors you took into account in making your decisions. For instance, I'm not sure if Isaiah's going to want this baby. Is that what you were thinking?"

"Just the opposite. Nicholas may not have wanted the baby, but he would've taken responsibility for the child. I decided that it was too high a price for him to pay. I didn't want to steal his dreams right out from under him; he had so many. I also feared that he'd insist on committing to me because it was the right thing to do, not because he loved me. What I feared most is that he'd later blame me for ruining his life. I now know that I was very wrong."

Torri's eyes widened with curiosity. "How do you know you were wrong?"

"Because of the things he just told me."

"Like what?"

Asia laughed. "You're not going to let me off lightly, are you?"

Torri shook her head. "I'm sorry, but our situations are so similar. I want to know what Mr. Nick was thinking back then. If Isaiah's anything like him, he may think the same way."

"Oh, trust me, Isaiah is very much his father's son. That's what makes me so sure that he's going to be thrilled about this baby. Torri, I hope what I'm about to say will reassure you. Nicholas said he'd already decided to do right by me if I ended up pregnant. He told me he would've stayed with me because he loved me, not because it was the right thing to do. Does that answer help satisfy your curiosity?"

"Wow! Only a real man decides that before the fact. How do you feel about it now?"

"Pretty stupid. While I didn't underestimate him as a responsible man, I put too small a price on his feelings for me. That's where I failed both Nicholas and Isaiah. It looks as if we could've been one happy family. But I have to put that all behind me now. Life has to go on even when we feel like we want to die from the embarrassment and pain of our past mistakes."

"Do you still love Mr. Nick, Miss Asia?"

Hearing movement near the door caused Asia to look behind her. Seeing Nicholas standing there kept her from responding to Torri's very pointed question. Though glad that she'd been forewarned of his presence, Asia still felt the rising heat of embarrassment in her cheeks.

He entered the room. "I'd be interested in hearing the answer to that question myself. Do you still love me, Asia?"

"I'll always love you, Nicholas. You're the father of my son."

"Yeah, I can tell that you're a very clever lawyer, Asia Morrell. You sure squirmed your way out of that one with ease. I'm happy that you love me as the father of your son. But I think Torri was asking are you *in* love with me? You know, the kind of deep connection, mental and physical, that occurs between a man and a woman. But you don't have to answer that. I wouldn't think of putting you on the spot." Much to Asia's discomfort, his eyes twinkled with devilment.

Asia narrowed her eyes at him as she got to her feet. "Thank you, Nicholas. I appreciate that. If you two will excuse me, I'm going down to the cafeteria and heat up the food. I never got a chance to eat with so much melodrama going on around here."

"What about warming mine up, too?" Nicholas couldn't help smiling at the mildly sarcastic comment that had been made with the intent of hitting him right between the eyes.

"Sure thing. I'll be right back. Torri, can I get you anything?"

"A bottle of cold water will work nicely for me, Miss Asia. I saw an Evian machine in the cafeteria. There's also one right down the hall, in the same room where all the other vending machines are located."

Asia removed a change pouch from her leather purse. With a slight nod toward her two companions, she stepped out into the hallway.

Nervously biting down on her lower lip, Torri looked over at Nicholas. "The press conference was so disturbing for me. To hear them discussing Isaiah and the use of illegal drugs in the same sentence was hurtful. Isaiah's not a drug user. Since I spend so much time with him, I think I'd know if he was ever under the influence of drugs. I've never known Isaiah to take so much as a sip of wine. He used to get upset at me for drinking any kind of alcohol until he saw that it was only an occasional thing with me."

"He told me he doesn't drink, Torri."

"He told you that because he doesn't. He's really an honest person. Isaiah is also very health conscious. It took him a while to recognize and admit that he needed to get counseling to help him manage his anger. Once he saw the need for him to get some help in keeping his temper in check, he didn't hesitate to go for it. He still blows up every now and then, but not as frequently as before. The only person he ever took his rage out on was himself, which came in the form of isolation. He'd just stay off by himself until he calmed down."

Her eyes suddenly filled with tears. "The stuff I heard today has me wondering if this was really an accident."

"What makes you say that?" Nicholas was very eager to hear Torri out.

"Everything about this case. Isaiah didn't take drugs, not so much as an aspirin. Not even the thought of suicide would ever cross his mind. None of it adds up."

"Do you have anything specific in mind?"

"Not really."

"Who do you think should I talk to first?"

"Troy, his best friend and confidant. Even though Troy is the one who told Miss Asia that I was pregnant, he'd never betray one of Isaiah's confidences. Those two are as thick as thieves. They've always had each other's back."

Nicholas looked perplexed. "Asia and I have also been wondering about the nature of Isaiah's accident. There are a lot of unanswered questions. However, I don't want you worrying about this to the point of it jeopardizing your health. You have to take care of yourself and the baby. If something is amiss, Asia and I have an entire police force to tap into, not to mention a host of other law enforcement agencies that we can count on for support."

"I didn't start wondering about things until I heard the reporters talking about the drugs. The stuff I heard at the press conference was an eye-opener for me. I'm happy that I have you to share my concerns with. You're so easy to talk with and to confide in."

"I'm happy you feel that way. The media enlightened us all to some vital information that we've never heard before today. Someone always sees fit to inform them before the victim's family hears anything. I'll get an official copy of the police report. It seems that one has already been delivered to the press. Asia and I haven't had an opportunity to discuss the things we heard from the media. I'll talk to her later, after she eats and gets a little rest. She's another one that's going to need to take good care of herself."

Torri smiled. "I, for one, am glad that you're here to help protect Isaiah and his mom." She grinned sheepishly. "Now, on a more personal note. Are you still in love with Miss Asia?"

"As a lawyer, I should heed the advice I occasionally give my clients on pleading the Fifth Amendment. But I'll just say this instead. I'm smart enough to know that we can't go back and retrieve or relive the past. We're a long way from where we used to be. Asia and I have changed significantly. At this stage in our lives, friendship is all that we can ever hope for. While we'll always have Isaiah in common, that's probably as far as it can ever go."

"Do you think you'll be able to become a close friend of Miss Asia?"

As her question sank in, he looked disturbed by it. "Why do you ask that?"

"I'm sure you're awfully upset with her for keeping you two apart. Forgiveness may come very hard for you if, God forbid, the unthinkable occurs with Isaiah. It would be very hard for me to forgive someone in that instance. That's only one of my numerous flaws, but I think it's just a part of human nature. I hate to be so painfully blunt. I'm simply a realist."

"It's already hard, Torri. On the other hand, I refuse to consider the unthinkable. Isaiah is going to recover. We have to put our trust in God. It's totally up to Him. He never puts more on us than we can bear."

"I second that," Asia announced, entering the room.

Getting to his feet, Nicholas took hold of Torri's hand. Once Asia set down the boxes of food and bottled water, he gripped her fingers tightly. "Let's kneel and have prayer."

CHAPTER SIX

Pastor Howard Jones, founding minister of the Hope of Trinity Church, wasn't in his comfortably decorated study when Nicholas stepped through the open door. Wondering if he was early or if the others were late, Nicholas glanced at his watch. The agreed-upon meeting time and the time showing on his watch were exactly the same. He was right on schedule.

Though he wasn't keen on meeting with the pastor and Miranda, especially for a marriage counseling session, he seated himself on one of the cloth-covered chairs. He didn't need Pastor Jones to tell him what his obligations and duties were, or the rules of God's law, as it pertained to marriage. The pastor couldn't provide him with any more information on marriage and divorce than what his Bible could. He'd already studied in depth the Scriptures that covered both issues. It seemed that Miranda was the one that hadn't done her homework in that area.

Nicholas still couldn't believe the nerve of her accusing him of committing adultery. Never once had he cheated on her, even after she'd moved into the guest bedroom. There were many times when he'd thought he'd go mad because he desperately needed to have his physical needs met, but he hadn't ever gone outside his marriage to do so. Nicholas looked over at the door when he heard footsteps, losing his train of thought.

Miranda had a heavy scowl on her face when she came into the room. She practically slammed her purse down on the floor as she took the chair in front of the pastor's desk. She didn't utter a word as she turned and stared hard at Nicholas.

She had a huffy air about her. Her mad-dog expression told him that no matter what he said it would be the wrong thing. His eyes had connected with hers, but he would wait for her to begin the conversation. Marriage counseling was her idea and he was content in letting her call all the shots. Besides, he didn't know what to expect from Miranda's new personality.

"You can't open your mouth to speak to me, Nicholas? That's not like you. Have you already changed that much?"

"Good evening, Miranda. With that said, I've always been under the impression that the person entering a room already occupied should speak first. But maybe I got it wrong."

"You're getting a lot of things wrong here lately."

His expression showed impatience. "I don't guess you'd care to expound."

"You guessed right. Before we go on, I have bad news for you."

His thoughts went straight to Isaiah, his heart racing.

"The pastor had to cancel our session."

Nicholas sighed hard, relieved to know the bad news wasn't to do with Isaiah. "When was someone going to let me in on it?"

"He called me and I was supposed to call you, but I got caught up in a problem needing immediate attention. When I couldn't get you at the office, I came on over to see if you'd made it here yet."

"My cell phone is always on, Miranda, and I'm spending most of my time at the hospital. But you already know that. Sorry for mentioning it to you as if you weren't aware of it." His sarcasm earned him an evil look.

"Well, it really doesn't matter one way or the other since I came here to tell you in person. Perhaps we shouldn't waste this opportunity to talk about our issues. But I'd rather discuss them over a hot plate of delicious food. Can I buy you dinner, Nick?"

He got to his feet. "Miranda, I don't think that's such a great idea. I also need to get back to the hospital. I pray to God that I'm there when Isaiah comes out of the coma."

"Why isn't it such a good idea? We've eaten together many times since we've been legally separated. Why is there a problem now?"

"The same reason it wasn't a good idea for you to talk to me at lunch the other day. I'm going through with this counseling session because it's what you want, Miranda. As far as I'm concerned, the marriage is over, and has been over for a very long time. We both decided that we're better as friends than we are as spouses. I've moved on, Miranda. Why can't you?"

"How can you think of moving on with another woman when you're not legally divorced from me?"

"Don't put words in my mouth. There is no other woman." His thoughts wrapped around the passionate kiss he'd shared with Asia. Guilt hit him momentarily. "I've moved on with my life. Does that make my meaning any clearer for you?"

It still surprised him that she could so easily twist his words. The fact that she totally ignored anything that had to do with his son hurt him. She hadn't offered him a sincere word of comfort since she first learned about Isaiah. Her coming to the hospital had nothing to do with compassion and concern. He knew her story about trying to reach him at the office was bogus. It seemed to him that she'd planned for them to share dinner together the moment she learned of the cancellation. Miranda hadn't ever before hesitated in contacting him on his cell phone. This time should've been no different from any other.

She took hold of his hand. "I don't like the way you've suddenly become so harsh with me. You've changed considerably. It seems that you're having a hard time being around me. What is happening to us, Nicholas? We hung out together on occasion until this Asia woman came back into your life, yet you continue to insist that there's nothing between you and her."

Nicholas removed his hand from Miranda's in a gentle way. He had no desire to hurt her feelings, but he didn't want to encourage her into thinking there was still a chance for them. He could forgive her for what she was doing to him, and he could forgive her for ignoring his son's dilemma. He couldn't stay married to her under any circumstances. He didn't know her anymore.

"Oh, there's definitely something between Asia and me. Something beautiful and magnificent: a son. But what's certainly not between us is what you've been suggesting. We're in no way involved on the physical and emotional level you seem to think. She's the mother of my child. That's an unbreakable bond, one we'll share forever. As for change, you've done the changing, a complete one-eighty if you ask me. I'm having a hard time accepting the new you. To be perfectly blunt, I don't like this new personality you're rapidly developing. I admired and respected the old you. That's the Miranda I care about."

Miranda rolled her eyes at Nicholas. "So, are you turning down my offer of dinner?"

Nicholas chuckled. "At least your determination in having your own way hasn't changed. I'll tell you what. I'll agree to eat dinner with you if you promise not to discuss our so-called issues. Deal?" Nicholas wanted to steer clear of any talk of them getting back together. It just wasn't going to happen. He hoped she'd come to realize that sooner than later.

"We can't make any headway in reconciling our relationship if we don't talk about it. I'm sorry, but I can't promise you that."

Nicholas shrugged. "In that case, I can't accept your invitation to dinner. Good night, Miranda. Drive safely." He got up and moved toward the exit.

"Nicholas," she shouted, "you can't just walk out on me. You need to show me more respect than this. I won't take this from you."

He turned around to face her. "Miranda, have you forgotten where you are? If so, let me remind you. This is God's house. And there's a Bible study session going on inside the sanctuary. So perhaps you should be the one to show some respect by lowering your voice." Without giving her a chance to retort, he moved quickly down the hallway and out the side entry.

Nicholas hated confrontation in his personal life, though he thrived on it inside the courtroom. He could hardly compare battling Miranda to some of the highly combative skirmishes he'd been involved in as an attorney, but he'd take legal fights over personal drama on any given day. There was something cowardly about fighting with a woman. Petty arguments of any kind were distasteful to him. The earlier argument he'd had with Asia had left him feeling like a silly, immature adolescent. It was rare for him to let his anger get the best of him. Whenever he let anger rule, he paid the price for it. Arguing was emotionally draining. He had a feeling that Miranda was about to declare war on him, which would only bring even more emotional distress.

* * *

Nicholas felt extremely fatigued and looked even wearier about the eyes as he entered the hospital room. He'd had too little sleep over the past few nights; too many important matters were on his mind. His heart thumped wildly at seeing Asia asleep in the extra bed that had finally been moved into Isaiah's room. It was his turn for all-night duty, but he didn't have the heart to wake her. She looked so peaceful, which was a welcome change.

Asia hadn't had a serene moment since she'd heard all the negative comments made at the press conference regarding Isaiah's alleged use of illegal drugs. The physician's doom-and-gloom announcements hadn't brought her any comfort either. Nor had Nicholas helped her situation by jumping all over her. He deeply regretted verbally attacking her, especially after the press had just dealt her a terrible blow. Her courage had weakened. His heart went out to her.

Careful not to wake her, he lifted the chair up, carried it across the room, and set it down at Isaiah's bedside. "Hi, son," he whispered. "How are things going?"

"Mom," Isaiah barely whispered in a dry, cracking voice, his eyelids fluttering slightly.

Nicholas jumped straight up and leaned over the bed. His heart was in his mouth. Unsure if Isaiah had actually spoken, he trained his eyes on his son's mouth. He nearly fell to his knees when he saw Isaiah's eyelids fluttering. Nicholas reached for the call button and pressed hard.

"Mom," Isaiah cried out, his voice coming in a tad clearer than before. "Mom."

Doing his best to contain his surging emotions, Nicholas shot across the room and shook Asia until she stirred. "Wake up, Asia. It's Isaiah. Asia, please wake up."

Asia finally opened her eyes and looked up at Nicholas. The expression on Nicholas's face scared her speechless. Fearing the worst, she muffled a scream as she got to her feet. With her legs unsteady, she almost lost her footing. Nicholas put his hands under her elbows and practically carried her across the room.

"My God, Nicholas, what's happening?"

"He's been calling for you, Asia. He was talking and his eyes were fluttering. Talk to him, Asia. See if he'll respond to you." He nudged her forward until she stood next to the bed.

Asia leaned over and took Isaiah's hand. She then kissed him on the mouth. The feel of his warm breath fanning her lips caused her hopes to soar. He was breathing on his own. "Isaiah, it's Mommy, honey. I'm here, baby. Please let me know if you can hear me."

Isaiah managed to squeeze her hand. "Mom . . . mom," he mumbled, his lips trembling, a single tear running from the corner of his right eye. The movement of his hand and fingers belied paralysis above the waist, but he hadn't yet moved any portion of his lower body, Asia noted.

"Oh, baby, Mommy can hear you! Oh, God, thank you for another miracle. Nicholas, he's come back to us." When Isaiah tried to speak again, she hushed him with a finger to his lips. "Save your energy, darling. You're going to need lots of it to get all the way back to us. You won't have to fight this battle alone. God is always with you. So are Daddy and I."

As if he had understood his mother, Isaiah appeared to give up the struggle to speak.

It felt as if her heart were trying to leap out of her chest. Taking slow, deep breaths, she tried to stabilize her pulse rate. Though euphoria filled her up, the emotional high was somewhat exhausting. She'd never felt weaker than she did right now. She wanted to shout out loud, but she didn't have the energy. As Nicholas's tender hands encircled her waist, she thrust her head back against his chest. Tears spilled out of her eyes quicker than she could wipe them away.

Nicholas couldn't speak. If felt as if his heart were wrestling with his tongue. He did his best to force his heart back into his chest so that he could talk to his son. Unchecked tears flowed from his eyes as he tried to get himself under control. His silent prayers of thanksgiving filled his head and his heart. God had heard him yet again. He had finally delivered His response to all the humble pleas. He had come through for him once more, just as He'd done so many times before.

Asia turned around to face Nicholas. Without the slightest hesitation, her fingers caressed his handsome face as she wiped away his tears. Her arms went around his neck in a warm, comforting embrace. "We need to get Isaiah's nurse in here. Would you mind going out to the desk and ask her to come see about him? I don't want to leave his side for a second."

He looked up and saw that the red call light was still on. Overwhelmed with emotion, he struggled to find his voice. Several seconds of silence passed before he felt like he could talk. He didn't know what his voice was going to sound like, but he had to try it out. Asia didn't need to worry about him, too. From the look on her face, he saw her deep concern.

"I buzzed the nurses' station when I first saw his eyes move," he croaked, swallowing hard, pressing the call button again. His mouth felt as dry as cotton.

Asia reached for a bottle of water and opened it. She then handed it to Nicholas.

He took several long gulps of the room-temperature liquid, wishing it were ice-cold. Nicholas felt instant relief as the water saturated his parched throat. "I'll go see what's keeping her." Bringing Asia back into his arms, he kissed her on the forehead. "God has answered our prayers, Asia. He has spared Isaiah's life. It looks as if we have a second chance to get it right." He kissed her forehead again and walked away, his heart feeling lighter than ever. He could feel God rolling his burdens away. He felt the power of the Almighty working within this room.

Asia looked after Nicholas for a couple of seconds, wondering what he'd meant by his last statement. *A second chance to get it right.* She didn't know his intent, but Isaiah and his dad had certainly been given another chance to see the sunrise on what she hoped would be a host of tomorrows to come. Her pulse quickened as she remembered Nicholas's heartbreaking words.

I've only just met my son; now tomorrow may never come.

Taking Isaiah's hand, she put it up to her lips, kissing each of his fingertips. "Continue to fight, baby. Fight for your every breath. There's a world of people out there rooting for you. And your daddy and I are cheering the loudest."

The nurse hurried into the room with Nicholas following closely on her heels. Without wasting a precious second, she began working on Isaiah immediately, taking his vital signs first. While checking his pupils with a penlight-like instrument, Isaiah's eyes squinted in resistance of the bright light, another good sign.

"He's breathing by himself. That's an excellent sign, but the respirator has to stay on until the doctor gives orders to discontinue its use. His heart rate is also normal. Blood pressure is high, but not extreme. I'm going to get the on-call doctor on the phone. Dr. Lowery will also want to know that his patient has come out of the coma. Spreading the good news to him will have to wait until in the morning since it's almost midnight. I'll return as soon as I speak with the doctor on call."

"I need to call, Torri, Nicholas. It's late but she'll never forgive me if I wait until morning. I have to get my cell phone out of my purse. I'll be right across the room. If there are any other changes in him, please summon me immediately."

All Nicholas could do was stare down at his son. He thought back to their first meeting. What a day that had been. He could never have guessed this outcome. He had looked forward to more dinners and great conversations, but he'd never dreamed that he'd end up being vigilant in any hospital's intensive care unit. Life with all its numerous twists and turns never failed to amaze him. No one knew what the next second would bring in a world as unpredictable as this one. Nicholas used bottled water to soak a washcloth in. He pressed the moist towel to Isaiah's lips to ease their dry, cracked condition.

Isaiah's mouth suddenly opened. As his tongue licked at the beads of water on his lips, Nicholas realized that he was thirsty. His first thought was to try and feed Isaiah water through a straw. He quickly thought better of it. Only the doctors could make that type of determination, clearly a medical decision. His desire to see that Isaiah got what he wanted could prove detrimental to his health. He could choke on the water and that would be disastrous.

Nicholas could hear Asia chattering away with excitement, but he didn't try to hear what was said. His rapt attention was kept on his son. Isaiah's every minute move was important to him. When Isaiah attempted to reach for his hand, Nicholas put it within easy reach for him, pleased beyond reasoning. His eyes became riveted to Isaiah's lips as he struggled to move them again.

"Dad, I . . ." Isaiah's voice had trailed off into nothingness, shaking Nicholas to his core.

Nicholas's barely contained emotions surged forth and broke loose, wreaking havoc on his weakened composure. That Isaiah had called out to him filled his heart to near bursting. That he even remembered him was nothing short of miraculous. His son calling out to him affected him significantly, making him one of the happiest fathers on the planet. Nicholas was too emotional to even try and summon Asia. Besides, this was his special moment, one that he desired to savor in private. Perhaps he and Isaiah would share a tomorrow after all.

Fear suddenly set in on Nicholas when it looked as if Isaiah was no longer breathing. Nicholas put his face close to Isaiah's mouth to see if he could feel his breath. Panic hit him when he didn't feel the slightest bit of air coming from his son's mouth. Instead of pressing the call button, Nicholas ran out of the room.

Alarmed by Nicholas's sudden flight, Asia rushed across the room and looked down on Isaiah. His lips now had a bluish tint to them. It looked to her as if he wasn't breathing. Trained in CPR, Asia rapidly put the railing down and leaned her head farther into the bed. Before she could settle her mouth into position, she felt herself being pushed out of the way.

A team of medical personnel quickly swarmed around the bed. Asia saw the crash-cart as it was wheeled into the room. *Cardiac arrest.* Then she saw Nicholas rush back into the room, his eyes wide with fear. He looked as if he'd aged ten years in less than two minutes.

Her hands flew up to her face; desperate screams pierced the air. Nauseated, she felt acid swirl in her stomach. Dizzy feelings danced inside her head. The floor, swaying back and forth, began to rise up. Blackness rapidly descended and completely engulfed her. As Asia plunged forward, Nicholas's body quickly settled between her and the hard surface.

Nicholas stood over the bed where Asia lay. Concerned for her health, he looked anxious. She had come around not long after she'd fainted, but Dr. Lowery had ordered a sedative to combat the hysterical blitz she'd fallen victim to. Asia had been completely knocked out for several hours now, but she had just begun to stir.

As Asia opened her eyes, Nicholas sighed with relief. "Welcome back, Isaiah's mother." Lifting her hand, he planted a kiss in her palm. "How are you feeling?"

Asia rapidly arose into a sitting position. Excruciating pain ripped through her head. She moaned as the pain forced her head back down on the pillow. Just before her head completed its descent, she saw the empty space that Isaiah's hospital bed had once occupied. Sharp talons of fear tore away at her insides. "Oh, God, Nicholas, where's my baby? Where's Isaiah? Please tell me where my child is." Her mournful cries rent the air.

He gripped her trembling hands tightly. "He's still with us, Asia.

They've moved him into the CCU, the cardiac care unit, where he'll be closely monitored around the clock. He went into cardiac arrest. It wasn't fatal but his condition has been downgraded from stable to critical. We're back to touch-and-go." Nicholas's voice had trembled while sharing the news with Asia. Concerned for her fragile condition, he had tried hard to keep his frazzled emotions from coming through in his tone. He wasn't at all surprised that he'd failed in his attempt. If only for her sake, he had to remain in control. He had to somehow find enough strength to sustain the both of them.

Torri bounced into the room, looking as happy as a lark. Seeing Nicholas comforting a tearful Asia, coupled with the missing bed, Torri froze dead in her tracks. The joy completely disappeared from her face, now replaced by an expression of utter shock. She looked back and forth from Nicholas to Asia and then over at the empty space. Torri suddenly dropped to her knees. Wailing like a wounded animal, she caressed her stomach.

Nicholas rushed over to Torri and knelt down beside her. "It's not what you think, sweetheart. Isaiah is alive." He went on to explain to her the same story he'd told Asia.

Feeling everything that Torri obviously felt, Asia looked helplessly on. Asia's fainting spell had kept her from calling Torri back after Isaiah had stopped breathing. How she wished she'd been able to prepare her for the decline in Isaiah's condition. The look on Torri's face was the same one Asia had on hers when she'd also feared the absolute worst. The nightmare that she thought might be coming to an end had started up all over again. Isaiah's breathing on his own had brought about the renewal of hope; now her optimism had been all but dashed away.

As if the situation with Isaiah wasn't complicated enough, her personal feelings for Nicholas, a married man, had come back at her in full force. Her love for him was stronger than ever before. The soul-deep feelings weren't the crux of the problem. The unrelenting desire to act upon them was her real dilemma. She hadn't been able to get his passionate kiss out of her mind. Her mouth had hungered for the touch of his since that magical moment. And now her body constantly ached for fulfillment from the only man who'd ever made her feel complete.

Turning off her torrid thoughts and her forbidden desires, Asia went over to Torri, who was still on her knees. Nicholas's every attempt to lift Torri from the floor had been thwarted by the girl, whose grief was becoming as unmanageable as Asia's had been earlier.

Tears flooding her face, Torri reached out for Asia. "Mommy-Asia, please hold me. I can barely breath. Mommy, I need you to take care of me and the baby until Isaiah can do it."

As her eyes filled with tears, Asia's breath caught at the name Torri had called her by. It sounded so beautiful to her ears. At the moment, she felt as if Torri were her very own daughter. Because she loved her son so deeply, Asia couldn't think of Torri in any other way. Asia truly loved Torri for who she was and not just because Isaiah loved her.

What a wonderful family this was going to be once Isaiah recovered. Torri had unwittingly restored Asia's belief that everything was going to turn out right. Nicholas might never be her husband, but he was not going to be denied the opportunity to be a part of Isaiah's family. That she was certain of. If nothing else, she and Nicholas were the natural grandparents of Torri and Isaiah's baby. No one could take that warm, loving title away, not even Miranda.

"Come to Mommy-Asia, darling," Asia whispered softly. Torri fell into Asia's arms, sobbing brokenly. Feeling the trembling of the youthful body, which was beginning to fill up with Isaiah's child, Asia rubbed her hands up and down Torri's arms in a soothing manner.

Nicholas decided to make another attempt to get Torri off the floor. This time she willingly complied, allowing Nicholas to lead her over to the extra bed, where he had her lie down so she could put her feet up. After folding two bed pillows in half, Nicholas lifted Torri's feet and placed them on the makeshift cushions. Torri thanked Nicholas and then closed her eyes.

Nicholas's loving demeanor toward Torri allowed Asia to see how caring he probably would've been toward her during her pregnancy. She couldn't help remembering what an awful time that had been for her, especially after her parents had turned their backs on her needs. There was no loving mother to comfort her as she'd just done with Torri. On many lonely nights, she'd found herself crying her heart out, but no one was there to whisper calming words, no one to soothe the pains of her tired body and aching heart. Nicholas was always there, but only in her heart and in her numerous memories of the unconditional love he'd once showered upon her.

Just as her parents had done to her, abandoning her during the most crucial time of her life, she'd deserted Nicholas at the most important time in a man's life. Why was his love for her so crystal clear now, when it hadn't been when she was right in the midst of it? She didn't know the answer to her own question, but she had to wonder if he could ever again love her in the same unconditional way. Even the thought of such an occurrence with a married man was sinful.

If the opportunity was ever presented to have him love her that way again, she'd have no choice but to engage in hand-to-hand combat with the devil. But there was one thing she wasn't sure about: whom she'd root for as the victor.

Nicholas came over to where Asia was seated and pulled out a chair. He stretched out his hand to her. Smiling, she placed hers within his. "I hope Torri can fall asleep," he whispered. "She has emotionally exhausted herself. It was hard to keep myself from falling apart with her. Our emotions are not letting up on us for a second."

Asia squeezed his hand. "I know. I'm hoping Torri will be okay. She has a lot to contend with. In many ways, she's still just a baby herself."

"That's a certainty on both of your statements. I noticed the shock and then surprise in your eyes when she called you Mommy-Asia, but I also saw that it touched you very deeply. I'm assuming that she's never called you by that name before today. Am I right?"

"Very much on target with your assumption. It went deeper than you can ever imagine. I'm worried about her. I don't know if she's even told her parents that she's pregnant. She talks about them very little." That was just another similarity between her and Torri, Asia mused. Asia hadn't talked very much about her parents either, especially to those who didn't know them.

"What about your parents, Asia? How did they react when you told them that you were having a baby?"

Asia realized by mentioning Torri's parents that she'd unwittingly set an inescapable trap for herself. She could lie or she could tell him what had happened with her parents, even though it would probably hurt him to know the truth.

She removed her hand from within Nicholas's and then formed a steeple with her trembling fingers. After pondering his question for a couple of seconds, she looked him right in the eyes. "My parents weren't there for me when I was carrying Isaiah. They turned their backs on me." Though he didn't so much as flinch a muscle or bat an eyelid, she instinctively knew that the unpleasant information had wounded him. His eyes had a way of telling on him, also.

"I'm not going to offer my apologies since it won't change anything. Is it too painful for you to tell me why they took that attitude with their only daughter?"

"Would you believe religious convictions?"

"Extremely easy to believe. There are many so-called religious people who stand in judgment of others. Does that mean you were totally alone during your pregnancy?" He had the answer yet she hadn't yet opened her mouth. The transparent pain in her eyes had already spoken for her. "You don't have to answer that. I can see how difficult this is for you."

She smiled weakly. "You know, I've held so much inside for so long. I'm beginning to think it would do me a lot of good to let go of all the pain." She laughed. "I actually thought I had worked through the indescribable pain of my past, that I was free of the bondage, but I'm still a victim. I don't know if this even matters to you, but I'm going to say it anyway. Other than Isaiah, there hasn't ever been anyone I've trusted enough to share my deepest secrets with. But of course, there are many private confidences that I'd never think of sharing with my son. I know now that I can trust you with anything. I'm so sorry that it took me this long to realize that you've always had my best interests at heart. I trust you explicitly, Nicholas Reynolds."

He engulfed her in his warm gaze. "It does matter to me, Asia Morrell. I'm elated to know that I've somehow earned your complete trust. I'll never do anything to lose it."

Blowing out a ragged breath, she nodded. "I believe that. As for my parents, they constantly preached to me about premarital sex, but never once did my mother sit me down and explain all the things young women need to know about their bodies. "Keep your dress down" isn't tantamount to a course in sexual education, a subject that wasn't taught in the schools back in our day. I'm not saying that I didn't know I could get pregnant if I had sex, because I did. I just think it would've helped if my mother had better prepared me for what I might one day experience as a young woman. Every mother owes it to her daughter to arm her with the knowledge that pertains to her body and all acts of sexual intimacy. I've always been shy and somewhat withdrawn. So you can imagine how I must've felt when my gym teacher had to assure me that I wasn't hemorrhaging to death, that it was only my cycle. Mrs. Craig is the one who told me the things I needed to know about menstruation, but even she had limitations."

"It happened during gym class?" Nicholas couldn't help feeling embarrassed for her. It was obvious to him that she was still humiliated by it. He fought the urge to hold her in his arms.

"Yeah, in my senior year. I don't want you to think I'm blaming my mother. I'm not. I'm sure no one in her family sat her down and explained the birds and the bees. My father was actually the one who turned his back on me and my mother went along with it because whatever he said became her order of the day. You know what the irony of the situation is? My mother was carrying me before she married my father. History does have a way of repeating itself."

"How do you know that? In light of what you've been saying, I'm sure she's not the one who'd tell you something like that."

"I overheard family members talking about it. But I never uttered a word to her."

"Not even when she was being hypocritical with you?"

"Not even then. If she'd known I was aware of her situation, she would've been mortified. I couldn't do that to her. She was my mother and I always respected her as such, just as I did my father. I didn't always agree with my parents, but I never verbally disagreed with either of them. Now, some of the things that went through my mind, often, would've gotten me slapped into another ozone layer. My tongue was quick, sharp, but only under my breath."

Nicholas laughed but he put his hand over his mouth so as not to disturb Torri, who had finally managed to fall asleep. He then felt guilty for laughing at all. But Asia was laughing, too, and that somehow made him feel a little better. "It's nice to hear you laugh. You should do it more often. All the confounded things going on around us aren't giving us much to laugh about. Don't want you to think I'm taking your anguish lightly, Asia. I wouldn't do that."

"I know, Nicholas. The laughter eased some of the tension for me. It's okay. I just pray that we aren't going to end up crying for the rest of our days. I like to laugh."

Unable to help himself from showing her compassion, he took her hand again. "When you feel like crying, try to think of the joy and laughter that'll come once our grandchild is born. Think of the happy times that lie ahead and take the liberty of including Isaiah in every one of those joyous occasions. Promise?"

"Promise."

Torri called out to Asia, bringing their conversation to an end, but Asia was eager to continue with it at a later time. It was time for her to tell all. Nicholas should know what she'd endured. But she'd make it clear to him that none of her suffering had occurred through any fault on his part. He deserved at least that much reassurance from her.

Asia hurried across the room and sat on the side of the bed. She gently pushed Torri's hair back from her face. "What is it, sweetheart? Are you feeling any better?"

Torri struggled to sit up. Physically weakened by the drain on her emotions, she laid her head back down on the pillow. "I'm okay, but what about Isaiah? Have we heard anything?"

Asia kissed the tip of Torri's nose. "Not a word. But it will come when it's supposed to. We have to be patient. There are just some things that can't be rushed. As much as I want to know what's going on, I'm trying my best to pray my way through this latest crisis." Asia lowered her head and rested her cheek against Torri's for a brief moment.

Several white-coated hospital staff members came into the room before Nicholas could offer Torri his words of comfort. Asia rushed to her feet and Nicholas came over to the bed and stood by her side. As weak as she felt, Torri managed to raise herself up into a sitting position. The three linked hands and all eyes fell on the visitors as each of the medical professionals introduced themselves. One of the African-American women was the on-call physician and the other male and female were residents. The male was Asian.

Dr. Johanna Blake, the on-call physician, extended her hand to each of Isaiah's loved ones. "I wish we were meeting under more pleasant circumstances, but I do have good news. Isaiah is once again holding his own. Our young man is breathing of his own free will and it appears that he hasn't completely fallen back into a comatose state. However, it's still too early to make that call one way or the other. He has suffered a very mild myocardial infarction, but no serious damage to his heart has occurred. His condition is still critical but we're very optimistic at this point. The doctors assigned to Isaiah's case have been advised of this latest incident and they are sure to make rounds by early afternoon. Do you have any questions for me?"

"When can we see him?" Torri asked, obvious signs of relief on her face.

The doctor smiled. "I can see how anxious you are for that, young lady. Unfortunately it will be a while before that can happen. The nurses will let you know when it's okay. Are you the sister of our super-star basketball player?"

Torri smiled brightly. "A lot of people think that. It's often been said that he and I look like we could be brother and sister, but I'm actually his girlfriend."

"How lucky for you! I hear that he's a fine young man. Have heard nothing but wonderful things about him," the female resident remarked. "He's certainly the most popular of all our inpatients. I can assure you that he'll be well taken care of in this hospital."

"Isaiah is pretty lucky, too. Torri is a very special young woman," Asia quickly offered.

The disparaging expression on Torri's face led Asia to believe that she didn't care much for the comments made by the pretty, very young female resident, who looked to be around the same age as Isaiah and Torri. It seemed to Asia that Torri sensed some competition might be at work here. Asia didn't think the beautiful model had a thing to worry about in that area. Isaiah was truly in love with his Torri.

The threesome hugged and kissed the moment the three doctors took their leave. Relief was etched on each of their faces as Nicholas led them in prayer. Knowing that Isaiah had pulled through this latest crisis had given each of them a reason to smile, an incentive to keep their hopes alive. It was almost 3:00 A.M., but it looked as if everyone had perked up as they seated themselves at the table to discuss the good news they'd just received.

CHAPTER SEVEN

Still wet from his shower, with a large fluffy towel wrapped around his waist, Nicholas dashed into the bedroom and picked up the bedside extension before it had a chance to ring again. After mouthing a silent prayer on Isaiah's behalf, he greeted the early-afternoon caller.

"Brother Nicholas, this is your pastor. How are things?"

"Brother Jones, nice to hear from you. Things are going as well as we can expect under the circumstances. What's on your mind this afternoon?" Nicholas had a pretty good idea of what was on the pastor's mind, but he hoped he was wrong. Because of his deep respect and admiration for his friend of numerous years, he'd listen to what Pastor Jones had to say regardless of the subject matter. Nicholas no longer tried to fool himself into thinking the call had nothing to do with his and Miranda's failed relationship. It was almost a certainty for him.

"Well, Brother Nicholas, there's a lot of things on my mind. Do you have a few minutes to chat with your good friend and pastor?"

"I'm getting dressed to go back to the hospital to be with my family, but I first have to drop in at the office to handle a legal problem. But, Howard, I can always make time for my spiritual advisor." Nicholas sat on the side of the bed and covered himself with the comforter.

Howard cleared his throat. "Nicholas, this family you just spoke of is the reason for my call, which you're probably going to consider controversial after you hear what I have to say on the matter. Miranda is very upset about your misuse of the term *family* at the recent press conference held in regard to your son's physical condition. The church family has been in constant prayer for the young man even before we were aware of your relationship. I also should first apologize for missing the counseling session. I had an emergency situation come up."

"That's understandable, Howard. No need to apologize. As for the use or misuse of the word *family*, Miranda has no clue where I'm coming from. Isaiah is my family; the only living being that has my blood running through his veins. Asia is included in that circle because she is the mother of my child, which makes her Isaiah's family. I consider Isaiah's girlfriend as such because she is carrying my first grandchild, who also shares my bloodline. All of this, to me, symbolizes a family circle. I have also shared my views with Miranda. Are we clear on my definition of family, which may not necessarily coincide with others' definition of the same?"

"I get the message that you've just conveyed in no uncertain terms. I'm feeling you, brother. To move on further into this conversation, Miranda came in to see me first thing this morning. In her state of mind I had no choice but to hold a session with her in your absence. I'm sure I don't have to tell you how distraught she is over this divorce filing. Nicholas, I know you're a man of God, but are you fully cognizant of the scriptures dealing with divorce? Do you completely understand how God's instructions apply in this instance?"

"I am weary with the knowledge. I know exactly what the Scriptures say. I've only referenced Matthew 5:31–32 and Mark 10:2–12 what seems a thousand times."

"I get the picture. I guess I shouldn't inquire as to the identity of the alleged adulterer?"

"That would be best for all concerned if an adulterer actually exists. You introduced the issue of adultery, not me. I never once used that term."

"As longtime friends, you and I have always been able to talk about anything and everything, whether we agreed or disagreed. Should I decide to further inquire into the matter of adultery, or the reasons for this divorce, would my queries be answered?"

"Not by me. But please understand this. I know that God knows the truth, that He knows my heart. Judgment on the issue of divorce belongs solely to Him. I answer only to God. I also take full responsibility for all my life's decisions with a complete understanding of the consequences for my every action. And I do hope you'll remember what I've said should you decide to continue your probe into my private affairs based on your assumptions."

"I hear you, brother, loud and clear, but I'm not basing anything on assumptions. I only bring this up to you because Miranda has accused you of carrying on an adulterous affair with the mother of your child during this marriage. These are charges that'll have to be answered by you at some point in time."

"You're absolutely right about that. And the appointed time is the Day of Judgment. I've already established that God is the only person I'm accountable to. No disrespect intended, but you've already overstepped the realm of your role as my friend and spiritual advisor. I may look to you for guidance in matters of the spirit and often call on you for your interpretation of the Scriptures, but I don't answer to any mortal man. God, in due time, will reveal all the answers to any questions that I may have. I just have to make sure that I give my very best as I continue on in my walk with Him. I will never attain perfection. And God will never reveal everything to us in this lifetime. You know that as well as anyone."

"Nicholas, my instincts are telling me that this particular conversation is over."

"Go with your instincts, brother. That's all we really have to go by in this crazy world. Once things settle down for me, how about getting together for dinner?"

Howard laughed. "You always did drive a hard bargain. Dinner sounds good. I'll even pick up the tab since you bought the last time."

"I'll hold you to it."

"Nicholas, one more thing. Any suggestions on what I should tell Miranda when she comes to me for further counseling?"

"Give her all the counseling she requires. But I suggest you make it clear to her that you can only deal with her issues in this matter, not mine. I'll do the counseling with you but on an individual basis. If I later see the need for Miranda and me to go into a session with you, I won't hesitate to holler. If my estranged wife has any questions that I can answer, send her straight to me. I'm going to be as patient with this process as I can. But, Howard, it's only fair that I tell you I'm not going to stay in this marriage. It's over."

"It's your world, brother. Sounds to me like you got your mind made up. With both of you as members of my congregation, I have to remain neutral. Don't forget to call me when you have time for dinner."

"That's a given, Howard, on both points. Have a great week."

Nicholas's naked body felt a little chilled, though it had been completely air-dried. Seated on the side of the bed, he massaged his body thoroughly with Vaseline Intensive Care lotion. In looking at the clock radio, he saw that he had to get a move on. He'd been on the phone longer than he thought. Although he was eager to return to the hospital, he still had to see how he could help out with the sudden problem that had come up at his office.

He wasn't the only one in the firm with a crisis. One of the other senior partners had an emergency situation arise with his youngest daughter who lived in Denver, Colorado. Emergency surgery was indicated, but Nicholas hadn't been given any information beyond that. He didn't know how long John Cothran would be away from the office, but his absence would no doubt require Nicholas to cut his leave time short.

Thank God that Asia, Torri, and he had committed to sharing in the time spent at the hospital. As it stood right now, no one had yet been allowed into the CCU to see Isaiah. Since Asia hadn't called as promised, he had to assume that nothing had changed. In this instance, he needed to interpret it to mean that no news was good news.

Asia couldn't believe the nerve of this woman. Miranda stood in the center of Isaiah's room as if she had every right to be there. It was obvious to both Asia and Torri that she had come in looking for Nicholas, but it should've been just as evident to Miranda that he wasn't there as she thoroughly scoped out the room. Her eyes searched everywhere but under the bed.

"Miranda, Nicholas is probably still at home. If he's not there, he did tell us that he had to go into the office for a short while. He'll be coming back here when he's through handling his business affairs. Can I give him a message for you?"

"What I don't need is a messenger. What I want to know is, since when did my husband start reporting his every move to you?"

"Since the moment our son landed in this hospital, Miranda. And furthermore, you don't want to start something with me that you don't have a chance in hell of finishing. I don't engage in petty feline spitting and scratching. Whatever your beef is it's not with me. I suggest you talk to your husband about why he's so considerate in letting me know his whereabouts should there be a significant change in his son's condition. In borrowing a few of your words, what I need is to maintain every ounce of my strength to be here for my son. What I want is for you to leave this room and not come back here until your agenda has changed. If you're not here out of concern for Isaiah, and to lift him up in prayer, you shouldn't be here, period. Now, if you'll excuse us, Torri and I were resting before you burst in here like a ball of confusion."

"I'm on my way out of here, that you can be assured of. But now that I've listened to your little speech, I'm going to have my say. Nicholas Reynolds is still my husband and don't you dare to forget it. And wherever he is, I shall be there also. Our marriage is not going to end because you've suddenly waltzed back into his life to announce that he has a son with you. You have his son; I have his surname. I will fight you to the death for Nicholas Reynolds. I will never let go of what belongs to me. In the eyes of God and the law of this state, Nicholas and I are husband and wife. Miss Asia, you have a good rest because you're going to need every ounce of your strength to fight a battle that you don't have a chance in hell of winning. Thanks for allowing me to borrow a few of your words."

Asia and Torri watched in stunned disbelief as Miranda turned on her heels and whirled away. Before they could comment, Miranda sashayed back into the room. "As for you not indulging in feline fights, Asia, your razor-sharp claws came out the same exact moment you opened your mouth." With that said, she blew out of the room in a huff.

Torri laughed. "Well, I guess we've been soundly informed of her intentions. I'm glad Isaiah wasn't here in the center of all her negative energy." Torri bit down on her lower lip. "Mommy-Asia, what's she talking about, anyway? Why does she think you're after Mr. Nick?"

Asia's loving gaze swept Torri's face. "What she's talking is crazy. According to Nicholas, she only started showing interest in saving their marriage once she found out about me. The divorce settlement had already been drafted and just needed their signatures. Then she learned that Nicholas had a son. Not only did Nicholas have a son living in the same city as he did, the mother of the son was living there, too. Apparently Nicholas had told her, when they first met, that I was the only one he'd ever loved. So, that's what she's all tied up in knots over."

"Ah, the picture is much clearer now. Still, I think she's going about things the wrong way. If she wants her husband back, she's not going to get him acting like that, especially at a time like this. He needs her full support and none of her ridiculous attitude."

Asia laughed softly. "Hey, you're sure sounding mighty grown-up all of a sudden, sweetie. Miranda should take a few notes from you. Eventually it'll all work itself out."

Torri curiously eyed Asia for a couple of seconds. "Maybe she sees what I see in Mr. Nick's eyes when he looks at you."

Asia looked surprised. "And what is it that you think you see, young lady?"

"Love! Crystal-clear love. The man still adores you."

"Now how would you know that?"

"Because I know what the appearance of love looks like in someone's eyes. I see the love I have for Isaiah in my eyes every single time I look into the mirror. Love wears a distinctive expression. Do you ever think about the possibility of you and Mr. Nick getting back together?"

Asia laughed. "Now that's what I call a loaded question. Normally this is something I'd only discuss with my mother, who's no longer living, or my best friend and colleague, Lenora, whom you've been in the company of on several occasions. But Esquire Antoine, the world traveler, is out of the country on a monthlong tour of Africa, which includes a safari. She probably doesn't even know what's going on back here. I would've heard from her by now if she'd somehow heard about Isaiah's accident. You know she loves Isaiah, like crazy."

"I already know most of what you've just told me, but you didn't answer my question."

Asia's eyes softened. "Torri, I love you like a daughter. Because you're the only confidante I have right now besides God, I'm going to answer your question. But you'd better not breathe a word of it to Nicholas or Isaiah, ever."

Torri laughed at Asia's menacing fistfight-like gesture. "I'm feeling you, Miss Asia."

"I haven't thought so much about us getting back together as I have thought of what it would feel like to be back in his arms again, if only for one night. And I know my torrid thoughts of him are sinful and dead wrong. However, I'd never go after Nicholas to try and win him back, at least not while he's still married. If he and Miranda can work out their marriage difficulties, I can most definitely be happy for him, especially if that's what he really wants. Yes, I'm still in love with Nicholas, have never stopped being in love with Nicholas. But he is off-limits to me in any romantic sort of way until his future is decided. And even if his divorce does go through, I'm not sure we can ever get back what we once had, not sure if he'd even want me back. But, sinful or not, I can still fantasize about him. Just as I've done so often over the past twenty-two years."

Torri giggled. "I've heard that the second time around in a relationship is always better. But I understand what you're saying about not making a move on him while he's still married. I imagine Isaiah must've thought about the possibility of such a union between you and his dad after he left Mr. Nick that night. To have his mom and dad back together would make him so happy. I'm sure of it. I'm willing to bet that, after he spent time with his dad, he'd no longer see him in a bad light. If he saw only half of the caring ways that I've already seen in Mr. Nick, I'm sure he could've quickly assessed how wonderful of a man his father is. Isaiah can easily determine a good spirit from a bad one. He does that on a daily basis in the type of evil, fast-paced world he lives in. I can't wait until he can talk to me and tell me all of his thoughts and feelings. I miss the sound of Isaiah's sweet voice." Torri's voiced cracked and her lower lip began to tremble. "I miss my boo something awful. The baby misses him, too."

Asia brought Torri into her comforting arms, in the same tender way she'd done so many times before with her son. *Isaiah has to be all right,* Asia mused. *So many people need him.*

Seated behind his desk, Nicholas observed the perplexed expression on the beautiful coffee-brown face of his female colleague, Taylor Whitfield. Young and impeccably dressed, Taylor stood in the doorway of Nicholas's private office. "What's on your mind, Taylor? You don't look too happy. Come on in and have a sit-down so I can try to help you solve your dilemma. Would you like Lynda to get you something to drink?"

Taylor, the youngest and newest attorney working in Nicholas's firm, sat down on the leather sofa. "Thanks, but I'm cool, Nick. I've already had two cups of coffee too many. I'm glad you were able to come into the office and talk with me. Knowing you'd taken an emergency leave, I doubly appreciate you being here. I'm just sorry I had to bother you at a time like this. How's your son?"

Nicholas nodded. "On my last inquiry, he was still holding his own. Thanks for caring enough to ask."

"Of course. I wouldn't think of not asking. I'm glad he's hanging in there. We've all been praying for him around here. How are you holding up under all of these incredible and continuously unfolding events? To learn that you have a son, no less a very famous one, must've brought you to your knees. Then you hear that he's been in a horrible accident, all of the incidents occurring within just a few hours of each other."

"Those are true enough statements. And I haven't been able to get up off my knees yet. That's the humble position I plan to stay in until he's out of the woods. Even then, I'll still be on my knees in my heart and mind as I endlessly sing praises of thanksgiving to my Father God. But I'm holding up as well as to be expected under all the pressure. Now that we've gotten that out of the way, let's get on with the business of practicing law."

Taylor held up the manila file folder she'd carried into the office with her. "Nick, this case shouldn't be handled by a rookie like me. I think John accidentally assigned this to my caseload. In no way am I prepared to take on a case of this magnitude. This one needs a veteran legal eagle, an extremely sharp mind like yours. I tried to pass it off to one of the other brainy attorneys, but everyone already has more than enough to handle. This one is a high profiler. That's why I was compelled to call and ask you to come in."

Nicholas stroked his chin thoughtfully. "Tell me what you got."

"Drug possession; illegal gambling, secret back-room variety; and solicitation of a prostitute rounds the charges out."

"What's so difficult about this case that you don't think you can handle? A gifted mind like yours can plea-bargain these types of offenses down to practically nothing."

"It's not the *what* that scares me, Nick. It's *who* the perpetrator is. In this instance, it's NBA superstar center Price Sheldon. And the press already has gotten wind of his arrest. The phones have been ringing off the hook."

Nicholas shrugged. "I've definitely heard the name but I don't even know who he plays for. I've also heard my son's name mentioned many times, but I've not seen a single game of basketball in I can't tell you how long. That should give you some indication as to what my life has been like. What pro team does the young man play for?"

"The California Wildcats, the same team Isaiah's on."

Nicholas sat straight up in his chair. As he thought about all the newspaper articles and magazine stories he'd managed to track down on Isaiah, he couldn't understand how he'd missed at least seeing the name of the center for the Wildcats. It was getting harder and harder for him to believe that he lived in Los Angeles, where professional basketball was all the rage, and to be so out of touch with names and faces of the players on the various California teams.

What had Nicholas even more concerned was the fact that Sheldon was one of Isaiah's teammates. He couldn't help wondering if his son was being considered by law enforcement as what was known as guilt by association. There was no doubt that Isaiah knew Sheldon, but it didn't necessarily mean he knew that Sheldon was involved in illegal gambling and drugs. From all indications, that wasn't the kind of world Isaiah lived and played in. Nicholas reached for the file and then relaxed back in his chair as he perused the details.

A few minutes later Nicholas looked up at Taylor. "Now I see what you mean. You told me about the drug possession, but you failed to mention him being charged with intent to distribute and sell rock cocaine. This is the most serious of all the charges, not to mention the mandatory sentence it carries if a conviction is won."

"I'm sorry, Nick, for excluding vital information. I guess I was a little hyped up about the case when I began rattling off at the mouth. I'm sure you read that he's been released on his own recognizance. That's a good indication that he doesn't have an arrest record here or in any other state, but we both know how that information has a way of not getting to us until after the arraignment."

"You're right, Taylor, but it's up to us to find out for sure before he's arraigned in court next week. Have you already initiated a nationwide search? The only thing I read over in the file was the charges."

"It's in the works, Nick. I've also met with Sheldon. He's good-looking and charismatic, but he can barely put a full sentence together. The brother splits verbs like you wouldn't believe. I found myself wincing every time he opened his mouth. If that wasn't enough, with all the trouble he's in, he had the nerve to try and come on to me. You know I had to put the brother in check, quickly and in no uncertain terms."

Nicholas smiled knowingly. "I can only imagine, but I know you handled your business. Don't ever take anything off these knuckle-heads, high profilers or otherwise, innocent or guilty." Nicholas raised an eyebrow. "I trust that his English skills, or lack thereof, aren't the reason you don't want this case." Nicholas laughed to show Taylor he was only kidding, but only after he saw the look on her face. It looked to him as if his question had offended her.

Taylor laughed, too, relieved that he was only joking. "I'll admit that it's embarrassing at times to be in the courtroom with some of these people, who never paid any attention to their teachers or just didn't bother to go to school at all. But I do my job no matter what the client is or isn't. Was I right to bring this one to you?"

"You'll be tackling cases like this with confidence in no time at all. However, you will need a seasoned coach for this ball game. But you'll act as the team captain, the ball handler, and the top scorer. I'll give you the various plays from the sidelines, but you'll articulate them to the judge, run the floor with the ball, and score all the points. I'll pass on my expertise to you, but your capable hands have to be ready at all times to receive the ball and do your best to slam-dunk it before the defensive opponents can stop you or cost your team a turnover. We must always try to keep the ball out of the hands of the defenders. More importantly, we have to keep their scoring to a minimum. Think you can handle it, young lady?"

"Sounds like I just received excellent instructions on how to play the game of basketball. Good thing I know something about the sport. But I'm always up for a challenge. Thank you so much for this golden opportunity, not to mention the fact that I'll be working side by side with the very best coach in the business of law. This is a dream come true."

Nicholas grinned. "Had the client been a football player, you would've heard instructions on how to play his game. I like to keep my analogies simple." He looked perplexed. "I don't know what's wrong with some of these young, wealthy professional athletes, especially the brothers. They don't get it. The world is their oyster, yet they're still out there in the darkness of the deep searching for unobtainable pearls."

"It's only because they don't know who they are yet and what their actual worth is to society and to their people. A lot of this criminal drug activity is born out of greed. I'm in no way assuming that our client is guilty of the charges, but there are so many of his peers who have already been convicted of the same or similar criminal activities. Can I ask you something, Nick?" He nodded. "What makes you so different?"

"Different from who or what?"

"Most lawyers wouldn't think of working behind the scenes on such a high-profile case. Some of the ones that I know would be climbing all over each other to land this type of case. These kinds of clients are what put lawyers on the high road to notoriety and financial success, but you've practically handed me this one on a silver platter."

"This is also the sort of case that could also have lawyers wanting to dig a hole and bury themselves in it if they fail to win. There are two sides to everything, you know. One side has to lose in order for the other side to win—and vice versa. For instance, take a negative or a positive; one can't exist without the other. I try all the time to get people to understand that. Make sense to you?"

"Indeed. But you still haven't told me why you choose to accept only the assist on this one when you have a clear path to the basket to score the points."

Nicholas laughed heartily. "I see that you do know a little about the game. Let me just say this. I don't want the publicity, nor do I need the press in my face at every turn. I've got enough of that going on with Isaiah's situation. And I don't need the money. But I also have another concern, a major one. Sheldon is my son's teammate. Some might consider that a conflict of interest. For my firm to even be involved in this case could be considered as such by those on the opposite side. Now, for the most important reasons of all: First, my son needs me. Secondly, it's time for you to sink your teeth into a big one. I have every confidence that you'll give it all you've got. Are we square on my reasoning?"

"All I can say is thank you. When do I start learning the finer points of the game of basketball?"

"That will all come soon enough. I'd first like you to set up a meeting between the two of us and your client. I can better advise you after I hear what he has to say for himself. I'm sure he knows by now that I'm Isaiah's father. In light of that, he may not want me in on the case. That will have to be determined by you after you give him a call and advise him of the strategy you plan on using. See what he has to say about your decision to have me confer with you on the matter—" The door burst open before Nicholas had a chance to wrap things up.

Nicholas frowned at seeing Miranda standing at his door. He guessed that it would do no good to tell her to wait until he finished up with Taylor. He also wanted to avoid a nasty scene in his place of business. Nicholas could only hope that Miranda hadn't already offended Lynda or any of his other staff members. But he had his doubts about that. Either Lynda wasn't at her desk, or Miranda had chosen to ignore what Lynda may have told her. No one got past Lynda with ease.

Nicholas looked back at Taylor. "Please excuse us, Taylor. Miranda looks like she has something important on her mind. I won't leave the office without seeing you. Use this time to try and get hold of your client. Thanks for bringing me your concerns."

"Okay, Nick. Nice to see you, Mrs. Reynolds," Taylor said, making a mad dash for the door. The scowl on Miranda's face was enough to have everybody running for cover.

"I guess it's a bit late for me to invite you in." Nicholas motioned for Miranda to take a seat. "Before you tell me what's on your mind, I'd like to lay down some ground rules. This is a highly respectable place of business, Miranda, and I happen to share the space with other professionals. I'm not going to let you put our marriage difficulties on display like one of those awful television episodes of *Divorce Court*. I'd never disrespect you, your office, or your employees, so I ask that you give me the same courtesy. Can we agree to that?"

She rolled her eyes at him. "Oh, but your stage was much bigger than this office space. You've only disrespected me in front of the entire world. I'm sure that press conference had a larger television audience than the one you've mentioned. Everyone in the United States is interested in what goes on with professional athletes. Most people know who your son is or have at least heard of him."

"True, but I can't imagine many of them knowing anything about who you are. Furthermore, your name was never mentioned during the press conference, because it doesn't have a thing to do with you or us. Nothing I've done has been with the intent to embarrass or hurt you, Miranda. I'm not trying to make your life miserable. Can you say the same?"

Nicholas wished that Miranda and he didn't have to be on bad terms. He didn't want bad blood between them, wasn't at all fond of how fighting with her made him feel. Being at odds with her wasn't a pleasant feeling. They'd been such good friends for a long time. He never dreamed that Miranda would ever feel so threatened by another woman. She'd been the type of person who exuded confidence and was always in control of herself, or so he'd thought.

"Look, I came here for one reason and one reason alone. You need to tell your girlfriend to watch her back. I'm also going to enlighten you to a few other important things. She'll never take you away from me. This marriage isn't going to be as easy for you to get out of as it was for you to get into. And I think the only way for us to have a fair shot at working things out is for me to move back into the house with you. I should never have moved out in the first place."

"That is not going to happen. This marriage is not going to continue. And I've heard enough from you for one day. The next time you decide to just pop in here, don't. Call and make an appointment. On second thought, I refuse to meet with you again in the absence of our attorneys. You're taking this madness too far. You may be able to delay the divorce; you'll never stop it. No judge in this country will force me to live under the same roof with you against my wishes. So you go ahead and delay it as long as you like. You won't benefit by doing so."

"We'll just have to see about that. Nicholas Reynolds, I have the power to ruin you, your career, and your woman's job as deputy D.A. Just a few calls to all of your enemies and the press to share some confidential info, and you'll be on your knees begging for mercy—"

Nicholas quickly jumped up from his chair. The room suddenly began to spin. It felt as if his blood pressure had gone through the roof. When the unexpected dizzy spell hit him again, he dropped back down in the chair. Beads of sweat popped out on his forehead, and his breathing was labored. Miranda saw how pale he was. She looked frightened as she ran to his side.

"Nick, are you okay? You suddenly look so ill. Can I get you something? Should I call 911?" When his eyes rolled to the back of his head, Miranda screamed bloody murder.

As Lynda Frasier streaked into the room, Miranda backed away. "What the devil is going on in here?" Concern for Nicholas's health brimmed in Lynda's eyes as she leaned over his chair and took his pulse. "Nick, you look horrible. What's happening? Your coloring is almost gray."

He held up his free hand. "I'm okay, just a dizzy spell of some sort. Can I please have you get me a glass of cold water?"

"I'll get it," Miranda offered.

Lynda frowned. "Your pulse rate is alarming. And what was that screaming all about?"

"More of Miranda's drama. She probably thought she caused me to have a heart attack when she was talking about how she should move back into the house with me. I still can't believe she even said it. I wish this wasn't happening. I don't know how much more of this I can take. My head is splitting. I'm not used to being this angry. If nothing else, it's exhausting."

"That might've caused your dizzy spell, Nick, but you still need to get your blood pressure checked. You're under a lot of stress from all this so-called drama. We don't want to see you in the hospital alongside Isaiah. Do you want me to make a doctor's appointment for you with your good buddy, Lloyd Walker?" Nicholas shook his head in the negative.

Taylor popped into the room carrying a crystal goblet of ice water. "This place is in an absolute uproar over the loud screaming coming out of here. What's up with Mrs. Reynolds? She handed me this glass of water to bring in here and then she practically blew out the front door."

Neither Nicholas nor Lynda offered a comment regarding Miranda's sudden appearance. Nor did they answer Taylor's question. Miranda running out like that during his dizzy episode was something else Nicholas would never have expected from her. He was grateful to have her gone since he had some recovering to do before he could deal with anything else.

Nicholas accepted the glass of water from Taylor, thanked her, and then gulped it right down. "Could you two ladies give me a minute to pull myself together? I'm still feeling a little shook-up. This has been one rough day."

Lynda affectionately squeezed his hand. "Okay, boss, we're out of here. Don't hesitate to buzz me on the intercom or yell for someone if you feel the least bit sick."

"Sure thing. Oh, Taylor, is it okay if I get back with you tomorrow regarding the Sheldon case? I'm not up to dealing with any more details today."

"Of course, Nick. You need to go home and take it easy. We'll check on you later."

"Thanks, ladies. I appreciate your concern. Once I'm a little calmer, I'll just slip out through the private entrance. Lynda, I'll be sure to make contact with you before I leave."

As soon as the two women cleared the doorway, Nicholas moved over to the sofa and stretched out on it. His head was still spinning like crazy. He had to admit to himself that this episode of dizziness had him scared. The fear of a stroke was weighing heavily on his mind. Nicholas didn't think it was such a bad idea for him to drop in and see Lloyd for a checkup. He hadn't had a complete physical in over a year, an unusual occurrence for him. Nicholas believed in staying on top of his health, but it was obvious he'd become negligent, allowing his busy schedule to interfere with his preventative medicine checkups. As Nicholas's thoughts turned to what had happened with Miranda, he shut them down. He didn't want to think about that while the throbbing pains still pounded inside his head. Nicholas tried to dodge anything with an unpleasant ring to it but he didn't see how he could continue to avoid his problems with Miranda.

Asia's fingers trembled as she dialed Nicholas's cell phone number. "We can see Isaiah as soon as you get here," she gushed the moment he answered. "He's coming around, but he's not yet fully conscious."

Nicholas's heart pumped frenetically inside his chest. "I'll be right there. But why don't you go on in and see him? I don't want to hold you back."

"He can only have one visit at this time. If Torri and I go in now, you'll have to wait until another visiting time is scheduled. We'll wait for you."

"Thank you, Asia. I'm on my way."

"Please drive carefully, Nicholas." Asia hung up the phone and turned to Torri. "He's on his way. It won't be long before we'll go in to see Isaiah."

"That was nice of you to consider waiting for him. If it were my child lying in an intensive care unit fighting for his life, I'm afraid I couldn't have waited. You're very thoughtful. I'm sure Mr. Nick is ecstatic about your decision."

Asia hugged Torri. "Isaiah has two parents in his life now. Besides, Nicholas would've done the very same thing for me."

Torri smiled. "You're probably right. I more than likely would've waited for my boo."

"Life is often unpredictable, hard as granite, and, at times, not very kind. But when it's within my power to try and make life easier for someone else, I go for it. It can be tough to do with some folks, but I try to show kindness to everyone I come across. You never know when you're entertaining angels. I'm certain that more than a few have crossed my path as guardians."

"You also know when you're entertaining devils, for sure! That was a crazy-talking demon up in here earlier." Asia laughed at Torri's comment and at the face she pulled. "I believe in guardian angels. One had to have been in that car with Isaiah, or outside it, slowing that fast-moving train down. If not, God isn't through with him yet. For whatever reason God spared Isaiah's life, I'm grateful for it. I just pray that God is going to bless Isaiah, the baby, and me with a future as a family, Mommy-Asia."

Asia brought Torri into her warm embrace. "Continue to pray, Torrianne Jefferson. That's all any of us can do. He hears our every utterance."

CHAPTER EIGHT

Nicholas hadn't skidded into the hospital room one moment too soon. Asia and Torri were on pins and needles when he first got there. While taking the long walk down the hallway, they held hands, something they'd become accustomed to. It actually brought each of them a touch of comfort: three people in the same boat, each needing the others to get through it all.

Asia squeezed Torri's hand when the younger woman moaned in despair. Not knowing what to expect had Torri terribly on edge. Seeing that Isaiah didn't look any worse than he did before he was wheeled away, Torri smiled, sighing with relief.

Asia and Nicholas also looked relieved.

Torri bent over and kissed her beautiful man on the mouth. "Hey, boo, when are you going to come back to us? We miss you out here. Promise not to scare us like that again."

I'm trying like hell, Isaiah's mind cried out. He had tried to speak so many times since he first began to come around, but he'd only managed to get a couple of words out. Mom, Dad. He could now hear everyone, but it sounded as if the voices were coming from out of a wind tunnel. That his dad was there with his mother had him dying to talk like he'd never talked before. He had so much to say to his parents and he couldn't wait to have a conversation with the woman he was crazy about. *Torri, I love you, baby,* he tried to say, but no sound came out. He could feel his frustration over the situation but he just couldn't voice it, no matter how hard he tried. *God,* Isaiah prayed inwardly, *please help me. I want to live. I need to apologize to my mother.*

"Isaiah, it's Dad. Torri was speaking for all of us, you know. We do miss you, son. Your mom and Torri need you out here with them. They're lonely without you. I know you're still fighting to come back to us. I saw that earlier, when you tried to speak. I also see your frustration. It's written all over your handsome face. Don't give up. I need you, too. We may've lost a lot of years, but we still have a chance to get our life going. I feel it in my soul. I love you, son. Hang in there, soon-to-be daddy! Torri's going to need you more than ever now that's she carrying your child. If you're anything like me, you'll want a boy. But more than that, you'll simply want your child to be healthy. I know that that's all I want for my son right now."

Hearing his dad's voice made Isaiah feel like crying. He was so glad his dad was there to look after his mother and Torri for him. Although he hadn't had much time with his dad, he'd gotten the feeling that Nicholas was a righteous man. Asia had admitted to keeping him out of his kid's life, unjustly so. That Torri was pregnant shocked Isaiah, but the news had him ecstatic.

Isaiah struggled hard to speak, to tell Torri how excited he was about the baby, and to tell her how much he wanted them to be a family; no child of his would be raised by only one parent. Torri's sweet name was right on the tip of his tongue. He could feel it, taste it, but he couldn't say it aloud. Having no voice scared him. If there were a way to recover it, he'd find it. If only he could get his parents' names out, as he'd done before, they'd at least know he still had a chance to recover. He had to pull through. Torri was carrying his baby and he loved them both.

"How's Mommy's boy-man?" Asia asked Isaiah. "You gave me a pretty good scare when you took a turn for the worse. Thanks for not letting go. If I thought you'd be better off with God, I'd give you permission to leave. But I don't feel that yours is a hopeless situation, my darling, quite the contrary. You've made me a grandma and Nicholas a grandpa, happy ones. Nicholas and I are having a ball with our new titles even if they do sound tired. Grandma and Grandpa can't wait to baby-sit and push a stroller around in the park on a sunny day."

Bending down closer to her son, Asia pushed Isaiah's hair back and kissed his forehead. "I need to ask your forgiveness for not talking to you about Nicholas sooner," she whispered. "He's a wonderful man, Isaiah. He will also be a great dad to you, just as you're going to be to your little one. If you have to be mad at someone or need someone to blame for your father's absence, I'm your girl. I promise to tell you everything about your dad and me but you'll have to come back home to us for me to do that. We'll be waiting for you. Please forgive me, son."

Mom, I do forgive you. I know you must've thought you had good reasons for keeping Dad a secret. I'm no longer mad at you, nor do I blame you. You're the best mom a kid could have. We did just fine, but I imagine we would've been a lot happier had Dad been around to help us out. I love you, Mom. And I am coming home, to all of you. Sorry I disrespected you.

"I'm sorry, but I have to bring your visit to end. Isaiah needs his rest. You can come back and see him tomorrow," the nurse said from the doorway.

"We can?" Torri asked.

"Yes, young lady, you can. In fact, Isaiah may be back in his old room by then. What do you think of that?"

"I think it's wonderful news," Torri screeched excitedly. "Did you guys hear that?"

Nicholas gently gripped Torri's hand. "I heard and I'm as excited as you are. Let's go, ladies, before we get thrown out of here on our ears. Isaiah needs his beauty sleep."

Torri and Asia laughed. So did Isaiah, within his heart.

Isaiah didn't want them to leave and he didn't want to be alone. If he somehow managed to start talking, there'd be no one there to hear him speak. He struggled fiercely in his attempt to ask them to stay, but all he could do was hear their footsteps as they moved away from the bed. Only seconds had passed when Isaiah felt too exhausted to keep on fighting. He then tried to move his legs; panic welled up in him when he couldn't do so. No one saw the look of utter horror on Isaiah's face; their backs were to him as they retreated.

It suddenly dawned on Isaiah that his lower body had been seriously injured.

Troy Dyson was standing outside the hospital room, the one Isaiah had been sent to the CCU from, when the threesome returned there.

Asia tenderly embraced the young, good-looking, well-dressed man. She then introduced Troy to Nicholas. Torri was still somewhat put out with Troy for telling Asia about her pregnancy. She greeted Troy, but her attitude toward him was a little cool and reserved. She didn't like that he'd given away her secret after she'd asked him to keep it in confidence. In her opinion, Troy was nothing more than a big egotistical blabbermouth. But he was also Isaiah's best friend, which she had to respect.

Troy shook hands with Nicholas. "It's nice to meet you. Isaiah talked to me about you after you guys had dinner. He didn't mention your last name, so I didn't know that his dad and Nicholas Reynolds, one of the most revered attorneys in this country, were one and the same."

"That we are," Nicholas remarked. "Being Isaiah's dad is the more important of the two."

Troy turned to Asia. "How is Isaiah, Ms. A? I wasn't allowed in to see for myself."

"He's coming along, Troy. No one but family is allowed into the CCU. According to the nurse, he might be back in this room tomorrow. Why don't we all go into the room and sit down?"

Nicholas took hold of Asia and Torri's hands. "Is anyone interested in getting something to eat? We can go down to the cafeteria for a quick bite."

Torri frowned. "No greasy cafeteria food for me and my baby. What about sitting down in a nice restaurant for a change? Since we can't see Isaiah again until tomorrow, we can get out of this hospital for a while. I think we can all use a break."

"That sounds nice," Asia said. "We need to make sure we can keep this room until Isaiah returns to it. Nicholas, is it okay if I make the inquiry? You're the one who got the extra bed."

"The census of patients was low when I obtained it. I'll take care of it for us, Asia You ladies go and do whatever you need to before we go out for a good meal. I know the perfect place."

Nicholas strolled up to the nurses' station. He was a little surprised when he turned around and saw Troy following right behind him. "Something on your mind, young man?"

Troy nodded. "Yeah, can we talk for a minute when you get through with your business here at the desk? There are some things I want to discuss, but not in front of Ms. Asia and Torri."

"I think I can manage that, Troy. I'll be right with you." Nicholas turned his attention to the nurse seated behind the desk. He then inquired of the room that Isaiah had occupied before his relapse. After learning that it was being held for Isaiah, since the staff expected him to return there the next day, Nicholas was glad that nothing had to change.

Nicholas moved down the corridor with Troy beside him. "Are you okay, son?"

"I'm fine, but my boy Price Sheldon seems to be in some kind of trouble. I heard that someone in your office is handling his case, but I don't know any of the details. Sir, can you tell me what he's been charged with?"

Nicholas directed Troy over to a visitor waiting area, where they both took a seat.

"I'm afraid I can't; attorney-client privilege. Besides, I'm not Sheldon's attorney of record, even though my firm has been hired to represent him. Sorry, but your pal is the only one who can tell you what the charges are. He's out on his own recognizance, you know. Perhaps you should be talking with him about this."

"I've been trying to get hold of him. He's not at home. No one seems to know where he is. Good thing the season is already over. I'm sure Price would've been suspended from the team if we were still playing. Our coach has no sympathy for anyone who runs afoul of the law, especially when it has anything to do with drugs. Upstairs management, now that's totally different. They want to win at all costs. We're going to struggle big time next season with Ike out, but we can't even make an attempt at a good season run if we lose Price, too. I don't think any punishment would come if only the front office had a say."

"So, I see that you do know something about the case. Are you saying that the powers-that-be would be willing to look the other way regarding Price's criminal case?"

"Mr. Reynolds, I know you didn't get to be a brilliant lawyer without knowing how all levels of the game are played. Price, just like any other superstar athlete, has major dollar signs on his head. He's one of the best centers in the NBA. The team needs him."

"You mentioned drugs a second ago. Are you involved in illegal drugs in any way, son?"

Troy was quick to shake his head in the negative. "Not even so much as a hit on a marijuana joint. I never touch any of that stuff and I didn't think Ike did either. That was your next question, wasn't it? If your son does drugs or not."

"No, that wasn't my next question. In fact, I didn't have a next one. I'm very much aware that Isaiah doesn't take or deal drugs. He told me that himself."

"But the newspapers and the sportscasters say differently."

Nicholas shrugged. "So they do. But that doesn't make it so. I believe my son's version. More than that, I believe in him. I'm glad to know that you're also drug-free. We'd better get back to the ladies before they think we got lost. Are you going to join us for dinner? My treat."

"Thanks for the offer, but I have to find Price. I'm sure he's going to need support. I was surprised at what I heard about Ike during the news conference. I've never known anyone to say or write anything bad about him. The reporters love the guy. That alone makes me wonder why they'd say all that negative stuff if there wasn't something to it."

"Where there's smoke, there must be fire. Is that what you're trying to say? If so, I'm surprised that you'd feel that way. As his best friend, you should know exactly what Isaiah's all about. Not only are you friends, you're teammates. A minute ago you answered a question that you'd assumed I'd ask. Your answer to that unasked question is synonymous with what you seem to be saying now. I'm curious. Do you believe the defaming stories that are out there?"

Looking embarrassed, Troy shuffled his feet. "He didn't appear to be on anything when he dropped by the house that night. Ike and me are boys. I'd never talk about him like that."

"I didn't ask you what you'd say about him, I asked what is it that you believe."

Troy stuffed his hands in the pockets of his pants. "I'm sorry if I gave you the wrong impression, Attorney Reynolds. I don't believe what's being said about Ike. None of it."

Nicholas didn't quite believe Troy. The young man's failure to make direct eye contact with him was only one of Nicholas's many reasons. Nicholas was a friend to many, but he only had a couple of guys that he could call best friends. If he did believe something bad about one of them, he'd never voice it to someone other than the friend in question. Troy may not have meant any harm by his comments, but to Nicholas they seemed to be of the back-stabber variety.

Asia wasn't at all surprised that Nicholas had chosen to bring her and Torri to the Italian eatery where he and Isaiah had eaten their first and last dinner together the same night of the accident. While there might be a significant delay in doing so, Nicholas felt confident that Isaiah and he would once again dine together at Tony's.

Nicholas introduced Tony to his female companions as the restaurant owner directed them to a booth that offered the most privacy. Nicholas saw that Tony was delighted to meet the mother of one of his favorite basketball players on his favorite team, Ike the Psyche. Although Tony hadn't mentioned anything about Nicholas being Isaiah's father, the two men had discussed it in depth not long after the press conference had taken place. Tony sat and chatted with them for a short time before summoning his waiter over to the table to take their orders. The waiter was told that the meal was on the house, compliments of Tony.

Most of the meal was eaten in silence. Nicholas saw that the women seemed tired and thought that maybe his idea hadn't been the best one under the circumstances. Torri looked like she could fall asleep right at the table, and Asia appeared to be having a hard time staying focused. He felt that it was time for him to get these two sleepy-looking beauties home where they could get into bed and relax. It had been decided earlier that no one was going to stay at the hospital overnight since they couldn't get in to see Isaiah until the next day. Torri had driven her car to the restaurant but Asia had driven hers home at Torri's prompting. Asia lived much farther away from the hospital than Torri, but the younger woman had insisted that she wouldn't mind driving Asia back home after dinner.

As they prepared to depart, Nicholas thought that it might be better for all concerned if he drove Asia home; Torri looked extremely tired. The thought of her falling asleep at the wheel was instrumental in his deciding to at least make the offer. However, the decision to accept or deny it wasn't up to him. Asia and Torri would have to make that call.

Nicholas pulled into the driveway of Asia's one-story home, constructed on a modest-sized property. The lovely home boasted beautiful landscaping featuring lawns manicured to perfection, trees, and colorful flower beds. Although it was dark, brightly lighted lanterns had been strategically placed up and down the driveway and around the sidewalk leading up to the house.

Nicholas turned to face Asia. "If it's okay with you, I'll walk you to the door."

Asia smiled at the fact that Nicholas was always the gentleman. She could make it to the door alone since it was only a few steps away, but it would be important to him to see that she made it inside safely. "Fine with me."

Nicholas cut the engine, got out of the car, and then walked around and opened the passenger door for Asia. "You have a lovely place here. Seems like a great neighborhood."

"Isaiah bought me this home. He even picked it out, but he also gave me the freedom to choose any house and in any city of my choosing. I realized how much our son really knew about me and my likes and dislikes when I stepped inside this house for the first time. Isaiah said every room in this house whispered my name to him as he was checking it out. He thought the house and I were a perfect fit. He was right. I fell in love with this place instantaneously."

"That's a wonderful story." Nicholas laughed. "I can see that Isaiah didn't want you too far away from him. His place is practically in walking distance of yours. Isaiah made his feelings for you very clear to me. Your son loves you dearly, Asia, and he appreciates all the sacrifices you've made on his behalf. He's also very proud of you and your accomplishments."

Asia stuck her key into the door lock. "I'm proud of him, too. I'm glad Torri agreed to your suggestion of driving me home. She was truly dog-tired. I'll call her when I get inside to make sure she got home okay. Thanks for the ride."

"You're welcome, Asia. Good night."

"Good night, Nicholas."

Just before Nicholas reached his car, Asia called out to him from the edge of the porch. He walked back to where she stood. "Are you having a problem getting inside?"

She shook her head. "If you're not too tired, I'd love to have someone to talk with over a cup of hot coffee or vanilla-flavored cappuccino. I promise not to keep you out too late."

Smiling broadly, he reactivated his burglar alarm. "I'm tired, but not so tired that I'd turn down an appealing offer from an attractive lady, such as my son's mother. Thanks for the offer. By the way, I prefer coffee over cappuccino."

Nicholas stepped inside the foyer after Asia deactivated her alarm system. Subtle track lighting allowed him to see the character of her living space. As a lover of antiques, Asia's timeless decor included solid wood furnishings and a variety of other traditional pieces. At her prompting, Nicholas followed Asia down the beautiful hardwood hallway and into the island-style kitchen. She motioned for him to take a seat at the bench-style breakfast nook built into one corner of the room.

Seated comfortably, smiling inwardly, Nicholas sat back and watched as Asia prepared the coffeemaker for brewing. As he looked around the room, he could see why Isaiah thought this house was perfect for his mother. It had a quiet allure, just like she did. The colors were soft and ultrafeminine, a lot like her. Despite the gentleness of the hues, a man could easily find comfort and relaxation in her space while reading the morning and evening papers. He couldn't count the number of times that he and Asia had sat at the table together in his dorm to study. He certainly wouldn't have minded being seated across from her during mealtimes. There was a time when he was so sure that they'd eventually take all their meals together, a lifetime ago.

Asia had to nudge Nicholas to get his attention. He looked embarrassed as he took the tray from her hands and set it on the table. Laughing at how distracted he seemed, she slid into the seat on the opposite side of the table. That left a lot of distance between them, close enough to hear each other but too far apart for rubbing elbows.

"Where was your mind, Nicholas?"

He nervously scratched a spot of skin over his eyebrow. "The truth?"

"Nothing less than."

"I was thinking of how comfortable a man would feel in your relaxing space. I also thought of all the countless times when we used to sit across from each other studying something or other. We didn't even have to talk. We were just happy to be in the same room. It was really nice for us back then."

"I can't argue with you on that. You've spoken nothing but the truth. I think of those times too, even more so since we're back in each other's lives. Torri had the nerve to ask me if I ever thought of us getting back together. I tried to skirt the issue, but she wasn't having it." Asia laughed as she recalled Torri's not-so-discreet interrogation of her.

"Care to share your answer to that question?"

"I guess it can't hurt. Of course I think about it, but you're married, and that makes you off-limits to me. That's what I told Torri. She already thinks the world of you. You really stole her heart in record time."

"Torri's a beautiful young woman. I'm very taken with her, too. It seems that Isaiah found a girl who's the mirror image of his lovely mother. I'm glad you've had an occasion to think of us, period. It's true that I'm married. And if Miranda could stop the divorce, she'd darn well do it. She even suggested that she should move back in with me. I'm glad you weren't there to witness my reaction."

"Bad or good?"

"Horrible. I actually experienced serious dizzy spells after the encounter. I couldn't believe she suggested it. Then she went on to tell me how she was going to ruin you and me with a few calls to the newspapers. I really believed I was having a stroke during that episode. But she was probably just rambling on. Miranda barks plenty but I don't think she knows how to bite."

"You gotta be kidding! Miranda has bitten into me on more than one occasion. Her teeth marks are still sunk deep into my flesh. She knows how to do more than bite all right. She has the grip of a pit bull or a nasty-tempered rottweiler. How are you feeling now, physically?"

"I'm fine. Nothing to worry about, but I'm going to see my doctor. I know the details of the first occasion with Miranda, but when did you have the second encounter with the new her?"

"It happened earlier today, when she came looking for you at the hospital. She was in one nasty mood. She had her say and I had mine. She left and came back with more to say. Then she finally flew off on the broom she must've parked outside the room."

Nicholas cracked up. "Don't fault her too much, Asia. She's going through some changes that I don't even think she understands. I have to believe that we'll work this all out eventually. She came to my office with the same foul attitude that you've described. Miranda's a good woman, though. I'm afraid I haven't had much patience with her lately. I probably need to work on that. I'd like to see us come out of this with our friendship intact. But the issues are serious."

"I try not to fault her at all. I know what it's like to be in love with a man who's no longer in your life. I think it's normal that Miranda would have second thoughts about giving you up. She's not doing anything that's so out of the ordinary, other than being confrontational with someone who has nothing to do with her marital problems. She has to know that I'm not to blame for her tribulations."

"She knows but she can't reason things out when her emotions are in control of her. That's enough about my problems for now. I'm sure you didn't invite me inside your home to discuss my ex-wife."

"So right you are. Would you like to see a few pictures taken of the different phases of Isaiah's life?"

"Nothing would make me happier. Before now I haven't had the chance to look at the ones you gave me already."

"Okay. I'll get a couple of the photo albums from the den and bring them in here. It won't take me long."

Nicholas was thrilled that Asia was willing to share with him pictures of their son taken throughout his life. He couldn't wait to see them, but he was worried about becoming too emotional. After all, he was going to visually review years and years that he'd missed out on, hundreds if not thousands of opportunities not afforded him, graduations from high school and college, twenty-one birthdays, and numerous other special occasions and events unattended by him, not to mention hours and hours of time that he hadn't been able to spend with his only son. Any way you looked at it, a majority of these events were all emotional ones.

The phone's ring and Asia coming back into the kitchen happened simultaneously. Her arms were laden with several thick-looking photo albums. She looked back and forth between the phone and Nicholas.

"Would you mind getting that for me, Nicholas? As you can see, no free hands at the moment."

Though surprised at her request, Nicholas reached behind him and retrieved the portable phone from the wall mount. "Hello." There was nothing but silence on the other end.

"I may have a wrong number, but I'm not sure of that. If this is the Morrell residence, I'm looking for Asia," the deep male voice remarked.

"You have the right number. Hold on a minute." Nicholas put his hand over the mouthpiece. "It's for you, Asia. Do you want to take it in another room?"

She shrugged. "No reason to do that." Asia set the albums down and accepted the phone from Nicholas. "Hello."

"Asia, it's Malachi Michaels. Am I catching you at a bad time?"

"Nice to hear from you, Dr. Michaels. How are you?"

"I'm doing fine. The question uppermost in my mind is how you're doing. I just heard about Isaiah. I've been out of the country at a medical convention. How are things?"

"They're looking up. Isaiah was in a deep coma, but now he's floating in and out of consciousness. He has also developed a mild heart problem. My son actually called out to me at one point. We talk to him all the time, but in your experience as a neurosurgeon, do you think he can really hear us?"

"I've talked to many patients who have told me they'd heard what was being said while comatose. Then there are others that don't recall hearing a thing while in the same state. It seems to be one of those case-by-case scenarios. Is there anything I can do for you personally?"

"Just keep my family in prayer, Malachi. We need every prayer that's available to us and then some. This is a tough ordeal to get through."

"I have been praying, constantly. Will do. By the way, was that a family member who answered the phone?"

"You could say that." Asia decided not to offer any more information than that. She had a feeling that Malachi was on a fishing expedition, sure that he'd heard or read the news regarding Isaiah's biological father, but she wasn't taking the bait. He was the jealous type, too, even without just cause. "Malachi, I do have to go. I don't want to be rude to my company by staying on the phone too long."

"How about lunch or dinner sometime this week? It's been a while since we've gotten together. I miss you."

"I'd love that, but finding the time for us to get together might be difficult. Why don't I call you when I see an opportunity for me to get away for a short break? Sorry I can't be more specific than that. My life is totally unpredictable right now."

"I understand completely. Whenever you call, I'll do whatever I can to make myself available to you, Asia. Have a wonderful evening. You and Isaiah will remain in my thoughts and prayers. Good night, Asia."

"Thanks for calling, Malachi. Talk to you soon." Asia hung up the phone, sat back down at the table, and pulled the albums toward her. The sudden blanket of darkness in Nicholas's eyes made her uncomfortable. "Are you okay?"

"I'm fine. What makes you think otherwise?"

"I don't know. Your eyes appear somewhat stormy. I'm sorry for being on the phone that long. Rudeness wasn't my intent."

"I didn't see it as rude. The doctor, a friend of yours?"

"A very old and dear one. Malachi and I go way back."

"Further back than we do?"

"Hardly. But if you're wondering if I'm romantically involved with the good doctor, you should just go ahead and ask me that question. Since you've never been one to beat around the bush, you don't have to start now."

"Are you?"

Asia laughed at his directness. "Why does it matter to you?"

"It doesn't. Just curious."

"Malachi and I have tried to be more than just friends, but we're not meant to be anything other than that. He's a wonderful man, but he hasn't yet learned how to conquer his bigger-than-life ego. I'm not a woman that likes to live in the shadows of a man's success or be so in awe of it that I may lose my own identity. That's the type of woman he seems to be looking for. I'm clearly not the kind of woman that fits into his specialty mold. Curiosity satisfied?"

"Quite. But answer me this. Since this doctor doesn't seem to do it for you, what type of man are you looking for?"

Asia frowned. "Who says I'm looking?"

"Isn't everyone looking for the right one?"

"Perhaps some, but not everyone is out there looking for a soul mate, Nicholas." *Besides, I don't think a person can have more than one soul mate. If such a thing does exist, you're the one and only that fits the mold.*

"Are you saying you don't want or need anyone special in your life?"

"I didn't say that at all. It seems to me that you're drawing your own inferences."

"Maybe so. Hand me one of those albums so that I can otherwise occupy my mind. Your love life isn't any of my business. The Asia I once knew would've told me just that, from jump."

"That Asia is all grown up now, but I think she has been telling you exactly that but in a rather restrained way. You just weren't catching the hints."

Nicholas grinned. "I see. You got me in check, justifiably so."

From the moment he laid eyes on Isaiah's first picture ever, taken less than twenty-four hours out of Asia's womb, according to the captions, Nicholas's breath caught. How he wished he could pick his baby boy up out of the picture and cuddle him. Isaiah was a beautiful baby, sweet looking, with quite a healthy appearance. Nicholas could only imagine what it might feel like to hold a baby in his arms, especially his own.

Asia guided Nicholas through the photos, explaining each one to him as he flipped through the pages. It looked to Nicholas as if Isaiah's first birthday party might've been the event of the year. Even real clowns and other costumed television and cartoon favorites appeared as a part of the festivities. Nicholas soon learned that basketball wasn't the only sport Isaiah played, as he looked at the various pictures of him wearing soccer, baseball, football, and track-and-field uniforms. Isaiah was quite the all-around athlete.

It seemed that Asia had provided their son with a well-rounded upbringing. The prom pictures reminded Nicholas of the first homecoming dance he and Asia had attended at Howard University. His mind took a brief spin back in time. He still remembered the stunning, delicately beaded number that Asia had worn to the dance. Fashioned in jersey knit, the white backless dress was sexy and downright provocative. Later, when it came time for him to separate it from her delicious body, he found that he wasn't ready for her to take it off. Before they'd gotten undressed, he had convinced her to parade around the room while modeling the dress for him. He remembered telling Asia that he never wanted to forget how beautiful she looked on that very special night. The memory of that night made him wish he could have that night all over again.

Isaiah playing the piano came as a shock to him. Nicholas had also taken piano lessons as a teenager, but it wasn't something he'd ever shared with Asia. Both he and his son as piano players amazed him in more ways than one: like father, like son.

Fighting back his tears while viewing his son's graduation ceremonies was especially hard for Nicholas. By the time he got to the pictures of Isaiah and Asia taken during NBA draft day, Nicholas could no longer hold his emotions at bay. He leaped out of his seat and quickly excused himself. Halfway down the hall, he realized he didn't know which room the guest bathroom was in, but he wasn't going to ask. He'd just open up the doors until he found it.

The third door Nicholas opened led into Asia's bedroom. As if he were rooted to the spot by some magnetic force, he drank in the simple elegance of the room. Decorated in only one color, various shades of soft white, the room had an ambience as gentle as a whisper, as beautiful as the woman who slept there. The mahogany wood furnishings were highly polished.

As he turned around to go the other way, he bumped right into Asia. His nose instantly caught the spine-tingling scent of her perfume as he kept her from falling down. Momentarily, he closed his eyes to savor the tantalizing smell. She was so close to him that he could almost feel her heartbeat; just the thought of them being only steps away from her canopied king-size bed had him backing out of the room in haste.

"Nicholas," she called out after him, "I assumed you were looking for a bathroom. Did you find one?" She laughed inwardly at his confused state.

He looked embarrassed. "I got completely turned around. Your house is much bigger than I initially thought. To answer your question, I didn't find what I was looking for."

"There are two bathrooms besides the one in the master bedroom. Since you're already right here in front of the master suite, you can use mine." She stepped aside for him to reenter her bedroom. "I'll wait for you in the kitchen. Think you can find your way back there?"

Smiling sheepishly, he nodded. "If I don't show up in the next few minutes please come looking for me. I have a tendency to lose my way when I'm in your presence."

"In that case, I'll keep an eye out for you. See you in a few minutes."

Asia cleaned off the table and then loaded the dirty cups and saucers into the dishwasher. She didn't turn the machine on since it wasn't full, but she turned over the magnetic sign that indicated whether the dishes inside were dirty or clean. Thinking of Isaiah caused her to put in a quick call to the hospital to check on him. She sat down on the bench seat and pulled her legs up under her while she waited for one of the nurses in the CCU to answer the telephone.

Nicholas entered the room just as Asia finished her call. He reclaimed his seat across from her, looking around for his coffee cup. "Did you throw the rest of the brew out?"

"There are two or three cups left, but I thought you were all through. As you can see, I cleaned the table off while you were gone. I'll get you a refill."

He stood up. "If you don't mind, I can get it."

"Help yourself, Nicholas. I think I'll have another cup, too."

"Coming right up."

"I just checked on Isaiah. He's resting comfortably. I hope I can do the same. Each night I find myself so anxious to see what the next day has in store for Isaiah. That makes it hard for me to get a good night's sleep whether I'm here or at the hospital. My body will be dead tired, but my mind just keeps on racing."

"Have you ever tried any aromatherapy products?"

"I can't say that I have. I've heard a lot about them, though. Do they really work?"

"Maybe you should find out for yourself. I replenished my stock a couple of weeks ago but I've never taken them out of the trunk. Would you like to try one or two of the products that I think will help you relax and get to sleep?"

"I'm willing to try anything at this point."

Nicholas's smile was devilish as he raised an eyebrow. "Don't say that unless you mean it. I have some surefire techniques that'll transport you right into dreamland."

"How well do I remember! As much as I'd like to have you work your magical massaging methods on me, I'd better settle for the aromatherapy treatment. We don't want to give Miranda any more ammunition to use on you in open court."

"What if Miranda weren't an issue? Would you let me work my magic on you then?"

Asia grinned. "She is an issue. A big one, so let's leave it at that."

"As you wish. I'll go get out of the trunk the next best thing to my wonderful techniques. Be right back."

CHAPTER NINE

Asia couldn't help wondering if Nicholas was okay. He had already come back inside from being at his car, but he'd excused himself again to go to the bathroom. Since he'd told her about the dizzy spells he'd experienced earlier, she was worried about his health. Her brow furrowed with concern as she tried to figure out what she should or shouldn't do.

Nicholas popped into the room before Asia could make up her mind about checking on him. Walking over to the sofa, he held out his hand to her.

Eyeing him with curiosity, she slipped her hand into his as she stood up. "I was getting worried about you, Nicholas. Are you feeling okay?"

"I'm fine. And you're going to be feeling even better than that in a few minutes."

Smiling, Nicholas led Asia down the hallway. When he stopped at her bedroom door and opened it, her heart began to hammer away inside her chest. Even though she thought she shouldn't do this, she followed him into her bedroom. The sheets and the comforter were already pulled down. All she had to do was climb right on in. As she turned to Nicholas for answers, he nudged her forward and on into the master bathroom. All of her questions were answered the moment she laid eyes on the drawn bath and the towels he'd laid out for her use. The scent of the candle he'd lit had a relaxing, gentle aroma. He'd even found her thickest terry cloth robe, which meant he'd taken the liberty of going through her closet. *How intimate is that?*

Her eyes closed as she inhaled deeply. "This is such a sweet gesture from you. I can actually smell the healing scents of the aromatherapy. It smells like eucalyptus and a touch of lavender. I can't wait to submerge myself in the swirling hot water."

"In that case, I'm going to leave the rest of the bathing process for you to tend to. Unless you want me to help you get into the tub." His eyes sparkled with devilment.

She arched an eyebrow. "Thanks, Nicholas, but I think I can manage that small feat."

He grinned. "I'll be waiting for you in your den. Mind if I turn on the television?"

"Of course not. I just hope I don't fall asleep in the tub. I'm that tired."

"If you're not out in a reasonable time frame, I'll come check on you."

"Nice try, Mr. Reynolds, but that won't be necessary. I'll just set the timer."

Nicholas laughed all the way into the family room. The look on Asia's face when she first saw his surprise for her was priceless. What a beautiful face she had: innocent, soft, and sweet. As the word *innocent* stuck out in his mind, he knew that the exchange between them was nothing more than that, nothing more than a mild flirtation. But others might see it differently, especially his estranged wife, not to mention his pastor. Miranda would serve him his own head on a silver platter if she somehow got wind of him running a bath for his ex-lover. For Asia's sake, he had to make darn sure that that never happened. The new Miranda would like nothing better than to continue her unjustified harassment of Asia.

Spotting the numerous videotapes Asia had stacked inside the glass case, he walked over to the entertainment center and chose a movie to look at while waiting for her. A closer look at her video collection revealed to him that these weren't just ordinary tapes, but recorded NBA games. His heart swelled to near bursting as he removed one of the tapes and put it into the VCR. He was going to watch his son play basketball for the first time ever. Just the thought of seeing Isaiah running up and down the hardwood court thrilled him to death.

Nicholas wasted no time in making himself comfortable in one of the reclining chairs. Eager to get on with watching the game, he quickly pushed the play button on the VCR remote. It looked as if Asia had started taping this particular game during the singing of the national anthem. His heart fluttered when the time came for the introduction of the team.

It was an away game, so Isaiah's team was the first to be introduced. As one of the starting five, Isaiah's was the second name called by the announcer. Nicholas fast-forwarded the tape to the beginning of the game. Then he thought of Isaiah's troubled teammate, Price Sheldon. Quickly, he rewound the tape to where Price's name was announced. He wanted to see what the guy looked like and how he carried himself before, during, and after the game. Price only got a few seconds of Nicholas's time since Isaiah was the star attraction for him.

Minutes later, Nicholas nearly came up out of his seat when Isaiah stole the ball from the contender and streaked down the floor like a bolt of lightning. Isaiah's spectacular slam-dunk score made Nicholas shout out loud as he joined the throng of fans in cheering his son on. Watching the game on video was the next best thing to being there, but Nicholas couldn't imagine anything more awesome than seeing Isaiah play in a live game. Time rapidly slipped away as Nicholas lost himself to the thrilling basketball game captured on video. So engrossed was he in watching his son play ball that he wouldn't even have heard a sonic boom.

While halftime festivities were being presented, Nicholas reclined the chair back another notch and closed his eyes to savor what he'd just witnessed. Isaiah *was* one heck of a basketball player and Nicholas now understood why his son was so cocky with confidence. He had certainly earned his superstar title. Isaiah was one of the best point guards that Nicholas had seen in a long while. If only he had known that Ike the Psyche was his son, he would never have missed a single game that Isaiah played in, as an amateur and as a professional.

Dressed in a beautiful designer robe, one that completely covered her anatomy, Asia entered the den. Her heart skipped a beat at the sight of Nicholas asleep in the chair. He looked as if he was at peace. The television screen was blank so she turned the set off with the remote. Nicholas didn't move a muscle as she moved about the room quietly. Her smile lit up her eyes when she read the label on the empty video case. Knowing that Nicholas had entertained himself by watching one of their son's basketball games brought her pleasure. After ejecting the tape from the VCR, she put it in the case and placed it back on the shelf.

Standing in the center of the room, Asia watched Nicholas intently for several minutes before deciding not to wake him. She gave a quick thought to covering him up with the colorful throw draped over the back of the sofa. Fear of disturbing him caused her to abandon the idea. The temperature of the house was relatively warm, which should keep him from catching a chill. Fighting the desire to kiss him good night gently on the lips, Asia turned off all lights but the one in the hallway. She then went back to her bedroom. Nicholas spending the entire night in her home was both intriguing and titillating. Her thoughts were downright iniquitous.

If only Nicholas Reynolds were a free man; he certainly wouldn't be sleeping in a chair.

The scent of freshly brewed coffee led Nicholas to the kitchen, where Asia was preparing breakfast. He came up behind her and blew a stream of even breath on the nape of her neck. As she turned to face him, he saw the pleasant smile on her lips.

"Good morning, Mr. Reynolds. Ready for a hot cup of coffee and a light breakfast?"

"The coffee smells great. What's cooking, Asia?"

"Eggs, turkey sausage links, and toast. Does that work for you?"

"Indeed it does. All I need now is the morning paper."

She pointed at the table where the folded *Los Angeles Times* lay. "Help yourself."

He walked over to the breakfast nook and seated himself on the bench seat. "Why didn't you wake me up last night and send my tired butt home?"

"You looked too peaceful."

"Maybe so. But if Miranda finds out I spent the night here, neither of us will ever have another moment of peace. As if she's not already screaming 'adulterer' at me. I can deal with her madness, but you shouldn't have to. Sorry for falling asleep but I have to blame it on the recliner. I admit to being very comfortable curled up in that chair."

"If you're so concerned with Miranda, perhaps you shouldn't have come into the house, period. We haven't done anything wrong, but I guess your wife's still not trying to hear that. But I must confess to thinking sinful thoughts. Seeing you asleep in my chair conjured up all sorts of wicked images. I should've covered you up but I didn't want to disturb you." Asia laughed at the expression of shock on his face. "Don't look so stunned. Just kidding with you. I never gave you or your sexy body a second thought after I turned out the lights and went to bed."

"Liar! You probably stayed awake all night thinking about what scrumptious things you'd do to my body and me if I were a single man." He howled at his own arrogant statement. "I remember how you loved Marvin Gaye's cut 'Sexy Woman Sure Do Love to Ball.' "

"I beg to differ. That was one of your favorite songs. My favorites were 'Let's Get It On' and 'Distant Lover.' All of them were already considered oldies to us."

"You're right. I recall how it used to drive your sweet behind wild— and it didn't matter where we were; you were going to dance to it no matter what. And we can't leave out War's 'Slippin' Into Darkness.' After you left, I completely wore out two copies of Aretha's 'Until You Come Back to Me.' The older the music, the more we loved it. Most people still love the oldies. I guess that's why I was so devastated when you just up and disappeared on me. I thought we had it all, that it would always be that way with us. We sure had a hell of a good time then."

Sadness flickered in her eyes. "Good times don't always conquer one's fears. Fearing that the guy might see their relationship as just a good time is often what causes deep concern for young women in the same situation I found myself in. I knew you cared about me, but I wasn't so sure you loved me deeply enough for any type of long-term commitment. Yet I knew you'd do right by me. If you were going to commit to me, I wanted you to do it because you loved me enough not to see marriage as a death sentence. I'm sorry I didn't recognize how much you really did love me. I'm sure had I known the depth of your feelings for me our outcome would've been totally different."

"Do you remember Donny and Robert's *Back Together Again*? I'm not sure when that album came out."

"Yeah, I remember, but why do you ask?"

"That's another song that I wore out while I was constantly wishing and hoping we'd someday get back together again. Now we are. In a different capacity than before, but nonetheless we're back together. Do you think we can become close friends again?"

"I don't have to think it, I know so; if that's something we both want. We just have to be careful not to ruffle the estranged Mrs. Reynolds's royal feathers any further. Hurting another woman is not something I would do knowingly or otherwise. If you two were living under the same roof, you wouldn't be sitting here at my breakfast nook."

"You sure about that?"

She chuckled. "If I weren't, you'd never know it."

He laughed heartily. "Now that I can believe. Where are those eggs?"

"Coming right up. You know I can't talk and cook at the same time. My hands have a way of expressing thoughts that I can't always articulate."

"Girl, you don't want me to go there. You have a great pair of hands! Do you know what song came to my mind the most when I thought of us, which was quite often?"

"I dare to say 'Then Came You' by Dionne Warwick and the Spinners."

"You go, girl! That's what I'm talking about! I didn't come alive until you came into my life. After our lives are more settled, we're going to have to get together one of these evenings and play some of those golden oldies we loved so well. My audio library has in it every song you and I ever listened to. Do we have a future date for an old-fashioned jam session? We can even cut a rug in my entertainment room."

"Depends on whether you go through with your divorce or not."

He frowned. "Why's that, Asia? The divorce is already final in my mind and it's almost as good as final on paper if Miranda would just go ahead and sign the original documents."

"Do you honestly think that we could listen to the kind of romantic music we used to love without it having any effect on us whatsoever? Just talking about them is already doing crazy things to me. Being alone with you is one thing, but being alone with you accompanied by all the soul-stirring music we once made love to is too dangerous to even think about."

"I'm hearing you, sweetheart."

"It wasn't one of our songs, but 'Still' by Lionel Richie and the Commodores has a way of putting me in a melancholy mood every time I hear it."

"How well do I know that one, Asia?" *It certainly speaks to how I still feel about you.*

She placed the food on the table and Nicholas went over to the counter to pour Asia and himself a cup of coffee. Once both were settled down, she offered the blessing.

As she was about to take her first bite, she looked up with a start. "In all our reminiscing, I forgot to call and check on Isaiah." She started to get up to retrieve the telephone.

Nicholas stayed her with a steady hand. "I've already called. No change other than him being back in his original room; that's better than good news. When the nurse told me that Torri was already there with him, I asked her to put me through to her. Torri says all three of the Morrell family members were just fine. She told me she was reading to Isaiah some of his old newspaper clippings. I think I've managed to convince her that he can hear us."

"You have done that. About his last name, does that bother you?"

"Of course it bothers me, but not to the point of it making me crazy. Our surnames are nothing but what were given to us by the slave masters. Isaiah has my blood running through his veins. That's what validates him as my son, not his last name. When I told him that Reynolds men don't quit, I was referring to our bloodline and our character. A name is just that, a name, which can be legally changed without any difficulty whatsoever."

"If Isaiah decided one day that he wanted to change his last name to Reynolds, how would you feel about that?"

"I'd certainly welcome his decision. But he'll never get any pressure from me regarding that. If he decides to change his last name, it'll be strictly up to him. I wouldn't try to influence him one way or the other. Isaiah Reynolds Reynolds sounds a little strange, though."

For the next few minutes Nicholas and Asia consumed their food in complete silence. Nicholas wasn't sure it had been the right thing to do in bringing up a lot of their old memories, but Asia was glad that he had. She'd never get tired of hearing Nicholas confessing his true feelings for her. Knowing that he'd loved her so deeply made all the things she'd gone through alone much easier to bear now. That Nicholas had loved her enough to want to marry her was the most wonderful part of it all, a miracle of miracles.

Nicholas cleared the table, poured each of them another cup of coffee, and carried them back to the table. "I'm going to get out of your hair in a few minutes, but first I want to discuss something with you. How well do you know Isaiah's teammates?"

"I'm more familiar with the starting five, and, of course, Troy. Why do you ask?"

"The Wildcats' center has gotten himself into some legal difficulties."

"Price Sheldon! What kind of legal troubles?"

"Possession of drugs with intent to distribute and sell."

"You've got to be joking!" Asia looked dumbfounded.

"You know me better than that, Asia. I wouldn't kid about something so serious. My firm is handling the case, specifically the newest and youngest lawyer, Taylor. She's a sharp cookie, but she didn't feel confident enough to take on such a high-profile case. I'm going to call the plays from the bench but she's going to run with the ball."

"I'm just so stunned by this. It's hard to believe. Have you already talked with Price?"

"Not yet, but I plan to. That is, if he doesn't oppose my involvement since I'm Isaiah's father. Taylor's supposed to talk with him about it and get back to me."

"He'd be a fool not to want you directly or indirectly involved. You're only the best defense attorney in the country. Thank goodness I work for a county other than L.A. I'd hate to have to prosecute that case. Isaiah would be so upset if he knew about this. Is Price in jail?"

"He's out on his own recognizance." He laughed. "I'm talking to a lawyer. I could've just said he's out on O.R. Troy wanted to talk to me about the case, but you know I couldn't do that. What do you think about Troy?"

"He's like a second son. I love him. A lot of people think he's where he is because Isaiah pulled strings to get him on his team. The two have been very close throughout their childhood. Troy comes off the bench as Isaiah's replacement. I get the feeling that playing behind

Isaiah frustrates him. He's every bit as good a basketball player as our son, but Isaiah seems to outshine him in other ways."

"Explain."

"Isaiah's very intelligent and charismatic and the media loves him. He's very personable, totally unpretentious, and he has a magnetic way of drawing people to him. Isaiah's love for kids and the time he donates to underprivileged youth certainly hasn't hurt his positive image. In short, Isaiah is a hard act to follow."

"You think Troy is jealous of him in some way?"

Asia shrugged. "Maybe a little, but that's only natural. There's no harm in being a little envious of a best friend and a teammate who seems to have it all. What are you getting at?"

"Just gathering information. Troy assured me that he isn't involved in drugs, but I didn't like the way he seemed to be unsure of what the media has been reporting on Isaiah."

"What do you mean by that, Nicholas?"

"I don't know. I got the impression he believed the negative news reports rather than in Isaiah's innocence. It kind of rubbed me the wrong way. But I have been edgy lately."

"That could be it. I can assure you that Troy's very loyal to our son regardless of any envy he may harbor. Will you keep me informed of Price's legal woes? If there's something I can do to help, please let me know."

"Sure thing." He snapped his fingers. "Mind if I borrow a couple of Isaiah's basketball game tapes? I promise to take good care of them."

"Help yourself."

Nicholas got to his feet and leaned over her. "Walk me to the door?"

"You bet."

As if deep fears, millions of tears, and twenty-two years hadn't come between them, Nicholas took her hand. It was as if nothing at all had changed. They had been extremely good friends and it seemed as though their friendship would continue in spite of everything they'd endured during the separation, in spite of Nicholas being married, in spite of spite itself. Nicholas waited while Asia gathered up a couple of the videotapes he'd asked to borrow before they moved on toward the foyer.

"Will I see you later, Nicholas?" Asia asked him as she opened the front door.

"You bet."

She laughed at the echo of her own words. "Still love to mock me, huh?"

"I can't think of anyone I love to mimic more than you." He kissed the tip of her nose. "See you at the hospital this evening, Grandma."

"Ugh! That name sounds so tired. I'll have to teach little Isaiah or baby Torri to call me Gamma, Grammy, or some other youthful name."

Nicholas cracked up. "And I just want to be called plain old Grandpa!"

Asia pressed her forehead into his. "Yeah, I like the sound of that. Grandpa it is!"

He kissed her lightly on the mouth. "Good-bye, Grammy. Hmm, now, I like that one."

The sound of Asia's phone ringing cut into their friendly farewell. Nicholas waved as she ran back into the house to answer the call. Nearly out of breath, Asia picked up the receiver, only to have the caller disconnect before she could get her greeting out. No sooner than she hung up the phone, the doorbell rang. Thinking that Nicholas may've forgotten something, she rushed back to the door and flung it open without checking to see who was there.

The beautiful smile on Asia's face quickly turned to a slight scowl.

"Sorry to see you looking so disappointed. I'm sure you thought it was Nicholas making a quick return since he just left here. Aren't you going to invite me in?"

"Why are you here, Miranda? I think we've already voiced what needed to be said. You and I aren't going to see eye-to-eye on any matter involving Nicholas."

"I just need a couple of minutes. I don't think you fully understand what Nicholas and I share. I sincerely want you to understand what's at stake here. Please, only a minute of your time. I need to talk."

Only out of sheer curiosity was Asia going to allow Miranda into her home. Asia stepped aside so that Miranda could enter the foyer. Asia then led the way into the family room, where Nicholas had slept last night. She realized she'd chosen the wrong room to entertain his wife in when she saw his tie on the coffee table. Asia tried to hide her embarrassment.

"You don't have to look like that. I know he spent the night here. You don't think I just got here, do you? I know what time he got here and I know what time he left." Miranda took an expensive-looking camera out of the large purse she carried. "This here baby has a time-date stamp on it. Nicholas won't be able to lie his way out of this one and neither will you."

Sorry that she'd let Miranda come in, Asia sat down. "It's not what you think, Miranda."

Miranda raised an eyebrow. "If it's not, then maybe you should tell me how it is. How is it that my husband spends the night in his baby's mama's home and I'm supposed to think it's not like that?"

"Because it's *not!* You know something? I really don't have to explain a thing to you. If you have a problem with Nicholas coming around here, you need to talk with your husband, not me. Nicholas and I share a child, and that's all, regardless of what you think or believe. We were good friends a long time ago and we're going to remain such. If you don't understand that, I'm sorry. He is my son's father and our child is in crisis."

"I'd say that you were more than just good friends. He's been in your bed in the past and he was in your bed last night. Pictures don't tell lies, girlfriend, and I have plenty of them to prove my point in court. You two have been flaunting your love affair all over the place. Taking your son's girlfriend with you to your rendezvous points as a cover isn't fooling anybody. You're either on some legal or illegal substance, or you think I am. I'm no fool. I know when a man and woman are having an adulterous affair."

Asia smiled wryly. "Miranda, are you and Nicholas presently living together?"

Miranda was caught off guard by the question but didn't make an outward showing. "We were talking of moving back in together before you came on the scene. Now he's not so sure anymore that he wants to do that. I wonder why. Maybe you can tell me."

"All I'm going to tell you is good-bye. I won't do this. You and Nicholas have to work this out between you."

"How can we when you're standing right in the middle of us? If you tell Nicholas that you don't want him, he'll accept that. He has a lot of pride. His sudden indecision about our future is because he thinks you and he might have another chance at a life together. If you're only friends, as you say, then you need to release your hold on him so we can get back what we've had for the past couple of years. I love Nicholas and he loves me. His mixed emotions all have to do with the turmoil over his son. Do you want to continue to play on his fragile emotions, Asia? Is that how you want to win him back, using your son's grave situation?"

"If what you've said is all true, I'd tell Nicholas to stay completely away from me. But I don't believe a single word of it. No matter what you may think, Nicholas and I aren't involved in an illicit affair. That's my last comment on this matter. I'll see you to the door now. And please don't show up on my doorstep again. I won't be so gracious as this the next time."

Miranda huffed and puffed. "Are you threatening me?"

"No, but your presence has been nothing less than threatening to me. Should you decide to show up here again, if need be, I'll file an immediate restraining order against you. That's not a threat, Miranda. Consider it a promise."

"Since we're making promises, let me make one. The time-date-stamped pictures I have of you and Nicholas aren't going to hurt me, or the divorce case. What you need to think about is if they might somehow hurt you and Nicholas, professionally or otherwise. Mr. Reynolds is the Johnny Cochran of the twenty-first century. Everyone is interested in what he's saying and doing. As you may already know, I'm not afraid to do whatever it takes to get Nicholas back where he belongs. Back in my life and in my bed."

"If he belonged there, have you taken the time to consider why he's been absent from both places for the last several months?"

"What you need to consider is that I won't hesitate to name you as codefendant in my divorce case, Miss Thang."

"In case you don't know, but I'm sure you do, since you seem to know everything there is to know about me, I'm a lawyer. A damn good one! So bring it on; make sure it's your best."

"Come on in, Taylor. What do you have for me?"

"The information I gathered on Price Sheldon. He has no problem with you being involved in the case. He actually sees it as a blessing." She handed over several pages of typed notes. "You can read the most recent discovery for yourself. The D.A.'s office sent the paperwork over this morning. I'm sure there's more to come. It doesn't look good for him. Apparently the Feds have been watching his every movement for a while."

Nicholas grunted. "Nothing we can't handle. Did you set up a meeting for us to talk to Price about the charges?"

"He can't meet with us until tomorrow evening."

Nicholas looked up from the papers he perused. "Say what? Who the hell does he think he is? He may be a superstar on the basketball courts, but his celebrity status won't mean a damn thing in the type of courts we do our thing in. Tell your client that he either shows up here first thing in the morning or he needs to get himself another lawyer."

Taylor was taken aback by Nicholas's tone and his remarks. It was rare for him to raise his voice, let alone resort to cursing. "Are you serious? That's a tough stand for us to take with him, don't you think, Nick?"

"That's the only kind you can take in cases like these. You're his lawyer, not a member of his fan club. You call the shots, not him. Make that clear to him up front and you won't have to worry about how to set him straight once you see he's trying to walk all over you."

Taylor nodded. "I see what you mean. Price is a big boy, at least a seven footer, but I can get my point across. I know how to make it plain to him in no uncertain terms if warranted."

"Good. Keep me informed. I only dropped into the office to pick up a couple of things. Call my cell and leave a message once you have the appointment set. Don't give that young man any room to wiggle out of his obligations to this case. If you have to, remind him whose butt is on the line. It sure isn't yours or mine. He may stand seven feet or better, but that won't help him behind bars if a group of his cellmates get together and decide to take his arrogance down a peg or two. If you can't get your point through to him, drop him like a bad habit. Let him find someone else to try and give a migraine to. There are plenty of lawyers out there who'd love to have a shot at defending this case. This firm is more interested in cooperative clients who want to help save themselves and are much less interested in those who think they're doing the firm a favor by letting us represent them. Many people think they're above the law—among them, superstar athletes."

"I hear you, boss. How are things going for Isaiah?"

"The same, but he's blessed. Things could be much worse than they are. Everyone here at the office has been so considerate of us and what we're going through. We do appreciate it. I'll show just how much when Isaiah's out of the woods."

"That's a nice thought but certainly not necessary. Everyone in this firm knows how much you appreciate what we do. Rather than just on special occasions, you show your appreciation for us every single day. I haven't been here that long, but you've already shown me the kind of great stuff you're made of. Plus, the others talk about your generosity all the time. How's Isaiah's mother holding up?"

Nicholas couldn't keep from smiling as he thought of Isaiah's mother. "Asia's a strong black woman. Still, she has her weaker moments. This isn't easy for her. Isaiah is and will always be her baby boy. Keep us all in prayer. This family needs to get through to God as many supplications as possible, even when we know that He has already predetermined the outcome."

"You guys are certainly in mine. I'll talk with you later, Nick."

"Have a good day, Taylor. Thanks for the nice comments. I like everything nice."

Taylor grinned. "You're welcome. You do the same regarding that good day, Nick."

"Taylor, please ask Lynda to come into my office on your way out."

"You got it, boss."

While waiting on Lynda, Nicholas unplugged the thirteen-inch television/VCR combination. Once he wrapped the cord, he stored it on the hooks in the back of the set.

"Hey, Nick, Taylor said you wanted to see me. What's up?"

"Come on in, Lynda, and have a seat. Just want to get an update on everything around here. Want to make sure I'm not putting too much of a burden on you."

"Oh, Nick, please don't go there. This has been some mild stuff around here compared to what we're used to dealing with. The office matters are completely under control. You're supposed to be taking a much-needed vacation, but every time I look up I see you popping your head in the door. Losing confidence in this old girl?"

"No way would that ever happen. I'm helping Taylor out with the Sheldon case. She doesn't think she's ready to take on a high-profiler such as this one. But I'm more out than in."

"Why couldn't one of the others take it on?"

"Too busy, from what they told her."

"Yeah, right! Who do you know in this firm that wouldn't jump at the chance to take on a high-profile case? After they think she's made herself look bad enough, then they'll consider themselves rescuing a damsel in distress. She's a woman and you have some guys working for you that think a woman's place is in the kitchen or lying flat on her back beneath them. Their chauvinistic attitudes are the real reason they're not helping her out. She has met with a lot of opposition from a few of them sexist lawyers already."

Nicholas laughed at Lynda's remarks, but he didn't think the situation was a laughing matter. "Write down the names on a notepad and leave it on my desk. I won't tolerate that type of behavior from anyone in my firm. I didn't know it was like that. But I'll get a handle on it."

"Of course you didn't. 'Cause you've never had a female attorney working here."

"You have a point. Once I know who's who, I'll make a few phone calls."

"Don't forget to mention that I'm the complaining culprit. I don't want them taking their anger out on Taylor. I can handle their arrogant behinds. I think she can, too, fearlessly so, but she's doing a bit of tiptoeing around them for now. She's still the new kid on the block."

"New kid or not, she's a member of this firm. And everyone that works for me will respect her regardless of their existing gender preferences."

"Oh, they all know what you expect from them. That's why they've been doing it behind your back."

"It's now out in front, and the unacceptable behavior has to come to a screeching halt."

"I know you'll make your demands known, Nick. I have every faith in you."

"Lynda, I need you to set up an appointment with Vann Orville. I have a few things I want to run by him regarding my son's situation."

"Okay, but what does consulting with a top private investigator have to do with Isaiah?"

"The drug issue. I need him to check out a couple of theories for me. My son is no drug user, abuser, or seller. Something smells to high heaven and I need the country's leading bloodhound to track down the origin of the funky odor."

"I see. But, Nick, are you sure there's no truth to Isaiah's involvement with drugs? You don't want to embarrass yourself without having all the facts. Since Isaiah can't provide you with the information, you're going to have a hard time proving or disproving things as they stand."

"Something Isaiah unwittingly said to me let me know that he's not involved with drugs or alcohol. He had no reason to make the comment he did if it weren't true. That still leaves the matter of the drugs found in his system, which may be in part or totally responsible for his paralysis. That's where the human bloodhound, Vann Orville, comes into the picture. If foul play is involved, Vann's extremely keen nose will pick up the scent. Call my cell as soon as you have a time for me and my man Vann to get together." He lifted up the television and set it on the corner of his desk while he gathered up his briefcase.

"Where you going with that television, Nick?"

"My son and I have a date to watch a basketball game together." Lynda looked nonplussed. "What?"

"Don't have time to explain right now, Lynda. I'll fill you in later."

Looking more puzzled than before, Lynda shook her head, looking after her boss as he cleared the doorway of the private entrance to his office. Fatherhood had him acting so strange.

Seated next to Isaiah's bed, Nicholas inserted the videotape into the VCR. In order for him to do the color commentating for the basketball game, he turned the volume down a bit. He thought that hearing the thrilling sounds of the game Isaiah loved so much just might be what his son needed to bring him completely out of the coma. He pressed the play button on the remote and relaxed back in his seat. Though he definitely thought it could get better than this for him and Isaiah, the reality of the situation was what he had to deal with for now.

"Okay, son, this is our first time sharing in a basketball game together. The Wildcats are playing the Denver Thunderbolts. You know all about the superstar they call Ike the Psyche. He's one heck of a point guard. 'The best in the business' is what he bragged to me. Now we'll get to find out if he's as good as he said he is.

"The Wildcat's center, Price Sheldon, has won the tip. Price has kicked the ball out to Ike." Nicholas jumped up. "Ike's streaking down the floor like he has a turbo boost attached to him. Slam dunk! Two points. Wildcats strike iron first." Nicholas sat back in his chair.

"Denver has the ball, but Ike is all over their point guard, Wesley Langston, like a cheap suit. Ike has cleanly stripped the ball right out of Wesley's hands. No harm, no foul, as Chick Hearn would say. Ike is leading his team in the fast break. He finds the center right under the basket and lobs it to him. Price scores and is fouled by the Denver center, Larry Brewkowski! Four to zip; Wildcats in the lead with a chance to go up by five if Price makes his free throw."

For over two solid hours, Nicholas commentated every aspect of the game for Isaiah in an extremely lively manner. Asia had edited the tape during or after the game to take out all the television commercials, which allowed him to go through the game without stopping. This was one of the best days in Nicholas's life and he hoped that it wouldn't be the last day he could enjoy watching a game with his son. His son might never play basketball again, but the recorded game tapes would furnish them with hours and hours of pleasurable viewing.

Nicholas had to take a minute to think of what it might mean for Isaiah if he couldn't ever play ball again. He knew what it would do to him if he couldn't practice law, but he was also cognizant of the fact that God didn't close one door without opening another.

Perhaps Isaiah could coach the game or land a place in management within the team's administrative structure. A player that was easy to coach often made a good coach himself.

The possibilities seemed endless as Nicholas reviewed them in his mind. Isaiah had stayed in college, had graduated at the top of his class, even though he'd constantly been enticed to join the NBA before he finished school, according to Asia. His entire life didn't have to end if his career on the floor happened to come to that. It would take everything Isaiah had in him to beat the odds, but there was no doubt in Nicholas's mind that his son could defeat them.

CHAPTER TEN

Nicholas and Vann Orville had just finished having a casual lunch at the L.A. Sports bar located right around the corner from Vann's private investigative agency, VO, Inc. Vann, a thirty-year veteran of the LAPD, was a tall, fifty-plus, physically fit African-American with a nice smile and keen brown eyes. As one of L.A.'s finest investigators, he'd opened his own private agency after his retirement four years ago. He was the best in his field, often contracted by various police agencies across the nation to come aboard to assist in hard-to-solve cases.

Nicholas stretched his arm across the back of the booth. "Keeping my son's stellar reputation intact is important to me, Vann. The media haven't declared outright war on him yet, but I expect it to come if some answers aren't forthcoming in explaining the drugs found in his system. Isaiah is not a drug user." Nicholas went on to explain why he felt that way.

Vann took a swig of his Diet Coke. "I'll do some preliminary snooping, Nick. If there's a scent to latch on to, you know I'll follow it right into hell if I have to. Where's there smoke, there's usually a spark of fire or two, yet you sound so sure that your boy is not involved in drugs. But have you asked yourself what you'll do with the information if you find out that he is? As a sworn officer of the courts, you'll have to uphold the law. If the train accident happened as a direct result of him being strung out on drugs, he could be in a heap of trouble. Then there's always the moral aspect for you to consider. In this instance, you've just met your son. You don't know a lot about him. At any rate, the parents are always the last to know when these youngsters get themselves into difficulties with the law. Are you prepared to deal with all the possibilities?"

Nicholas looked Vann dead in the eye. "You haven't mentioned anything that I haven't thought of. I can't explain to you how I know. I just know what I know. Isaiah wasn't on drugs when I had dinner with him several hours before the incident. I know he could've taken something after he left me, but I think not. The last place he visited that night is the first location to begin this investigation. Do you agree?"

"Wholeheartedly." Vann briefly looked at the information Nicholas had written down for him. "This Ladera address? Is that the best friend's residence?"

"That's where Troy resides. He also plays for the Wildcats. Those two have been the best of buddies for years. Isaiah called his mother and his girlfriend to inform them of his destination. He was supposed to go see his mother after he left his friend's place. He never made it."

Vann eyed Nicholas with curiosity. "Do you think his best friend is somehow involved in this accident or with drugs? If so, I'm just curious as to why you feel that way."

Nicholas shrugged. "I don't know either way. I'm just playing out a hunch. My curiosity was aroused about Troy before I learned that the center for the Wildcats has been brought up on drug charges, possession with intent to sell. My suspicions have more to do with Troy's willingness to believe the media story regarding Isaiah's drug use. That doesn't sound like something a best friend would even consider. If he were that close to Isaiah, wouldn't he know for sure? Why would he have cause to speculate?"

"Maybe he does know for sure, Nick, and it's the reason he believes the media reports."

"I don't think so. Also, there's something about Troy that doesn't sit well with me. Just can't put my finger on it. Isaiah's mother thinks I'm way off the mark, but we'll have to wait and see. I don't know how she's going to take what I'm doing, but I feel obligated to let her in on it. I'll tell her over our dinner date this evening. She's also an attorney, a prosecutor. I'm hiring you to dispel or confirm my suspicions, Vann. If I'm wrong about my theories, I'll be the first to admit it. You can send your expense reports to my office."

"This one is on the house. I've never forgotten how you came to my son's aid when he unknowingly got mixed up with that car theft ring. You were able to prove far beyond a shadow of a doubt that he was set up, that he had no knowledge of what was going on when he was paid to drive one of the stolen cars to the storage garage. I had the means to pay your legal fees, but you wouldn't accept one red cent from me. Good deeds have a way of coming back to you when you least expect them."

"I wasn't looking for something back when my firm represented Tommy, but I'm going to be gracious about your offer and accept it. If there's any expense that's too large for you to swallow whole, don't hesitate to holler at me. I know firsthand that private investigations don't come cheap. I also have the means to pay your fees."

"You got it, dear friend. We go way back, inside and outside of this legal business, Nick. That also counts for something with me. You've been a good friend to me over the years. I'll do my part in clearing up the fog for you. It'll be about a week before you get my first report. I can't say how long the entire case will take. But I like to solve things in a minimal amount of time."

"Thanks, Vann."

Vann suddenly looked uncomfortable as he studied Nicholas's profile. He fumbled with the Diet Coke can after he took another swallow. "Nicholas, I need to know something. Are you happy about being united with your boy?"

"Extremely happy! I thought it was apparent. But why do you ask?"

"'Cause I'm the investigator he hired to locate you."

Nicholas's eyebrows shot up a good inch as he looked at Vann in bewilderment. "So you knew all about my relationship to Isaiah before you took this meeting? Why didn't you tell me?"

"I'm doing that right now. Of course I had no idea who the boy's father would turn out to be when I first met with Isaiah. I had a hard decision to make when I learned it was you. I thought of giving him all his money back and telling him I couldn't get the job done. But this young man was so urgent about finding his father that I just couldn't ignore it. Knowing you as well as I do, I figured there had to be a darn good reason for you not being involved in your son's life. Now that I've laid the cards out on the table can you please tell me what that reason was?"

"I didn't know about him until the very day he walked into my office ready for battle. I know you may find that hard to believe, but that's how it happened. His mother wanted it that way because she didn't want to stifle my career goals. That was the one woman I would've married in a heartbeat, but I was waiting until I had more to offer her. We were still in college."

Vann looked relieved. "Knowing of the kind of man you are, I can believe you with ease. I wrestled with so many questions about you when I found out you were the man in question. You were an upstanding citizen; a successful, brilliant attorney; and an all-around great person; and I just couldn't imagine you running out on your kid. It didn't add up for me from what I knew about you. The kid was angry as hell. That was easy enough to discern. He told me he just wanted to meet the sperm donor and get the chance to tell him to go to hell. It was something he'd dreamed about since the day he was old enough to understand that the man who'd fathered him had simply abandoned him and his mother. He called me the day he came to your office, but I didn't hear back from him after that. Then I heard about the accident. I wanted to come to you, but I still didn't feel it was right for me to discuss with you anything that had to do with your son hiring me to locate you. So I just sat on my hands until now. Tell me. How did that meeting go?"

Nicholas had to take a minute to calm down his heart. It was beating way too fast. But that wasn't his only problem. The pain of Isaiah's words to Vann had shaken him. It hurt to know that Isaiah had considered him as nothing more than a sperm donor. He began to feel much better when he thought of how their meeting had ended rather than how it had begun.

"Badly at first, Vann. Like you said, he was angry. The built-up anger and frustration was apparent in every word he spoke. Then we got into talking about a few things and I later invited him to dinner. Though reluctant, he accepted the invitation. Before that evening was over, I was holding tightly in my arms the son I never knew I had. We were two adult men crying and moaning like blubbering idiots.

Several hours later I found myself crying and howling even harder than before. That's when I learned about Isaiah's accident. I had just met my son and then I was suddenly faced with the fact that for us tomorrow might never come. But tomorrow did come! Isaiah survived the accident. And when he gets out of that hospital, we hope to have a multitude of tomorrows ahead of us. I'm also going to be a grandfather! Can you even imagine that?" Nicholas beamed with pride from head to toe.

"God is good, isn't He, man? You and your son are blessed. I wish you nothing but the best and I hope this investigation turns out the way you're hoping. If your son is being falsely accused of using drugs, I'll do everything in my power to clear his good name. Man, it must be something else to find out that you have a son and that he's none other than the famous Ike the Psyche of the California Wildcats. I don't have to ask if you're proud. I can clearly see that you are. Good luck, man. I'll keep your family in my prayers."

"Vann, thanks for all that you've done and all that you're going to do. Knowing that you were the one that Isaiah hired to find me, I can now put this incident to rest. I didn't know who might have so much personal information on me and if they would decide to use it for monetary gain once they knew about the professional credentials of both father and son. I'm relieved to know that you're the man and I no longer need to have those concerns. God bless you."

Seated at the table in her kitchen, Asia poured a second glass of wine into a crystal goblet for her visitor. Lenora Antoine, her best friend and Isaiah's self-appointed godmother, had only been back in town for a short time. As soon as she'd heard about her godson, she'd immediately phoned Asia from Africa to make plans for them to get together soon after she landed back in California. Lenora had first seen the story on Isaiah on the front page of a newspaper.

Lenora wiped more tears from her caramel face, deeply tanned from her monthlong rendezvous with the African sun. Her hazel eyes carried a disturbing glint, so different from the spicy twinkle of laughter they normally carried. Her champagne-like personality had no fizz or bubbles left in it whatsoever.

Hearing the bad news about her godson and then seeing him lying so lifelessly in that hospital bed had affected her more than she wanted Asia to know. She could already see how fragile Asia looked and she didn't want to add any other burdens to her load. If Lenora weren't so concerned for her dear friend, she'd fall out in the middle of the floor and wail until her voice was hoarse, just like she'd done in her hotel room when she'd first read the story, the same as she'd wanted to do when she laid her eyes on the seriously injured Isaiah. Isaiah Reynolds Morrell had become her son, too, from the very first moment she'd laid eyes on him.

Lenora took a long sip of her wine. "How are you really holding up, Asia? You don't look as if you've been getting much sleep."

"I'm doing okay. I don't get much rest, but I don't expect that I will, at least not until Isaiah comes out of the coma. This has been an ordeal that I wouldn't wish on my worst enemy. I just talked to my boss this morning about taking a leave of absence. It's hard for me to concentrate on my work, especially on this murder-one case I'm involved in. Nicholas offered to help me out with this, but I didn't feel that I was the one to prosecute this case because of my own personal traumas. It's already been reassigned, thank God. I start my leave tomorrow."

"Who's this Nicholas person you just mentioned? Is he new to the D.A.'s office?"

"Nicholas Reynolds, as in Isaiah's biological father, and also as in the famous attorney."

"The nationally acclaimed defense attorney Nicholas Reynolds and the Nicholas Reynolds you fell in love with in college, Isaiah's father, are the same exact man?"

"One and the same."

Lenora's eyes widened. "I had no idea that the man you've been telling me about for the past couple of years is the same brilliant legal mind so many have come to revere. This is too darn amazing! But wait a minute. You told me that Isaiah's father didn't know about him."

"He didn't. Isaiah went to see him for the first time the same day of the accident. They had dinner together only hours before the tragedy occurred. I didn't know exactly where Nicholas was practicing law when I moved out here. His career has taken him all over the country. I'd read many articles about him, but not in recent times. If Isaiah hadn't insisted on me moving to California after he signed with the

Wildcats, I'd still be in Ohio. Isaiah actually hired a private investigator to find Nicholas. The retired cop knew exactly where to find him."

Lenora crossed her legs. "Girl, pour me another glass of wine. I want to hear every detail of this juicy story. I'm not leaving here until you have completely filled in all the blanks. In fact, I'm staying over the entire night. I've already had more wine than I dare to drive under the influence of. Police officers love to give tickets to drunken lawyers and judges."

Asia laughed from deep within. It felt good to her as it eased the knotted tension in her stomach and neck. She hadn't done a lot of laughing lately, except for when Nicholas was around. He always did have a way of bringing out the sillies in her. She and Isaiah had always found something to giggle about, too. Her son had the same type of entertaining personality that Nicholas possessed. Both men were effervescent beyond words, and the stories or outright exaggerations they sometimes had a tendency to tell were often downright comical.

"Tell me something, Asia. Is your Nicholas still married?"

"That's another amazing story. Although I heard a long time ago that Nicholas was getting married, he tells me the wedding never happened. He's only been married for two years but he's in the process of getting a divorce."

"Ooh, this story is getting better and better! I know the brother looks as fine as you said he did back then, because I've seen his picture numerous times in several different newspapers. Just had no idea that he was the same man you were in love with. The Nicholas Reynolds that I'm thinking about is actually too fine to fit any description. Do you think he still has a thing for you? Any chances of you two getting things back together? Would you get romantically involved with him again if he wanted to take up where you two left off?"

"Whoa! Slow down, Lenora, girl. You're getting way ahead of me and of yourself. You've rattled off a battery of questions without giving me the chance to answer the first one. Didn't you hear me say the man is still married?"

"But you also said he's getting divorced. Right?"

"Yeah, but the estranged Mrs. Reynolds has changed her mind about setting him free. And it seems like her change of heart only came after she learned about Isaiah and me."

"That's not too hard to figure out. She must feel threatened by you, that is, if you two have met. I would feel that way about my husband's ex-girlfriend, especially if she's as beautiful and intelligent as you are."

"Boy, have I met her! On more than one occasion, unpleasant ones, I'd have to say. Miranda had the nerve to pay me a surprise visit a couple of days ago. She also threatened to name me as codefendant in her divorce after she found out that Nicholas spent the night here."

Lenora nearly choked on the wine she had in her mouth. It took a couple of seconds of spitting and sputtering for her to clear her airway. "You're sleeping with a married man! No, not the Asia Morrell I know. Girl, you have to hurry up and tell me everything before I go crazy over here. Break out another bottle of these fermented grapes. I want to hear it all before I crash into the twilight zone! In fact, let's go into my favorite guest bedroom so you won't have to carry me in there when I pass out. 'Drag' might be a better word. I'm too heavy for you to carry."

Asia had to laugh at her girlfriend, though she knew Lenora was simply trying to dull the acute pain she felt over Isaiah's medical condition. Lenora's bubbly personality was back but only because of all the wine she'd consumed. No way was she going to bring out another bottle of silly liquid since Lenora had already drunk more alcohol in this one day than she'd ever seen her drink during their entire friendship. They'd met in Ohio before Lenora had moved to L.A.

Asia helped Lenora out of the chair. "I think getting you into the bedroom is a great idea. Steady, girl. I got you, Lenora. Away we go off to your favorite room in my house."

Nicholas closely studied Asia as she sat across from him in the dimly lit restaurant booth. Something was bothering her. She hadn't been herself at the hospital when she and her friend had shown up earlier in the day. It concerned him that she hadn't made direct eye contact with him once since he'd picked her up at her home. Asia had looked everywhere but at him. During their earlier phone conversation, he'd had to practically beg her to keep their previously scheduled dinner engagement. She had simply refused to give him a reason for wanting to cancel in the first place, but her strange behavior had made his curiosity grow tenfold.

The waiter placed the prime rib entrées, with all the trimmings, in front of each of them. Nicholas had ordered the king-size cut of ten-

der, juicy beef, and Asia had requested the petite cut. The baked pota-
toes were piled high with sour cream and butter, and the fresh vegetables consisted of bright orange baby carrots, deep green broccoli
cuts, and delectable pearl onions.

Without comment, he bowed his head and asked the Lord to bless
the food before them.

Nicholas allowed Asia to eat her food in total tranquility, but he
couldn't stop wondering why she seemed so sad and withdrawn. This
type of terribly awkward silence hadn't occurred between them since
they were reunited after being apart for twenty-two years. Communication hadn't posed a problem for them until today. She had barely
spoken five sentences to him at the hospital and she'd said even less
on the drive to the restaurant. It now looked as if she wasn't going to
speak to him at all this evening. He had no clue how to break into the
silence of her thoughts, but that wasn't going to stop him from at least
trying to converse with her.

"How's your food, Asia?"

"It's delicious, Nicholas. This is a first-class restaurant. I'm glad you
talked me into coming out to dinner with you. The atmosphere is
calming."

He put his forefinger up to his temple. "Hmm, that wasn't as hard
as I thought it might be. I've been sweating bullets for nothing."

"What do you mean?"

"Do you realize you haven't spoken a word since we sat down and
you've only made eye contact with me once? That occurred while we
were outside in the lobby waiting for our table. Why don't you tell me
what's happening over there with you? I'm concerned."

"I've been trying to think of how I can tell you that I'm not going to
be seen out in public with you like this again. It's not what I want, but
it is what's best for both of us."

"It seems that you managed to tell me that with ease, but why would
you stop if it's not something you want? What has happened to make
you come to this conclusion? It doesn't seem to me that you came to
this end without some sort of coercion. Miranda?"

"Coupled with the fact that I don't like to have pictures of me
taken, especially those I haven't posed for. She has you and me on
film, or so she says. She knocked on my door right after you left the
morning you spent the night at my house. We're being stalked by
your wife."

"Soon-to-be ex-wife. Why are you letting that bother you?"

"Why shouldn't I?"

"Because we aren't doing anything wrong. I slept at your house but I didn't sleep in your bed. We both know that for a fact. You and I have been joined together at the hip because we have a son who's in a serious crisis, a son that needs to have both his mother and father around him until he's up and running again. Miranda is going to have to deal with that. Are you going to let her dictate your every move? She'll do it if you let her. I've said this before."

"I told her I wasn't going to give up our friendship."

"Then why did you just say you were giving us up?"

"I'm not sure. I guess I don't want to cause you any more trouble with Miranda. I have to respect the fact that you're still married to her."

His eyes grew soft and liquid. "And if I wasn't? What would it be like for us, Asia?"

"I don't know how to answer that, Nicholas."

"How about honestly?"

"You haven't asked a specific enough question."

"Okay. I can work with that. Had I not been married, where would I have slept the night I stayed at your house? Is that specific enough for you?"

Asia tried hard not to show embarrassment but she felt the hot color staining her cheeks. She couldn't believe Nicholas went there, but she had opened the door for it. "Nicholas, it's been twenty-two years of separation for us. Where do you think you would've slept?"

"I only know where I wanted to sleep that night: in your bed and in your loving arms, Asia Morrell, the only place I've ever wanted to sleep. That's as precise as I know how to get."

"Nicholas, don't. We shouldn't be talking about sex under the current circumstances."

"Who said anything about sex? It was never just sex with us. We made sweet, sweet love. The deep desires I now have for you have little to do with the physical. Don't you remember all the nights we slept together without even attempting to make love? Every time I lay in bed with you I got the same thrilling sensations as I did when we came together in passion. What I want from you has nothing to do with sex or us making love. Do you want to know what that something is, Asia?"

Asia couldn't look him straight in the eyes. He would see way too much emotional turmoil in hers. Her flesh was on fire for him but she couldn't stake a claim on what belonged to someone else. She loved him more than ever, but he was no longer hers for the taking. She wanted to know what that something was more than anything in the world and she hoped it was the same as what she desired from him, his unconditional love.

"I think you'd better call for the check, Nicholas. It's getting late and I still have a houseguest. Lenora is probably awake now and worrying about where I am at this hour."

"Didn't you tell her you'd be with me, your baby's daddy?"

She laughed at how Nicholas sounded just like the women she'd heard on one of the talk shows using the phrase "my baby's daddy." "She knows where I am."

"Then sit back and relax. I'm sure she knows you're safe with me. You've made her privy to our history. I promise not to tell you what I want from you until you ask. Fair enough?"

"Fair enough."

He smiled at her in a knowing way. "On to safer topics but nonetheless explosive. I hired an investigator to look into Isaiah's accident. You might find it interesting to know that my investigator is the same man Isaiah hired to find me. How's that for coincidence?"

"That is an incredible twist of fate. Where are you starting with this investigation?"

"Troy Dyson."

"Oh, Nick, I can't believe you're still hung up on the theory that Troy had something to do with this. I know that boy. Have known him for a long time. He's not the type of kid that would resort to something as evil and criminal as wanting to take out his best friend. Isaiah would not only object vehemently to this investigation, he'd resent it."

"Well, since Isaiah's unable to give us any input into what happened to him, I have to go with my instincts. You have to trust that I can sense the devil in someone. Troy's personality borders on evil. Add the letter 'd' to evil and you have the word *devil*. Whether this accident stems from jealousy of Isaiah or not, I don't know. But it's my duty as his father to find out. If you know a better way to do this, please share it with me."

She shrugged. "I wouldn't know where to begin. I guess I'll have to do as you ask. Trust you. I pray to God that you're dead wrong. But if that turns out to be the case, the Nicholas Reynolds I know will be the first to admit it. Are you the same man that I came to know?" *And love like crazy,* she added in her thoughts.

Nicholas shook his head. "I'm afraid not. I've changed considerably. I've matured and I'm a hell of a lot wiser. If you're asking if my heart and morals are still the same, those qualities haven't changed. My heart is still in the right place and I somehow manage to live by the same moral codes I've lived by my entire life. That's why I know I'd never indulge in an illicit affair or another type of affair with any other woman until my divorce is final. But you're not just any other woman. You're my first love, my only love, the mother of my son, my only child. The reason no other relationship will ever work for me is that the first time I fell in love was also the last time. Every woman I've been with has been cheated simply because my heart was elsewhere. I don't expect that to ever change. I'm too old to change my way of thinking and feeling. So let me put you on notice. When this divorce mess is done with, I'm coming after you with every ounce of strength I've got in me. If you don't want to be caught, you'd better run as fast and as far away from me as you can."

"Thanks for giving me a head start should I decide to run." *But I promise I won't run so hard that you can't possibly catch me. I not only desire to be caught, I want to be overtaken.*

"You're welcome. Back to this issue with Troy. Since his house was Isaiah's last known stop, we have to begin there first. What do you think?"

Asia had the strangest look on her face as she thought about Nicholas's remarks. She momentarily pursed her lips as she looked up at Nicholas. "I'm not sure that Troy's was his last stop. My house might've been."

Nicholas looked perplexed. "I thought he only called you. What exactly are you saying?"

"He did call. Then he decided to drive out to the house when he couldn't contain his excitement. By the time he got there, he had brewed up quite a storm out of his anger for me. For the first time ever, he actually yelled at me. It hurt like hell, even though I deserved to have him unleash his fury against me. I've never seen Isaiah that much out of control."

"You're his mother. No matter how angry he was, he was wrong to disrespect you. He's going to hear that from me the next time I visit him, coma or not. And he won't do it again."

"As I told you before, he isn't upset about what I told him. It's those things I didn't tell him. He feels that I cheated him. I was the last person he'd expected to rob him of the one thing he needed the most, his natural father. When he got through shouting and ranting like a madman, he stormed out of my house. It was the last I saw of him or heard from him until I got to the hospital emergency room. So you see, I'm afraid that I may have caused Isaiah's accident."

"Take yourself off the medieval stretching rack, Asia. Isaiah did go to Troy's. He told us that he talked with Isaiah."

"But he could've done that over the phone. Isaiah was calling everyone he cared about after he left you at the restaurant."

"Troy specifically told me that Isaiah stopped by his house."

"After he was at mine?"

Nichlolas shrugged. "I'd have to say I'm not sure about that. But that bit of information is easy enough to find out. Everything still starts with Troy. If he's in any way involved in this incident, Vann Orville will find it out." Nicholas folded his hands and put them on the table. "Why didn't you tell me about your fight with Isaiah before now?"

"I'm not sure. I blamed myself for what happened to Isaiah and I thought you might hold me accountable, too. I'm responsible for everything that has gone wrong in that boy's life. So why would this latest tragedy be any different?"

Nicholas covered her hand with his. "You are not to blame for any of this. Isaiah turned out to be the successful man and wonderful human being he is today because of you. If it's confirmed that Isaiah had drugs in his system, you didn't put them there. Our son took them by choice, someone forced him to take them, or they slipped the substance into his drink or something else he consumed. I don't believe he took them voluntarily. However it happened, we're going to get to the bottom of it. Stop shouldering the blame for something you had no control over."

"One day I'm going to stop keeping secrets, especially from those I care about and know I can trust with my life. I tend to clam up on the issues I should be open and honest about. I don't know why that is. I suspect it has a lot to do with my strict upbringing. When you're forced to keep normal, everyday occurrences from your parents, things most girls can happily share with their families, you learn to become extremely secretive about everything, especially the serious stuff. The truth is this. I've really had no one to share my deepest secrets with, not until Lenora came along. We became instant friends. Still, there are times when I don't open up to even her."

His expression was soft with understanding. "You're opening up wide to me right now. Why do you think that is, Asia?"

"You're one of the few people I can trust with my life."

"What about with your love?"

"That, too. Now, we really should be getting out of here. If I tell you all my well-kept secrets at once, I'll have nothing intriguing to share with you on our next outing."

"In view of the way this evening began, I'm thrilled to pieces to know there's going to be a next one. I'm glad you're going to keep your word about not giving up our friendship."

"Yeah, me too. I need your friendship, Nicholas. It's one of the few things in my life that I can claim as being true-blue."

"I've always been loyal to you, Asia."

"I know that now. That's why I'm able to trust you implicitly."

"I only wish you'd known that about me when you found yourself in deep trouble. Carrying a child without any support from the father couldn't have been an easy feat. I'm here now to help you carry the heavy loads. You can always count on me."

"Thanks, Nicholas. I promise not to ever again ignore your loyalty as my friend."

Instead of waiting for him to do it, Asia summoned the waiter to request the check.

"The dinner is on me, Nicholas."

"Thank you, Asia."

Looking surprised, she grinned. "I'm glad to see you're not going to put up a fight over who pays the check. Men have a tendency to think they should pay for everything. Then they turn around and call the woman a gold digger. After she's walked out on him or left his behind for someone else—and he's gone stone broke from trying to impress her."

He chuckled. "It seems to me that someone's been hanging out with the wrong men. Besides, I'm a lover, not a fighter. I'm a man who loves to have his peace."

* * *

After opening Asia's front door for her, Nicholas's good night kiss fell lightly on Asia's lips. Although it wasn't the type of kiss that could be misconstrued as anything other than friendly, Asia looked around to see if the lens of Miranda's trusty camera had caught them.

"Sleep tight, Grammy Butterfly. See you at the hospital sometime tomorrow."

"You bet, Grandpa Moth." Smiling broadly, Asia stood by quietly, listening to Nicholas's gentle laughter as he made his way back to the car. When he looked her way and waved, she blew him a kiss and went inside. Then she heard the phone ring. Hoping the noise hadn't awakened Lenora, Asia dashed inside.

In a matter of minutes Asia ran back outside, even though she was sure Nicholas had already pulled off. With tears streaming from her eyes, she immediately went back inside, picked up the phone, and hit the code that would connect her to Isaiah's father. Her heart thundered inside her chest as she waited for Nicholas to respond to his cell phone.

"He's awake!" she cried into the phone. "Though somewhat groggy, our son is awake, Nicholas. Torri just called. He's asking for us. I'll meet you at the hospital."

"Thank God!" Nicholas shouted. "Thank you, Jesus! I'm just at the gas station around the corner. I'll be back for you, Asia. You sound too upset to drive and it's also too late for you to be out alone." He hung up the phone before she could object.

Asia felt horrible that she hadn't been there for Isaiah when he came out of the coma. But Torri was there. That brought her a huge amount of comfort. Someone that loved him as much as she did was with him; that's what mattered most.

Asia fell on her knees to give thanks to the Creator, the only one who could've brought Isaiah safely though the valley of the shadow of death. "The Lord is my shepherd, I shall not want," she whispered. She kept her eyes closed as she continued to recite the twenty-third Psalm. "I will fear no evil. Thou art with me. Thy rod and Thy staff they comfort me . . ."

The moment she got off her knees Asia made a mad dash for the guest bedroom to share the good news with Lenora. Much to her surprise, the room was empty. Then she thought about where Nicholas had parked: in the driveway, where Lenora's car had been when they'd left for dinner. As she turned to leave, she saw a note propped up on the pillow. Asia knew her friend had left before she even read the note. She was sure that Lenora had wanted to give Nicholas and her some privacy should he come inside after their dinner engagement.

CHAPTER ELEVEN

A jubilant Torri met Nicholas and Asia at the doorway of Isaiah's room. She then led them over to Isaiah's bedside. Leaning over the bed, Torri gently kissed Isaiah's lips. "Boo, your Mom and Dad are here. Are you going to make them proud by saying hello to them?"

Isaiah struggled to open his eyes. Once he managed to accomplish that, he could only make out the figures in shadow. It was like he had a film over his eyes. He tried blinking to gain better focus. A slight smile crinkled at the corners of his mouth when Asia leaned in closer to the bed. The old, familiar, sweet scent of his mother filled his nostrils.

"Mom, Mom, hi." Isaiah's speech pattern was slow and slurred and it frustrated him.

Asia nearly came unglued at the sweet sound of her name on his lips, but she quickly composed herself. "Mommy's here, baby. Welcome back once again. We've missed you. Please stay with us. Your daddy's here, too."

"Dad, can . . . you . . . come closer? I can barely see . . . you," Isaiah stammered.

Nicholas wiped the tears from his eyes before moving closer to where his son lay. "Hey, champ, it's good to see you with your eyes open. I thought we were going to have to change your nickname to Sleeping Beauty."

"Yeah, how about that?" Isaiah rasped painfully.

Isaiah's struggle with his speech concerned Nicholas. "Maybe you'd better wait until you're a little stronger before you try to get too vocal. You don't want to strain your vocal cords." Nicholas leaned over and kissed Isaiah on the cheek. As Nicholas drew back, he saw the holy terror in his son's eyes. "What is it, son?"

"I can't move my legs," Isaiah managed in whisper, biting back a broken sob. "I'm scared, Dad. I haven't been able to move anything below my waist. Please don't tell Mom or Torri. I don't want to upset either of them."

Nicholas didn't know what to say, but he knew he had to say something comforting. He leaned over the bed and put his mouth to Isaiah's ear. "You've just come out of a coma. Everything is probably rusty from nonuse. Give it more time. You have to regain your strength before you start moving all over the place. Don't worry. This is our secret." Nicholas couldn't help thinking back on Asia revealing a few of her secrets to him at the restaurant. He hated the fact that more covert matters had to come into play, as if there hadn't been enough of hush-hush topics already.

Isaiah nodded gingerly. "Yeah, maybe that's all it is. Torri, where are you?"

Torri immediately responded to Isaiah's call. "I'm right here, Mr. Man. I was just talking to Mommy-Asia." His hand trembled as he placed it against Torri's abdomen, causing her to draw in a deep breath.

Isaiah managed to pull off a weak laugh. "Where'd that name come from? I like it."

"I just called her by that one day. I liked the way it sounded. Miss Asia has always been an acceptable title, but not as personal as the new one. Are you okay with me calling her that?"

"I'm fine with it. Mommy-Asia! I like that name, Torri."

Asia was holding on to Nicholas's hand with all the strength she had in her own. Feeling a mixture of euphoria and fear, she looked on as her son talked to his beautiful girlfriend. Though he hadn't voiced it yet, Asia was sure that Isaiah knew about the baby Torri carried for him. The way his hand was gently fondling her abdomen was a good indication, but Torri seemed oblivious to everything but her man's handsome face. All Torri could see was the reflection of her love for Isaiah in his eyes. He was Torri's hero, just as Nicholas had been hers.

Asia was thrilled to see him awake and talking, but her mind and heart couldn't grasp the real possibility of paralysis and what that would mean for her once vibrant-with-life son: total devastation. The lack of movement from Isaiah's lower extremities hadn't gone unnoticed by Asia. Isaiah's life was his athletic prowess. It would darn near annihilate him if he wasn't able to return to the world of sports as a top-notch competitor.

"Nicholas," Asia whispered, pulling him out of earshot of Isaiah, "he hasn't moved a muscle below his waist. I'm scared for him. Please ask God to save him from further trauma."

"I'm already doing that, Asia. I've been in constant prayer from day one. We have to let go of it so God can work it out. We're powerless in this situation, other than in continuing to use the unshakable power of prayer. Keep your chin up. You don't want Isaiah to sense your fear."

"He looks so tired, Nicholas. It appears as if he hasn't had a moment of sleep. My poor baby has been through pure hell and his journey is nowhere near over yet."

"We don't know what being in a coma actually means. Everyone seems to think it's the same as sleeping. But I have to wonder since I believe that some comatose patients can hear what's going on around them. If that's the case, it means they're not always asleep, which might explain his fatigued look. It could've been tiring for our son as he fought his way back to us."

Asia smiled. "You love saying that, don't you?"

"What?"

"Our son."

"Oh, yeah, those are the sweetest two words recently added to my vocabulary. I'm either saying my son or our son. I love saying it, love the way it sounds, thrilled by the way it makes me feel. I can't imagine ever getting tired of saying it. Isaiah is my son, our son!" Since Asia had mentioned her concerns, Nicholas was glad. He didn't want to break Isaiah's confidence.

"Mom."

Isaiah's voice reached out to Asia and wrapped around her like a warm embrace. She couldn't get to his side fast enough. Her baby was calling out to her and she had to answer. Torri moved back a little to make room for Asia at the bedside. She understood their great relationship.

Asia leaned over Isaiah. "You rang, darling. What's on your mind?"

"I'm getting sleepy. Before it takes me over, I want to apologize for the way I talked to you." His eyes filled with tears. "I'll never do that again, Mom. I hurt you. I know I did. Pain was all over your face. Please forgive me for causing you that kind of distress, Mom."

Asia couldn't stand to see the tough struggle he had to endure just to speak. "Shh, Isaiah. There's nothing to forgive. That's all over with. Do you remember what happened after you left my house? Do you recall who you were with?"

He closed his eyes and she took hold of his hand to wait for him to think about her questions. Several minutes passed before she realized he had slipped away again. Panic quickly arose inside her because she didn't know if he'd fallen back into the coma or if he was just asleep. Her lips moved rapidly as she mouthed a silent prayer.

Asia turned to Torri. "Do you think he's only asleep? Should we call the nurse and have her check on him?"

"He's probably asleep, Mommy-Asia. He said he was sleepy before he began talking to you. But I'll get the nurse so we can make sure everything is okay."

"I'll get the nurse," Nicholas offered. "But I'm like Torri. I believe he's just worn out."

"Would you like to come in for a minute or do you have to get going?"

Nicholas looked at his watch. "It's not past my bedtime yet. I think I can stay awake a little longer, but a cup of coffee will help."

"I'm not going to drink any tonight. I want to get to sleep at some point."

"Maybe I shouldn't come in if you're sleepy, Asia."

"Oh, no, I'm wide awake, way too keyed up to sleep. I'd love to fix you a cup of coffee."

Nicholas parked the car in Asia's driveway and then got out. Asia waited for him to come around and open the passenger door for her. Nicholas loved being the gentleman and she loved that about him. It didn't take away from his manhood or her status as an independent woman.

It only took a few minutes for them to get inside the house and make themselves comfortable. Asia didn't blink an eye when Nicholas went into the kitchen and began to make coffee. He hadn't asked if it was okay for him to putter about in her kitchen and she'd offered no objections. They were merely good friends who were once lovers. Asia wanted him to make himself at home in her residence. Though it felt like old times, she knew better.

She seated herself at the breakfast nook. "I'm worried about Isaiah, Nicholas. Like I told you at the hospital, there doesn't seem to be any movement in his lower body. I think he's aware of it, too. He has to be told that he could be permanently paralyzed, but I don't want the doctors to tell him; that's too impersonal and insensitive. I think we should be the ones to tell him, Nicholas. He may take it better coming from us."

"You could be right. But I'm not sure it should come from me either. He doesn't know me well enough, Asia, for me to spring something like that on him. I'm not being a coward in this. Just considering his feelings. I think someone should tell him the news other than his doctors. And that only leaves you, the one person he trusts without question or thought."

"Oh, Nicholas, I can't tell him something like that without you being there to support both Isaiah and me. It would be much too difficult." She took a moment to ponder. "I guess I'm leaning on you too hard. I'd have to do this alone had the accident occurred before you two met. How does a mother tell her child that he may never walk again, let alone run up and down the hardwood? His contract is fully guaranteed, yet being financially stable won't mean a darn thing to him when he learns he's physically incapable of doing what he loves best."

"That's a tough question for me to answer, Asia. There's nothing easy about the task. As for you leaning on me, that's what I'm here for. I promised that I wouldn't let you hit the ground, and I won't. Even though I'm concerned about how Isaiah will take such horrific news coming from a stranger who just happens to be his father, I'll be there with you every step of the way. We're all going to get through this. God will see to it."

"Thanks, Nicholas. I definitely needed the reassurance. If you don't mind, I'm going into the bedroom and put on something comfortable. The waistband on these pants has dug into my flesh long enough for one day."

Nicholas grinned. "Not something too sexy, now. My heart couldn't stand to see you looking too provocative for words," he joked. "As a married man, I have to be on my best behavior. But seeing you in something hot would certainly lift my spirits."

"In your dreams. Besides, I don't own anything like that."

"You've occupied plenty of my dreams, girl. Sure you don't want a cup of coffee?"

"Positive. But a hot cup of tea might hit the spot. I'll make a pot when I get back."

"Consider it done. Go ahead and do whatever it is you do to relax. This has been one crazy day. I can't thank God enough for bringing Isaiah back home to us. He'll help us get over any hurdles we need to jump. The Lord won't desert us."

"I know what you mean about this being a crazy day. I also know that the Lord will give us strength to handle everything that comes our way. Be right back with you in a couple of minutes. Try not to miss me too much," she teased in parting, making him laugh heartily.

Without missing a beat, Nicholas went straight to the cabinet where Asia kept the nondairy creamer and removed the plastic container from the lower shelf. While practically watching her every move the last time he'd sat in her kitchen, he'd paid close attention to where she'd removed this, that, and the other from. Spotting a box of herbal teabags, he chose a packet called Evening's Delight. He filled the teapot, set it on the burner, and turned on the gas flame.

Everything in the bright, cheerful room was neat as a pin and sparkling clean. He saw that Asia took care of her house the same way she took care of herself, extremely well. Her body was every bit as firm as it had been in college, despite the fact she'd carried and delivered a baby.

Twenty minutes had passed since Asia left the kitchen and Nicholas was concerned about her failure to have returned by now. This time she wasn't soaking in a hot tub of water to lose track of time. She was only changing into comfortable attire. He checked to make sure he'd turned off the gas under the teapot and then he took to the hallway with long, purposeful strides.

Nicholas stopped in front of her bedroom door. Though it was closed, the sounds of hard sobbing reached his ears with crystal clarity. With no thought to her privacy, he opened the door and entered the room. His heart broke at the sight of her anguish.

Huddled on the bed, sobbing her heart out, Asia didn't even hear Nicholas come in.

As he advanced toward the bed, he stopped dead in his tracks. The birdcage he'd given her so long ago hung in the corner closest to her bed. That she still possessed it after all this time astounded him. Seeing something he'd made for her with his own two hands brought on a tidal wave of emotions. It looked as beautiful as it did the day he'd given it to her. The silk flowers she'd filled it with still looked vibrant and appeared dust free. He didn't know how he'd missed the birdcage on his prior visit to her bedroom, but he was thrilled to see where it hung.

After seating himself on the bed, he brought Asia into his arms.

Her head immediately sought out the comfort of his chest. Nicholas had arrived to rescue her one more time. All these years she'd thought she had rescued him from a terrible fate; how wrong she had been was far beyond explanation.

It seemed to him as if she were coming apart at the seams. He had expected her emotional release to come long before now. But she was a tough one, had held up admirably well until now. He was proud of the stamina she'd shown thus far. To prepare herself for the next several rounds of Isaiah's prizefight for the quality of his life, she would no doubt build herself back up. In order for her to do that she had to release the anxiety to make way for what was yet to come.

Nicholas just held Asia tightly in his arms, gently stroking her hair, without any verbal attempt to calm her down. Peace would come soon enough, but the storm had to completely run out before that could happen. None of the sun's rays would beam brightly in her heart until the rain went away. He prayed that a rainbow would soon appear on the horizon; without the rain, a rainbow was impossible.

The last thing Nicholas had expected was for Asia to fall asleep in his arms, but she had.

She had worn herself completely out. What to do next was his real dilemma. Also, the coffee pot was still on in the next room, but he had turned off the gas under the teapot. Her coffeemaker was very similar to the one he had at home, so he was able to easily convince himself that it was programmed to turn off after a certain amount of time. With that in mind, he lay back on the bed and made himself comfortable.

To once again have Asia asleep in his arms was exactly what he'd prayed for from the moment he realized that she had left him, that she wasn't coming back. He'd never be able to forget that day as long as he lived.

Nicholas had gone straight to her dorm room after basketball practice on the fateful evening. No one had answered the door, so he'd gone back downstairs to the recreational room, where he had a perfect view of the entrance she normally came through. He'd been waiting for over an hour when Asia's roommate finally came inside the building. After Nicholas had asked her about Asia, she had invited him up to the room to see if Asia was in the room asleep and simply hadn't heard his knock.

A quick sweep of the dormitory room had left them both in shock. It was if she'd never occupied the space that she'd once claimed as her own. She hadn't left a single article of hers behind. Nicholas first thought it was a joke that Asia and her roommate were pulling on him. After seventy-two hours of Asia's absence, he began to accept the fact that she had left school; her reasons completely eluded him and everyone else who knew her. Asia hadn't breathed a single word to anyone about her plans. All he'd ever learned was that she'd decided to drop out of college. Privacy laws prohibited the powers that be from telling him anything.

Miranda screaming at the top her lungs brought Nicholas and Asia out of a deep sleep. Nothing could've prepared Asia for seeing Miranda standing in the middle of her bedroom. When she had awakened in the middle of the night, and found herself in Nicholas's arms, she hadn't been ready for that either. But the shock of it all didn't stop her from promptly laying her head back down on his chest, which was where she eventually fell back to sleep with ease.

In Asia's mind, it was the first time in over twenty-two years that she'd slept in his arms. Since she thought it might be the last, she had taken full advantage of the complicated situation. Now she was paying the price for her sins. Miranda looked as if she was ready to kill her and Nicholas. *Have mercy, Lord,* Asia prayed silently. *Have mercy on our misguided souls.*

As Miranda's claws went straight for Asia's face, Nicholas moved in front of Asia to protect her. The scratch landed near his right temple.

Even as the cut oozed a razor-thin line of blood, Nicholas didn't retreat or retaliate. This was an unfortunate incident, one that he blamed himself for. He knew what it looked like to Miranda. It wasn't what she had to be thinking of, yet Miranda's thoughts more than likely matched his desires. He'd always wanted Asia, had never stopped wanting her, didn't think his desire for her would ever cease. That's just the way it was.

Totally out of breath, carrying a large butcher knife, Lenora suddenly popped into the bedroom. Seeing Asia and Nicholas on the bed together helped her to figure out who the strange woman might be, the daredevil that had zipped past her when she'd opened Asia's front door.

Lenora put her hand on her hip as she waved the knife back and forth. "Lady, I don't know how you had the nerve to run in here like this, but you'll have to explain that to the police." Lenora looked at Asia. "I'm sorry, girl. I left an important legal brief in your guest bedroom. With it being so early, I decided to use the emergency key you gave me to just slip in here quietly and retrieve the documents I need for court this morning. I saw the car in your driveway, a clue that you had a guest, but I didn't give it much thought since I wasn't going to disturb you. Still, I had no idea this woman was lying in wait to rush your house. I didn't come inside right away because I didn't know what she was capable of. I was going to wait for the police until I heard the loud screaming. After arming myself, I rushed in here to rescue you. That's why I'm holding this here knife. And I wouldn't have hesitated to use it if I'd had to," Lenora said, looking dead at Miranda.

Asia would've thought the situation was darn near laughable if it weren't so serious. She couldn't fault Miranda for how she felt, but her tactics left a lot to be desired. This was something she was going to let Nicholas handle since she didn't have a clue how to explain what Miranda had come upon. She and Nicholas in bed together was actually unexplainable. But the fact that they were fully clothed should exonerate them regarding any charges of engaging in sexual misconduct. They had slept in the same bed, in each other's arms, but sex had nothing to do with what had occurred between them. Had that been the case, Asia thought, Miranda would've found them under the sheets, butt naked, not on top of the comforter, dressed.

"This is not about you," Miranda shouted at Lenora. "This is about

Asia being in bed with my husband. Nicholas, you'd better talk to me, and you need to make it quick. You owe me an explanation. The police will be here any minute and they're bound to lose respect for you as an officer of the court. This should make all the local papers without any assistance from me."

Nicholas wrung his hands together. "You're right about our needing to communicate, Miranda. Let's go outside to my car where we can talk this over calmly."

Miranda shook her head. "I'm too far past calm for that to happen. I want to hear what you have to say for yourself and I want you to say it in front of your girlfriend. It seems to me that you're telling me one thing and her something else. How can we work on our marriage if you keep these unthinkable deceptions going?"

"Miranda, you're just plain delusional, 'cause you're sure not as clever as you might think! You can come outside and talk to me in private or you can get into your little Lexus and move on down the highway. Your choice."

Miranda looked at Asia. "I can't believe you're not going to open your mouth and at least apologize to me for sleeping with my husband. I guess you're going to blame this one too on your anguish over your ill son. What kind of woman are you? How could you use your son's tragedy to get what you want from his father? You're nothing more than an educated slut."

The look on Asia's face clearly spelled out her deep regret over what Miranda must be going through. She truly felt sorry for the woman even if she did think Miranda a hateful witch. Asia also felt ashamed because she could've asked Nicholas to leave when she'd awakened in his arms. Both her behavior and Nicholas's had been inappropriate any way it was viewed.

Lenora grabbed Miranda by the arm. "You're out of here, Ms. Ann! We've heard enough from you to last us a lifetime. Nobody gets away with talking to my girl like that. If you know what's good for you, you'll take your husband's advice and find the wind at your back. I'm not the one to be toyed with," Lenora warned in a no-nonsense manner. "You don't want to try me."

Miranda gave a quick thought to a physical fight until she saw that Lenora still had the knife in her hand. Still, she found the nerve to violently snatch her arm away from Lenora's tight grasp and then turn to Nicholas. "Let's get the hell out of here, Nick. I can't wait to hear how you're going to explain this one away. I already know it's going to be weak and tired."

"I need to speak with Asia for a second. I'll be right out, Miranda."

Although Miranda clearly showed her dislike for his consideration of Asia, the stern expression on Nicholas's face brooked no argument from her as she stomped out of the room.

Lenora followed right behind Miranda to make sure she went outside to wait for Nicholas. She also wanted to clear things up with the police. If it were up to Lenora, the officers would never get an opportunity to interview Nicholas regarding the incident. Miranda was right on the money about him losing face with those who held him in high esteem. Nicholas was an icon to his peers as well as law enforcements officers all over the country.

Nicholas took Asia's hand. "I'm sorry, sweetheart. I take full responsibility for this fiasco. My intentions were honorable but my uncontrollable feelings for you will always get in the way of my using better judgment. That's not an excuse. It's a fact. I hope this bothersome episode doesn't cause you to run away from me again. If it does, remember what I told you. You can't run fast enough or far enough away. I'll find you." He kissed her forehead. "Hope to see you at the hospital later on. Nothing can alter the fact that we're Isaiah's parents and good friends."

Asia watched Nicholas as he walked toward the bedroom door. Something about his demeanor disturbed her. His head wasn't hung low, but she felt that his spirits were. Without bothering to dig any deeper into her thoughts, she ran out of the room, catching up with him in the hallway.

"Hey, Reynolds, since you slept in my bed last night, can a girl who's a dear friend and your baby's mama get more than a sweet-but-sorry kiss on the forehead? This old girlfriend is in dire need of a warm hug from her baby's daddy."

Nicholas's face beamed as he turned back to Asia. "Girlfriend, we're going to get into a lot more trouble. But it's all worth it. Just to hold you in my arms for another second is worth walking through hell for." His arms reached out to her, pulling her into the safety of them.

Asia gave a deep sigh of satisfaction as she glowed within the warmth of his embrace.

* * *

"Thanks for explaining everything to the police, Lenora. You saved Nicholas's sweet butt from a royal roast. Miranda has threatened to go public with an illicit affair that we're not having. I'm sure she wasn't too happy about you smoothing things out with the officers."

Lenora stirred a teaspoon of sugar into her coffee. "You're welcome, but I thank God that I knew one of the cops. Their willingness to accept my call as a false alarm was nothing short of a blessing. But I need you to talk to me. What is really going on with you and that fine Nicholas Reynolds, Asia? The fact that the man was in your bed with you can't be denied. How did all of this early morning's madness come about?"

"I don't even know where to begin, but I'll take a shot at it. Miranda is obviously tailing his every move, which she is in no way trying to hide. It all started out so innocently and would've ended that way had Miranda not shown up. I was crying my eyes out. Nicholas came into the bedroom to comfort me. I fell asleep in his arms but not intentionally. Sheer exhaustion and the familiar comfort of his chest proved to be a deadly combination. I should've asked him to leave when I woke up during the night, but I didn't. And there's nothing I can do about it now. I deeply regret the incident but I can't erase it. If Nicholas told me that he wanted to work things out with Miranda, I'd hate it but I wouldn't interfere. If they were living as man and wife, I could see why she'd go through all this. They're not together like that. I'm not going to give him up as a friend unless he asks me to. That's not something either of us wants to happen."

"Friends, my foot! You two are still madly in love with each other. Anybody with eyes can see that. But I'm fearful for you. That woman he's married to is a little off her rocker. Something serious is driving her to this end, more than what clearly meets the eye. Miranda Reynolds has some dark secrets. I'm willing to bet my diamond Rolex on it. Mark my words."

"Oh, Lenora, your theory's too wild. Miranda's just crazy over the fact that Nicholas has a child with a woman he was once in love with. If he hadn't told her about Isaiah and me, he believes the divorced would've gone forward as planned."

"Was in love with? Please! If anyone can convince me he's not in love with you, I'll eat my car keys. Whatever you do, girlfriend, make sure you watch your back. I've got to get to court. I have an important case to argue. I'll call you later on. Give my godson my love. Tell him I'll be up to see him before the day is done." Lenora blew Asia a kiss as she rushed out of the kitchen.

Nicholas was frantic as he tried to calm Isaiah down. In the absence of the family, certain members of the medical staff had informed his son that he might never walk again. Nicholas couldn't believe that medical professionals, especially doctors, could be so insensitive and downright cold. He thought of all the painful moaning sounds and gasps of torment that he'd heard coming from Asia and himself over the past weeks. The anguished moans from Isaiah were the worst Nicholas had heard yet. His son was broken in every way a man could be. Isaiah was a young man who'd had it all. Now it seemed that he'd lost everything he had become in his deep agony. Isaiah was tormented inside and out.

"Dad, this can't be! How can they say these untrue things?" Isaiah cried. "If I can't walk or run, I don't think I want to live. What good am I to anybody if I'm no good to myself? My legs are how I make my living. It would've been better if I had died."

"Don't talk like that Isaiah. God will have the last word on this."

"How dare you talk to me about God! Where was He when this was happening to me? Dad, I've not only lost my ability to walk, jump, and run, I can't remember a damn thing that happened after I left my mom. I've lost my memory, too. How's Torri going to love me now?"

"The same exact way she loved you before. Your profession is only a fraction of who you are, Isaiah. Torri's not the type of woman who'll run out on a man when he's down."

"Exactly my point. She'll stay with me out of obligation and pity. I won't have that. I refuse to see her again. I want you to tell those nurses not to let her in here again. Tell them now. I can't stand the thought of seeing pity in her eyes for me." Isaiah's tears streamed down his face.

"I'll tell them no such thing. If you want them to know your wishes, tell them yourself. I want no part in this selfishness."

"Selfishness? Look who's talking! How can you stand in judgment of me when you couldn't see that my mother needed you? If you hadn't been so selfish, maybe you could've realized that she was in real trouble. You failed her and me, yet you can tell me I'm being selfish. How does that come to be?"

Nicholas put his arms around his son. "You're angry, son. And I understand it. But I'm not going to let you tear me down because of it. I won't stand by and watch you destroy the people you love, the people that love you. I accept that your dagger-sharp comments are a part of your anger. Had I known about you, there's not a person on this earth that could've kept me away from you. I don't know if Torri told you she's carrying your baby or not since you've been awake, but she is. She told you when you were in the coma. Don't do what you've falsely accused me of for so long now. You didn't get where you are by being a coward. If you run out on Torri, you run out on the woman you love and you run out on your own flesh and blood. The difference between us is this. You know Torri's pregnant. I didn't know that Asia was."

Isaiah's tears came faster. "I thought I was dreaming when I heard that she was having our baby. I heard a lot of things while I was in the coma. I fought to respond, but I couldn't. There are many hours out of my life that I've totally lost, but I'll always have that one precious moment with me. Torri deserves the best. If I can't take care of myself, I'm not the best for her. Torri needs a whole man, not a half of one. My upper body works, but the lower part has no feeling in it whatsoever. How fair is that to a woman her age? Torri is too beautiful and far too sensuous to live a life of celibacy. I can't do that to her. She deserves to continue with her colorful life. The only colors I can offer her are various shades of the blues."

"Son, why don't you let Torri decide what she wants for herself? Besides, the paralysis may only be temporary."

Isaiah's eyes widened with disbelief. "How do you know that? Did the doctors say that?"

"I'll explain everything to you in a minute. I want to ask you something first and I need you to be completely honest with me."

Isaiah nodded but was unsure of where Nicholas was headed in his line of questioning.

"Were you on an illegal substance the night of the incident? Have you ever taken any kind of illegal drugs, including marijuana, for recreational purposes or otherwise?"

Isaiah looked his father straight in the eye. "No, never."

"Then that means the drugs found in your system were put there by someone with sinister motivation. We just have to find out what their motive was. Can you remember anything about that night? I need to know the last place you were and the name of everyone that you came into contact with before the accident."

Isaiah shook his head, as if he were trying to clear the cobwebs. He struggled hard to remember his every movement that night. A look of frustration crossed his features when he failed to recall anything that might've occurred after he'd seen his mother, yet he felt sure that Asia wasn't the last person he'd made contact with on that fateful evening.

"I don't remember anything that happened beyond seeing Mom. But somehow I don't believe that she was the last person I was with. Maybe when some of this medication wears off my full memory will return. This is so frustrating for me. Can this situation get any worse?"

"It could've been much, much worse! Count your blessings, son. There have been many. What about your friend Troy? Did you recall seeing him after you visited Asia?"

"I just don't know." Isaiah shrugged. "I keep drawing blanks."

"He said that you were at his place. I intend to get clarification from him regarding that statement. I also believe that whatever happened to you occurred after you left Asia's house. I feel that Troy has the key that could unlock this case. Your mother thinks not. I know Troy's your best friend, but is there any reason that he might want to see you hurt, or worse, dead?"

Isaiah looked horrified by the question. "What are you getting at? What are you trying to say, Dad? If your theory about the drugs is correct, how could you think Troy is somehow involved with what happed to me?"

"I don't know. That's why I asked you those questions. You're the only one who knows how deep Troy's loyalties to you run."

"We've been friends forever. Every now and then he grumbles about coming off the bench for me, thinks he should be a starter, but that's only natural when you're as good a ballplayer as he is. He makes jokes out of his grievances, but I get the feeling he's serious at times. But that's not enough motivation to commit a serious crime."

"It's not? Sounds like the perfect motivator to me."

"Troy's not at all like that. Our relationship has always been solid. He'd never do anything to bring harm to me. I'm sure of that."

"I hope you're right. We'll find out soon enough. I'm having him investigated."

"What? Why are you doing something like that? I think that's going too far without a shred of evidence of any wrongdoing on his part."

"Maybe so. You don't know this, but Price Sheldon has been brought up on drug charges, possession with intent to distribute. I'm trying to find out if there's possibly a link between his charges and what happened to you."

"I'm amazed!" Isaiah looked troubled as he racked his brain regarding any drug use or other involvement with illegal substances by his teammate. Unable to draw anything but blanks, he sighed out of deep frustration over his loss of memory. "Price may or may not be involved with drugs, but that has nothing to do with Troy. He wouldn't be involved with something like that, nor would he try to hurt me."

"Okay, but I'm still running a check on him. If he's so squeaky clean, there's nothing to worry about, right?"

"You're so determined!"

"Yeah, just like you. And your determination is what's going to see you through this worst of times. Be just as indomitable about walking again and see what happens."

"You mentioned the paralysis might be temporary. Where'd you get that from?"

Nicholas explained what the doctors had told him regarding the fact that the drugs in his system might actually be responsible for his condition. Nicholas had then taken it up on himself to do his own research on the different kinds of drugs that could cause problems with motor skills. There were numerous drugs that could induce paralysis with both short-and long-term effects on a person's ability to move. The most puzzling thing was that only the lower half of Isaiah's body had been affected, which still might suggest spinal cord injury. Only time and further medical testing would determine the final results.

Throughout their conversation, Nicholas observed Isaiah's struggles with his speech and his valiant fight just to stay awake. Now his eyes were staying closed for longer periods of time, a good indication that he had tired himself out. Nicholas concluded that his son should rest. He'd need to be well rested and to have his physical and mental strength restored in order to fight all of his uphill battles.

Nicholas took Isaiah's hand. "We'll have prayer and then you need to get some rest. You can barely keep your eyes open. I'll be right here when you wake up."

With tears in his eyes, Isaiah looked up at his father. "Why are you doing all this for me? Why do you even care, especially after the way I treated you in your office?"

"Whys and wherefores are questions that don't need to be answered when a man loves his son as much as I love you. Now that you're going to be a father, you'll come to know one day exactly what I mean. I can promise you that."

"But how can you just say you love me without really knowing anything about me?"

"Son, there are some things that simply come without the knowing. Loving you came naturally for me, instantaneously. One look at you is all it took. When you see your baby boy or girl for the first time, you'll experience the same extraordinary feelings I did at seeing you. I can't explain it any better than that, Isaiah. Just know that I love you in every way that it's possible for a parent to love his child. You are my flesh and blood. That alone makes you very much a part of me."

Unable to maintain control any longer, Isaiah let his tears spill over. "How could I have been so wrong about you? Why did Mom let me think you were just another deadbeat dad?"

"Is that what she made you think? Did she ever tell you I was an irresponsible parent, one that had shirked his responsibilities? Or are those the types of things that were easy for you to believe about me?"

"She never said anything about you, good or bad. I was scared to ask her a bunch of questions because I didn't want to cause her pain. And I was also fearful of the answers. If she'd told me you didn't want me, or that you didn't believe I was yours, that would've hurt too much. I was in enough pain. Why add more to it?"

Nicholas's emotions were tugging hard at him for liberation. Seeing his son so emotional was hard for him. He hated what Isaiah had had to endure because of his absence in his son's life. He should've been there from the moment of Isaiah's conception. No child, male or female, should have to grow up without both parents. Asia had been the one to make the decision, but all three of them were paying the high cost of her making the wrong one. While he now understood her reasoning, the excruciating pain of her resolution was nonetheless hard to bear.

"Isaiah, I want you to close your eyes and go to sleep. Your emotional state will only deplete what little energy you're operating on. We'll have many more conversations just like this one. I'll be here to answer all your questions from now until I take my last breath. I plan to be an immovable force in your life. Think you can manage to take a short nap for now?"

"Knowing that you'll be here when I wake up makes everything easier for me. I never thought I'd hear myself saying this, just like I never dreamed I could bring myself to call you Dad. But here goes. I love you, Dad. I don't know much about you either, but I felt an instantaneous connection with you the day we met for the first time, the same type you've already talked about. With that said, I'll do as you suggested. See you when I wake up?"

"Without a doubt, son. I'll be right here. I love you, too."

CHAPTER TWELVE

Nicholas listened intently to every word Vann Orville had to say, glad that he was receiving the information before his later meeting with Price Sheldon. Vann had certainly done his homework. He wasn't known as the best human bloodhound in the business for nothing. Vann had brought Nicholas more news to digest than he'd expected, but of the unsavory variety.

It seemed that the Wildcats' center was involved in more than illegal drugs and petty gambling. The serious things Sheldon was implicated in couldn't be pulled off without having a partner or perhaps a couple of partners in crime. Troy Dyson was the first accomplice that came to Nicholas's mind. It certainly would explain a lot of the things that Nicholas felt about Troy.

Nicholas wished Asia were there with him to hear what Vann had to say, but she had wanted to be at the hospital with Isaiah when he had to undergo a special medical procedure on his spine. The delicate testing procedure wouldn't take place until late in the afternoon. Isaiah's nurse had made Asia aware of the fact that it could happen before or after the scheduled time. Nicholas hoped for the latter, since he also planned to be there for his son. Being at the hospital was the most significant issue, but finding out what happened to his son was nearly as important.

"These are some incredible findings, Vann. If what you've said

can be proven as true, we may have found the motive for what occurred to my son. This revelation is mind-boggling but certainly
believable. Illegal crap like that happens more often than people
can imagine. Let's continue to keep this quiet for a while longer. I
want to make sure I have a winning combination before I show my
hand."

"Aren't you now more concerned about conflict of interest since
your firm is representing the young man in question?"

"Yeah, much more than before. I have to take myself completely off
the case but I'm thinking Taylor can still be his attorney. But we could
have some major trouble as it pertains to the issues of discovery. I certainly can't tell Taylor what I've learned from you without compromising the integrity of her case. Boy, this is even more complicated
than I thought just a moment ago. This so-called great legal eagle will
have to get outside legal advice on this one before I can make any
final decisions. I'm too emotionally involved in this to do otherwise. I
have to make all the right calls. There's no room for mistakes, especially those that could allow technicalities to be entered into the playing field. Got any suggestions?"

"Drop the Sheldon case altogether. Let me be the one to present
my findings to the D.A. That way, there's no conflict of interest. My
desire to anonymously help out a friend is a good enough reason for
me to be involved in this. Or I can wait until the D.A. commissions my
office. And they probably will. That's the beauty of being able to work
both sides of the fence."

"You might be on to something." Nicholas consulted his watch.
"We have a meeting with Sheldon approximately two hours from now.
Should I have Taylor cancel it?"

"Right away!" Vann handed his cell phone to Nicholas. "Make the
call."

"Thanks, but I have mine handy."

Nicholas put his call through to Taylor. After talking with her for
several minutes, he disconnected the lines. "We just received another
blessing. Sheldon cancelled on us. Even when Taylor told him she
couldn't represent him if he didn't show up at the scheduled time, he
refused to commit. According to Taylor, his arrogance over the matter was somewhat unbearable."

"I'm not surprised by that. Some athletes think they're gods. Looks
like he just handed you your out. Is your attorney prepared to tell him

she can't take him on as a client if he calls back? This is a high-profile case, one that most lawyers would love to take on for publicity's sake."

"She'll have no problem with it after I share with her what you've told me. Knowing Taylor, she's probably relieved. Thanks for the advice, old-timer. I owe you."

"You don't owe me a thing. Just do what you got to do to help your boy out of this mess. I'm going to pull myself off the case where you're concerned. But you can rest assured that I'll still be out there sniffing out as much evidence as my old smeller can get a good whiff of. Another word of advice: I wouldn't tell your colleague anything. No client—no faulty discovery or conflict of interest can come into play. What has gone on between you and me is nothing more than just two old friends talking over possible theories. Understand what I'm saying here?"

"I see what you mean. Thanks, Vann. I know I can always count on you."

Asia was beside herself with a mixture of worry and rage. When she'd first gotten to the hospital, she was told Isaiah had requested that no visitors be allowed in to see him. No one on the staff could explain the reason for his strange instructions because he hadn't given any. Since he was an adult, Asia had no recourse whatsoever. That her only son would exclude her from his visiting list hurt more than anything else she'd ever experienced. She was even more saddened knowing that he also desired to cut off all communication with both Nicholas and Torri. Asia wasn't at all sympathetic to his unreasonable request, but she'd have to find the opportune time to enter his room without the permission of the nursing staff. She didn't want to make a scene, but she wasn't going to let these restrictions stay in existence another day.

Asia jumped up from her seat in the waiting area the moment Nicholas exited the elevator. It didn't take her long to explain Isaiah's position on visitors. Nicholas looked as stunned as she felt. Unlike Asia, he had no intentions of waiting for an appropriate time to get past the nursing staff. He didn't care about not making a scene, either. Taking hold of Asia's hand, he strode into the dark room.

Isaiah was definitely surprised to see them walk in. He had been so sure that his mother would honor his wishes, but he could see by the look on Nicholas's face that his father had no intention of doing any such thing. Nicholas pulled up two chairs and waited until Asia was seated before he sat down. He felt Asia's fingers trembling in his own hand as he held hers again.

Nicholas leaned over the bed rail. "If this is just your way of getting attention, Isaiah, you have certainly gotten ours. I expect the nurse to come in here any minute to throw us out. So, if you don't want to see me get arrested, I suggest you call the nurses' station and lift this silly visitation ban. I just pray that Torri hasn't already been subjected to this indignity you've chosen to impose on those of us who love you."

"Dad, you don't understand."

"I understand all that I need to." Nicholas heard the shuffling of feet at the door. "Your nurse is here to enforce your rights. If you really want us to leave, tell us that to our faces right now. Don't take the coward's way out by having someone else do the dirty work for you. Be a man about it, son." Nicholas didn't take his piercing eyes off Isaiah for one second.

Isaiah lifted his hand in a halting motion. "It's okay," he told the nurse. "They can stay."

"Thank you, son," Asia said in a shaky voice. "I don't understand why you'd do something this cruel to us, but it might help if you'd explain your actions. I need to know what's going on with you."

"I don't want anyone's pity, Mom, especially from you and Torri. I'm not the man I was and I never will be again. I know you have high hopes for my getting better, but it's not going to happen. You and Torri need to face that. I don't need or want to be pitied."

"So, what *do* you want from us?" Asia asked. "Pity isn't what we've given you thus far."

"I just want to be left alone until I can come to grips with what's happening to me. It's not going to help me one bit if I have to continuously look at sad faces with tears running down them. Please let me keep as much of my dignity as possible. Don't make me endure your heartache along with my own. I have to get my pain under control before I can even begin to deal with yours. I don't want to hurt you, but I know it'll happen if I don't take some time to try and pull it together for myself. I'm feeling like I'm only half a man right now."

Nicholas stood up. "You've made your point, Isaiah. Let's go, Asia. We may not like what he's proposing to us but we do have to respect it."

Asia started to protest but there was something in Nicholas's eyes that caused her to change her mind. She decided to hear Nicholas out before she told Isaiah what she really thought about his asinine request. More than for herself, she was concerned with what Isaiah's decision might do to Torri, the woman who loved him with all her heart. It wasn't like Torri didn't already have reservations regarding Isaiah's wanting to be saddled with their unborn child at the height of his career. Asia was sure that this bit of more bad news would positively crush young, beautiful, pregnant Torrianne Jefferson, the popular international supermodel who was loved by everyone that got to know the real her. She and Nicholas had worked so hard at convincing Torri that Isaiah would be ecstatic about the baby. What were they to tell their precious Torri now? That was the one question burning in Asia's mind.

Nicholas leaned over the bed and kissed Isaiah on both cheeks and his forehead. "Good luck in working everything out. Your mother and I will keep you in prayer."

Asia didn't understand the method to Nicholas's madness, yet she also embraced her son as she said her heartbreaking farewell. She managed to keep her emotions at bay as she walked out of Isaiah's room not knowing when she'd see her baby boy again. He had asked for space and had pretty much left them with no choice but to give it to him. Asia wondered how long Isaiah would keep them out of his life. She prayed for it not to be too terribly long.

Nicholas squeezed Asia's hand as she came up to him. He'd waited for her out in the hallway so she could have a private moment with their son. "It's going to be okay."

"Is it? Our son just practically threw his mother and father out of his room. How can I deal with that? And why did you give in to his ludicrous demands so easily? I thought we were going to put up one hell of a fight, Nicholas. We just threw in the towel without even trying to talk some sense into him. How in the world do we tell Torri—"

"Tell Torri what?"

Nicholas and Asia turned around as Torri's voice reached them. Attired in a beautiful silk dress, fashioned in bright colors, Torri looked like a fine spring day. As soft as a summer breeze, her light kisses fell on Nicholas and Asia's cheeks. "Is Isaiah okay?"

Asia looked to Nicholas to save the day. She didn't have the guts to tell Torri what they'd been told by Isaiah.

"Isaiah is fine, Torri. How are you doing?"

"I'm fine. But I'll even be better once I see my boo. Have you been in to see him?"

"We just came out," Nicholas responded. "Asia and I were just taking a break."

"Let me get out of your way. Take all the time you need. I'll be with Isaiah for a while."

Nicholas stopped Asia from revealing Isaiah's request to Torri. It was as if he'd seen Asia's apologetic words written in her eyes. Nicholas didn't feel that it was their place to enlighten Torri. That was Isaiah's job and Nicholas was content to let him handle it. Personally, he didn't think Isaiah would dare to send Torri away knowing she carried his baby. In fact, he was counting on him not being able to. That's why he'd asked the nurses to enforce his desires.

"I'll see you two a little later. Perhaps we can eat together after the visit."

"We'll be right out here for a while. If we decide to leave, we'll let you know," Asia said, glad that Torri hadn't pushed for an answer to her question about Isaiah being okay.

Nicholas and Asia watched as Torri bounced into the room, smiling like the first rays of a morning's sunshine. They could actually hear her gushing over Isaiah as she greeted her lover.

Asia turned to Nicholas. "I want you to answer the questions I asked before Torri showed up. Why did you allow him to have his way without a fight?"

"Battling with him wouldn't have done a bit of good, Asia. I don't feel that we did give in to him. Isaiah's being a bit selfish right now and we just have to let him work it out. If we coddle Isaiah and treat him like a baby, he's going to stay weak, without the least attempt at fighting to grow strong. We have to let him make his own decisions. He's a man, but you heard what he said. He feels as if he's only half of one. We have to allow him to find the other half of himself, the part that he thinks he's lost. I'm dispensable in Isaiah's life simply because I've never been there for him to lean on and for him to receive guidance from. As for you, that's a totally different story. You've always been there for him—and in every way imaginable. He moved you out here to California because he needed you to be near him. He can never ignore what you mean to him. Once he has to do without you for a few days, he'll come to his senses. I'm willing to bet my practice on it. It's up to him to tell Torri everything that's going on."

"But he has done without me for days and weeks at a time. When he's on the road with the team, I'm not there for him then. He also attended college away from home for four years."

"A completely different set of circumstances. There are times in situations like these when you just have to walk away and let God have complete control. We're not walking out on him. Just giving his spirit time to heal. His needs aren't the same now as when he was at college or away with the team. He needs you now more than he's ever needed anything in his life, Asia."

"Besides you, because he definitely needed you while growing up. I just ignored all the obvious signs."

"We've settled that issue between us. There's no need to keep revisiting it. We're now living from moment to moment and in those moments. Let's not bog ourselves down with the past when Isaiah's future is still at risk. You're going to have to ride this current storm out, too. Don't think for a minute that Isaiah can cut you out of his life just like that. It's impossible."

"I bet you once thought it was impossible for me to cut you out of my life with such ease, but I did it. There was nothing easy about it, yet I somehow managed to pull it off."

He shook his head. "I'm not going back there with you. Stay grounded in this moment, Asia. I'm going to keep reminding you of that until you see that the past is best laid to rest."

"Okay, so let me change the subject. What eventually happened with you and Miranda after you left my house? Did you two finally get your issues resolved?"

Nicholas threw his head back in laughter. "Miranda is also in the past, Asia, my past. But I'm going to share something with you that you might find very interesting. I can promise you that you'll receive crystal clarity regarding what's really going on with Miranda. I'm only asking that this conversation stay between us. I've never breathed a word to anyone of what I'm about to tell you—and I have no intentions of addressing this matter ever again. Can you keep my confidence in what I'm about to share with you?"

With her curiosity fully aroused, Asia nodded at the same time she gave a verbal agreement to his conditions.

Nicholas began his story by going back to the beginning of his history with Miranda. He wended his way through their later decision to marry, Miranda's request for a legal separation, and then his decision to file for divorce, both parties in agreement.

Asia couldn't help having jealous feelings over the time, however brief, he'd shared with Miranda, knowing she herself had been the only one Nicholas had ever wanted to share his entire life with. He didn't want her to live in the past but it was hard to let go of. It was even harder for her to stop riding her own back about the unspeakable decision she'd made that had significantly altered three lives, not just hers.

Asia stared at Nicholas in disbelief. "You're kidding! I don't believe it."

Nicholas shrugged. "It's true, every bit of it. So, if I were you, I wouldn't continue to worry about what Miranda thinks or feels at this point. What I've told you is the reason I don't let her not-so-little, treacherous escapades get completely under my skin."

"Does she know that you know?"

"Like I said in the beginning of this conversation, I've never breathed a word of this to anyone until now."

"Amazing. You are truly an amazing man. I can't believe you haven't said a word about this, especially to Miranda."

"It's time for us to change the subject again. I've washed my hands of that one." He looked at the large wall clock. "Torri hasn't come out yet and it's been over twenty minutes since she went in. I didn't think Isaiah would be so insensitive as to send her away knowing she's pregnant. I hope I'm right."

"Torri is a lot like me, stubborn as can be. So, she could be telling him she's not trying to hear a word of what he has to say. I wouldn't be a bit surprised at that."

After pondering it for a couple of seconds, Asia wasn't so sure about what she'd just said to Nicholas. Torri could be very stubborn, but her emotions were rather fragile even before her pregnancy. If Isaiah gave any indication that he didn't want her around, she would probably take it to mean that he didn't want the baby either. What else could she think? Asia prayed hard that Isaiah wouldn't make the same mistake with Torri that she'd made with Nicholas. That history kept repeating itself in this instance was a mind-blower for Asia. At her every turn, Asia's past mistakes were right before her, glaring brightly in her face like a neon sign.

* * *

"Torri, I'm not saying I want our relationship to be over. That's not it."

"Then what is it, Ike? You have to spell it out for me. I'm not going to stand here and try to guess at what you're saying. I shouldn't have to do that. We've been together too long for that kind of nonsense."

Isaiah sighed hard. "It's just that I'm in no position to make a commitment to anyone or anything. I don't know how long I'm going to be laid up."

"Do you consider our baby anyone or anything, Isaiah? You said you were happy for us."

"Torri, no! I didn't mean to imply that." He pressed his hand against his forehead. "Girl, I just need some space to figure this all out. Can you give that much to me for now?"

"I can give you all the space you need, Isaiah Reynolds Morrell. In fact, you can have this whole damn planet to yourself. Is that enough space for you? I hope so, 'cause I can't give you any more than I've already given." Without waiting for any response from Isaiah, Torri hurried from the room, tears blurring her vision.

As Torri swept past Nicholas and Asia, stumbling about as if she were drunk, Nicholas immediately went after her. At the elevator, Nicholas's arm snaked around her waist and turned her to face him. "Don't run away from this, Torri. He's not himself."

"Oh, he's himself all right. His arrogance is shining like a newly minted coin. After all the time I've put into this relationship, he had the nerve to ask me to give him space. I've given him nothing but his space ever since he entered the NBA. He can't have any more. There's no room left for me to operate outside of his space now that we're having a baby. He doesn't want this baby but he's too morality-conscious to tell me that. If this doesn't take all."

Nicholas rubbed her back in a soothing manner. "His fear is doing the talking, Torri. Knowing he may never walk again has him feeling like he's not whole . . ." The look on Torri's face was downright alarming to Nicholas. Her healthy complexion had turned pale in a matter of seconds. Then it dawned on him that Isaiah hadn't told her why he'd made the request. He hadn't told her he was paralyzed. But it had been days since he was told. How could she not know?

"Did I hear you right? Isaiah may never walk again? Please tell me I didn't hear you say that." Tears glistening in her eyes, she turned and looked back down the hall at the entry to his room. "I . . . I had . . . no idea. Mr. Nick, he . . . never . . . uttered a word." Torri appeared to be in a state of shock. Her hand went to her stomach in a protective gesture. "Oh, no, I yelled at him. He was only trying to shield me from the truth. That has to be it. His behavior makes sense now. I've got to go back to him. He needs me whether he wants to admit it or not. Both the baby and I need him regardless of his physical condition. We love him and that's not going to change ever."

Nicholas stayed her with a gentle hand when it appeared she might tip right over. Asia joined them at the elevator just as Nicholas steadied Torri on her feet.

"Take it easy, sweetie," Nicholas soothed. "Let's sit down over here until you regain your composure. Asia, take care of her while I go get some water. She just learned the truth about Isaiah's medical status. He didn't tell her, but I assumed he had." Feeling horrible about his blunder, Nicholas walked away from the waiting room area in haste.

Asia sat down with Torri and took hold of her trembling hand. "I'm sorry you had to find out like that. Nicholas is blameless. We both thought you knew by the way you stumbled out of the room and down the hallway. Nicholas and I have been worried about the lack of movement in Isaiah's lower body for some time now. We didn't want to give cause for alarm since a firm diagnosis hadn't yet come from his doctors. That's why we haven't said anything to you."

"Do we have one now?"

"He's paralyzed from the waist down, Torri. I'm sorry to be the one to tell you—and I understand why Isaiah couldn't. He's not taking this very well right now. We have to give him time to get used to the idea."

Torri frowned. "Do you really think he should do that? Get used to it?"

"Oh, not at all," Nicholas interjected as he handed Torri a bottle of water. "That's not something he should ever get used to. To me, that means he has to think and act in the negative to try and arrive at a positive. It won't work. For him to get used to and accept his condition shouldn't be an option for him. He can only believe that he's going to walk again despite what the doctors say. They're not God. They cannot determine the outcome of any part of his life. Only the power of God can do that. But we do have to give him a little time to think things through. Then we have to be there to help him, encourage him to only think positive, and then to rely on and trust in God to pull him through. There's still a good chance that he's paralyzed from the drugs, which may mean his condition isn't permanent. We can't rule it out."

Torri looked puzzled, so Nicholas took the time to explain to her what he'd learned about certain types of drugs and how they had a tendency to induce paralysis, especially when administered in large doses. He didn't tell Asia or Torri that he now had a motive for what could have possibly happened to Isaiah and that he believed his prime suspects were Troy, Sheldon, and possibly a few others. If Vann's investigation proved true, the heads of the major players involved in this incident were definitely going to roll.

"Thanks for the information and also for caring. I understand the risk you've taken. No one will ever find out from me that you called."

Nicholas hung up the phone and then stretched out on his bed to ponder the conversation he'd just had with one of Isaiah's nurses. Fearful of losing her job for providing him with privileged information on a patient, she had sworn Nicholas to absolute secrecy. He couldn't believe that Isaiah had lasted this long without at least reaching out to his mother. Nearly a week had already passed and not a word had come to anyone from his son. Both Torri and Asia were devastated by Isaiah's refusal to see them, but Nicholas had been able to convince them to wait it out. As things stood now, he didn't see Asia waiting too much longer. In fact, as far as Nicholas was concerned, the waiting game was over, period.

The time for stalling his family had run out on Isaiah. He was taking this madness too far. Determined that nothing would get in his way of seeing his son, Nicholas got up from the bed and headed to the shower. Isaiah's refusing to do recommended physical therapy, according to his nurse, was the last straw. Isaiah's feeling like half a man or no man at all wasn't going to stop Nicholas from giving Isaiah a verbal butt-kicking to the curb.

Isaiah had stated that he didn't want anyone's pity, but it was obvious to Nicholas that Isaiah hadn't included himself in that statement. His son was guilty of throwing a private, ongoing pity party for himself. Nicholas's last thought before stepping into the shower was that Reynolds men don't quit at anything.

Miranda was about to ring the bell when Nicholas opened the door to retrieve the morning's newspaper. His expression told her that she was the last person he wanted to deal with at the beginning of his day. "Did I come at a bad time, Nick?"

"Lately there hasn't been a good time for us, Miranda. I can't imagine this morning being any different. What happened to courtesy calling? Is it unfashionable these days to call someone's house before you show up there? You seem to pop up all over the place, uninvited."

She shrugged. "We're not just someone to each other, Nick. We're husband and wife."

"Ah, yes, lest I should forget, Miranda will constantly come around to remind me of that legality without the reality of such. You and I have not been a husband and wife to each other for quite some time now, even before you moved downstairs into the guest bedroom." He threw up his hands. "I don't know why I keep repeating the facts since you know them as well as I do. Good morning, Miranda. So nice to see you. What can I do for you on this wonderful day?"

She ignored his sarcasm as she pushed past him.

Before she could get too far into the house, he grabbed her arm, spun her around, and then led her the few steps back to the entrance. "To answer your earlier question. Miranda, you have come at a very bad time. I'm on my way out."

"You didn't look like you were on your way out to me. It seems to me you were getting ready to read the newspaper, a part of your normal routine. Are you trying to hide something? Did your little girlfriend spend the night here instead of you staying with her?"

"Girlfriend! Oh, Miranda, we're not in high school or college. We're supposed to be grown folks leading adult lives. Maybe you're living back in the day, but I'm not. Perhaps you've forgotten your age. I don't know, but you're sure not acting like a mature woman."

"What's that supposed to mean, Nick?"

"Maybe you should tell me. Perhaps it wasn't you I saw mooning over a young man half your age, a teenybopper of some sort. If not, it sure as hell looked like you."

Miranda looked stunned. "I don't know what you're talking about.

If you saw me with any man, it had to be about business. Or he was a patient."

"I'm not sure it was business, but you were certainly busy enough. As for him being a man, he looked as if he'd barely cleared puberty."

Miranda's face turned beet red. "I'm not going to get into some bull like this with you. You're trying to accuse me of something vulgar to use against me in court because I've caught you with that woman on several occasions, including the compromising position of you in her bed. And I also have pictures. I'm out of here. I won't allow you to falsely slander me."

"Just what I thought you'd say. Sure you don't want to stay and talk this over? Maybe we should take those marriage-counseling sessions after all. I'm sure our pastor is still willing to counsel us. What do you say to that, Miranda? Still want to try to make something good out of what's been absolutely nothing but bad for us, which we both agreed upon?"

"Go to hell, Nick!"

"Doesn't feel so good to have someone degrade you and try to make you feel smaller than small, does it, Miranda?" he yelled after her retreating back. "It can feel even worse when it's done in the eyes of the public. You'd better be careful out there. It's a cruel, cold world."

Asia had been concerned about Torri all day. She realized Torri was not her usual bubbly self as she watched her closely. Seeing the sweat trickling down Torri's face gave Asia cause for alarm. Practically leaping out of the chair, Asia rushed to Torri's side when it looked like she might topple over. After helping Torri to get situated on the sofa, Asia sat down next to her.

Asia pushed Torri's hair back from her sweat-drenched face. "I'm really worried about you, Torri. You're looking so pale. Do you think I need to call your doctor?"

Torri shook her head gingerly; it felt as if her brain had exploded inside it. "I'm fine. Just a dizzy spell, probably brought on from not eating. Haven't had much of an appetite for anything lately. I'll be okay in a minute or two."

Asia removed two pillows from the ends of her couch and plumped them. "Here, lie back on the sofa and prop your feet up on these two pillows. I'm going to fix you something to eat. I'll set up a snack tray and bring your food to you here in the den. I don't want you to move a fraction of an inch." Asia thought of the similar experience Nicholas had had while under stress.

Torri nodded. "Okay, Mommy-Asia. I won't flex even a single muscle."

Torri smiled but Asia noticed that it had failed to light in her beautiful eyes. Asia was worried about Torri and the baby. She was under way too much stress. Isaiah cutting off all communication with his girlfriend had her more than a little skittish. Asia could tell that the young woman hadn't had much sleep by the slight bags under her eyes. And Torri had just openly admitted to poor eating habits. Isaiah's stubbornness was taking everyone on a wild ride.

"The soup and the sandwich were really good. What kind of meat did you use?"

"Smoked turkey. I'm surprised you haven't tasted it before since it's one of Isaiah's favorites for sandwiches."

"You know that I'm not too much into eating animal flesh. I'm not a total vegetarian, but there are times when I don't touch meat for weeks."

"I haven't forgotten how careful you are about your diet. I just thought Isaiah might've fixed a sandwich for you at some time or other at his place. He keeps smoked turkey on hand. Are you feeling any better, Torri?"

"I am, thanks to you. What time is it?"

Asia looked down at her watch. "Just a little before noon. Do you have something to do?"

"Not really. I came over here because I wanted to talk to you about the baby and a few other personal matters." Torri looked apprehensive. "I need some advice. Since you've been in the position I'm now in, I thought you might be able to help me out. How did your parents take it when they first learned you were pregnant?"

Asia smiled gently, hating to bring up all the bad memories of that horrific time, yet knowing Torri wouldn't have asked the question without good reason. "Not very well. My father actually disowned me.

My mother went along with his appalling decision because what he said was more important to her than how her only daughter felt. My dad's feelings meant more to her than how her only child, a pregnant one, was going to manage without the love and support of her parents. I somehow get the impression that you haven't told your parents that you're carrying Isaiah's child. Am I right?"

Torri looked abashed. "Mom and Dad love Isaiah but they are going to throw multiple conniption fits if I ever find the nerve to tell them. My mom is puritanical and my dad is something of a charlatan. She hasn't always been so morally strict and he's not all that he pretends to be. I've actually heard Mom tell some of her female friends stories about herself as a young, wild, out-of-control woman. I've not only heard crazy stories about my dad from his brothers, I've seen him in action for myself. My parents weren't born with and didn't grow up with any sort of social standing. But you wouldn't know that if you heard my dad tell some of his outlandish stories. You'd swear the man was born with a silver spoon in his sometimes less-than-truthful mouth. Their bourgeoisie attitudes are nothing more than an acquired taste rather than any family legacy. But they have always loved their baby girl to death. I'm ultrasecure in that."

"I'm not an envious woman by nature, but I certainly envy you that kind of assurance. How I wish I could've boasted of my parents' love for me, and done it with so much confidence. That must be an amazing feeling. If you're that secure in their love, what are you afraid of?"

"I'm not exactly fearful of telling them about the baby. It's their deep disappointment in me that I fear most. I have already imagined seeing the unhappiness in their eyes a thousand times. Knowing how they've had to work hard to purchase their prestige and social standing, in their sight, I came by it naturally. I'm their free pass to high-society social events."

"I can understand why you'd fear the disappointment, Torri. Been there, done that."

"Ashton and Saressa Jefferson's daughter is the famous supermodel whose photographs grace the inside pages and outside covers of top publications all over the world. That's the kind of legacy they couldn't lay claim to, yet their daughter can. They wear my so-called celebrity status better than I do. Isaiah would make them the perfect son-in-law. He also has a wonderful legacy to offer, not to mention his own superstar ranking. But would they feel the same way about him if he were a sanitation technician or a maintenance man? I don't know. In light of the fact that the story of my pregnancy is probably going to receive worldwide attention, they're not going to do well in handling what they'll consider public embarrassment." Torri sighed heavily. "You see what I mean?"

"Clearly. I've come to learn that the people who are the most critical of others are carrying around the same kind of heavy baggage as those they criticize. They can point our your flaws with ease but fail to see their own. My parents were deep into their religion, but they failed to adhere to one of God's most profound messages: love one another."

"Are you very religious? We haven't ever talked about that subject."

"I'm more of a spiritual being than a religious one. I believe in God with all my heart and soul. I have a very personal relationship with Him, but it's carried on within me rather than inside the church sanctuary. I'm not much of a churchgoer. But I do believe people should attend worship services for fellowship and numerous other benefits. I just haven't found a place that I can call my home. My parents lived in the church, but I'm not so sure what good it did them, especially when they could so easily harden their hearts against their own flesh and blood."

"I hear you. My parents attend church every week, and they raised me in the church, but they're hardly religious or spiritual. They're really good people and I love them as much as they love me. However, being overly status-conscious and keeping up with the Joneses are their biggest issues. I've never had to concern myself with how Mom and Dad treat me, but I don't like how they sometimes treat others, especially the people they feel are beneath them. It's not a pretty sight."

Torri suddenly got a funny look in her eyes. Her hands then flew up to her face. "I'm so embarrassed. I think I peed on myself and I didn't even feel it coming." She jumped up from the couch and twisted herself at an awkward angle trying to see the stain on her pants. The bright red spots caused her immediate alarm. "Oh, no, I'm spotting!" she cried out. "The baby!"

Asia leaped into action the second she realized what was happening with Torri. Keeping Torri calm was a must in this delicate situation. Spotting didn't necessarily mean she was having a miscarriage, but it was certainly an indication of something seriously wrong. Asia believed that Torri's professional training as a nurse would be helpful in her keeping her wits about herself. She knew that Torri losing control might prove disastrous for her and her unborn child.

Nicholas waited a few minutes after the nurse left the room before he approached Isaiah's hospital bed. The young man had his eyes closed, but it didn't appear to his father that he was asleep. Nicholas stood by and quietly watched his son for nearly a full minute, praying within his heart that this meeting would go well. Even though he was prepared to take Isaiah to task over his unreasonable behavior toward his family, he hoped it didn't have to come down to that. Nicholas was still extremely mindful of the seriousness of what his son had to cope with.

Mentally and emotionally ready to get on with what he'd come there for, Nicholas leaned over the bed and grazed Isaiah's lips with his own. Isaiah slowly opened his eyes and then tried to bring into focus the shadowy figure leaning over him.

"Dad," he said in a raspy voice, "you don't give up, do you?"

"And neither should you. How are you feeling?"

Isaiah flexed his fingers, wishing he could do the same with the lower part of his anatomy. "I guess okay. No use in complaining. It's not going to change anything."

Nicholas immediately recognized the sound of defeat and hopelessness in Isaiah's voice. It seemed as if he'd totally given up, that there was no fight left in him. Nicholas figured that Isaiah's decision to give up was the reason it no longer mattered to him that his father had violated his right to privacy. Isaiah hadn't called on his family simply because he'd thrown in the towel, believing the game was over and that he couldn't possibly win.

"Your attitude about this can change everything, son. How have the parties been going?"

Isaiah frowned. "What parties?"

"The pity parties you've been throwing for yourself ever since you came out of the coma. You tell us you don't want to be pitied by us, but you need to stop pitying yourself. You're alive, man! Doesn't that count for something?"

"Not when you're looking at a fate worse than death. Dad, my legs are how I make my living. Without them, I can't take care of me or anyone else."

"Don't you have a brain? Are you saying you think with your legs and not your brilliant mind? Aren't you the one who was boasting to me about your high grade-point average? Didn't you earn a degree in communications?"

"That was the old Isaiah inside a healthy body. The body I'm in now is useless."

"Isaiah, give yourself and me a break, will you?" Nicholas snatched a cafeteria menu off the bedside stand and slapped it down on the tray table. Taking an ink pen out of his pocket, he put it in Isaiah's hand. "Write down your name for me."

Isaiah looked at his father as if he'd lost his mind. "For what?"

"Just do it," Nicholas thundered, shouting to make a point.

Curious as to what Nicholas was after, Isaiah did as he was told. When he finished, Nicholas had him read some of the items listed on the menu. He then put a glass of orange juice into his son's hand and told him to drink a few sips of it. Once that was accomplished, Nicholas challenged Isaiah's on his other senses: sight, smell, hearing and touch.

"What are you trying to prove by all this?"

"That your body is not useless, Isaiah. You can still see, taste, smell, and hear, and you have feeling in your upper body. You possess a brilliant mind and you are certainly employable with the impressive credentials you've earned through your college studies. You can't define yourself by your career choice. Basketball may be all you want to do, but you can't play the game forever no matter how healthy you are. There is life after basketball and you're already educationally qualified to handle another professional career. If you can't play the game, you can always call it. There's nothing wrong with your voice. It might be a little weak right now, but that's to be expected. Though he's gone now, if Chic Hearn got back into the swing of things despite his age and serious health issues, so can you. God rest his soul."

Nicholas got right up close and personal with Isaiah. "Are you hearing me, son? If you're not, you'd better get your butt in gear. Just as I'm in your face now, I'm going to stay there until you decide to jump back into the game of life. No ban placed on me by you or anyone else in this hospital is going to stop me from exercising my rights to act like any other responsible father when his son's very existence is at stake. Together, with God, we can beat the odds, or at least lower them. That's what we're shooting for. We will do what we have to do."

Isaiah wanted to protest but he knew nothing he had to say would make one ounce of sense to his father. Besides, his father was absolutely right. How could he argue with the truth? He couldn't. But his courage was practically nonexistent. How could he regain his valor in the face of such incredible adversity? He didn't know the answer, but Isaiah had just received the blessed assurance that his father would be around to help him figure it out, a comforting thought.

Without taking his eyes off his son, Nicholas answered his cell phone. His eyes clouded with concern as Asia informed him that Torri was in the emergency room at Valley Memorial Hospital, right around the corner from Asia's home. He gasped when he got the full impact of what was happening. "I'll be right there."

"What's wrong, Dad? You look like you just got some bad news."

"I've got to go, but I want you to think long and hard about what I've told you. Torri needs you. She's in Valley Memorial Hospital threatened with the possibility of a miscarriage. Asia's with her. It's time for you to start thinking about someone other than yourself for a change. Your family needs your strength. You don't want to fail them at a time like this."

Nicholas walked out of the room despite Isaiah shouting for him to come back and explain things to him. He never would've walked out on his son after delivering such bad news, but Nicholas thought Isaiah needed an even harder, colder dose of reality than that of his own situation. It just might be what he needed to get himself motivated into fighting his way back to life. He needed to let the possibility of Torri losing their baby sink into his head and inside his heart until he couldn't stand not knowing her fate or that of his child. Perhaps Torri's own medical dilemma would force Isaiah to do something about his negative attitude. If that didn't do it, Nicholas was determined to try anything and everything that would eventually make Isaiah see the light.

The war for his son's survival was on; any means necessary would be the weapons used.

CHAPTER THIRTEEN

A sia couldn't have been happier or more relieved to see Nicholas enter the hospital ER waiting room. Medical emergencies were happening way too often. Medical facilities were a scary thing for her to have to wait in alone. This trip to the hospital with Torri reminded her so much of the time she'd recently spent waiting to hear the least bit of news about Isaiah. She had waited for hours before someone on the staff came out to talk with her regarding his condition. Torri had already been in the examining room for over an hour and no one had made any attempt to speak with Asia.

Nicholas bent over and hugged Asia before seating himself next to her. "What's been happening? Have you heard anything yet?"

"Not a word. I'm extremely worried."

"Tell me about it. Does anyone on the staff know you're here with Torri?"

"I assume so. I came inside with her but they immediately whisked her away."

"Maybe I should inquire about her. It looks like a really busy time for the ER staff. This room is packed."

"That might not be such a bad idea, Nicholas. I probably should've done that already."

He leaned across the seat and kissed her forehead. "Be right back. Hold tight."

Asia watched after Nicholas as he made his way to the registration desk. He was such a confident man. There were so many things that still made Nicholas such an appealing man. He was a very caring soul, a genuine human being. But she'd thrown that all away in the midst of her fears while at the same time misinterpreting his true feelings for her.

Asia had just recently begun to realize that the reason she had had no idea Nicholas loved her was that during that time she often felt unlovable. She didn't know what it was to be loved or how it actually felt, so how could she have recognized it when it came knocking? While she believed her parents loved her in their own strange way, there was never any outward show of it. Rarely were hugs and kisses exchanged between them; even when she'd gotten up the nerve to ask for affection, her request had always been totally ignored. It was as if she were invisible. So she'd gotten in the habit of staying in her room and only coming out for meals or when her presence was required or requested, which wasn't very often.

The years of her youth had rolled by, with her enduring interminable silence and unfathomable sadness. Just thinking of those yesteryears made her shrink inside. It was only with Nicholas that she had learned to receive and give affection. Her need for love and affection was nearly insatiable back then. After learning she was pregnant, she'd made a promise to shower her child with constant love and adoration, a vow she'd never even come close to breaking.

Asia thought of her earlier conversation with Torri. If Torri's parents were to turn their backs on her, Asia vowed to give Torri everything that she herself had been denied by her own parents. Torri would not suffer like she'd been made to, not for one solitary moment.

Nicholas lowered himself back down into the seat. "The doctor is still in with her. I had to lie to get that little bit of information. I told the desk clerk I was her dad. Hopefully Torri understands it's just me when they mention that her father is anxiously waiting to see her."

"She'll know it's you. I told her I planned to call you and that I was sure you'd rush right over here. She's so scared of losing the baby and Isaiah. It was all she talked about on the drive here." Asia's voice weakened considerably as she warred with her emotions.

It was rare for Asia to be angry with her son, but she was irritated and saddened by his selfish behavior. She didn't blame her son for

Torri's present situation, but she was holding him fully responsible for the emotional pain he'd unnecessarily inflicted on the mother of his baby. Asia was also aware that Torri had gotten very little rest since Isaiah's hospitalization, which could count in part for her medical problems. Her poor eating habits and the constant stress she appeared to be under were the other culprits. Dealing with the question of how she was going to break the news to her parents could've pushed her over the edge.

"I guess we weren't prepared for lighting to strike twice in such a short span of time. You going to be okay, Asia?" He reached up and wiped her tears with the pads of his fingers.

"I hope so. I was thinking about Torri. I just can't get over the similarities of the circumstances surrounding our pregnancies. She's fearful of telling her parents about the baby, just as I was. Torri says their disappointment in her will be deep. But she's also certain of their love for her. I wish I could've said that. But that's all in the past."

"No, it's not; not when it still hurts you the way it does. Letting go means total absolution for everyone or everything that has hurt you. Have you truly forgiven your parents, Asia?"

"There were times when I was sure I had. Then, on the times when I'd do a total recall of my life with them, I'd have a tendency to let resentment rule my heart. It's no longer like that. Although I'm deeply saddened when I think about certain painful instances, I no longer hold them accountable. To answer your question, yes, I have truly forgiven my parents. In my growth, I've come to know that my happiness is totally my responsibility. I'm the only caretaker of me."

"That's good to hear. Now we have to get our son to adopt your philosophy. He has to take total responsibility for any and all decisions pertaining to his future. Being happy or sad is his choice to make. I hope he makes the right one. Paralyzed or not, he still has a lot to offer."

"Oh, my goodness, Isaiah doesn't even know what's happening to Torri. Do you think we should break his visiting ban so that we can inform him of her medical situation?"

"He already knows about it."

"How? Did you go there after I talked with you?"

"I was already in his room when you called."

Asia raised an eyebrow. "You broke the ban?"

"I did my best to destroy it. I received a confidential call this morning from one of his nurses. After she told me Isaiah had refused to begin physical therapy, I went there to speak my mind." Nicholas gave Asia a thorough rundown on what had transpired between himself and Isaiah. "I had just finished verbally kicking his butt when you called. I said a couple of other things to him and then I told him about Torri. I intentionally walked out on him before he could say anything. He yelled for me to come back and explain, but I kept going like I never heard him. I thought he needed time to worry about someone other than himself. If my plan worked the way I hope for, he may already be trying to get out of that bed."

"What if your plans backfire?"

"I won't bother to think about that until it actually happens. I take on things as they come. If we take on the burden of everything that might or could happen, we'd be too worn out to deal with the things staring us right in the face. Torri and the baby are my priorities right now. What about you?"

"The same. Your ideology has been rubbing off on me. I'm starting to believe in the method of your madness."

"Why not think of it as the method to my sanity? I refuse to go mad regarding things I have no control over. I can't change the color of the sky. Recognizing that I'm powerless to do so means I realize I can't control it. Knowing what I can and can't control helps me in making wise choices and decisions. Isaiah may not have the power to change his physical condition, but only he can control how he's going to handle it."

"Is it really that simple for you?"

"Most of the time. It only gets complicated when I forget to include God in my daily routine. I very seldom start my day without Him, or end it without prayer to Him. But on occasion I have allowed myself to get too busy to talk to God. Very little goes right for me when that happens." Nicholas nudged Asia. "Here comes a nurse." He jumped to his feet. "Are our girl, Torri Jefferson, and our grandchild doing okay?"

Nurse Rayburn smiled as she introduced herself. "Both mother and baby are doing well. However, we're going to keep her overnight for observation. Once she goes home, she's going to need complete bed rest for a while. She'd love to see you if you're up to it. You two have a lovely daughter. She's been very brave."

"We're up to it all right," Asia responded. "We can hardly wait."

The nurse took a note out of her uniform pocket and handed it to Nicholas. "This is for you. It's from your son. He phoned the ER desk. He was very concerned about Ms. Jefferson."

"Our son?" Nicholas asked, puzzled by the remark.

"That's who he said he was. If you'll follow me, I'll take you to your daughter. She's anxious to see you."

Nicholas exchanged bewildered glances with Asia. "Did you actually talk to our son?"

"The gentleman only told me that his parents were probably in the ER waiting room or possibly in with Ms. Jefferson. He didn't give me your names. I just assumed you were the couple since I was told you were here with Ms. Jefferson. Was I wrong?"

"No, you have the right people. I'm just surprised that my son called himself. You see, he's in the hospital too, Cedars Sinai. He was hurt in a terrible car accident," Nicholas said.

The nurse's eyes clearly showed her sympathy for the couple. "I'm sorry. You two really do have your hands full. I'd better hurry and get you in to see your daughter before you have to leave for the other hospital to see about your son."

Relieved to see Nicholas and Asia, Torri broke down and cried. Asia sat down on one side of her and Nicholas took the other side. Each of them touched and caressed her in their own soothing ways. Asia was crying too, on the inside, but she couldn't let Torri see her vulnerability.

"I was so scared," Torri sobbed. "I was sure I was losing the baby when I saw the spots of blood. Thank God that I didn't miscarry. I'm going to do everything the doctors tell me. I couldn't go on if I lost my baby. I was uncertain about this pregnancy in the beginning, but I want this baby more than I've ever desired anything. I will also be the very best mother that I can." Torri's sobs weren't coming as hard as before but her tears hadn't slowed a bit.

Nicholas dabbed at Torri's eyes with a tissue. "It's going to be okay, sweetheart. You're going to be a great mom. Just like your Mommy-Asia." He gave Torri a warm hug.

Asia squeezed Torri's hand. "I hear they're going to keep you here overnight. Do you need us to do anything for you? Anyone you want us to call?"

Torri shook her head. "Thanks, but I don't need a thing. I'll call my parents when I get home tomorrow."

"You'll have to call them from my house. You're coming home with me for a few days. I'm going to take care of you until you're feeling much better. I'm going to cook for you, too, and you're going to eat," Asia said firmly. "Bed rest will be the only thing on your agenda."

"Sounds like someone has some pampering coming. Wish it was me," Nicholas teased. "I could use some looking after, too, Mommy-Asia." Asia cracked up at Nicholas's comment.

Torri laughed but it was short-lived. Her face clouded as she thought about Isaiah asking for space. "If and when Isaiah ever decides to see or speak to you, I don't want him to know what happened to me. Since he's asked for space, I'm sure he doesn't care one way or the other about the baby and me. I know he's not in his right mind, but that's when you're supposed to draw close to the people you love, not push them away. I wish Isaiah needed me the way I do him. I once thought that everything about our relationship was mutual. I guess I was wrong."

Asia ran her fingers through Torri's hair. "He does need you, desperately so. He just doesn't know how to admit it yet, to you or himself."

"Torri, Isaiah already knows what's happening. I told him. I was in his room when Asia called. I went to see him without his permission, deciding I didn't need his approval any longer. I'm the parent and he's the child regardless of how old he gets. But you know what? The nurse gave me a note saying he wants to see us. Torri, he called himself. That speaks volumes to me. He could've had one of his nurses call, but he didn't. We'll have to wait and see to be sure, but I think this might be the spark needed to get his engine revved up. Think you can hang in there with him a bit longer? He does need you as much as you need him, if not more." Nicholas went on to explain to Torri how he'd intentionally ignored Isaiah's attempt to get more information regarding her hospitalization. "I won't ever give up on him, but getting him not to give up on himself is the concern. I sort of kicked him to the curb with my mouthy threats."

Torri managed a weak smile. "You're a tough-love daddy, aren't you, Mr. Nick? What you did probably didn't make sense to anyone but you. I didn't get it at first, either. But I can now see how it might help to motivate Isaiah. If he thinks his own daddy sees his actions as wimping out, he just may put up a fight to try and prove you wrong. Let's hope so. To answer your question, I can hang in there with Isaiah for an eternity. The question should be this: Does Isaiah want me to hang around? He's the one who all but told me to get lost."

The trio looked up when Nurse Rayburn came back into the room. The seriously troubled look on her face put everyone on high alert. It seemed she was at a loss for words as she stood in the center of the room, staring at them like they were alien escapees from *Men In Black II.*

Nicholas got to his feet. "Is something wrong? Are you okay?"

She looked at Nicholas for a couple more seconds. "Your son called again. He inquired of Miss Jefferson's health and that of his child. I asked him if he meant to say his nephew or niece, but he made it clear that he was the father of Miss Jefferson's son . . ."

Nicholas's loud laughter turned all eyes on him. "I think I know what you're thinking. Let me assure you that Isaiah and Torri are not sister and brother. Isaiah is our son and Torri here, his girlfriend, is carrying our first grandchild. We love her as if she were our daughter. I told the desk clerk I was her father to learn about her condition. I'm sorry for the duplicity that led you astray."

Asia's body tingled all over at Nicholas's use of the word "our." He seemed so proud when proclaiming what belonged to him and her, as if they were still one. Asia wasn't a bit surprised by him professing his love for Torri. It was apparent in his every interaction with her.

The nurse looked 110 percent relieved. Then her face broke into a huge grin as her body shook with laughter. "You have no idea how many prayers I sent up for you all between the nurses' station and this room. I feel like an old fool. But I'm glad to have made a fool of myself rather than to have confirmed for me what I so foolishly thought. This situation is a perfect example of how rumors get started." She winked at Nicholas. "Thank goodness I'm a Christian woman. No gossip gets past these sweet lips."

The others laughed as the nurse rolled her eyes to the ceiling.

Asia smiled with warmth. "I'm glad things were cleared up for you. I can see why you came to that conclusion. We did say our son was in another hospital. Sorry for the confusion."

Torri giggled. "What you thought is too wild for me. Isaiah and I are often told we look like sister and brother, but you now know that we're not. You really would've flipped out had you seen him before you found out the truth." Torri suppressed another bout of giggles.

"Okay, now that we've painstakingly established how foolish I was, it's time for me to get back to the business of taking care of our patient. Miss Jefferson, you have to say good-bye to your boyfriend's parents for now. We need to get you up to your room on the fourth floor. They can sit with you later on, during the evening visiting hours."

Asia and Nicholas were shocked by what they saw upon entering Isaiah's room. Everything that had once been near his bed or stationed on his bedside table had been knocked to the floor, including the pillows. Both the plastic water cup and pitcher were cracked and the clear liquid had spilled. Isaiah was lying flat on his back staring up at the ceiling. He didn't so much as bat an eyelash when they came and stood over him.

Nicholas grinned. "Looks like you've had a great time in here. You must've worn your body out. Finally knocked yourself flat on your back, huh? Sure hope you can afford to pay for the cup and pitcher you've broken."

"Mom, see if you can get Mr. Funny Guy an audition on *BET Comic View*. Maybe he can take his comedy routine to someone who might appreciate it. I don't."

"Oh, so you're talking to Mommy now? It's nice to hear your voice and even nicer to be summoned to your room. What's up, Isaiah?" Asia smiled and was glad she'd taken the risk of reading a chapter from Nicholas's self-help book.

"Maybe you should audition, too, Mom. Why you all fronting me like that?"

"Ooh, the boy done went into his sack of slang and pulled out some words he thinks we're too old or not fly enough to decipher," Nicholas joked. "Your daddy may have been around the block a few hundred times, but he keeps up with the happenings. Now that we know you think we're good enough to appear on *Comic View*, why don't you tell us why you called us to the center of your stage?"

Isaiah finally looked up at his parents. "I can't believe you all came in here joking with what's happening with Torri. Can somebody please tell me how she and the baby are doing?"

Nicholas stroked his chin. "Why do you care? Didn't you recite to her that tired speech about your desire for space? If you take a look around this huge room, you don't have anything but space, empty space. Is that what you want your life to become like? Do you want to spend the rest of your days locked in a room devoid of natural sunlight? If that's your desire, you just continue to lie in that mechanical bed and surf the channels with that trusty remote as your only companion. If it's not your desire, then you'd better start doing something about it today. Torri is doing just fine, but you can't take any credit for that since you haven't been there for her."

Asia put her hand on Nicholas's shoulder. "Don't, Nicholas. Getting angry is not going to solve anything. Isaiah may need more time."

"I'm way ahead of anger. I'm pissed! As for time, he doesn't have the luxury of that. The longer he lies there feeling sorry for himself, the more time he's allowing to tick off from his precious life. The world will just pass him on by as he stands still and watches."

"Lies still," Isaiah corrected. "Have you forgotten that I can't move?"

"How can anyone forget it when you're using the paralysis as a weapon against everyone who gives a damn about you? What are you going to tell your son or daughter when he/she asks you why you checked out on him/her, his mother, his grandparents, your teammates, your coach, and the rest of the world? What sorry excuse will he or she hear coming from your lips?"

"Dad, could you shut up long enough to hear what I have to say?" Isaiah shouted.

Nicholas gave his son a warning look. "You better watch how you talk to me. I had to warn you about that the first day we met. If you feel good enough to disrespect me, I won't feel a bit of remorse when I don't hesitate to fatten your lip. Your mouth isn't hurting, but it will be."

Asia stepped forward. "Come on now, you two. Let's get a grip."

"I'm sorry, Dad, but will you please hear me out? I have something important to say."

Nicholas nodded but his eyes held a clear warning about his intolerance for disrespect.

"I told the nurse to set up the physical therapy sessions. I'm not going to lie to you; I'm terrified of doing this, more so of failing." Isaiah began to cry. "But I got a family to think about now. I don't want anyone taking care of them but me." His upper body began to tremble.

Asia put her arm around her son as she gently stroked his hair with her other hand. "Baby, we all have to take care of each other. Torri's strong. She and the baby are fine."

"I sure hope so. I'm really worried about not being able to be there for my family in every way. It scares me that I might not be able to live up to their expectations of me. Mom, I'm not blaming you for the decisions you made regarding Dad and me, but you'll never know how I felt growing up without my father. It was hard. On special occasions, and when other kids had their fathers at school or at sporting events, I didn't. Uncle Thomas attended functions with me, but it wasn't the same. Most of the guys I came up with considered their dads heroes."

Nicholas sat down on the bed and rested his hand on Nicholas's numb thigh. He wished he could rub out the numbness and replace it with the flexibility of strong, healthy, muscle tissue; neither was within his power or control. Isaiah was hurting something awful and there wasn't one thing he could do to ease his pain and suffering. All he could do was love him.

Isaiah looked at his father, his eyes full of liquid sadness. "I was constantly teased about your absence. I didn't dare hit any one over it; I would've hurt them too bad. I don't want my child to know that kind of raw pain. I couldn't scratch the itching ache, couldn't pull off the nonhealing scabs on my heart. And I couldn't conjure up my daddy's face to bring me comfort, especially when I couldn't sleep at night. I didn't even know what he looked like. But I had visions. Never in my wildest dreams did I think I would look so much like you. Even though I said differently, I'm proud that people can look at us and instantly know our blood relationship without asking. I'll never forget the look on Lynda's face after I told her I was your son."

A tear escaped the corner of Nicholas's right eye. It killed him inside to know the kind of pain his son had endured. He still didn't feel bad for coming down so hard on Isaiah. That's what a father was supposed to do for his son. Mental toughness was needed when a man was physically put to the test. No pain, no gain. Isaiah might not fully understand why he had challenged and criticized him so harshly, but Nicholas was certain that he'd get it one day.

"I don't know if I'll ever fly above the rim again, but I know my son or daughter is going to make my heart soar just like a 777 sails through the clear blue skies. Dad, thanks for the verbal challenges. Without them, I don't know if I could've gotten my head straight this soon. I'm still pretty messed up, but you've given me plenty of options to think about. Torri and the baby have given me a reason to make the best of what I have to work with."

Asia's heart grew full as she listened to her son. The strain in his voice was clearly heard, but she also could hear the resounding positive notes, music to her ears. He had some major hurdles to leap over, no doubt, but she felt confident in his ability to do so. She'd never known Isaiah to give in to defeat. Up until the last second ticked off the clock, Isaiah was in the game to win it; no matter how many points the team may've been down. If there was a way to win this competition he'd been forced to enter, her bet was squarely placed on her son.

Isaiah took Asia's hand in his and kissed the back of it. With adoration shining in his eyes, he stared up at her for a couple of seconds. Her beauty never failed to mesmerize him. "Mom, you're still my sweet angel of mercy, goodness, and pure love. I can't love you more than I already do. Guys, I've decided that I'm going to stand tall. Even if I have to do it seated in a wheelchair, my family will be taken care of. Dad, do you think God can grant me another miracle? He's already given me three mega ones in just a little over a month. You, the baby, and then he saw fit to spare my life. I've been counting the miracles to help me keep the faith."

"God is in the miracle business, son. There's nothing too hard for our Father God." Nicholas encompassed both Asia and Isaiah with his arms. "Just look at what He's done for the three of us. He brought us together after twenty-two years. And He did it when we needed it the most. If our being here like this isn't one of His miracles, the devil surely got one over on us this time. But I don't believe for one second that old Satan had anything to do with pulling this grand party together. He's definitely involved in the tragic things that have occurred, but he'll never best the Master. God's tender mercies will forever remain unrivaled."

"Amen!" came a strong voice from behind them.

Nicholas looked up and saw his pastor, Howard Jones, entering the room. Tall and sturdily built, Howard had wavy hair that had completely turned a shocking white before he'd reached forty. The neatly trimmed beard and mustache he wore were the same color as his hair.

Nicholas quickly crossed the room and then shook the hand of his friend and spiritual advisor. He then introduced Howard to Asia and Isaiah. Nicholas could tell by Howard's expression that he was rather stunned to see that Isaiah looked so much like his old man. It was one thing seeing separate pictures of them; in person, the resemblance was uncanny. Laughing inwardly, Nicholas pulled up a chair for Howard to be seated. He then reseated himself at Isaiah's bedside.

"Son, it's so nice to meet you. I've heard nothing but good things about you, yet I never dreamed you were the son of my dear friend Nicholas. How are you coming along?"

"I'm paralyzed. I may've lost the use of some of my motor skills, but all my other senses are intact. Dad has challenged me to use my brain to get over in whatever I choose to do instead of play basketball. He's been here to harass me every chance he gets. Without his tough but positive approach, I'd still be thinking of my situation as hopeless."

Asia looked dazed by Isaiah's remarks. It wasn't so much what he'd said as it was how readily he'd spoken about it. She was proud of how he'd handled his response to the pastor's question. Isaiah was going to be just fine with the passing of time, she mused.

"I'm glad to hear it, but what has he told you about the power of prayer?" Howard asked.

"His speech on that subject was first and foremost. And he's not just talking, either. Dad believes wholeheartedly in what he's saying. I can tell. I've been around countless people throughout my short life span, good and evil ones. For whatever reason, I'm able to instantly recognize the good spirit from the bad one. I also get certain vibes from the misguided spirit."

"Care to go into more detail on the misguided spirit?" Pastor Jones prompted Isaiah.

"You know, the ones who are really good spirits but painful and unpleasant circumstances have caused them to ignore and try to cover up the good inside them. Take my best friend, Troy, for instance. He's a great guy, but he allows the bad guys to influence him simply because he's desperate to fit in and wear the tough-guy image. That's the one area where he and I are as different as night and day. I talk to him about it constantly, but he's not trying to hear it. I tell him that if a man or woman wants to be successful, they have to surround themselves with successful people. It doesn't mean that we're better than anybody else; we just have a different agenda. Troy occasionally hangs out with some pretty shady characters."

Nicholas was surprised but intrigued by Isaiah's detailed assessment of Troy. "Have you met Troy's family, Isaiah?"

"Of course I have, Dad. We went all through school together. Troy's dad was once a street thug involved in a lot of petty crimes. They lived in a bad neighborhood before his dad decided he wanted something better for his family than what he'd had while growing up. Troy's the youngest out of five boys. The next-to-youngest brother was already nine when Troy came along. All but one of his brothers has gone back to the hood they grew up in. Drug-dealing gang bangers; they're always in some kind of mad trouble."

Nicholas stroked his chin. "I see. Interesting background. What about his mother?"

"Mind you, everything I'm saying to you guys is in strict confidence. She's an ex-prostitute and a recovering crack addict. But both of his parents are in the church now. Troy's parents were in a much better social and financial situation by the time he was born. He doesn't know that kind of tough life except through his brothers' lifestyles. But there are times when he seems fascinated by it. So much so that I worry about him."

Several more interesting facts, Nicholas thought. The fact that Isaiah was even talking about his friend made Nicholas wonder what had prompted him to do so. He then thought that Isaiah could still be trying to show him he was wrong about Troy. If that was the case, it had backfired. Nicholas felt that the new information gave his theory more credence. Troy sounded like a wanna-be that would do whatever it might take to fit in with a particular group of people.

As Pastor Jones got around to making polite conversation with Asia, Nicholas saw that his friend was finding her not to be anything like the woman Miranda had painted a picture of. In his opinion, Howard seemed taken by Asia's graceful charm and effervescent personality.

As much as Nicholas loved his old friend, Howard had chosen a bad time to pop in to see Isaiah, since his visit had ended their emotionally charged family session. Nicholas had asked Howard to come and pray with his son long before Isaiah had kicked everyone off the visiting list. But it seemed that he was just now getting around to it.

By the time Pastor Jones got to his feet, Nicholas was of the mind that he wasn't ever going to leave. It wasn't that he didn't appreciate him coming. Nicholas just wanted them to get back to sharing as a family unit. Talking about the past seemed to be good for Isaiah. Nicholas thought that if enough blank spaces about his dad were filled in, Isaiah would come to know that he had a father who would move heaven and earth in order to try and meet his every need.

"Well, it's time for this old boy to move on. It was nice meeting both of you. Young Isaiah, you take care of yourself. Everyone in my church is praying for you. Miss Asia, it was a pleasure getting to know you. We have you in our prayers as well."

Asia smiled. "Thank you, Pastor Jones. The pleasure was all ours."

Isaiah extended his hand to the pastor. "It was nice of you to come and see me, sir. We were talking about miracles when you came in. I take your presence as a good omen."

"Your daddy and I know firsthand about the miracles God performs. Nicholas, buddy, I've got to run, but can you and I have a few moments in private? It seems we haven't found the time to get that dinner engagement in so we could sit down and catch up."

Nicholas started to ask if they could talk over the phone later but he then thought better of it. Whatever Howard had to say, Nicholas thought it was best to let him go ahead and get it out of the way. He just hoped it had nothing to do with Miranda. If so, the conversation would be short-lived. Her last visit to his house still rankled Nicholas from deep within.

After telling his family he'd be right back, Nicholas led the way to the nearest waiting room. He didn't bother to seat himself because he wasn't planning to stay that long. He looked to Howard. "What's on your mind?"

Howard grinned like the Cheshire Cat. "Man, she's some looker. Sure there's no truth to Miranda's stories? She might be a hard one for any man to resist."

"Including you?" Nicholas asked pointedly.

Howard looked abashed. "Now you should know better than that. I am a highly respectable man of God."

"That doesn't make you any less human. You're a man and you still have warm blood running through your veins. So we know you're not dead."

Howard cracked up. "You've made your point, Brother Reynolds.

Weakness and other matters of the flesh are still man's most committed sins."

"Asia is a beautiful woman, a good sister. She's done a wonderful job raising our son."

"That's quite a young man you have there." Howard's brows knitted together as his expression grew somber. "Nicholas, I know I don't have to preach to the choir. But I have one or two things on my mind. First of all, I haven't seen you in church since your son got hurt. And then, there's still the matter of this pending divorce—"

"Hold up, hold up," Nicholas interrupted. "When two or more are gathered in His name, His presence is felt. Besides that, I hold worship service in my heart twenty-four-seven. That other matter you mentioned: not open for discussion. Anything else you'd like to say?"

Howard couldn't do anything but laugh. Nicholas had always had a knack for being a man of few words—no uncertain ones, when he deemed it necessary. It was one of the numerous things Howard respected and admired about Nicholas Reynolds. "I can see that you're still a point man." Howard embraced Nicholas. "Good to see you, man. We're going to have that dinner yet. Time just hasn't been on our side."

"It'll happen. Thanks for coming. Come again when you find a minute. Isaiah can always use someone to pray with as well as someone to pray for him."

Nicholas stopped dead in his tracks just as he cleared the doorway. His eyes filled with tears as he looked at the beautiful sight before him. With their heads touching, hands entwined, Asia and Isaiah had fallen asleep. His family had abandoned him in exchange for the sweet arms of peace. He couldn't help smiling through his tears as he wondered if one day they'd ever be a real family united by love and joined together in holy matrimony. Isaiah was their son but he and Asia weren't husband and wife. Did he dare to dream that such a thing was possible? His question was answered for him when he recalled their earlier conversation about miracles.

He hadn't been gone that long, but exhaustion must have claimed Asia and Isaiah soon after he'd left the room. Although it looked as though Asia might fall out of the bed if she moved over the slightest bit, he decided not to disturb her. Quietly, he tiptoed across the room and then stretched out on the other bed. Closing his eyes, he fell into a silent, prayerful session with his Maker. Not long after voicing his silent amen, Nicholas fell asleep, too.

Carrying a large vase of pink roses, Asia and Nicholas swept into Torri's room with just twenty minutes left to visiting hours. They hadn't awakened in time to make it to the hospital any sooner. Nicholas or Asia couldn't believe how long they'd slept despite their known states of fatigue. Isaiah was still asleep when they'd left his room. Then freeway traffic had been a nightmare when Nicholas had done his level best to get them across town to where Torri was hospitalized before visiting hours were up.

Asia laughed softly. "Looks like we did all that rushing for nothing," she whispered. "She's asleep. It's seems like the sandman made his rounds to all of us at practically the same time. I don't think we should disturb her."

Nicholas was careful not to wake Torri as he placed the vase of roses on the bedside stand. He then tiptoed back across the room to where Asia stood. "I think you're right," he said, speaking in a hushed tone. "She needs as much rest as she can possibly get. Torri's going to have a lot to cope with over the next six months or so. Let's go. We can ask the nurse what time she'll be discharged tomorrow. We can come over here together to pick her up."

"I think she'd love that, Nicholas. Thanks for being so caring. I don't know what we'd all do without you."

"Survive, just as you've always done. You're tough enough to handle anything. As for caring, I've never stopped."

"I'm sure I'd survive, but I like having you around to help me through the rough spots. Isaiah and Torri seem to also love your being here for them."

They both had to stifle laughter at how funny their hushed conversation sounded.

Asia dug around in her purse and came up with a notepad and a pen. She wrote down a loving message for Torri and then handed the pad and pen to Nicholas. "I know she'd love to have a little note from you, too. We're all the family she has here in California."

CHAPTER FOURTEEN

Seated on the sofa in his family room Nicholas was busy reading over Vann Orville's latest investigative report, which FedEx had just delivered to his home. Nicholas was especially interested in the portion where Vann talked about his visit to Troy Dyson's residence. According to the report, Vann stated that he found Troy to be less than honest in his verbal depiction of the night that Isaiah had come to his home. His story was inconsistent and full of gaping holes. It seemed to Vann that Troy had more information about Isaiah's visit than what he'd divulged. He also believed that Troy was withholding information pertaining to Isaiah's car collision with the commuter train. His extreme nervousness was indicative of a person riddled with fear and guilt.

One of the most interesting facts that Nicholas had read thus far was that Price Sheldon had been at Troy's house when Vann first arrived, but that he had hurried away when he learned why Vann was there to see Troy. Vann had asked Sheldon to stay on and participate in the interview since he was also a teammate of Isaiah's, but Sheldon had refused Vann's request without any sort of explanation. Vann summed up this portion of his report by saying that Troy was a poor liar and that he definitely had something he was hiding. He believed that Sheldon was also hiding something and that he might possibly be involved or perhaps know what had happened to Isaiah.

The next two pages in Vann's report addressed his visit to Isaiah's head coach, Walker Fitzgerald, fondly referred to by his players and peers as W.F. According to Fitzgerald, he couldn't think of any reason why someone would want to bring harm to his star point guard. He spoke highly of Isaiah as a professional basketball player, and as a community servant, mentor to youth, and man. Fitzgerald's deep respect for Isaiah's extraordinary work ethic and his phenomenal skills on the basketball court had come through quite loud and clear. His personal assessment of Isaiah Morrell was heavily favorable.

Vann stated that the coach had also voiced grave concern for Isaiah's refusal to take visits from himself and his teammates. Isaiah was very much loved and missed by everyone who knew him in the California Wildcats organization. Vann was told by Fitzgerald that the news media had backed off thus far because of their genuine like and respect for Isaiah and also because the team owners requested it. A press conference was promised as soon as all the facts were in.

Tears came to Nicholas's eyes when he read that the head coach had mentioned loving Isaiah like a son and that the pride he felt for Isaiah had been visible and unquestionably sincere. Nicholas was glad that he didn't just have to settle for loving Isaiah like a son, Isaiah was his son. He was Isaiah's father, one that couldn't be prouder of his only child.

"You guys didn't have to go to all this trouble. I can't believe all these fresh flowers you two put here in this guest bedroom for me to look at and smell. I feel like I'm in a spring garden. Thanks, Mommy-Asia, for inviting me to stay here with you. Mr. Nick, I want to thank you, too. You've been so sweet. This is a special treat. I promise to be the perfect recovering patient."

"I'm thrilled to have you here, Torri. Just buzz me on the intercom when you need something. There are speakers in all the rooms except for the laundry room and the garage. Are you hungry yet? Nicholas and I stocked the pantry and refrigerator with some of your favorites."

Torri shook her head. "I had lunch just before you guys came to get me. You've put this nice pitcher of ice-cold water here on the nightstand so I'll be content with that for now. I didn't know riding in a car could be this exhausting when you're not feeling well. I guess it has more to do with being pregnant than anything else since I'm certainly used to long drives in a car."

Asia bent over the bed and kissed Torri's cheek. "We'll go in the other room and let you get some rest. I hope you don't get too bored being here with an old lady."

Torri laughed. "You're not an old lady and there's no way I can get bored with all the different types of reading material and videos you've furnished me with. I do love to read. But I think I'm going to first try and take a quick nap. Is that okay?"

Nicholas gave Torri a quick hug. "Of course. See you later on."

The phone rang before Asia and Nicholas made it out of the room. Asia picked up the bedroom extension and cheerfully greeted the caller. Her eyes lit up when she heard Isaiah's voice telling her "hi" and that he loved her. "Yes, yes you may," she happily responded to his request to speak with Torri. "Hold on." Asia handed Torri the receiver. "It's for you."

Torri looked bewildered. "For me? Who could possibly be calling me here?"

"Why don't you say hello and find out?" Asia took Nicholas by the hand and hurried him toward the bedroom door.

"It was Isaiah calling for Torri," she whispered to Nicholas as they walked down the hallway. "His voice sure sounded nice and strong."

"All right! Our boy is coming back to us."

Nicholas desperately wanted to kiss Asia but he knew it would be wrong of him to do so. Spending so much time with her had only strengthened his feelings for the mother of his child. She was an amazing person and he still loved everything about her. The fresh scent of her skin and hair excited him and he never grew tired of looking into her beautiful, expressive eyes. Her smile had a way of lighting him up on the inside. Her touch, no matter how slight, made him tremble both inwardly and outwardly.

Never taking his eyes off Asia, he seated himself at the breakfast nook, just one of the places in her home that had become familiar to him. As his thoughts turned to Miranda, he felt a sudden flash of emotion streak right through him. He hadn't heard from her in the last forty-eight hours and he found it strange that it actually concerned him. Every single day she'd leave two or three messages on his answering service concerning one thing or another, none of it ever that important. He still believed that something had to be bothering Miranda for her to act the way she had been. He just wished that he knew what it was, though he now had a pretty good idea.

Maybe he shouldn't have been so crass to her. Nicholas began to think that it might behoove him to try and sit down and really talk everything through with Miranda and to do it in a much calmer manner. Even if she had brought it on herself by her bad attitude, he hadn't been as kind and understanding with her as he normally would've been. So many unpleasant things had occurred between them. He had simply run of out patience with her much too quickly, especially knowing Miranda had serious issues, too, which he had failed to address.

"Hey, are you over there thinking of some other woman while you're with me?" Asia teased, smiling brightly at him. "You've been daydreaming for a long time now."

His embarrassment was apparent. "As a matter of fact, I was thinking about Miranda. I haven't heard from her in a couple of days."

"Oh, I see." Asia hid her disappointment very well. She had only been teasing, but there was no denying that she'd hit the nail right on the head. His thinking of Miranda caused a dull ache in her heart. Asia thought it would've been nice to hear him say that he was thinking of her. Like Nicholas, the more time they spent together, the more in love with him she fell.

"Don't you want to know why I was thinking about her?"

Asia scowled. "Pray tell, why would I want to know that?"

He grinned. "Because you care about anything and everything that has to do with me."

Asia did her best to keep a straight face but all she wanted to do was laugh with wild abandonment despite the pain she felt at his thinking of his estranged wife. "Nicholas, I hate to tell you this, but you're starting to smell yourself over there. And I can sure catch your heady scent from way over here. Your stuff is getting might funky, brother."

He came up behind her and wrapped his arms around her waist, nudging the side of her neck with his nose. "You know I smell exceptionally good. You used to say that all the time."

She tried to twist her way out of his hold, but the strength in which he held her close to him was too much for her to overpower. Asia had the desire to put her head back against his chest, tilt her head upward until their lips met, and engage him in the hottest kiss he'd ever gotten from her. Closing her eyes, and for the umpteenth time, she conjured up an excitable vision of him kissing her breathless, the way he used to do. Her inner thighs trembled at the memories.

As he turned her to face him, their eyes met in an intense, candle-melting gaze. On fire for each other, they could only stare into each other's eyes. Making love wasn't in the cards for them as long as Nicholas had a wife, estranged or not. But there was no doubt each of them wanted that very thing to happen, badly. Asia stepped slightly back from him and he quickly released his hold on her. To keep her captive in his arms a minute longer would make him go completely insane with longing. He was already half-crazed in both his emotional and physical desires for her. Nicholas could no longer deny his physical need for her; it had grown stronger.

Asia jumped when the intercom buzzed. It had scared her, but she was grateful for the badly needed intervention. Torri was awake and wanted something, and Asia thought it was the perfect excuse to get out of the kitchen and away from Nicholas's sexually arousing presence. Without uttering a word to him, Asia took off like a fireball blazing a trail through dried brush. Another moment with him would've had her begging him to take her right there on the kitchen floor. Now how Christian-like was that? Her thoughts had her feeling ashamed.

"For Pete's sake," Nicholas muttered to himself as he sat back down at the breakfast nook. "What are you trying to do here? This is not like you. You darn near seduced Asia without thinking about what it would mean in the eyes of God. Talk about weakened flesh!"

Nicholas bowed his head, confessed his sin, and asked for forgiveness.

In all the time he'd been separated from Miranda, he hadn't given serious thought to sleeping with another woman. It was morally wrong, not to mention sinful. The fact that he was too busy with his work to think about other women had also helped to keep him an honest man. After nearly sixteen hours of work practically every day of the week, Nicholas was usually too tired to do anything but exercise, go home, grab a bite to eat, shower, and then fall right into bed.

Then Asia had come back into his life. Nothing had been the same for him since.

Having composed herself as best as she could, Asia smiled at Nicholas as she entered the kitchen. "Our girl is hungry for a grilled cheese sandwich. Want to do the honors while I make her a garden salad? I remember the killer ones you used to make for us?"

"That will certainly give me something sinless to do. Forgive me for continuously coming on to you like an oversexed teenager looking to score for the first time ever. I said I wasn't going to do this again, but I seem to keep at it. Are you offended?"

"Oh, Nicholas, you've not done anything I haven't encouraged in some way. We're simply human beings with adult desires. It's as hard for me as it is for you to be in the same room together and not think of all the love and passion we once shared. I'm haunted by our erotic adventures constantly. The fact that we made a child together on one of those passionate occasions makes it doubly hard for us to ignore it. But taking no notice of it is a must."

"Yeah, easy for you to do."

"I wouldn't bet on it if I were you. The desires of a woman are no less demanding than a man's. If we're going to feed Torri, you'd better start rattling those pots and pans, Mr. Reynolds." She smiled. "I got the job of making the salad. How easy can that be?"

"You're such a forgiving spirit. Thank you, Asia. And you're still a pro at changing the subject with grace."

"Thank you for being just who you are, Nicholas. Thank you for allowing me to be me."

Nicholas and Asia sat at the round table in the bedroom watching and listening to Torri as she ate and talked at the same time. The fact that she was merely pinching off tiny pieces of the grilled cheese sandwich didn't hinder her ability to speak. She hadn't touched the salad yet, and Asia hoped the lettuce wouldn't be soggy from the ranch dressing by the time she got around to it. For Torri's drinking pleasure, Nicholas had poured an entire bottle of cranberry-apple juice into a glass pitcher filled with crushed ice. He had also garnished the refreshing liquid with several thin slices of fresh lemon.

"If it's not too personal, Torri, how did your conversation with Isaiah go?"

Torri smiled brightly. "It didn't go too well in the beginning. I purposely made it difficult for him to talk to me. My one-syllable answers and contrary attitude frustrated him, but he didn't give up trying to get through to me. When he started blaming himself for my medical problems, I couldn't let him do that. He doesn't need to feel any worse than he already does. I quickly let him off the hook. And I later put him at ease by telling him how much I love him." Torri suddenly looked embarrassed. In the next second she giggled out loud.

The telltale blush in Torri's cheeks tickled Asia's funny bone. "I guess there's a part of the conversation that you need to keep to yourself, huh?"

The color in Torri's cheeks deepened. "Yeah, I think so. I wouldn't want to embarrass anyone. Isaiah can be so silly at times. He had me laughing so hard."

Nicholas laughed heartily. "I think you're the only one who seems discomfited. But the intimate secrets between you and Isaiah should be kept. We're just happy to see you smiling. To hear that our boy's feeling well enough to act silly is kind of thrilling, especially after seeing him looking and sounding so depressed all this time."

"Nicholas is so right. I'm happy you two were able to talk and get back to being playful with each other. I've been around you guys enough to know how silly you both can get. And I also know how much love you share between you, Torri. Everything is going to be just fine."

"I hope so. There's been somewhat of a serious development that I'm very worried about," Torri told Nicholas and Asia.

Asia looked alarmed. "What do you mean? Are you cramping again?"

Torri shook her head. "Oh, not that. I'm sorry. I didn't mean to scare you. It's just that Isaiah insisted on being the one to call my parents and tell them everything."

Nicholas looked puzzled. "Why should that worry you? That's a highly commendable thing for him to do, as well as it being very responsible."

"My parents will positively flip out over hearing that I'm pregnant. Dad is known to be less than tactful in saying what's on his mind. In fact, he can be downright crude despite his pretense at social refinement. I'm worried that Isaiah might get his feelings badly hurt. They might say anything as a result of their initial shock; more than likely, they won't be thinking of his own medical problems at the time."

"Isaiah has pretty thick skin, Torri," Asia assured her.

"I agree with his mother. And she knows him better than anyone. If he's the kind of man I believe he is, he'll know how to handle himself with your parents."

Nicholas's thoughts took him straight to what he would've done had Asia told him she was pregnant with his child. His father had taught him that youth was never an excuse for not being accountable for your actions. Adult behaviors required mature resolutions. Although he knew that a person could never reach back into the past and snatch it into the present, he wished that he and Asia had it to do all over again. If that were possible, he'd pay much closer attention to everything that had to do with her. He still found it hard to believe that he'd never guessed that she was pregnant, that he hadn't seen coming her disappearing act from school.

"I just hope they don't say anything to hurt him. He's tough but he's also sensitive. I know Isaiah won't disrespect them either, but neither will he back down from my dad if he gets verbally abusive toward him. 'Your dad was never in the navy, but he can sure cuss like a sailor,' my paternal grandmother used to say about her son. I've heard my father say things that some people wouldn't dare to think of, let alone voice. My mother also has an unkind tongue. I guess I'll have to pray for the best possible outcome."

"Prayer is the best way to handle every problematic situation. It's the answer for everyone to everything," Nicholas said with strong conviction.

"Thank you, Mr. Nick. By the way, Isaiah asked me if you two planned to visit today. I told him I didn't know, but I couldn't imagine your not visiting. His godmother was there earlier. He said that he'd had a good visit with his Auntie Lenora. Troy also came by, but Isaiah didn't want to go into the details of their visit. He actually sounded upset, but I didn't try to pry into his business since he'd already said he didn't want to talk about it. He'll call back after he talks with my mom and dad. Are you going to the hospital? If so, I can tell him when he calls."

"Nicholas is stopping by there. I'm staying here with you. You shouldn't be alone at a time like this. Isaiah will understand. I'll call him a little later."

Nicholas got to his feet. "I'd better get on over to the hospital if I'm going. More than three-quarters of the day is gone. I'll ring you two beauties before I leave the hospital to see if you need anything. Torri, continue to take it easy. Grammy Asia, don't you overdo. You should get some rest, too."

"I plan to. Torri and I are going to chill out while we watch a couple of movies." Asia pointed to the overstuffed lounge chair with the matching ottoman. I'm going to curl up in that comfortable spot and hope I stay awake through an entire movie. If not, oh, well!"

Nicholas and Torri laughed at the comical expression on Asia's face.

"What movies did you rent?" Nicholas asked Asia.

"None other than the ones featuring the best actress and best actor Academy Award winners. *Monster's Ball*, with Halle Berry, and *Training Day*, with Denzel Washington. I didn't get to see either one on the big screen. I'm eager to see what all the negative hoopla's been about. Did you get to see them, Nicholas?"

"I didn't see either one. I'm not much of a moviegoer anymore."

"Really? You used to love to take in movies every chance you got."

He looked at Asia in a knowing way. Frequent trips to the movies had nothing to do with watching the picture. He simply loved to make out with Asia up in the balcony seated in the very back row. Something about kissing and hugging her in a darkened movie theater had turned him on back then. Rarely was either of them able to tell anyone what the show had been about when it was over. The only stars they'd ever cared about were the ones they'd frequently seen in each other's eyes.

"Don't have time for the movies these days. Come on and walk me out, Asia. We don't want Isaiah champing at the bit if he thinks we aren't going to show up." Leaning over the bed, Nicholas placed a gentle kiss in the center of Torri's forehead. "Have fun watching the movie."

"Thanks, Mr. Nick. Mommy-Asia and I plan to have a ball over the next few days, but in a quiet way."

"A very quiet way," Asia added. "I'll be back in a minute, Torri. Can I bring you something from the kitchen?"

"More cranberry-apple juice would be nice, please. I practically drank the entire pitcher all by myself. It was that good."

"Coming right up, sweetie," Asia said, looping her arm through Nicholas's as they left the room.

* * *

Asia opened the door for Nicholas only to come face-to-face with Lenora. The two smiling girlfriends exchanged greetings and warm hugs. Lenora then spoke to Nicholas in a very familiar way, acting as if she'd known him all her life.

"Hey, Lenora, I'm glad I got to see you. I never had a chance to thank you for smoothing things over with our cop buddies. You saved my behind from a good skinning."

"That's what friends do for friends of friends."

They all laughed at how Lenora had so cleverly voiced her remark.

"Asia, are you and Nicholas leaving?"

"Nicholas is. He's on his way to see Isaiah. Torri's here with me so I have to stay home."

"How is the poor darling? I should've paid her a visit long before now. All Isaiah could talk about was her near miscarriage. Is she really going to be okay?"

"The doctor says she'll be fine with plenty of bed rest. Why don't you go on into the guest bedroom and see her?"

Lenora turned her palms faceup and drew them back in dramatic fashion. "Oh, I can't believe you let someone else sleep in my room. I love Torri, but she can't have my favorite room. Please tell me she's in the smaller guest bedroom before I faint."

"Your room is vacant, silly darling, with the exception of a few spiderwebs," Asia joked.

Lenora clapped her hands like a small child. "I knew you'd never betray me." Lenora had to laugh at her own silliness. "Let me get in there and see Torri so you two can say your good-byes. Nicholas, you have a great evening. Hope to see you again soon."

"Same here. I'm going to have to check out that room and see what's so spectacular about it. Mind if I one day take a look around your special room?"

Lenora grinned mischievously. "Not a problem, but I'm sure you prefer sleeping in the same room and the same bed you were in the last time you stayed over." Lenora slapped her hand over her mouth. "Did I say that? Oh, my, I did." She howled as she turned to walk away.

"Lenora, please stop in the kitchen and pour Torri a glass of juice from the pitcher in the refrigerator. I'll join you guys shortly."

"Sure thing," Lenora shouted over her shoulder.

Asia took Nicholas's hand. "Sorry about that. She can be positively tactless at times. But she's so darn lovable. She didn't mean any harm."

"She was right, you know—"

Asia put two fingers up to Nicholas's lips. "Taking no notice is a must."

He smiled as he recalled the same words that had come from her sweet mouth earlier. He pressed her fingers firmly into his lips and kissed them, allowing their eyes to connect for a few brief moments. He ran his fingers through Asia's hair before walking out the door and closing it behind him. Leaving her was hard to do but necessary. She just wasn't his to have and to hold.

Regretting all the things that stood between them, Asia stared at the shut door as if she expected Nicholas to run back through it. Her thoughts tried to take her back in time, a time when he was all hers, but she valiantly resisted the temptation to stroll down memory lane.

Nicholas felt Isaiah's disheartened spirit the very second he walked into his son's room. The deep misery Isaiah was experiencing also showed on his face. The salt from his dried tears had left streaks on his cheeks. Nicholas softly greeted Isaiah as he pulled up a chair to the bedside and seated himself. Out of respect for Isaiah's obvious torment, he sat quietly to wait for his son to open up to him.

Several minutes of complete silence had passed when Nicholas removed the Bible from the nightstand drawer. Understanding that Isaiah was suffering from depression of spirit, he turned to those passages that he thought would offer relief to his son's despondent mindset. In reading examples of depression experienced by noteworthy characters in the Bible, Nicholas hoped that his son would come to understand that he was not alone in his feelings of despondency. Greater men than he had fallen victim to depression, but God had been there to see them through, just as he was there for Isaiah.

Nicholas began his reading with scriptures pertaining to Elijah, Kings 19:4, 10. "But he himself went a day's journey into the wilderness, and came and sat down under a juniper tree: and he requested for himself that he might die; and said, It is enough now; O Lord, take away my life; for I am not better than my fathers." He never once looked up at his son as he continued on with a verse from Jeremiah's story in Jeremiah 15:10. Nicholas's eyes were teary as he controlled his emotions through tribulations of Job found in Job 7:4–7. By the time he had finished his profound journey, he had also read scriptures from Jonah 4:3, 8, Joshua 7:7–9, Numbers 11:10–15, and Luke 24:13–17.

Silence still permeated the air, but the look on Isaiah's face had changed. The anguished appearance had turned to one of utter amazement. Fresh tears rolled down his face as he allowed the readings to sink in, praying all the while for a thorough cleansing of his spirit. The words read by his father had reached him and had touched him way deep down inside. He saw that Nicholas had more messages in store for him when he began to read aloud once again.

Nicholas read softly the story of the invalid man cured at the pool of Bethesda solely by the miracle of Jesus' love and His healing powers, John 5:1–9. He included in his ministry to Isaiah the story of two blind men cured, Matthew 9:27–31, and the tale of ten lepers cleansed in Luke 17:11–19. Last but certainly not least, Nicholas revealed the parables and miracles pertaining to the bread of life, which leads to eternal salvation through Christ, John 6:25–59. At the conclusion of his ministering session to Isaiah, Nicholas led them in reverent prayer.

After father and son embraced at prayer's end, Nicholas took his seat.

"Dad, thanks for being intuitive enough to know that I needed to hear the things you just read to me. I'm amazed that you recognized my state of mind from the moment you stepped foot into this room. How do you do it?"

"Through the power of God, son. I felt your restless spirit before I ever saw the anguish written upon your face. God reveals messages to us in so many different ways. If we take the time to seek Him out, and then sit still and listen, we'll hear Him as He whispers a response. His distinct voice can be heard in both the quietest and the loudest of atmospheres. We have the luxury of calling on Him no matter where we are or what the hour or situation is. He instantly hears our cries. He comes to our aid in His time, which is normally right on time."

"Mom read the Bible to me and she always talked about believing in God and praying to Him, but we didn't go to church that much. It was like she held something against attending, but she never discouraged my Uncle Thomas from taking me to worship services with him. I took my first formal Bible training class in college, which required me to be present, study the Scriptures, and verbally participate in classroom discussions. I took the course more out of curiosity than anything else, but I'm glad I did so. I can see how it will help me get through these fiery trials I'm faced with. What I heard on the phone today from Torri's mom and dad came straight from Satan. I'm shocked. I never knew they were that evil. Torri never mentioned to me that they had something of a dark side until I told her I should be the one to talk to them."

Nicholas knew exactly why Asia didn't attend church with any regularity, but he wasn't going to get into her reasons with his son. However, he thought of suggesting to her that she tell Isaiah why she had a tendency to reject worship services. Asia's strict upbringing had soured her on matters of religion as a whole, but she believed in God. Her parents hadn't practiced what they'd preached, yet her faith in God had remained strong and steadfast. Since Torri had earlier shared with him and Asia some confidences about her parents' personal deficits, Nicholas decided it best not to comment on that either. Isaiah and Torri would eventually work it all out.

"Isaiah, people are often good at hiding their evil spirits behind smiling faces, heavily veiled eyes, and false representations of themselves. There are many false prophets in the world today."

"I know that. And just the other day I told you and Pastor Jones that I'm good at differentiating between the spirit of evil and good. I admit to only being around Torri's parents a couple of times, but I didn't feel then what I heard from them today. They even told me I should suggest to Torri that she have an abortion if I wanted what was best for her. I was told in no uncertain terms that Torri was too young to be saddled with a permanently disabled spouse."

Isaiah instantly reacted emotionally to the pain of those words as if he were hearing them for the first time. His shoulders convulsed as his emotions erupted once again.

Nicholas rushed to his son's side and enveloped him in his arms. "Words of men will sometimes inflict hurt and leave deep wounds upon your heart and inside your soul. Words of God will ease the worst of hurts and heal the deepest of wounds. All you have to do is trust in Him as your Lord and Savior and believe in His healing powers. Don't be afraid to ask Him for what you need from him, Isaiah. God's desire is to fulfill your heart's every yearning with things that are good for you. He sent His only begotten Son into this sinful world to die so that you and I and the whole of mankind might have eternal life. Imagine that if you can! Son, even in the darkest hour of night always remember that the sunlight of joy comes in the morning."

For the next several minutes Isaiah continued to release his anguish against his father's chest. Surrounded by the miraculous love he could actually feel as it emanated with fervor from Nicholas, Isaiah was comforted by the presence of two fathers, his biological one, and his spiritual Father in heaven. Knowing he had many trials yet to face, Isaiah also felt safe in the knowledge that he'd never walk the path alone, whether he was walking under his own power or in a wheelchair. Once Isaiah had fully composed himself, Nicholas sent up another fervent prayer.

Nicholas rocked back in his chair. "So, is there anything else new with you?"

"I start my physical therapy tomorrow morning. Will you be here, Dad?"

"As early and as long as you need me to be. I'm excited about being there for you."

Isaiah's expression was sober. "It bothers me that I can't remember anything about how the accident occurred. Yet I keep having these recurring dreams. I stand corrected, nightmares. I wake up sweating profusely."

"Do you remember what they're about once you wake up?"

"Yeah, vividly, but I can't make any sense of them. I seem to wake up at the point where the nightmare might make some sense if it continued. Troy and an angry, faceless person are surrounding me in these dark dreams. When I try to get up and run away from them, they join together in holding me down. I feel something cold but tasteless going down my throat, and that's the point where I always wake up. Every attempt I've made to remember what happened to me has been futile."

"Do you recall being at your mom's house?"

"I can easily recall what happened earlier: all the time I spent with you before and after dinner, and then seeing Mom. Whatever happened after that is anyone's guess, yet I strongly sense there's more that went on." Isaiah's frustration began to set in again.

"Don't go and get yourself all worked up. Things will unfold at the appropriate time. I believe that whatever happened to you was the work of some evildoers and that justice will eventually be served."

"Then I'll have to try and believe that, too. Troy's behavior is what's blowing my mind. He acted so strange when he was here earlier. Dad, I know I was upset about your hiring a private investigator, but now I'm glad you did. When Troy told me the guy's name, I nearly flipped out. Dad, Mr. Orville is the same person I hired to find you. Did he tell you that?"

Nicholas nodded. "You hired the very best in the business. Vann and I are old friends. I helped his boy out of a jam a few years back and now he wants to help me with my boy. He's a good man. What did Troy have to say about Vann?"

"He's doesn't like the guy. He thinks he had a lot of nerve coming to his house to question him. He said if Mr. Orville came to see him again that he'd refuse to talk to him. I don't think Troy knows that you hired Mr. Orville, and we should keep it that way. If Troy is some-how mixed up with whatever happened to me, I don't want him to know you're involved in an investigation."

"Are you conceding to my theory that Troy knows something about the accident?"

"I guess so. All I know is that his behavior has made me suspicious of him. I'm not distrustful by nature, but I'm feeling extreme nega-tive vibes from Troy. No matter who's involved or what happened, I collided with that commuter train, and there's no reasonable expla-nation for why it happened. If drugs played a part in it, I don't do il-legal substances or anything that alters my ability to think clearly and act responsibly. I didn't take those drugs."

"Following your instincts is a good thing. When Troy visits, try not to show your dubious feelings about him. If he suspects you suddenly don't trust him, he'll be on guard. Keep things between you two as natural as possible. Did he tell you that Price Sheldon was there when Vann first came, but that he hurried away after refusing to be inter-viewed by him?"

"Never mentioned a thing about Price, not even his arrest. How's his case going?"

Nicholas shrugged. "Don't know. He called and cancelled his scheduled appointment and we dropped him like a bad habit. Un-cooperative clients, the firm can do without. If it turns out that Sheldon is involved in your situation, the decision to lose him will turn out to be a darn good one. If not, we're still better off. He has an ego the size of Texas. I haven't met him personally, but I've heard enough about him to know he would've been a nightmare to deal with."

"His uncontrollable ego is the very reason Price and I aren't close as teammates. But it's understood that we need each other on the court in order for us to be a top-contending team. I do my job and he does his. When the game is over, we go our separate ways."

"How does he get along with the rest of the team?"

"You're always going to have the suckups who think the center is king of the hill. In my opinion, to be king, you have to be a leader. Price Sheldon has no leadership skills. We can't do without his scoring, but it would sure help if he took seriously his role as team captain."

"Well, with all the trouble he's in, he may end up playing center for the state or even the federal pen. There may be more darkness to Mr. Price Sheldon's personality than what meets the eye. And now I'm sorry that I didn't meet him. It would've been an interesting meeting." Nicholas glanced at his watch. "Looks like it's time for me to go, champ. But I'll be here first thing in the morning for your therapy."

"Dad, before you go, how is Torri really doing?"

Nicholas grinned. "She was as happy as a lark when I left her and Asia. Those two had plans to watch a couple of movies. Your godmother showed up just as I was leaving, so I imagine things are pretty lively around your mom's house about now. As for Torri's health, she seems fine. Asia's making sure she gets plenty of rest and Torri has vowed to do whatever it takes to make sure she keeps healthy for herself and the baby. She's a beautiful young woman. You're blessed to have her."

"That's for sure. You got a hug for your only son before you shake spot?"

The hug Nicholas gave Isaiah was indicative of a man who loved his son with everything in him. Isaiah's return hug matched the strong feelings his dad felt for him.

CHAPTER FIFTEEN

Lenora scrambled the eggs while Asia made the grits and toast. Torri was only allowed to stay seated at the breakfast nook and look beautiful. Dressed in the cute cotton pajamas and robe that Lenora had given her as a get-well present, Torri was now looking the perfect picture of health. A few days of Asia's pampering and showering much love and compassion on her had done wonders for her. Five or six daily talks with Isaiah had also brightened her outlook.

The one thing that periodically darkened Torri's mood was the upcoming visit from her parents. Their flight from Chicago was scheduled to land in Burbank in approximately an hour and thirty minutes. Much to Torri's dismay, Seressa and Ashton had insisted on picking her up from Asia's house and driving her back to her own place.

"You got everything ready, girl?" Lenora asked Asia. "Torri's sitting over there drooling. Smells good, huh, Isaiah's girl?"

Torri cracked up. "You look like you can't wait to dig in, either. I'm sure enough ready."

"After all the champagne I drank last night, I'm more than ready to pig out. What about you, Miss Asia?" Lenora asked. "Ready to get your Miss Piggy act on?"

"I'm starving. Remember, I didn't eat any dinner last night."

Asia quickly joined Torri and Lenora at the table. The blessing was voiced and then the food platters were passed among the three women.

Lenora looked across the table at Asia. "Yeah, you didn't eat dinner because you were too busy pining over that fine man you've been constantly hanging out with, your baby's daddy. I bet last night was the first time he didn't come over here to visit. I know you were on the phone with him for over two hours before you went to sleep, but that's not the same as looking into each other eyes, is it, girlfriend?" Lenora teased Asia.

Asia snorted as she rolled her eyes. "Lenora, you need to quit. Nicholas and I are always together because of Isaiah, and you know it. All we talked about was Isaiah and the visit he had from his best friend a few days ago. Our son is all we ever think and talk about."

Torri's shoulders shook as she laughed at the two friends' haughty but comical exchange.

"You all weren't thinking of Isaiah the two times Nicholas spent the night with you."

Torri gasped in disbelief. "You and Mr. Nick spent the night together, Mommy-Asia?"

Asia couldn't help laughing at the shocked expression on Torri's face. "It's not what Lenora's trying to make you think, Torri. It was all very innocent." Asia took a minute to explain how Nicholas had come to spend the night in her home. "Lenora loves to get a rise out of me."

"Oh, I see. That *was* innocent." Torri snickered. "I bet you two must've been sweating each other like crazy. Both of you seem to still such have a thing for each other. I know why Auntie Lenora is saying what she does. You two belong together. You make the perfect couple. You're so beautiful and he's too, too handsome, looking like the mirror image of my boo."

"Yeah, he for sure spit your boo out. I've never seen a father and son look alike as much as those two men do. It doesn't appear that Asia had any input whatsoever into the creation of Isaiah," Lenora joked. "I'm surprised I didn't put two and two together as many times as I've seen pictures of Nicholas Reynolds in the newspaper. My godson looks just like his daddy and has one of his names to boot."

"Can you answer a question for me, Auntie Lenora?" Torri queried. Lenora nodded. "Since you didn't meet Mommy-Asia until long after Isaiah's birth, how did you become his godmother? I've wondered about that, but I always forget to ask Isaiah," Torri added.

"I fell in love with Isaiah the moment I laid eyes on him, Torri. There was never any official ceremony or anything formal to set it in stone. I just started calling him godson and he began addressing me as Auntie Lenora. He was already a big boy when I first met Asia back in Ohio. Any particular reason you were wondering?"

"No, not really. Usually the godparents are friends of one parent or both long before the baby is born. I don't have anyone that close to me to consider as a godparent for our child since Mommy-Asia is the grandmother. I've never had a real girlfriend to develop a relationship with like the one you two have. I'm a loner. I wouldn't normally share this with anyone, but I didn't try to strike up any real friendships because of my parents. I didn't want to bring anyone home, because if they didn't have some type of social standing, my mom and dad would look down their noses at them. I didn't want the embarrassment for myself or others."

Asia choked back her emotions. Every aspect of Torri's life was practically a carbon copy of her own. She had been a loner too, a very lonely loner. Asia hadn't brought others home because of her parents' attitude about what type of home her peers came from. If it wasn't a Christian family, she wasn't allowed to socialize with what her parents referred to as the nonbelievers. Asia had often wondered how you could share your love of God with nonbelievers or tell those who didn't know about Him if you weren't able to communicate His goodness. As for boys and young men, it didn't matter what type of background they came from. Asia wasn't permitted to mingle with the male species, period. Her pregnancy had been an insult to her family.

"You're a world-renowned model and you don't have a close girlfriend? I find that unbelievable," Lenora remarked. "But I guess I can understand it. Most women probably hate you because you're so beautiful. I've even been a little envious of your wholesome beauty and that gorgeous figure you're famous for flaunting down the runways of the world."

Torri laughed. "I'm no one to be envied. Everyone thinks I lead this glamorous life. But the glamour is all in the fabulous clothes I'm privileged to wear. I'm happiest dressed in jeans and a T-shirt. Designer jeans, mind you, but comfort works best for me."

The three women cracked up.

"Okay, now! I heard you when you said it," Lenora chimed in, throwing her head back in laughter. "Designer labels work for me, too."

"I think most women like to be a little fashionable," Asia added, taking a sip of her coffee. "Simple elegance is my preference. Complicated clothing is what never worked for me. I like to be able to slip on my attire with ease and hit the door running. But I do have an occasion to wear my power suits in the courtroom. Talking about powerful clothing, Lenora goes to court dressed to impress everyone present. Her professional attire makes an awesome statement."

"Definitely," Lenora agreed. "But it's the after-hours attire that can knock a brother right off his feet. In the courtroom I'm a confident, independent woman and a tough opposing counselor. I know my legal stuff and I don't have a problem letting everyone know I know it. In the evening time, I'm all feminine fluff. I love to be sweet-talked and romanced, even when I know it's nothing but a bunch of bull. I'll swoon at his big feet in a heartbeat while making darn sure I fall right into his strong arms. In the lovemaking department, I want to be tenderly touched and caressed until he makes me want to holler 'please don't stop' at the top of my lungs. I'm as good at giving a man what he desires as I am at receiving what he does for me. Ooh, can't you just feel the touch of your man tingling all through you?" she screeched, laughing heartily.

Torri and Asia howled out loud. Lenora was the type who always knew how to get a party started. She'd kept them laughing the previous evenings and she already had them going in the morning hours. Lenora didn't have to work at being funny. She was a natural at it. She was as sweet as she was comical. She hadn't married, but she'd had her share of good and bad men.

Torri's heart fell the moment she heard the doorbell chime. She figured it was her parents. "Mommy-Asia, please don't take it personal if my parents say things they shouldn't. And if you don't mind, I'm going to revert back to calling you Miss Asia. Mom won't like me calling you by the new name. She's also the jealous type. What's hers is hers alone."

Lenora wiped her hand across her brow. "It sounds like your parents have lots of issues. I better not meet them. I've never been known to take any stuff off of anyone. I'm going to clean up the kitchen and then slip out through the garage door. I'll call you all later."

Asia gave Lenora a pleading look. "Please stay for me."

Torri's expression was grim. "For me, too, Auntie Lenora."

"Oh, please, get rid of the pitiful looks, you two! I'll do it, but once I meet them, I'm coming right back here to the kitchen. Maybe they'll think I'm Asia's maid and that she's upper crust." Lenora laughed at her own comment, making the other women laugh as well.

"Come on, Torri, we'd better get the door," Asia suggested. "I don't want to start off on a bad foot with your mom and dad by leaving them standing outside too long."

"Come on, Isaiah, you can do it," Nicholas encouraged. "Try to pull yourself up again."

Isaiah appeared exhausted as he looked up at the metal contraptions that had recently been installed above his bed. He groaned. He'd been pulling up on the silver bar for a solid thirty minutes and he felt like he couldn't lift his arms high enough to grab on to it for one more try. He stared it down as if it were the enemy, a formidable foe that he wasn't so sure he could conquer. The gleaming metal seemed to be challenging him to grab hold if he dared to.

"Once more, Ike," Walter, the physical therapist said, "and we'll call the session to an end."

While licking his dry lips, Isaiah closed his eyes. He then began to pray for the strength to pull up one more time. His loud groans and grunts resounded off the walls as he slowly reached up and finally grabbed on to the bar. For several seconds, his hands just gripped it. Sweat poured from his face and body as he slowly pulled himself up, his arms aching like a bad tooth.

Having achieved his goal, he inched back down until he felt his upper body make contact with the mattress. Isaiah suddenly broke out in a cold sweat, his body shaking all over. As he engaged in deep-breathing exercises to try and calm his body down, the hard trembling of the muscles on his upper anatomy appeared uncontrollable.

To Nicholas it looked as if Isaiah was having a convulsion or seizure of some sort, but the therapist didn't appear panicked by the sudden violent twitching. In fact, he didn't seem at all concerned by it as he watched Isaiah closely. Nicholas couldn't believe the therapist's apathy.

"What's happening?" Nicholas finally asked. He was worried by what he was seeing.

"His muscles are only reacting to the strenuous use from such a long period of nonuse. The body is a wondrously complex. I don't think we'll ever learn all there is to know about the miraculous workings of the anatomy. In many instances the body can heal itself. But modern medicine is too impatient to let the natural process of healing occur. Besides that, there's minimal financial gain in allowing nature to take its course. The almighty dollar is the driving force in medicine and every other profession you can think of. Profit and loss statements are important, sometimes more significant than the welfare of the patient. There are more good doctors out there than quacks, but the dollar has a way of influencing even some doctors who started out with the very best of intentions. Money pays the bills."

"Ever worry about getting fired for voicing what your peers might consider your twisted point of view?" Isaiah asked, his breath coming in short, shallow gasps.

"I guess I'd worry about it if I weren't telling the truth. If I were lying, then I could be sued for libel," Walter responded to Isaiah. "There's nothing twisted about the facts. Now let's get on to other topics. You did extremely well today, my man. You should be real proud of yourself. I'll be back to work with you first thing in the morning. Be ready for me." Walter Jackson threw up his hand in a farewell gesture as he left the room.

Nicholas made direct eye contact with Isaiah. "He's right, you know. You should be proud. I'm proud of you, too. Is there anything I can get you?"

"How about a new pair of legs, Dad? I sure could use them. As strong of an athlete as I've been most of my life, I can't believe how much pain those few pull-ups caused me. It was excruciating. I'm as tired now as I am after playing forty-eight minutes of basketball. I don't know how I managed to do the little I did. And what's going to happen to me tomorrow?"

"You'll find the strength tomorrow just like you found it today, because you prayed for it. If you ever feel like giving up, just take a second to think of Torri and your unborn child. Thoughts of them should help you get through the rough spots."

"How do you know I prayed for strength? I didn't pray out loud."

"I saw your need to pray in your eyes just before you closed them. It was plain as day."

"You're right, as usual. Why didn't it work all the times I prayed for my dad to come and visit me? Why didn't God hear me when I cried myself to sleep every night for years, right after begging Him to make you love me?"

"I can't answer for God, Isaiah. You'll have to ask Him to tell you what you want to know. But He did answer your prayers."

"How's that?"

"I'm here now and I do love you, only God didn't have to make me do so. No one has to make me do something that comes as natural to me as breathing. But you already know that, don't you, Isaiah? I've told you enough times. And I'll never stop telling you."

Emotionally full, Isaiah smiled. The miracle of having his dad in his life still overwhelmed him.

Nicholas looked on as Isaiah's eyes drooped shut, and then popped open, only to close again a couple of seconds later. The questions Isaiah had asked him fleetingly crossed his mind.

Envisioning a little boy huddled in the corner of his bed wishing his dad would visit him and then begging God to make his dad love him caused Nicholas's heart to wrench. If he could take on every ounce of Isaiah's pain, he'd do it in a second. He'd also take his son's place in that hospital bed if it meant Isaiah would walk again. Nicholas knew that neither of those things was possible, but that didn't stop him from wishing they were.

Torri's introductions of her parents to Asia and Lenora had gone very well. It didn't seem as if politeness was being forced. When Nicholas had arrived, Torri had introduced him to her parents as Isaiah's father. Seressa and Ashton Jefferson were impressed as they mentioned to him that they'd heard many great things about him. Everything had been fine up until this point. But then her parents had stated they needed to be open about a few things regarding their concern over her relationship with Isaiah.

Seated on the sofa beside Nicholas, Asia looked mighty apprehensive. On the other hand, Nicholas looked keenly interested in what they had to say, since Isaiah had already told him what they'd dared to say to him over the phone. Lenora's eyes had narrowed to tiny slits and she'd also moved forward to the edge of her chair. Torri sat in the recliner, and her parents were seated opposite her on the love seat.

"Mom and Dad, I think Isaiah and I are the only ones who should be discussing our relationship. We're adults and we can make our own decisions. We don't want any outside influences. He and I know what we want."

Seressa sucked her teeth. "Torri, you're too young to know what you want. You're not thinking clearly and neither is Isaiah. It's selfish of you two to bring a child into the world where the father can't actively participate in their life. The child will only suffer if you don't abort."

Asia darn near bit off her tongue to keep from responding in haste. It was in her best interest to take a minute and let Seressa's inappropriate words settle into her head. To overreact wasn't going to resolve anything, and Torri didn't need to be upset in her delicate condition.

"What makes you think Isaiah won't be able to participate in his child's life?" Nicholas asked Mrs. Jefferson.

"I'll take this one, baby," Ashton offered his wife. "Your son is paralyzed, Mr. Reynolds. He can't run, jump, climb, or play any athletic games, which are all things children love to do. And neither he nor Torri is mature enough to handle the responsibility that comes with a baby. They're still babies themselves."

"Oh, I'm mature enough to run all over a strange world alone but not responsible enough to take care of my child in my own backyard. Is that what you're saying, Dad?" Torri asked.

"Those are two totally different things, Torrianne Jefferson, and you know it. There's no comparison between traveling the world and staying at home changing diapers and making formula. You need to wake up and see what disasters are waiting to happen for you," Ashton scolded. "You're not going to have just one baby to take care of, you'll have two if you insist on staying with a man who won't be able to do a darn thing for himself."

Torri gasped and Asia winced from her own inner agony. Nicholas felt like he could commit murder, and Lenora was out of her seat and heading straight for Mr. Jefferson.

Standing over Ashton, Lenora had the fire of Hades in her eyes. "Who the hell do you think you are? How can you come in here and talk to your daughter like that about the man she loves? And to insult Isaiah and then make a mockery of his medical misfortune in his mother's house, with both of his parents present, is downright appalling. You and your uppity-behind wife are the shallowest people that I've ever met."

"Lenora," Asia called out to her, "don't let this upset you. They have a right to say what's on their minds. But we don't have to agree with them or their opinions."

"Oh, I'm not upset, just ready to kick some high-and-mighty butt. I believe they have a right to say anything they want, but not here. So, Miss Asia, if you don't tell them to get the hell out of your house, I'll have to do it for you. I love Isaiah, too, and I'm not going to sit by and let someone put him down because of an accident he couldn't help."

"He could help it, all right. If he hadn't been high on drugs, none of this would've happened. He acted irresponsibly and he's paying for it," Ashton shouted. "A drug addict. What kind of man is that for a child to have as a father? He's suffering the consequences of his own actions and he expects my daughter and grandchild to go through hell with him."

Nicholas quickly got to his feet. "Mr. and Mrs. Jefferson, I'm a very peaceful man, but I'm not feeling any serenity at the moment. You obviously don't know my son very well. If you did, you wouldn't be making slanderous remarks. There are three attorneys in this room, and we know what slander sounds like. I hear you talking about your grandchild as if you care about him or her, but only minutes ago your wife was talking about Torri aborting the baby. Do you believe in God, Mr. and Mrs. Jefferson?"

The Jeffersons looked at each other in disbelief. Neither of them seemed to know how to answer Nicholas's question. It was so silent in the room you could've heard a pin drop. With bated breath, everyone waited for a response from the couple, one that didn't seem forthcoming.

"What does God have to do with this?" Ashton queried in anger.

"If you have to ask that question, I feel sorry for you. God has everything to do with everything. It seems that you've come to the conclusion that Isaiah has no future if he can't do all the physical things you've mentioned; therefore, your daughter won't have one if she stays in a relationship with him. Knowing how brilliant my son is I have to disagree with you, but I don't think stating Isaiah's case will do anything to change your mind about him. What's so sad about the whole thing is that your beautiful, talented daughter lacks the support of her own parents."

"That's a lie! We have supported everything our daughter takes on. We've always been there for our child and we always will be," Ashton countered.

Torri looked at her parents through her tears. "This is so sad for me to see you two acting this way with people who have been nothing less than wonderful to me. I don't dare to disrespect you because it's not the right thing to do, but I can tell you that I'm very ashamed of this kind of behavior. Like it or not, Isaiah is the man I love, the man I will marry should he ask."

"Torrianne, I think deep down inside you know we're right," Seressa said, "but you're not going to admit that in front of Isaiah's family, probably out of respect for them. I understand that. But you have to realize that you won't ever be able to have any sort of intimacy in your life if you marry a physically handicapped man. Physical intimacy is a very important element in a marriage. I don't think I need to remind you that he's paralyzed from the waist down. You need to think about all that you'll be sacrificing to be with this man, young lady. A man who gave not a minute's thought to you and his baby when he was partying and getting high. He doesn't deserve your loyalty."

Nicholas sucked in a deep breath. "I agree with Lenora about Asia telling you to leave. But my wi— son's mother is too polite for that. So I'll tell you for her. It's time for you to go. I won't stand by another minute and allow you to insult our son or us any further." Nicholas hoped that no one caught his blunder. He had nearly called Asia his wife. Wishful thinking and a strong desire for such had found a way to escape his heart and exit his mind through his lips.

Both of Torri's parents leaped to their feet at the same time. Torri got out of her chair, too.

Her deep embarrassment and heartfelt pain were obvious to everyone in the room but didn't appear to affect her parents in the least. It appeared that they still had numerous insults to deliver to Isaiah's family.

Torri crossed the room, sat down next to Asia, and reached for her hand. "I'm sorry about all this. Will you help me get my things out of the bedroom? I hate to leave, but I don't have a choice since my parents came all the way from Chicago to take me home. Thanks for taking such good care of me. I won't forget how sweet all of you have been to me." Torri's warm, tearful gaze encompassed both Nicholas and Lenora.

Asia kissed Torri's forehead. "You should never apologize for something you've had no part in. It's been a pleasure having you here with me. I feel blessed because of it." Asia got to her feet and then reached back for Torri's hand. "Come on. Let's get your bags together, sweetie."

Lenora got up from her seat and followed Torri and Asia out of the room.

Left alone with the people he didn't think he'd ever come to understand, Nicholas's heart wrenched as he thought of what Isaiah had had to endure at the wicked tongues of Torri's parents. When Isaiah had told him the horrible things the Jeffersons had said to him, he hadn't imagined that such rudeness and downright ignorance had come down so hard on his son in such a vile way. Their nastiness and evil spirits were hard to ignore. Still, he felt obligated to pray for their salvation. The Jeffersons obviously couldn't differentiate between God and Satan. Because Nicholas could, he felt that they needed him to pray to God for them.

Looking as if her world had come to an end, Torri dropped down on the bed where she'd spent the last few days being loved and pampered. "Mommy-Asia, do you see what I'm talking about regarding my mom and dad? They're impossible."

"Torri, it now seems to me that they only accepted Isaiah as a superstar basketball player. I don't think they really got to know him as a person. Their opinion of him is so harsh."

"You're right. He's only been around them a couple of times, but they didn't act like this on either occasion. They were proud and boastful, as if they'd actually had something to do with him being a star athlete. They hadn't been able to introduce him to all the people they'd wanted to due to time constraints. Isaiah was definitely put on public display during those brief visits."

Torri looked to Lenora. "I need to apologize to you, too. I know how much you love Isaiah. The things they said had to hurt you, too. I'm sorry for them and their bad attitudes."

"This isn't a battle you've started, Torri. Don't gear up for it. What bothers me more than what happened out there is this: Would they dare to say these things to Isaiah's face?" Lenora asked. "Torri, honey, only you'd know if they were capable of saying those heartbreaking things to him. Would they do that?"

Tears bubbled on Torri's lashes as her lower lip trembled. "I think they may have already done so. Isaiah insisted on calling to tell them about the baby. He thought it was his responsibility as a man to take that task on. He was supposed to call me back after he talked with them, but he hasn't. I believe his call to them is what prompted their sudden visit to L.A."

Asia and Lenora both looked horrified at the thought of the Jeffersons spewing out that kind of damaging talk to Isaiah. Asia hoped with all her heart that Isaiah hadn't made the call to them yet, but she didn't feel optimistic. When her son made up his mind to do something, he wasn't known to waste time in getting it done. Their despicable comments could set his progress way back if he took them to heart. He didn't need to hear that kind of negativity from anyone. Asia's heart ached sorely for her only child's predicament. It seemed to her that he wasn't getting any breaks at all. As if he didn't already have enough to deal with, he now had to deal with Torri's uncultured parents.

The tapping on her shoulder brought Asia out of what seemed like a nightmare to her.

"I've got to be going now. I know you're not the type of person to hold my parents' behavior against me, but I can't explain how sorry I am. Can we still visit with each other after they've returned to Chicago? I'll miss you."

Asia took Torri into her arms for a brief moment despite the fact the model was much taller than she. "Nothing has to change between us, Torri. I'm your friend and the baby's grandmother. Your parents haven't affected our relationship one iota. If anything, they've strengthened it. You're welcome in my home any time you want to visit. Okay?"

"Okay. Thanks, Mommy-Asia." Torri turned to Lenora. "Auntie Lenora, I hope nothing has changed between us, either."

"Not a chance. You take care of yourself and our baby. If you can't think of someone to be a godparent to your child, don't hesitate to ask me. I found out recently that I'm not able to have children of my own, but I've always had very strong maternal instincts. I certainly know how to give love and to receive it from little children. Just as I've always had Isaiah's back, Auntie Lenora has yours, too."

Asia looked hesitant about what she wanted to say to Torri, but it had to be said. "Don't let anyone talk you into an abortion if that's not what you want. No one has the right, parent or not, to tell you what you can and can't do with your body. And one other thing. Please don't take your parents to the hospital to see Isaiah. No good can come of it for either of you."

"Everything you just mentioned is completely out of the question: no abortion, no visits to the hospital for them. You have my word on it."

Asia just had to hug Torri again. This young woman already had a lot to contend with before her parents arrived; her troubles had now tripled. Asia was proud of the fact that Torri hadn't disrespected her family when it could've been so easy to accomplish, especially with parents like that. Asia had never disrespected her parents either. It was a forbidden act.

"If you don't mind, Torri, Lenora and I are going to stay in here. Going back out there will only complicate matters. I'm sure Nicholas has remained in control of himself. Otherwise he would've come back here by now. Please call me tonight when you're all settled in bed. I want to know how you're doing."

"Will do. Bye for now," Torri said, looking ready to cry again.

Asia and Lenora carried Torri's suitcases to the end of the hallway and then summoned Nicholas to get the bags and take them out to her parents' rental car. After their final farewells to Torri, the two women turned around and went back into the guest bedroom.

Badly needing emotional release, Asia fell onto the bed and let her tears flow free. Lenora sat down on the side of the mattress and gently stroked her friend's hair. She also had to let go of the anger still boiling inside her. Crying for release was Lenora's only option as well. If she'd been able to do what she'd wanted to earlier, Lenora knew she wouldn't be seated in Asia's bedroom; she would've already been arrested and charged with assault and battery on the Jeffersons. But Lenora was also a person who knew what she could and couldn't control.

* * *

Things had heated up considerably when Nicholas met with Vann Orville for the third time. He had learned that the case against Price Sheldon was even more serious than originally thought, which alone had been bad enough. According to Vann's account of Sheldon's legal troubles, Vann had managed to get access to irrefutable proof that the Wildcats center was involved in shaving points to predetermine the outcome of basketball games. Vann had named Troy as Sheldon's accomplice, but there wasn't enough evidence to implicate the two teammates in what had happened to Isaiah.

Unless Isaiah's memory of that night returned, the two men couldn't be charged with a crime against him, if they were in fact involved in that incident. Both basketball players were out on quarter-million-dollar bonds. Once the new evidence had been introduced to the presiding judge, Sheldon was arrested immediately and bailed out almost as quickly. Sheldon had already implicated Troy in the hope of being offered a decent plea bargain, not so unusual when it came down to saving one's own butt.

Nicholas knew that Sheldon and Troy were nothing more than sacrificial lambs for a mobster gambling organization operating out of Las Vegas. The case file suggested that Sheldon had run up exorbitant gambling debts with the loan shark organization. When he couldn't pay his debt, he was offered a sure-fire way out of his gambling troubles, shaving points. Why Sheldon had solicited Troy's help in pulling off his duplicity was not yet known.

Troy's involvement with Sheldon was what made Nicholas even surer that the two men had something to do with Isaiah's accident. Since Troy only came into the ball game when Isaiah was on the bench, he wouldn't have been Sheldon's first choice in an accomplice. With Isaiah out of the game due to injury, Troy would be the one to take over the starting position as the team's point guard. Nicholas realized his theory was just that without concrete evidence against the two basketball players to support it. But if he was correct in his theory, Sheldon and Troy had to remove Isaiah from the scheme of things for their plan to work.

Nicholas could only wonder if Isaiah had met with his end when he refused to go along with Sheldon's plan to shave points for monetary gain, or in the center's case, to get himself out of serious debt. Perhaps Isaiah had been solicited by Sheldon and had not only turned him down, but also threatened to go to upper management regarding the elaborate scheme. Nicholas felt that this particular assumption provided him with a very realistic motive.

Unable to sleep with so many theories rolling around inside his head, Nicholas decided to put a call through to Asia. He wasn't ready to share with her all that he'd learned until his conjecture was either proved or disproved. Talking with her might calm his nerves and perhaps help him get to sleep once the call ended. He and Asia had been soothing each other since the nightmare of their son's accident first began.

The sound of the ringing phone pounded in his ears as he waited for Asia to answer. When she finally answered his call, she didn't sound the least bit drowsy. "Hey, you sound pretty good for it being after ten o'clock at night. How are you feeling?"

"Nicholas, you must have ESP. I was thinking of calling you, but I'd decided it might be too late. I'm feeling okay. How has your day been?"

"My day has been busy, busy, busy. Too late doesn't count between us. It's never too late when we need to talk with each other. I thought you knew that by now."

"I do know. Just was feeling a little guilty for needing to lean on you again. But I did think you might've called it an early night, so I decided it was best to talk to you tomorrow. You're up at the crack of dawn to make Isaiah's therapy sessions and you're back to work now, even if it is only part-time. It's also Wednesday, so that meant you probably went to Bible study at your church this evening. But I'm glad you found the time to call me. How about having lunch with me tomorrow?"

"Sorry, but I'm seeing Miranda during the lunch hour. I've decided to try and work out everything with her. I'm long overdue on getting back with her as it is. How about a nice, early-evening dinner? I'll even let you choose the restaurant. Sound good to you?"

Asia had never expected Nicholas to get back with Miranda, not after all the negative stuff that had occurred between them. She was practically in shock over his announcement. The casual remarks had come right out of the blue. Although she was highly curious about his serious change of heart in regards to his marriage, not to mention devastated by it, she wouldn't touch that topic with a ten-foot pole. At the moment, all she really wanted to do was cry. But she'd never let him know that her heart was broken over his decision. She'd have to support his choices, but she was going to miss him; Miranda would never let them continue to have the type of relationship they'd enjoyed over the past few months. Not in a million years.

"Asia, are you still there?"

"I'm here. I just got lost in my thoughts."

"What's your answer to dinner?"

"I've already been invited to dinner tomorrow evening; that's why I asked about lunch. My doctor friend, Malachi, has finally pinned me down for a dinner date." She hadn't exactly given Malachi a definitive answer, but she didn't see any reason not to go out with him.

Now that Nicholas would no longer be unavailable to her for casual outings, she had to get a life. Being around him had aroused her needs and desires for an intimate relationship with a man, feelings that she didn't want to continue to suppress. Having Nicholas back in her life had caused Asia to become aware of all the things she'd been missing out on by continuously denying herself the love of a good man. That was all about to change. Just because she couldn't have Nicholas didn't mean she had to go back to the lonely existence she'd lived before he'd happened along. That was an unfulfilled life that she never wanted to go back to.

"Is that the same brother that called when I answered your phone?"

"That's him."

"I thought you two were just friends, Asia."

"We are, just two friends who've decided to take an evening meal together."

"I hope you have a good time. How was Isaiah when you left the hospital?"

"He was in better spirits than what you said he was like when you saw him early in the morning. Still not very talkative, though. He seems to be sulking because Torri's visits to him have been short lately. With her parents still here, she tried to explain to him that it was hard to get away from them for any length of time. And she doesn't want to run the risk of them asking to go out with her if she tells them she'll be gone all day or all evening. It's their attitude toward his disability that's the real issue for him, but he won't admit that to her. He's of the mind that Torri should choose him over her parents, but he'd never come right out and ask her to do that.

"But he did say it would please him if she decided that on her own.

Of course, I didn't encourage him in that way of thinking. Torri shouldn't have to choose one or the other. But she might have to keep the two relationships separate," Asia told Nicholas.

"He's still not taking his therapy in stride. He's having an extremely hard time with it. I think his anger is building again. I hope if he explodes that it's one of us that's there when it happens. I don't want Torri to have to bear the brunt of his rage. Her parents have managed to really set him off, Asia. I hear doubt in his voice once again. His resolve has weakened a lot over the past week. I keep talking to him about hanging tough, but I don't think I'm getting through. So I have to rely on the only resource that's one hundred percent reliable, prayer."

"The vulgar things the Jeffersons had the nerve to say have set us all off. He'll come around. We just have to keep reminding him of how blessed he is, Nicholas."

"He is definitely that."

Nicholas fell into a moment of silence as he thought about Asia's dinner date. He didn't like the idea, but he had no right to protest it, especially in view of his desire to resolve things with Miranda. Until he found out where he and Miranda stood, he had no say in what Asia did with her life or whom she did it with. How had his life gotten so complicated? Asia's yawning cut into his thoughts. "Sounds like somebody has gotten sleepy. You get a good night's rest, Asia."

"I'm sorry for yawning in your ear. I'm beginning to feel exhausted. Good night."

"Good night, Asia."

After hanging up the phone, Nicholas immediately began to put a plan into action to try to get Troy to fold. He couldn't execute the plan himself; Taylor was the perfect person to get the ball in play for him. Troy had to know by now that Sheldon had rolled over on him, which would make him game to get some sort of break for himself and to return the favor to his disloyal teammate. Working over Troy Dyson should be a piece of cake for Taylor, once Nicholas told her what she needed to do to get him talking about his legal troubles. Taylor would have to be a really good poker player. She would have to bluff her way into getting information. They somehow had to make Troy think they knew all the details of what had happened while Isaiah was at his home, but that they needed to hear his side of the story before they could even try to negotiate a plea bargain on his behalf. If Isaiah couldn't remember what happened to him, then Nicholas thought it was up to him to reenact that night by any means necessary. It was imperative to Isaiah's future.

Truth, justice, and complete vindication for his son would prevail, Nicholas vowed.

CHAPTER SIXTEEN

Taylor listened intently to Nicholas as he laid out his plans for her to execute. He went through every scenario he could possibly think of. Taylor was surprised to learn that Nicholas didn't want to see Troy hang, that he just wanted to vindicate his son. That he actually wanted to help the young man he thought might be responsible for nearly killing his son had Taylor admiring her boss even more. Nicholas knew Troy would get some time if found guilty on the crimes he'd already been charged with; it was how much time that Nicholas was concerned with. He didn't want to see the kid spend the rest of his life in jail for something he might not have known was going to happen; that was a question that still had to be answered.

After reading the case file, Nicholas's gut now had him feeling that Troy hadn't expected things to go as far as they did with Isaiah. He somehow didn't think Troy knew that the plan would lead to killing him. That's where Sheldon came in. He was the one with the most to lose. Whatever drug Isaiah had taken wittingly or unwittingly had wiped out a portion of his memory. Isaiah remembered everything that had occurred earlier in the day and after he'd left his mother's house. That puzzled Nicholas. If he was given something after he got to Troy's house, he should at least remember arriving there. All of this was speculation on his part.

He pulled out the lists of paralyzing drugs that he'd been told about and had read about and handed it to Taylor. "Get this list to someone in one of the labs we use." He pulled out another report. "Isaiah's blood and urine tests are conclusive for drugs but inconclusive as to identifying the actual drug that was taken. Have the lab go through that list and identify any drugs that might cause the kind of outcome that's on that report. I need to get the results as quickly as possible."

"Yes, sir." Taylor chewed on her lower lip. "Can I make a suggestion, Nick?"

"Let's hear it."

"In order to keep you and our office out of this altogether, I think someone else should talk to Troy. I still see an issue of conflict of interest with our office getting involved in this."

"Like who?"

"Isaiah's mother. She's knows Troy extremely well and has spent countless hours with him. He's her son's best friend. She would know Troy better than anyone. I think he would open up to her more than he would with someone else. She's your point man, Nick. She can appeal to Troy as Isaiah's mother and also as Troy's friend, a loving woman that Troy can believe has genuine concern for him since she's known him for many, many years. Asia is also a prosecuting attorney who can spell out for Troy all the legal ramifications."

Nicholas stroked his chin. "See, that's one of the reasons I hired you! I think you have something here. But will Asia do it? We are talking about the possibility of Troy being involved with a plot to kill her son. Asia is a mother first. But then again, she's also a Christian. She would be able to forgive Troy even if it took her a little while to finally come to that end."

"But, Nick, I see how her brilliant skills as a prosecutor can make Troy clearly understand what he's up against. She can certainly convince him that's he's not going to win against the system. No matter how much money he has, he will be made an example of by the court if he doesn't get the right advice and sound representation from his legal defense team."

"I see what you mean. Asia can easily convey that message to him. You're right about him being able to see her genuine concern for his welfare. She cares a lot for this young man. I'll talk to her and get back to you. Thanks for coming up with a great solution to our dilemma.

If we can convince Asia to take part in this, I think your fantastic idea is doable."

Nicholas's cell phone rang. "Hold on a minute while I get this." He greeted the caller with enthusiasm, smiling broadly when he recognized his son's voice. "Hey, what's up, champ? How's it going for you over there?"

"Dad, I need to see you right away! I've remembered a few things about the night of my accident. These strange memories were triggered by the nightmares I told you about. Can you come to the hospital now? Also, I want to share with you what the doctors just told me."

"I'm on my way. Hold tight until I get there." Nicholas disconnected the line. "That was Isaiah, Taylor. Says he's remembered some things from the night in question. I need to get over there as soon as possible. Call me if you get any new information before I get back. Thanks for everything. It's been a pleasure working with you on this case."

"The pleasure's been all mine. It's not often a rookie lawyer gets to work with one of the best legal minds in the country. Go on and get out of here. I'll keep you posted."

Asia felt so sorry for the young man seated in her family room. He looked more depressed than she'd felt since the moment Nicholas had announced his intent to work things out with Miranda. Troy had come to her for advice. He'd already told Asia that he was in deep trouble and that he knew it. He couldn't see any way to get out of the serious mess he'd gotten himself into. Asia suspected that he might've been drinking or taking drugs before he came to her house. His words sounded a little slurred. His bloodshot eyes had narrowed to tiny slits and were glazed over. Fear and crying could bring about the same effects to his eyes and the defects in his speech, so she couldn't be 100 percent sure of her suspicions.

"Troy, how can I help you with your situation? You know I'm not a defense attorney."

"Yeah, but you're a prosecutor, so you should know how the prosecution is going to proceed in their attempt to bring me down. Do they have a case, Miss A?"

"I can't determine that. You haven't told me anything about your case. What I know about it is what I've read in the papers and what Auntie Lenora has shared of her knowledge of the situation. In order for me to advise you, you're going to have to come clean with me regarding your involvement in the alleged illegal gambling and drugs. I can't possibly get a read on your situation without knowing the facts."

"I'm not being charged with drug possession or intent to distribute. That's Sheldon's rap. They've only charged me with illegal gambling, as it pertains to shaving points to try to control the outcome of a sporting event for monetary gain."

"Are you guilty of the charge, Troy? I have to know the truth."

"Do I have attorney-client privilege with you?"

"I'm not either a defense attorney or yours. You have my word that what you tell me stays with me, unless the defense or prosecution subpoenas me. Is that good enough for you?"

"Why would one of them subpoena you?"

"Simply because I know you and you're my son's best friend. The defense attorney may want me as a character witness, which means I'd testify to your character in open court. The prosecutor will get a chance to redirect and try to discredit any information the defense gets from me. It can also work in the reverse. The prosecutor can call me as a witness and then the defense gets its shot at me. I'm not saying I'll be hauled into court, just that it could happen," Asia advised him. "Either way, I'd be obligated by law to testify. I'd have no choice."

Asia could see that Troy looked scared to death but also reluctant to open up to her. She was sure that he knew he could trust her, but she understood his need to weigh out his options.

"Troy, how did this all get started in the beginning? How did you get involved with something you had to know would carry dire consequences? This is a serious crime we're talking about. And if you're found guilty it will bring about a stiff penalty! At any rate, even if you're found innocent of the charges, your pro basketball career may already be shot. Sometimes just the suggestion of criminal intent can ruin a high-profiler's lifestyle."

Troy's eyes started to tear up. "So, it looks as if my life is over anyway. If I can't play ball, I may as well be dead. Basketball is my life. I'm nothing without it."

"From what I've heard many inmates say, being locked up can often be worse than being dead. If you have information that might help the prosecutors bring down the bigger fish involved in this case, you might be able to save yourself from some really hard time. Through the legal grapevine, I understand that Sheldon has been willing to roll over on you to save his own hide. Have you already gotten wind of that vital piece of information?"

Troy looked distraught by what he'd just heard. "Yeah, I know about it. I can't believe it either. I thought he was my boy. As you know, I've been around crime all my life by having brothers involved in every kind of illegal thing you can imagine. I've tried to avoid getting caught up in their criminal activities, but I've also been somewhat fascinated with that kind of lifestyle. My older brothers always made it sound so exciting and fairly easy when they bragged about the bad things they'd done. Even jail and prison time didn't deter them from seeking thrills from their crimes. This situation I'm in now all started with Sheldon asking me to do him a favor. Apparently he had gone to Isaiah—"

"What does Isaiah have to do with any of this?" Asia quickly interjected.

Troy jumped to his feet and began to pace the floor. He suddenly became highly agitated, which was evident in his punching his fist into the palm of his hand and his pacing turning maniacal. Asia began to feel a little frightened by his odd behavior.

Her next thought was to make an excuse to slip away so she could call Nicholas to come over there just in case Troy's behavior became violent. She could handle herself, but she didn't want to have to. While she kept a gun in her nightstand drawer, she knew she'd first have to be able to get to it. Why she was thinking these kinds of things eluded her, but then she quickly chalked it up to basic instinct. Her natural instincts were actually alerting her to the fact that Troy might become a danger to her in his altered state of mind. She quickly sent up a silent prayer.

When Troy came back and sat down in the recliner, the look in his eyes frightened Asia even more. It appeared to her as if he had lost touch with reality. Then tears suddenly started running down his cheeks. The unexpected pounding of his fist on her coffee table caused her to jump with a start. With her heart beating erratically inside her chest, she moved to the other end of the sofa just in case she needed to make a mad dash for the front door. Wondering if he had a weapon had her scanning his clothing for unusual bulges, especially around his waistline.

"This is all Isaiah's fault. If only he'd done what Price asked him to do, all this wouldn't be happening. Ike is selfish and he only thinks of himself. Price came to him as a friend in trouble and Isaiah turned his back on him. How do you ignore someone in big trouble?"

Asia knew the charges against Isaiah weren't true, especially where Troy was concerned. Troy was playing for the Wildcats organization because of Isaiah's generous spirit toward him and the recommendations he'd made on his behalf. Isaiah had often carried Troy on his back.

Asia willed herself to calm down. Nicholas had been right, she mused; Troy seemed to know something about what had happened to Isaiah. Though she still found it hard to believe he could be involved in harming her son, she had to remain cool if she was to get any more information. Troy sounded desperate to rid himself of the details that might have led up to his arrest. And she was more than eager to receive any and all information he might give up.

"What did Price ask Isaiah to do?"

"The same thing he asked me to do. He just wanted to shave the points on a couple of games so he could get out of having to pay back a high gambling debt. He needed some help, badly. Price didn't think he was asking too much in light of what could happen to him if he didn't figure out a way to come up with the cash."

"So, I gather that Isaiah turned him down. Am I right?"

"Yeah, but he didn't let it go at that. He threatened to tell the head coach and the people upstairs in the head office what Price had gotten himself involved in. That really scared Price. I never met the people Price was into the money for, but he said they'd kill him if he didn't either pay up his gambling loans or settle his debt with them on the basketball court."

"Troy, I need you to tell me what happened after Isaiah threatened Price with exposure."

Sweating now, Troy rubbed the palms of his hands up and down his face. Then his hands flew up and came to rest on the very top of his head, where he entwined them.

"Price told me he was only going to try and scare Ike into keeping his mouth shut. He said he needed me to help him out. Before I agreed to assist him, I made him promise me that Isaiah wouldn't get hurt. One thing led to another as Price planned out what we could do. Then he suddenly came up with the idea that if Ike were out for a while with a minor injury that he could pay up his debt. He said I'd be able to help him out then; he was sure I'd be moved into the starting lineup. It seemed like an okay plan to me since Ike wouldn't suffer a serious injury."

"How was the minor injury to occur?" Asia asked, her heart beating harder than earlier.

"That's where the problem came in. Price couldn't come up with anything that would make it seem accidental. But if the accident occurred while Isaiah was under the influence of a strong sedative Price had in his possession, Price thought we could pull it off. Once Isaiah was out cold, he planned to sprain one of his ankles by twisting it around with his bare hands until it began to swell or a tendon popped."

Asia winced in pain. Just the thought of their cruel and unusual plans hurt her deeply. Price was a big man who had the physical strength to pull off what he'd suggested. Seeing that Troy was up pacing around again like a caged lion caused Asia to instantly return her full attention to him. His rapidly changing mood swings let her know she needed to stay alert.

"Since Isaiah didn't suffer that type of damage, I'm guessing you didn't execute that particular idea. What happened next, Troy?"

Visibly nervous, Troy began popping his knuckles. His sweating had also increased.

"Why did your son have to resist Price's attempt to get help for himself? Isaiah always thought he was better than the rest of us. He never wanted to go with the team when we all decided to go out for some fun. Rarely did he socialize with his teammates . . ."

"He hung out with you quite a bit. When you say he didn't want to socialize with his teammates, you seem to be including yourself in that. And we both know that's not a true statement. What is it that you're really holding against Isaiah? It has to be something serious for you to agree to be a part of a plot to harm him."

Troy stared hard at Asia as he gathered his thoughts. "I don't have anything against Ike. It's just that no one ever thought I measured up to him on or off the basketball court. But I knew better. My skills on the court are just as honed as his, but I never got the call as a starter."

"Isaiah was the starting point guard when you came to the team last season. It's not like you two were rivals for the starting position and he was picked over you. The position was his from the day he was drafted and signed with the Wildcats. It has to be something else."

"There's nothing else. Ike is the man and I've always had to live in his shadow. I bet you never knew that I was interested in Torri first. But, as usual, she was just another of many women who automatically gravitated to him. He had it like that and I didn't."

"Are you saying you dated Torri?"

"We never did that. No chance for it."

"Did Isaiah know you had an interest in her?"

"I didn't tell him after the way I saw her looking at him when I introduced them at a party. He never knew I liked her."

"I'm sorry, but I don't understand. How can you hold that against him if you never bothered to tell him you liked Torri? Isaiah told me that you were there when they met, but that was the extent of it, other than him saying that Torri was with a friend of yours. I was under the impression you met Torri the same time he did, but that it was through your friend."

"That's true. But I'd seen Torri's picture at my friend's place, and had asked her to bring Torri to the party so I could meet her. I would've eventually asked her out had she not shown immediate interest in Isaiah. The come-on looks she gave him couldn't be misinterpreted."

"Then I don't think you can hold Isaiah responsible for the outcome. Maybe if you had told him you wanted to ask out Torri things might've been different. Troy, we've gotten completely off the subject. I'm interested in knowing what you know about my son's accident."

Asia's question triggered his agitation anew. He didn't get up and start pacing the floor, but his right foot started going up and down like mad. He was getting hyper again. "You have to understand that I was lied to. I didn't know Price had changed plans. I was given this clear liquid to slip into Isaiah's drink, but it was only supposed to knock him out. But later, when his body started shaking all over, like someone having a grand mal seizure, Price panicked big time."

The phone rang, scaring both Asia and Troy. His hand instantly went to his side and then he lifted up his shirt. That's when she saw the gun. Intense fear gripped her. It suddenly felt like a million razor-sharp claws tearing away at her insides. Slowly, Asia got up to reach for the phone, keeping her eyes locked on Troy.

"Don't answer that," he shouted at her. "I'm not through talking to you. I have to make someone understand what happened. I'm not going to get a second chance at this. No one wants to hear what a lying criminal has to say. I know you will give the newspapers and the media an accurate account of what I'm telling you. Price is lying about me and I want everyone to know that. When this horror story is finally reported, I want the truth to be known."

"Troy, you'll get a chance in court to tell your own story. I think people will believe you. I do. Everything you've said seems true to me. Why don't you think anyone will listen?"

"Because I'm not going to be around to tell my side of it. That's why I'm telling you everything so you can do it." He pulled the gun out of his waistband. "Once this little soul-cleansing interview is over, I'm out of here. I have no intention of going to prison, ever."

Asia was horrified at his remarks. He hadn't said outright that he was going to kill himself, but her gut and his unstable demeanor clearly spelled out his intent for her. Troy wanted the truth of his actual involvement to be recorded by a reliable source, one that he could trust. Like it or not, Asia realized that she'd been appointed to act as his voice for him to be heard from the grave. Her insides quivered at such an unsavory revelation. That he hadn't intended to kill her, too, brought her a touch of solace, but the thought of him killing himself nearly destroyed her emotionally. To have him do it in her house caused her anguish to deepen.

Off and on, the phone rang, stopped, and rang again every thirty seconds or so. To silence the annoying sound, Troy reached over and snatched the receiver off the hook and tossed it on the floor. Asia's heart was now in her mouth as beads of sweat popped out on her forehead.

Troy now held the gun to his head. For several seconds he just sat there expressionless.

"I'm ready to finish my story. No more interruptions from you. This has to be done."

Asia was on the edge of her seat as Troy spelled out for her in painstaking detail what had occurred next at his home in Ladera. She fought back her tears as her son's best friend explained how a liquid sedative or muscle relaxant of some sort was then poured down Isaiah's throat to try and stop his body tremors. Price had told Troy that he had been prescribed the substance to use to relax the muscles when severe spasms occurred in his back.

Asia was even more concerned that Price had continued to use the sedative without seeking further medical advice. Instead of getting it from his sports physician, he had gotten into the habit of purchasing it on the black market. That made the substance and the purchase illegal.

As if she hadn't been shocked enough, Troy practically stunned her into cardiac arrest when he told her how Isaiah had finally ended up on the commuter train tracks. The hell her son was put through prior to the accident had been catastrophic.

According to Troy's account, Price thought Isaiah was going to die from the drugs he'd given him, so he decided he had to make things look like an accident. With Troy following Price in his own car, Price had driven Isaiah's car onto the tracks and had somehow jammed the gearshift, knowing Isaiah was out cold and that he'd never make it out alive. The fact that he'd checked the train schedule before taking him to the tracks proved to Asia that Price was a calculating, cold-blooded killer—and not just a man desperate to rid himself of gambling debts.

The thought of Isaiah's teammates, one of whom was supposed to be his best friend, leaving her son on the tracks to get run over and killed by a fast-moving train made her violently ill. Taking deep breaths was all Asia could do to keep from regurgitating. She couldn't pray hard or fast enough for deliverance. If Troy had gone along with such an evil plot to kill his best friend, she was in no doubt that he could easily change his mind and decide to murder her, too.

A sudden flurry of activity caused Asia to run for cover. As she ducked down behind the sofa, she got a glimpse of Nicholas. Where he'd come from, and how he'd gotten in, she didn't know, didn't care. He was there, and that was all that mattered—until she heard the gunshots.

Paying no heed to her own safety, she came from behind the couch intent on rescuing the man she loved. Seeing him sprawled out on top of Troy caused the screams to rip away from where they'd settled at the top of her lungs. As she made her way over to where Nicholas lay, she could barely see for the sea of tears flooding from her eyes. Asia then spotted the silvery glint from the barrel of the gun, which was lying a couple of feet away from where the two men lay on the floor. She quickly secured it and then dialed 911 before moving any closer.

As she bent down beside Nicholas, she heard barely audible cries. Not knowing if they came from Nicholas or Troy, she tried to lift up

Nicholas's head. That's when she recognized his anguished voice praying over Troy's body, yet she could still hear the muffled cries. Nicholas couldn't be praying and crying at the same time, so she figured the other sounds came from Troy. That meant he was still alive. Giving no thought to Troy's crimes, she began to pray for him, too.

When one of Nicholas's arms reached out and pulled her close to him, Asia slumped the rest of the way down to the floor. Both Asia and Nicholas were crying now as he lifted his weight off of Troy. In one quick movement, Nicholas cradled Troy's head in his lap. As he began to pray fervently for the lost soul of his son's best friend, he thought of how Isaiah could've so easily died alone in that car, without his father or mother to hold him in his arms. He wasn't a parent to Troy, but he couldn't deny the young man a comforting presence despite the things he'd done to bring serious harm to Isaiah. The kid was obviously troubled, deeply so.

It took several minutes for Asia to discover that no one had been shot. Nicholas had apparently saved Troy's life by getting to him in time to knock the gun away. And he had put himself in harm's way. It was that kind of a thing that made Nicholas such an extra-special man.

Troy began to wail at the top of his lungs. He then switched back and forth between cursing both Jesus and Satan. Nicholas pulled Troy's head upward until it reached his chest. While holding Troy in his arms, Nicholas prayed for both Troy and Price, asking God to forgive them for their sins against Him and his Son, Jesus, and for the crimes against Isaiah.

Nicholas stayed right by Troy's side when the police showed up, giving him as much moral support as he could. He was convinced that Troy didn't really believe Price intended to kill Isaiah up until the very second that Price drove Isaiah's car onto the commuter tracks. Troy wanted off the bench for a game or two, and Price felt he had to kill to keep from being killed. Isaiah had stood between Price and his last chance to live rather than die at the hands of the people he was into the money for; the major obstacle in Price's way simply had to be removed.

The police had come and gone, taking a handcuffed Troy away with them, but Asia still felt terribly unnerved by the earlier events.

The inhuman things the distraught Troy had revealed regarding Isaiah's nightmarish scenario with him and Price Sheldon were horribly upsetting to her, not only as a mother, but also as a compassionate human being. What Isaiah had endured at the hands of people whom he'd believed to be friends of his had turned her emotions inside and out. The gut-wrenching experience had left her drained and so weak that she could barely stand under her own power. All that had happened to her son had occurred within just a couple of hours.

Asia had held up all through the police interviews, which, in her opinion, had bordered on biting interrogations. But only seconds after the police had cleared out of her home she'd begun to fall apart. The look on Troy's face as they took him away haunted her still. He would definitely have to be placed on suicide watch at the county jail. If she had it to do over again, had she known no one had been shot, she wouldn't have called 911. It was neither her nor Nicholas's desire to see Troy punished too severely. Inpatient psychiatric treatment would serve him better than long-term incarceration. As for Price, the cold-blooded mastermind, Asia hadn't determined what his fate should entail. It was hard for her to even think of him without getting all worked up.

Nicholas came into Asia's bedroom carrying a wicker tray laden with a white ceramic teapot and two matching mugs. He set the tray on the nightstand. After filling the two mugs with the hot liquid, he stirred a teaspoon of sugar into each one. He handed Asia one of the cups and then pulled up a chair and situated it close to her bed.

The look on his face showed his deep concern for her. At one point, during a scary bout of near-uncontrollable hysteria, Nicholas thought he might need to transport her to the local emergency room. This was the second time he'd seen her come unglued, but this one by far had been the worse of the two. It had taken much longer to get her to calm down than it had before.

"You feel up to talking, Asia?"

"Not really, but I know I should. Since you heard most of what I told the lead detective, do you have any other questions about what happened in here with Troy?"

"None that I can think of. You gave a pretty detailed account of your frightening experience with him. My theory about the accident, which we now know was planned to look like one, was practically right on the money. Coupled with the few things Isaiah remembered about that night, I have a clear enough picture. Taylor thought you should be the one to talk to Troy about his situation, but it's apparent that he came to you of his own free will. If Troy hadn't called Isaiah and told him he was coming over here to see you, there's no telling what might have happened."

"Please don't feel guilty about that. It was logical. His call to Isaiah was probably just another cry for help. Although Troy doesn't seem to realize it, our son has had his back all though their relationship. Troy's deep envy of Isaiah seems to have destroyed his ability to use better judgment. I can't imagine being that jealous of someone I consider a best friend. And I didn't see that strong type of envy in Troy. What made Isaiah think I might be in danger?"

"Isaiah knows Troy well enough to recognize it when he's not himself. The stress in his voice, as well as his slurred speech, alerted Isaiah to the peril you could be in, especially with Troy sounding as if he was under the influence of a mind-altering substance. I'd been at the hospital for over an hour when the call came in to Isaiah's room. Troy must've been right at your doorstep when he phoned."

"Troy was inside a long time before the phone rang. But there are times when my answering service picks up before the phone actually rings. I don't know why it does that."

"The service activated on the first ring, repeatedly. After we tried to get you on your cell phone several times, but couldn't, Isaiah thought I should come over here and check on you. He told me where you kept the spare keys in case of an emergency. I broke the speed laws getting over here, but I shudder to think of what could've happened had I arrived only seconds later than I did. Troy's still alive because I dared to break the law at God's commanding voice. Troy is also alive because, by the grace of God, our son was intuitive enough to realize that his best friend was unstable and behaving irrationally."

Asia took a sip of her tea. "I agree with all of that. But he more than likely survived because God isn't through with him yet. I'm sorry I balked at your suggestion of Troy's involvement in Isaiah's situation. It was so hard for me to believe. And even after I've seen firsthand what he's capable of, I'm still having a hard time accepting it. This boy was like family to me. Not knowing a thing about Troy, how did you see the dark side of him when I had no clue that he possessed one?"

"Power of the Holy Spirit combined with gut-level instincts is the best I can come up with. I felt an instant wariness of him only moments after he opened his mouth. I was uneasy around him just taking a short walk down the hospital corridor. I felt negative vibes."

As he sipped on his tea, Nicholas thought of how God always gave his children a safe way out of every situation. But there were many who willfully ignored His directions in order to take their own path, even when they knew it might lead to destruction. Both Troy and Price had choices; both had made the wrong ones. The consequences for their actions would be costly, but it was obvious that they hadn't given any thought to the extremely high price they'd eventually have to pay for their sins. The more a person got away with simply meant that he or she was just closer to getting caught. There were many escape routes in life, but no one could evade God's judgment, which would be swift and absolute.

"Up to hearing some good news, Asia?"

"Always."

He took Asia's hand. "Isaiah's doctors came in to see him today. The medical tests have positively ruled out any injuries to his spinal cord. Isaiah's paralysis is a direct result of the drugs he was given. Also, with intense therapy he should regain the use of his lower body. Isaiah can make a full recovery. You should have seen the look on his face when he realized what the doctors were saying. His initial shock gave way to hysterical laughter. And then the bittersweet tears flowed like the river Jordan. God is good!"

Asia couldn't speak, not just yet. She had to let Nicholas's comments sink in for a couple of minutes. Isaiah's having a chance to make a full recovery was a miracle. Their prayers had worked. God had heard their cries and their humble pleas; He had blessed them yet again. Hot tears poked at her eyes but she blinked them back. This was a joyous, hallelujah occasion, not a sad one by any means. Though there were happy tears, she didn't want to cry her joy out.

As her arms went around Nicholas's neck, her shouts of sincere praise to the Father above filled the air. With his fingers entwined in her hair, Nicholas held Asia tightly against him while thanking God for sparing Isaiah's life and making him whole again. No one other than God could've brought Isaiah through the fire. While Nicholas understood that Isaiah still had a rugged obstacle course before him, he also knew that his son would rise to the occasion.

All the glory belonged to their loving Father God.

Nicholas and Asia only pulled apart when the doorbell rang.

Appearing confused, she looked over at the clock. Then her hands went up to her face. "That must be Malachi. In all this chaos, I forgot we had a dinner date."

Asia's comments triggered Nicholas's memory regarding his appointment with Miranda.

He slapped his forehead with an open palm. "It looks like we both screwed up. I was supposed to see Miranda today. She must be furious at me." He jumped up from the bed. "I'd better get over to her place right now. I'll let your date in on my way out if that's okay with you."

Knowing she didn't have much of a choice, she nodded. At any rate, she wouldn't be going out with Malachi or anyone else this evening. Too much had happened for her in one day. She needed to take time out to recover from the trauma. With him being a doctor, Asia was sure that Malachi would understand her state of mental and physical fatigue.

As Nicholas rushed out of the bedroom, she felt like a part of her had left with him. He hadn't even given her so much as a backward glance or a good-bye. Nicholas's running off to be with Miranda crushed her. However, Miranda was still his wife. He'd made his choice and she'd just have to learn to live with it. The question singeing her mind was how she was ever going to manage to live her life without him there by her side. How could she go back to those lonely days and nights she'd had before he came back into her life? How could she go on, period?

Asia had once again become accustomed to Nicholas's handsome face and loving ways.

CHAPTER SEVENTEEN

"I'm sorry, Nick, I can't see you right now. You had your chance to talk to me yesterday but you blew it when you stood me up. I have a new patient due in any minute now."

Nicholas grinned. "I'm him."

Miranda looked puzzled. "What are you talking about?"

"I'm James Whitaker, your new patient."

She looked at her schedule and saw that her patient's name was the same one that Nicholas had just given. "I don't understand. Why would you make an official appointment to see me? Surely you don't need a psychologist."

"That's exactly what I need. I also have every intention of paying your hourly fees. I have to get some help with several personal issues, ones that are affecting me psychologically. Think you can stand to hear me out?"

"I'm all ears, Nick."

"Okay. I'll get right to the point. I want an old friend of mine and me to get back to being amicable pals. It's seems that we've run into all sorts of problems over the last few months. She's changed a lot and I don't understand why. We'd come to an agreement that we should divorce, had decided that our marriage had fallen short of our expectations, but she backed out at the last minute and refused to finalize the settlement. She then began to make me out as one of the world's worst cheaters and liars. What advice can you give me on how I can get my friend to understand that I never did the things she accused me of, that I never lied to her or cheated on her during our marriage?"

"Nick, I don't have time for these silly games of yours. What's this all about?"

"I just told you. I need your expert advice."

"Well, I'm not sure you're going about it the right way. It seems that your old friend and wife are one and the same. If your wife accused you of cheating on her, I'm sure she had just cause. Women have a way of feeling it when her man is having an illicit affair. No wife likes to learn that her husband is sleeping with his ex-girlfriend. And if she happens to see his infidelity with her very own eyes, like finding them in bed together, she can feel that her whole world has been destroyed. Any woman would find that kind of intimate betrayal very hard to forgive."

"What if the wife is having an illicit affair on her husband while they're living under the same roof?" He studied her reaction very closely. "Should he find it hard to forgive her?"

"Infidelity is hard to forgive no matter who's doing it. A marriage is supposed to be sacred and both parties should honor their vows. What point are you trying to make, Nick?"

"I think I could forgive my wife if she cheated on me. However, what I'd have a very hard time with is her projecting her wrongdoing onto me. For her to accuse me of something she's actually guilty of would be unconscionable. What advice can you give me about confronting her if I thought she was carrying on an extramarital affair behind my back?"

"Nick, I don't know what's going on here, but your time is up. I have no advice for you."

"I believe you know exactly what's going on. You'd better look at your schedule. I'm down as your next two appointments and each is booked for an hour long. So you see, we have plenty of time for you to answer my last question and all the ones that I intend to ask."

"Why don't you just go ahead and spell out for me what you're trying to get at? I've grown impatient with this entire matter. And I'm also sick to death of your juvenile games."

Nicholas sat back in the chair and crossed his legs. "Since you asked me to spell things out, let's get on with it. Your fees are expensive even if I can afford them. You see, my wife doesn't know that I'm well aware that she'd taken on another lover. Then I wondered if perhaps she'd already grown tired of the lover whose bed she'd shared while still living under my roof when she decided to back out of the divorce settlement we'd already reached.

"My wife is the one guilty of adultery, yet she has constantly projected her wrongdoing onto me. How stupid would she feel if she knew that I'd seen her go into a motel with her lover, right after they'd had a cozy dinner for two in a popular restaurant, one that I frequented?"

Nicholas immediately thought back on the evening that he'd seen Miranda in a restaurant with a man much younger than himself. He'd never seen the man before then. To him, they'd looked pretty cozy with one another. Out of curiosity, he'd followed them from the restaurant to the motel. He didn't know what had gone on once the door closed, but he'd been a witness to the passionate kissing and heavy petting before they'd entered the room. It had shocked him to learn of Miranda's extramarital affair. It had hurt him despite their decision to divorce.

"While my wife and I were no longer sharing a bed at the time of the incident, I still saw it as a betrayal. I thought she could've at least waited until she moved out of my home. I would've tried harder to remain true to our vows, per the instructions given on divorce in the Bible, but her affair had spelled out the end for me. I didn't see any sense in trying to hold on to something that hadn't been working out even before I knew about her affair. Though I've often itched to call her out on her secret rendezvous, I'd always think better of it.

"Even after she went to our pastor and told him I was an adulterer, I didn't give up her secret. I didn't ever want to throw her illicit affair up in her face, but then I started to see it as the only way to have her back off. My wife had become a reckless mudslinger, and an unbearably nasty, uncaring person. I later came to the conclusion that perhaps it was time to wash her face in the same wet dirt she seemed hell-bent on smearing me and my character with. But I could never do it because that's not the type of man I am. I still want us to make a clean break and for us to try and remain friends. What's your take on this story, Dr. George? Do you think it's possible for my wife and me to divorce and continue to have a friendship?"

Miranda was sick with shame. The pain in Nicholas's eyes made her feel even more humiliated. She didn't know what to say to him, especially when there was nothing she could say to ease his hurt. His torment was clearly visible to the naked eye. There was no way she could ever live this down. The fact that Nicholas knew the truth about her scandalous behavior had her grief-stricken. That he hadn't thrown her adulterous affair up in her face, especially when she had blatantly accused him of being an adulterer, reflected his true character.

Nicholas Reynolds was simply a man of inexhaustible integrity.

He looked her dead in the eye as he got up from the chair. "Please send over to my office your professional assessment and recommendations on how to keep further psychological damage from occurring. I'm interested in your response. Thank you, Dr. George. God bless."

"When was the last time you saw your dad, Isaiah?"

"He's here every day, Mom. Haven't you seen him or talked to him?"

"Actually, I haven't, not since we went to the jail to see Troy several days ago. He's probably busy trying to get his marriage back on track. Did he tell you that he decided to try and work things out with Miranda?"

"Not once has he mentioned his wife to me. I don't even think he ever said he was married, just that he didn't have other children. I only know what you and Torri have told me about her. You seem unhappy about him getting back together with his wife. Are you?"

Asia smiled softly. "Unhappy might not be the right word for what I'm feeling. Perhaps I'm just a little disappointed. I think I always knew that he and I didn't have a future, but I can't say that I didn't find myself hoping for that once or twice. The disappointment I'm experiencing is over the loss of our close friendship. As well as lovers, Nicholas and I were the best of friends when we were in college. We seemed to have picked up right where we left off—and now it looks as if we're back to where we were when I disappeared on him without a word. Talk about poetic justice!"

"Why do you think your friendship with him is lost? Dad is a loyal man and he's been a true friend to both you and me. He won't turn his back on us. He's just not like that, Mom."

"No, he isn't, but his wife is. Believe me, if they're working out their problems, Miranda won't want him anywhere near me."

Isaiah looked fearful. "Do you really think Dad will stay away from us if she asks him to? Does she have that much influence over him?"

"Not us, just me. When it comes to you, no one has any influence on him whatsoever. You're his boy-man and he loves you the way a father should love his son, unconditionally, with every fiber of his being." Asia's eyes filled with tears as she kissed the top of her son's head. "If you could've only experienced the magnificent things he shared with you when you were comatose. But you still have a lot of wonderful things to look forward to with your dad. Nicholas Reynolds is not about to lose any more time living his life without you in it. Where you're concerned, his love and his time come with automatic and unlimited overdraft protection. That's the kind of bank deposit that can't be withdrawn nor overdrawn."

"Thanks for that, Mom. But I think that deep down inside I already knew it. I don't just see my dad standing or sitting here with me, I feel him. His spirit touches me so many places deep in my heart and soul. The man I wasted all those years hating with a passion, crying buckets of tears over, and losing total control of my temper about, is nothing like the man I've come to know, respect, and love over the past few months."

Asia looked at Isaiah in adoration. "I'm glad you got to see for yourself the wonderful man Nicholas is. I should've told you about him. Maybe I didn't tell you about him because I knew you'd come to desperately want to know the man that I'd only have great things to say about. What good was it to tell you about him since I had convinced myself that he would do the right thing by us, but only out of feeling obligated to do so? I knew he was a good man, I just didn't know how good he was. I completely underestimated his true feelings for me. I regret it all."

"I'm sorry that you didn't tell us about each other, but I now believe that it happened the way it did for a reason, the way it was supposed to. We may never know the why of it, but like Dad has told me numerous times, God sent him to me when I needed him the most, not a moment too soon or too late; right on time. He said we shouldn't waste a minute dwelling on a past that we can't change, but that we should make darn sure to focus on each future moment we're granted by the grace of God. Dad is awesome! His apparent love for God makes him even more amazing. He's a man who walks his talk, without stumbling over his feet or any stuttering with his tongue, an absolute rare breed."

"Is that so?" Nicholas asked as he entered the room, smiling at the things he'd just overheard Isaiah saying about him. "My son is a mighty awesome man himself!" Nicholas went over to the bed and embraced his son, kissing and hugging him. He then turned and embraced Asia. "You're pretty awesome, too, Isaiah's mom. This room is overflowing with amazing grace. How are two of my favorite folks doing today?"

"Hey, Dad, I'm all good. I can feel my limbs getting stronger every day. As that continues to happen, my confidence will also strengthen. Since my paralysis is due to the drugs, I'm on the road to recovery. It's going to take even less time for me to be up and about, according to the doctors. Good mental health will play a big role in my recovery. My drive and determination will keep me from losing this battle. The therapy is also getting easier. Everything is looking up. Dad, every single day I think about what you once said to me: totally surrender your will to God. I have surrendered all."

Nicholas hugged his son and then turned to face Asia. "Asia, you want to tell me how you're doing?" he asked.

"Blessed. And it feels so good to find favor with the Father. Seeing the unbelievable progress Isaiah is making helps keep me upbeat." Asia looked pensive. "I know we're all on a natural high, it seems, but have you heard anything at all about Troy?"

"The D.A.'s case is mostly based on circumstantial evidence and hearsay. The only eyewitnesses to the crime against Isaiah are Troy and Price Sheldon, which comes down to one's word against the other. You, Isaiah, can't testify to what happened because you're only able to recall bits and pieces, very small ones at that. Until your memory fully returns, you're no good to the D.A. as an eyewitness. As for the illegal gambling issue, Price is going to have a hard time making the D.A. believe that Troy was the mastermind since Troy has never met the major players who are behind the operation. Every aspect of Troy's involvement was based on the information he received from Price."

"Dad, are you saying Troy could get off scot-free?"

"I'm only explaining how tough a case the D.A. has to prove. If Price hopes to get a plea bargain, rolling over only on Troy isn't going to cut it. There are bigger fish to catch in this deal, and Price is the only one who can reel them in. What do you want to see happen to Troy?"

"I would've been lenient on him had I been the only one he tried to hurt. But when he went to Mom's house with a gun, he crossed too far over the line."

"He wasn't going to harm me, Isaiah. You know that he had the gun to kill himself."

"Maybe so, Mom, but he intimidated you with it when he showed it to you and then told you not to answer the phone. He's not my friend, not when another joker can come to him and ask him to help get me out the way. Even if only a minor injury was suggested, Troy agreed to it, and that's why it was able to go much further than originally planned. And even when he realized that Price had decided to off me, Troy did nothing to try to stop it."

"I hear what you're saying, son. But do you know and understand God's law on forgiveness?" Nicholas asked Isaiah.

"I know to be forgiven that I have to forgive those who sin against me, but I don't have to hang out with them. I don't even remember Price coming to me and asking me to do something like that. Furthermore, I don't think he'd dare to ask me to participate in any type of crime, no matter the reason. He'd know better than that. My guess is that he lied to Troy about me to get him involved. Price was aware that Troy had a few insecurities that had to do with me. I know Troy has said things from time to time about coming off the bench for me. Everyone on the team has heard his grumbling about it, and Price used it to his advantage. Dad, to answer your question, I can forgive Troy, but I'm not going to hang out with someone who was willing to let someone else kill me. I agree that Troy needs psychiatric help, but he should also do some time in jail. He committed a serious crime."

"Well, you've definitely shed a lot more light on this for me," Nicholas said. "I never thought of Price lying to Troy about you turning him in. But it makes perfect sense now that I think about it. If you threatened to turn him in, you certainly would've done it right away. Wow, he really did do a major snow job on Troy. Price lying to Troy about asking you to help him out never crossed my mind. That's something major that I didn't figure into my theory. I just wanted to know what you thought should happen to Troy since the word around the halls of justice has it that he's planning to cop a plea. Now that I have your answer, I can offer my legal input."

Asia shook her head. "I still think he needs psychiatric help. Locking him up before he gets proper treatment is not going to help him with his serious problems. Just think about it; he has to be terribly disturbed to go along with a plot to harm his best friend. I don't believe he knew Price planned to kill until the very moment the crime unfolded. But like you've already pointed out, Isaiah, he didn't try to stop it. Do you have any objections to your father and me counseling Troy on his legal options?"

"Are you talking about representing him, Mom?"

"No, Isaiah, but he doesn't know what he's up against. The history his family has with the law could also hurt him. He needs someone to guide him in these matters."

"Someone other than my parents! He has the money to buy a great legal defense team. I don't think it's sinking in for you, Mom. He was an accomplice in an attempt to murder me. You need to stop trying to convince yourself that you need to help him because of the relationship we once had with him. He's not the person you thought you knew, not the kind of friend we both believed he was.

"His desire to take my starting position by any means necessary was what drove him to participate in this heinous crime. Dad, do you understand what I'm saying? If you do, you need to explain it to Mom. None of us are responsible for what Troy chose to do. He has to be held accountable. And how do we know Troy isn't the one lying? Maybe at the last minute he convinced Price to off me and not the other way around. He had as much to gain as Price."

Nicholas couldn't believe how well Isaiah had thought through Troy and Price's attempt to kill him. He also saw that Isaiah had gotten himself all worked up. "Okay, calm down, Isaiah. I think your mother gets it now that you've explained your feelings about Troy in no uncertain terms. I believe she just wanted to make sure that he gets a fair shake. Everything you've said sheds more light on those two. Both are liars, so we may never know who did what."

"I do understand what you're feeling, Isaiah. What I really wanted was to make sure that you had come to terms with what should happen to Troy. I see that you have. I won't go to see him again, or try to have any influence on his case, but I will continue to pray for him. Is that okay with you?"

"Mom, I'm praying for him, too. I don't mean to sound this bitter, but I'm hurt by his involvement in something so horrific. As Dad has said, I need to ask God to deal with my heart where Troy is concerned. I believe that will happen, but I still have to get through the challenges I'm faced with in the meantime. I have Torri and the baby to think about. And that's what makes what Troy did even worse. According to Torri, he knew she was pregnant before he set me up. Maybe he wanted Torri just as much as my starting position."

Asia thought it best not to comment on what Troy had told her about his interest in Torri. Isaiah was already close to blowing a gasket. She'd eventually tell him, but not now.

"I'm glad you brought that up. Torri was worried about something that was going on with you and your teammates. She said you'd been upset by it, and that you mentioned you were no whistle-blower. Whatever that was about, she thought it might have something to do with what happened to you. Can you tell us about that?"

"I can't believe Torri connected that situation with this one. That wasn't even serious. It had more to do with team effort. Someone complained to the coach that everyone wasn't giving it their all in the practice sessions and in the games. The coach came down hard on all of us. But one of my teammates later told me that I was the one who'd been accused of blowing the whistle. That's what Torri must've misinterpreted, because I did refuse to talk to her about it. In looking back on it now, maybe Price and Troy had already started to set me up to take a fall. Still, I don't know how Torri connected that incident with this one. It doesn't even come close."

"Did I just hear my name being mentioned?" Torri asked as she strolled into the room. "Hey, family. Nice to see you." Taking long, graceful strides, she quickly made her way to Isaiah's bed. In one fluid motion, her lips connected with his. The kiss was deep and passionate. "Hey, boo! You're looking good today. I missed you."

Isaiah had a funny expression on his face as he looked up at Torri. He struggled to find his voice, but all he could do was swallow hard. All eyes were on Isaiah as he appeared to go through some sort of strange metamorphosis. "Dad," Isaiah finally managed to say, "can I speak to you in private? Mom, Torri, could you give us a minute?"

Asia and Torri looked puzzled, but they hastened from the room without question.

Nicholas rushed to Isaiah's bedside. "What is it, son? Your eyes look haunted."

Isaiah crooked his finger for Nicholas to bend down closer. When Nicholas obliged him, Isaiah whispered something into his father's ear.

Nicholas's eyes brightened with surprise. "Are you serious?"

"Yes, but I'm having a hard time believing it myself. When Torri kissed me, I got a sensation! I actually felt it. What do you think that means, Dad?"

"It means your girl still excites the heck out of you. It also suggests that the lower half of your body responded to the intimacy of her kiss. I'd say that's a darn good thing to have happen." Nicholas laughed heartily. "Looks like you're finally able to get it up."

"Dad, this isn't funny." Isaiah looked thoroughly embarrassed.

"No, it isn't. It's beautiful. All you have to do now is talk to your doctors and see what they tell you. You should be ecstatic."

Isaiah gave a slight chuckle. "I guess you're right. But can we keep this under wraps until we're sure? I don't want to give anyone false hopes, including myself. Okay, Dad?"

Nicholas smiled gently. "Okay, champ. Should I call the girls back in?"

"I'm all right with that, but I hope you can keep a straight face."

"You can count on it, son."

Asia looked concerned when Nicholas summoned them back to the room. Seeing that Isaiah was all smiles helped her to relax. She could see that he was okay, but she was curious about him dismissing them in the first place. Knowing he was fine allowed her to drop the matter altogether, for now. She had every intention of later finding out from Nicholas.

Torri bent over the bed and kissed Isaiah. "I'm not going to stand for you kicking me out of here too many more times, buster. You promised me that we would share everything from here on in. But it looks like you're still keeping secrets."

Isaiah had a hard time keeping a straight face, especially after he looked over at Nicholas and saw the comical expression on his face. Isaiah stifled his laughter.

"Torri, it was just something personal I had to talk over with my dad. You know, men stuff. Nothing you ladies would be interested in hearing."

Nicholas chuckled under his breath. In his opinion, what Isaiah had said was an interest to any woman who loved her man enough to share her intimate treasures with.

"Whatever, boo. But just know that I'm going to hold you to your promise. Have you told your parents about what we've been discussing?"

"No, but now is as good a time as any. Mom and Dad, Torri and I are talking about getting married. We want the baby to have both his parents around. But that's not the only reason, or the main one. We love each other."

Asia was happy despite her concerns for the futures of both her son and his girlfriend. They were doing exactly what she and Nicholas should've done, had she given him the opportunity. Unlike what her parents had done in her situation, she was going to stand by her two kids 100 percent. If they fell, she'd be right there to help them get back up.

Asia embraced Torri first and then her son. "I'm thrilled for you. Congratulations!"

Isaiah looked up at his mom. "I saw the concerned look you had, Mom. Just know that Torri and I are going to take this one step at a time. We both understand what we're up against. We're both ready to deal with whatever comes our way. Torri has also accepted the fact that if I can't share in a physical relationship with her, I'm not going to tie her down like that. Regardless of her loudly voiced objections, it wouldn't be fair to either of us. But physical intimacy has nothing to do with me being a good father to our child and to continue to be Torri's best friend. We have to work this out so that everyone benefits, not just me."

"That's a very mature approach you two have decided on. I'm happy for both of you! We are a family, one that has done a lot of praying together over the past few months. God will take care of us. And I'll be here for you guys all the way. This papa you got here ain't no rolling stone," Nicholas joked.

Everyone laughed as they gathered around Isaiah's bed for a moment of prayer. While holding hands, Nicholas prayed for each person in the room and then prayed that Torri, Isaiah, and their baby would have a happy life together.

* * *

"You're kidding, Nicholas. He told you that?"

"Why's that so hard for you to believe? I'm his father. Or are you thinking he should've told you instead of me? Feeling a little left out, Asia?"

Asia took a sip of water. "Yeah, I guess you could say that. At any rate, he tells me a lot of things, and at times he gives me way too much information. But I don't think he would've told me he got a sensation from kissing Torri. At least, not in the same terms as he told you. It's been three weeks now and he hasn't said a word to me yet. But I can tell you this: I'm thrilled to know he's feeling something below the waist. It's a good sign, isn't it, Nicholas?"

"A darn good one. If I hadn't been around, he definitely would've told you what was up, no pun intended."

Asia laughed at Nicholas's comments. "Interesting choice of words."

He grinned. "I understand Isaiah tells his mom everything. But he was somewhat embarrassed by it. He doesn't like me laughing and joking about him being able to get it up. He's had a few more erections since that first one, each coming after an intimate encounter with Torri. But he still wants to wait until he's able to move his legs and all before he tells her." Nicholas chuckled as he looked over at the refrigerator. "Mind if I get something cold to drink, Asia? I've gotten a little thirsty all of a sudden. It's getting hot up in here."

"I wonder why. And are you sure it's just your thirst you're trying to cool down? But, no, I don't mind a bit. You've always been free to make yourself right at home when you're visiting me."

He laughed hard. "I'm going to leave that one alone. Thanks for making me feel at home. You want something other than the water you got there?"

"Nope. I'm fine. Water is good for me, but I don't drink enough of it."

Nicholas came back to the table carrying a large glass of cranberry-apple juice. While he was taking a long gulp of the ice-cold liquid, his eyes connected with Asia's. He thought about how much he needed to say to her, but he didn't know where to begin. They hadn't been alone like this in a while—and he didn't know when another opportunity might present itself. Life had become complicated for all of them, but the raging storms appeared calmer. The dark gray skies were starting to make way for the softer hues of blue.

It looked as if Isaiah was coming along just fine; his attackers had finally had their day in court. Both Price and Sheldon had pleaded no contest in hopes of receiving lighter sentences. The judge had recommended psychiatric inpatient treatment facilities for both men. The sentencing hearings in the criminal case wouldn't be held until after six months of psychiatric treatment was received. While Asia and Nicholas thought the judge's recommendation was the best course of action, for the time being, Isaiah had to continuously pray for his heart to soften against the two men who'd tried to kill him.

Torri's pregnancy had stabilized, but her parents weren't happy about her decision to stand by Isaiah. But she'd made it clear to them how much she loved him, that she was going to have their baby, and that the three of them were already a family. The Jeffersons had gone back to Chicago disappointed and unhappy. Their attempts to get their daughter to go home with them and have the baby there had also failed.

It seemed to Nicholas that everyone's personal future had been decided but his. The last time he'd seen Miranda was during the appointments he'd scheduled with her for himself several weeks back. He hadn't heard a single word from his estranged wife since he walked out of her office that day. Every attempt to communicate with her had failed.

"Are you okay, Nicholas? You look like you're in pain."

"I am. I ache to kiss you until our lips are swollen with passion. But I don't dare take possession of your sweet mouth. I'm still a married man." He got to his feet. "I'd better go while I have the willpower to do so. I'm sorry things couldn't be different for us. I've always loved you, Asia Morrell, and I can't imagine that ever changing. I can't ask you to wait for me; I don't know how long the wait would be. Thank you for giving me such a beautiful son. You've done a marvelous job with him. He's a strong black man and I think he's going to pull through nicely. He has inherited both our determination and strong will."

"Why do I suddenly get the feeling you're telling me good-bye? Are you, Nicholas?"

He walked back to Asia and pulled her into his arms. "There can be no good-byes when you share a child. I'll just venture to say so long."

"Nicholas, why now? What's making you walk out on our friendship now?"

"I'm not doing that. I'll always be here for you. But until I work out everything in my personal life, I need to make myself scarce. I still have Miranda to consider. I have a lot more thinking and soul-searching to do."

As he gently kissed her forehead, his heart hammered away inside his chest, and his desire for her had increased at an alarming rate. Unable to control his need for her, he claimed her mouth with his, engaging her lips in the most staggering kiss ever. The moment he released her, he then walked away. As he reached the kitchen entry, he turned around. "Until whenever, Isaiah's mom. I love you, Asia Morrell."

With tears in her eyes, she blew him a kiss. "I love you, too, Nicholas Reynolds."

"It's good to finally hear you say it, Asia. But I've felt the power of your love from the moment I walked into that hospital room. On that fateful night I was scared that tomorrow may never come for Isaiah and me. But I downright refuse to believe that another tomorrow may never come for you and me. Until our tomorrow comes, please keep me close to your heart."

EPILOGUE

Nicholas had tears in his eyes as he conjured up all his beautiful memories of Isaiah and Torri's magnificent wedding day. He'd never seen a lovelier bride before the moment Torri had walked down that aisle where Isaiah awaited her. Ashton and Seressa Jefferson had finally come to their senses in realizing there was nothing they could do to thwart what destiny had created. He could still envision the bright tears in Isaiah's eyes as Ashton gave him Torri's hand.

Nicholas had to close his eyes as the next memory hit him with full force. He also had to cover his mouth so his cries wouldn't be heard. He felt every bit as emotional as he did on that special day, the most important day in his son's life. While seated in his wheelchair, Isaiah had reached for Torri's other hand. Without hesitation, Torri had placed it in his.

Isaiah then kissed the back of each of her hands as he got to his feet under his own willpower. Just as he'd made an oath to himself that he would do so, Isaiah stood before the altar of God and exchanged wedding vows with the woman he loved with all his heart and soul.

The memories were indeed powerful, but what was even more powerful was the memory of what had occurred after Isaiah and Torri were pronounced husband and wife.

This was one memory he didn't want to share alone. He climbed back into bed and gently pulled his wife into his arms. "Good morning, Mrs. Reynolds. How about taking an amazing trip down Memory Lane with me? Afterward, I promise to give you an encore of our honeymoon night, one of the most sensuous nights we've ever had, and continue to have every time we make love. Do I have a date for a stroll down Memory Lane?"

Asia kissed her husband full on the mouth. "As long as those memories only include you and me. The very best of you and me."

"I know what you mean. When I received those divorce papers all signed, sealed, and delivered from FedEx, after waiting nearly four months without knowing what was what, I promised myself to think of nothing but my future from that moment on. I've always known that you were my destiny; I just didn't know it would take so long for it to become our reality."

"Just as your tomorrow came with Isaiah, our tomorrow finally came. Now from what address on Memory Lane do you want to start our little stroll?"

"At the church, right after Isaiah and Torri exchanged vows. Right where Pastor Jones shouted, 'Hey, why don't we make this a double wedding ceremony?' "

Asia laughed heartily. "My heart was beating so fast I thought it was going to pop out of my chest. I thought the pastor was joking. But it didn't take long for me to realize that you, your son, and Torri had planned a double wedding from the start. That entire day was packed with wondrous surprises, me being the most surprised of all. I could stay at that address on Memory Lane for the rest of my days."

"I hear you, but I'm ready to move on to the next address."

"Which one this time?" Asia asked.

"The honeymoon suite at the Bona Venture Hotel."

"Hey, you, we made other stops before we got there, Nicholas."

"Yeah, but you just said you only wanted us to remember the very best of us. Now that's an address that I could stay at forever. Shall we go there?"

Before Asia could respond, the phone rang.

She laughed at the expression on her husband's face. "We'd better get that first."

Nicholas groaned as he picked up the receiver. Then a huge grin broke out on his face as he listened to the caller's enthusiastic voice. "Hold on so Asia can hear what you're saying." Nicholas pressed in the button to activate the speaker. "Your mom can hear you now, Isaiah. Tell us what's up."

"It's twins! Torri and I have twins, Mom and Dad," Isaiah screeched. "A boy and a girl! The babies and their beautiful mom are doing very well. Torri sends her love. The Reynolds name will live on through our son. Thanks, Mom, and Dad, for helping to make that happen. In legally changing my name, I was able to pass on my real surname to my children. The Reynolds clan couldn't be happier."

"Congratulations!" Asia and Nicholas said in unison, hugging each other tight.

"So, when are you guys going to get down here to the hospital to see your first grandchildren?"

Nicholas chuckled. "Son, we'll be there shortly. As soon as we leave our special visit to an address up here in the clouds on Memory Lane!"

Once Nicholas hung up the phone, Asia turned off the speaker, while her new husband wasted no time in working feverishly to turn her on and relive the very best of their memories.

Dear Readers:

I sincerely hope that you enjoyed reading TOMORROW MAY NEVER COME from cover to cover. I'm very interested in hearing your comments on the story of this father and mother who prayed continuously and fought courageously alongside each other to help bring their loving son back from the brink of death. I love hearing from my readers and I appreciate the time you take out of your busy schedules to respond.

Please enclose a self-addressed, stamped envelope with all your correspondence, and mail it to: Linda Hudson-Smith, 2026C North Riverside Avenue, Box 109, Rialto, CA 92377. Or you can e-mail your comments to *LHS4romance@yahoo.com*. Please also visit my Web site and sign my guest book at *www.lindahudsonsmith.com*.

ABOUT THE AUTHOR

Born in Canonsburg, Pennsylvania, and raised in the town of Washington, Linda Hudson-Smith has traveled the world as an enthusiastic witness to other cultures and lifestyles. Her husband's military career gave her the opportunity to live in Japan, Germany, and many cities across the United States. Linda's extensive travel experience helps her craft stories set in a variety of beautiful and romantic locations. It was after illness forced her to leave a marketing and public relations career that she turned to writing.

Romance in Color chose her as Rising Star for January 2002. ICE UNDER FIRE, her debut Arabesque novel, has received rave reviews. Voted Best New Author by the Black Writers Alliance, Linda received the prestigious 2000 Gold Pen Award. She has also won two Shades of Romance Magazine awards in the categories of Multicultural New Romance Author of the Year and Multicultural New Fiction Author of the Year 2001. Linda was also nominated as the Best New Romance Author at the 2001 Romance Slam Jam. Her novel covers have been featured in such major publications as *Publishers Weekly, USA Today,* and *Essence* magazine.

Linda is a member of Romance Writers of America and the Black Writers Alliance. Though novel writing remains her first love, she is currently cultivating her screenwriting skills. She has also been contracted to pen several other novels for BET Books.

Dedicated to inspiring readers to overcome adversity against all odds, Linda has served for the past two years as the National Spokesperson for the Lupus Foundation of America. In making lupus awareness one of her top priorities, she travels around the country delivering inspirational messages of hope. Her Lupus Awareness Campaign was a major part of her ten-day book tour to Germany in February 2002, where she visited numerous U.S. military bases. She is also a supporter of the NAACP and the American Cancer Society. She enjoys poetry, entertaining, traveling, and attending sports events. The mother of two sons, Linda shares residences with her husband, Rudy, in both California and Texas.